The First Horseman

The First Horseman

D.K. WILSON

SPHERE

First published in Great Britain in 2013 by Sphere

A CIP catalogue record for this book
is available from the British Library.

ISBN 978-0-7515-5035-1

Typeset in Goudy by M Rules
Printed and bound in Great Britain by
Clays Ltd, St Ives plc

Papers used by Sphere are from well-managed forests
and other responsible sources.

MIX
Paper from
responsible sources
FSC
www.fsc.org   FSC® C104740

Sphere
An imprint of
Little, Brown Book Group
100 Victoria Embankment
London EC4Y 0DY

An Hachette UK Company
www.hachette.co.uk

www.littlebrown.co.uk

For Suzannah, a real Tudor gal

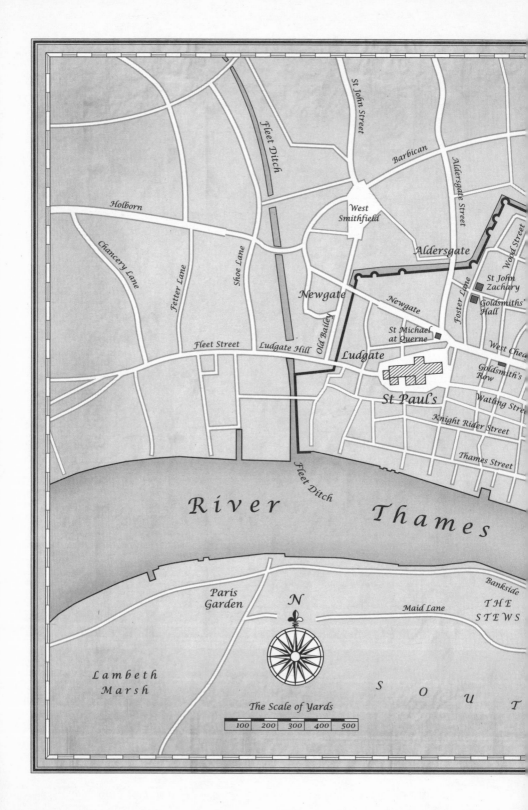

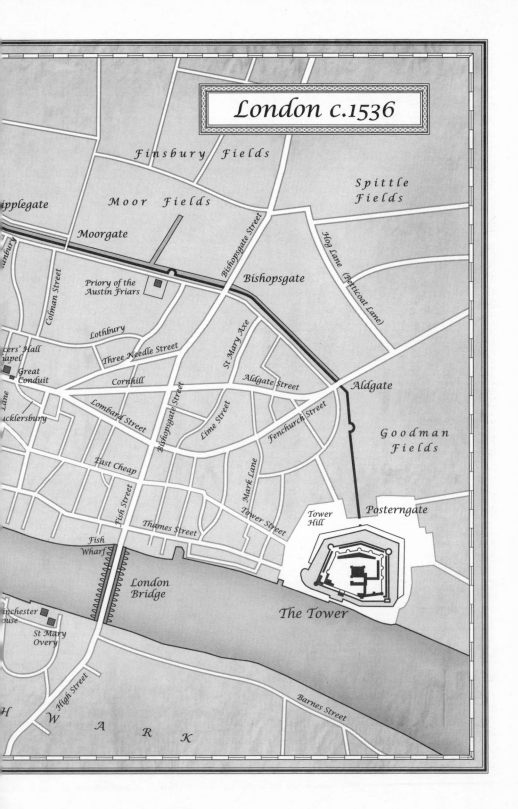

London c.1536

Finsbury Fields

Spittle Fields

Moor Fields

ipplegate

Moorgate

Bishopsgate Street

Hog Lane (Petticoat Lane)

Bishopsgate

Colman Street

Priory of the Austin Friars

Lothbury

Three Needle Street

St. Mary Axe

Aldgate Street

Aldgate

Goodman Fields

cers' Hall
hapel

Great Conduit

Cornhill

Bishopsgate Street

Lime Street

Fenchurch Street

ucklersbury

Lombard Street

Lane

East Cheap

Mark Lane

Tower Street

Posterngate

Fish Street

Tower Hill

Fish Wharf

Thames Street

London Bridge

inchester ouse

St Mary Overy

The Tower

High Street

H   W   A   R   K

Barnes Street

And I saw, and behold there was a white horse,
and he that sat on him had a bow, and a crown
was given unto him, and he went forth
conquering and for to overcome.

– *The Revelation of Saint John the Divine,* in the
1534 translation by William Tyndale

In this year, Robert Packington, mercer of London, a man of
great substance, yet not so rich as discreet and honest, dwelled
in Cheapside and used daily at five of the clock, winter and
summer, to go to prayer at a church then called Saint Thomas
of Acres, but now named Mercers' Chapel. And one morning
amongst all other, being a great misty morning such as hath
seldom been seen, even as he was crossing the street from his
house to the church, he was suddenly murdered with a gun,
which of the neighbours was plainly heard and by a great
number of labourers there standing at Sopers Lane end.

He was both seen [to] go forth of his house, and the clap of
the gun was heard, but the deed doer was never espied nor
known.

– John Foxe, *Acts and Monuments of the
Christian Religion,* 1563

Friday 19 May, 1536

Someone was shaking me.

'Master Thomas, Master Thomas, rouse yourself!'

Master Thomas had not the slightest intention of rousing himself.

'Sod off, Will!' I thrust my throbbing head deeper into the pillow.

I only half heard another voice. 'Stand aside, Will. Give me that bowl.'

The wave of icy water that crashed over my head brought me, gasping and coughing, into the garish daylight. The shutters had been thrown open and Robert Packington's thin, grave, disapproving countenance seemed etched on parchment. He bent over me.

'Jesu, but you stink! Have you brought the Stews home with you? At least you were too drunk to undress. That will save us time.'

'Leave me alone.' I rolled over to face the undrawn curtain on the far side of the bed.

Robert grabbed me by the collar and yanked me into a sitting position. 'You've an appointment at the Tower and I'm going to make sure you keep it – though the Lord knows why I bother.'

I struggled but there was little strength in my arms and legs. Aided by my servant, Robert had little difficulty getting me on my feet. As I swayed, half-conscious, he tackled my unfastened doublet, doing up the points. 'Will, fetch his best livery gown,' he ordered. 'We have to cover up these disgusting stains.'

'Why all the fuss?' My tongue seemed swollen to twice its size in my dry mouth.

'You know why – we've been nominated to be among those representing the City companies. Fortunately it's been postponed to a later hour. That's more luck than you deserve. Don't press it any further.'

Slowly, grindingly, my memory's clockwork whirred into action as the two of them wrapped my blue goldsmith's gown around me. I recalled what 'it' was.

I scrabbled for an excuse. 'The king won't—'

'The king certainly won't be there. But his eyes and ears will be. Your absence would be noted. There will be many who'd happily put their own interpretation on it in order to make trouble for you with your superiors. You're already in bad odour in the Goldsmiths' Company because of your recent behaviour. Any suggestion that Thomas Treviot was sympathetic to her—'

'That's absurd,' I protested.

'We live in times when many absurd things happen,' Robert muttered bitterly. He stepped back as Will fastened the clasp of my gown and set a cap on my head. 'Jesu, what a sight. It's a mercy your father isn't here to see you thus. Come on.'

He half-steered, half-propelled me through the doorway and down the broad stairs to the shop, then out into Goldsmith's Row. Our horses were waiting and with a shove from Will I scrambled aboard Dickon, my grey gelding. West Cheap was alive with its usual hubbub, the stalls already set out and people and horses moving along the paved thoroughfare. Despite the crowds, Robert insisted on leading the way at a bustling trot that jarred all my bones and rattled my still aching head. We must have completed the journey in a fast time, though it seemed to me as long as purgatory.

I was certainly unwilling to arrive at our destination. Anyone hungover, melancholy or otherwise out of sorts should keep away from the Tower of London. I suppose my nurse must have planted the seed of fear in me. The threat 'I'll take you to the Tower' was her standard way of dealing with naughtiness and it was usually effective. It was all too easy to believe that anything could and did happen within the walls of this monstrous soaring pile that crouched like a malevolent stone beast, keeping watch on the capital.

My stomach churned as we emerged from Tower Street and jogged along the well-worn track across the green. We joined a file of other travellers on foot and horseback, most of whom attached themselves to a small crowd that surrounded the Bulwark Gate. I looked about as we pressed our way through. My bleary gaze passed over the mixed throng – a quiet, expectant blob of humanity. A hag thrust a grubby kerchief at me. 'Fetch me some of the blood, Master,' she screeched.

We paused at the gate to have our credentials checked and were waved on to cross the causeway. We were stopped again by guards at the Middle Tower and the Byward Gate and I

3

swear that if my hands had not been trembling on the reins I would have turned Dickon's head and fled from the ordeal. Never before had I come this far within the concentric cordons of the fortress. Occasionally business took me to the Royal Mint but that was situated within the outer wall. As we dismounted I inadvertently cringed away from the uprearing stonework. It seemed to sway, as if about to crumble on top of us. Robert grasped my arm and urged me briskly forward. We entered the inner ward through yet another gateway and followed a path beside the White Tower – its pallid complexion pockmarked where the paint was flaking. And so to the green, the theatre where the tragedy was to be performed.

An arena had been created in front of St Peter's Chapel, Tiered staging arranged on three sides of the black-draped platform. The seats were already almost full. Prime positions were occupied by courtiers and government men. The upper levels were for prominent citizens, like ourselves. We clambered up and found two spaces at one end of the topmost bench. An elderly alderman grunted and grumbled as he made room for us. Clamped between him and Robert, my stomach still churning, I wanted it all to be over. Wanted to be back in the warm anonymity of my own bed.

'Have you ever seen the new man, Cromwell?' Robert asked, pointing to a thickset councillor seated next to the familiar figure of Lord Chancellor Audley.

'No.'

'Well, take a good look and remember what you see. Cromwell's the future. He has more brains than all the rest of the king's council put together. He's climbing fast to the top. You'd do well to cultivate him.'

I was scarcely listening. 'How long is it going to be? Much longer and I'll throw up.'

But the waiting was over. The buzz of conversation stopped and all eyes turned towards a gateway beside the White Tower. It was a small procession: two pikemen, four female attendants, then the Constable, Sir William Kingston, and beside him a woman, small but walking very erect, in an ermine mantle over a grey gown, her face framed by a gable hood. Queen Anne of England, going to her death.

She was helped on to the platform and spent some minutes talking with her ladies, two of whom seemed on the point of collapse with grief. One was on her knees clutching the queen's gown and had to be pulled aside by a guard. Anne turned away and came to the edge of the dais. Not a flicker of movement from her audience as she lifted her head to speak. I leaned forward, focused on the slight figure. My head seemed suddenly clear.

'No priest, Tom,' Robert muttered in my ear. 'No priest. Mark that.'

It was a brief speech but I don't recall all the details. I know what she did not say – the silence all London was abuzz with for days after. She did not confess her adulteries. She bade us pray for the king and for herself. Then the women helped her remove her cape and her headdress. Her long hair gleamed in the sunlight before she tucked it into a little cap. As she was composing herself, a tall figure stepped on to the stage behind her.

I turned to Robert. 'Who—'

'The executioner. Brought specially from France. They say he's very good. Pray God it may be so.'

One of the ladies came forward with a blindfold. Before it was fastened, the queen looked around the ranks of men happy or content or indifferent to witness her destruction. As her gaze reached the end of the line, it rested on me for a long moment – or so it seemed. I could not tear my eyes away from the slight figure, who now knelt, her head bent slightly forward, her lips moving in silent prayer. Up to that moment the performance had proceeded at a slow, almost stately pace, like a sinister pavane. But now the Frog took a stride forward, swinging his large sword as he did so. It flashed down in a wide arc. The capped head fell to the floor, bounced and rolled a few feet. The body, fountaining blood, remained upright for several seconds before tumbling sideways.

That was when I threw up all over the smart black gown of the man sitting in front of me.

Chapter 1

The nauseating scene I was obliged to witness that May morning was the first in a series of violent acts that would change England for ever and involve a very reluctant twenty-two-year-old merchant in that revolution. The sequence of events would rob me of my truest friend, turn my life inside out and, in very fact, almost bring it to a precipitate end – and that more than once. Of course, I could not know that at the time. The queen's death had no relevance to me, Thomas Treviot, freeman goldsmith of the City of London. I had no interest in the affairs of the royal court. For all I cared, Lecher Harry could have been a Musselman with a dozen wives and decapitated every one of them. I had problems enough of my own. Grief enough and to spare.

A mere eight months before Queen Anne's execution I had been one of the most fortunate young men in London. And I knew it. I was the only son (in fact, the only surviving child) of Thomas Treviot Senior and his wife, Isabel. My father was one of the leading City goldsmiths and, at the age of ten, I was apprenticed to him. Nine years later, having served two years as a journeyman, I was admitted a freeman of the Worshipful Company of Goldsmiths of the City of London. I worked beside my father to build upon an already flourishing business. My life lay before me like the map of a familiar land. There were no spaces marked '*Terra Incognita*' or peopled with speculative monsters, such as one sees on new charts of Africa or America. One day I would take over the business operating from the sign of the Swan in Goldsmith's Row, continue running it on the lines laid down by my father, assume my place among the mercantile nobility of the City, grow into an old and respected member of the Worshipful Company and eventually be laid to rest with others of my peers in the Church of St John Zachary, next to our company hall. Life became even more agreeable a year later when, in May 1534, I married Jane Coutray, a daughter of one of the London aldermen. It was in every way a suitable match. Suitable, not only because it greatly pleased our families, but also because we were very much in love. Jane, with her flowing fair hair and heart-melting smile, was everything a successful young businessman could want in a wife. She kept house immaculately and presided with charm and wit over our table when we entertained. There was only one thing we lacked – children. But we were young and time was on our side. Or so, in the careless arrogance of youth, we thought.

It was in December 1534 that Jane became pregnant. Any parent will know the joy and excitement that filled us over the following months. Yet no one was happier than my father. The prospect of a new generation to carry on the business delighted him. He dismissed as nonsense our protests that the baby might be a girl. He was right, but would never know it. The following summer he fell victim, like hundreds of others, to an outbreak of quotidian fever. Suddenly I was left alone, shouldering all the responsibilities of running the business, supporting my grieving mother and ensuring that Jane had everything necessary to bring her to term successfully. Her time came in early September of 1535. She was delivered of a healthy boy. Three days after the birth my lovely Jane was dead of the fever that kills many new mothers.

Everyone was very kind. John Fink – my journeyman apprentice, who had been with the firm as long as I could remember and knew the business as well as I, if not better – eagerly took on fresh responsibilities – I knew I could leave much of the day-to-day running in his hands. I could also rely on the Goldsmiths' Company's excellent record of looking after distressed members. For several months brother craftsmen kept an eye on the workshop and supervised my accounts. Neighbours were sympathetic. But sympathy is a flower that soon fades and grief is a much hardier plant. Perhaps I might have come to terms with it more rapidly had I not had so much support. If I had thrown myself into supervising the workshop, the heat and din of precious metals being melted, hammered and fashioned into jewellery and table plate might have driven other thoughts from my mind for much of the working day. Discussing their needs with clergy commissioning chalices, patens and altar furniture, with courtiers wanting to impress the king with the New Year gift of an embossed cup and cover, with newly rich merchants wishing to adorn their tables and court cupboards with silver plates and dishes or young gentlemen seeking expensive love pledges would have kept me in the world that goes on despite all our personal tragedies. But I was left much to my own memories and they were unbearable.

I fled from them. I had to escape from the everyday, the familiar. All that I saw, heard, smelled and felt reminded me of what I had lost. They spoke of happy days now gone beyond recall. My home at the sign of the Swan had become a mausoleum. The shop and the atelier were filled with my father's shrewd, energetic presence. The parlour and especially the bedchamber enshrined the very essence of Jane. She had been my light, my warmth. Without her all was like a cold, blackened hearth on which no fire would ever burn again. Escape seemed to offer the only way to keep a semblance of sanity.

So I took myself out. Out of the shop. Out of the house. Out of the City. Away from anywhere that conjured up images of lost happiness. I rode about aimlessly, steering Dickon along the solitary heights of Hampstead or the marshy banks of the Lea near Hackney village. I had no care for where I was; no interest in the things I saw and heard. Sometimes I shouted my rage into the empty autumn air. Rage against a cruel God, who had given me everything and then taken a perverse delight in snatching it all away. I even complained to the yellowing woods and new-ploughed fields about well-meaning friends who tried to comfort me with platitudes, sympathy and advice.

Everyone warned me about riding unaccompanied along roads around the City infested with highway robbers. My response was that anyone killing me for my purse would be doing me a service. Colleagues urged me to put the past behind me, to abandon self-pity and look to my responsibilities. My son needed me, they said. But I could not bring myself even to look at him. To my distraught mind he was his mother's murderer. Or, if he was not, then I must be, for I was responsible for the condition that had killed her. My mother and her ladies had decided that the boy was to be baptised with the name Raphael. Our parish priest had advised that the name of the archangel meant, in the original tongue, 'God heals'. It was, he said, a good omen. I raised no objection. I was too much out of my wits to listen to any counsel. The counsellors themselves were abhorrent to me. I shunned them and wanted only to be alone. That was why I failed to notice the change in my mother. She, who had always been so calm and strong, was being destroyed from within by the canker of a grief even more virulent than my own. She became vague and absent-minded. Sometimes she spoke as though her husband were still alive. I should have seen the signs if I had not been blinded by my own feelings.

My random wanderings seldom took me across the river but on a crisp January day in 1536 I stuffed half a manchet loaf and a flask of Canary wine into my saddle bag and set out across London Bridge. Islands of ice were drifting slowly downstream to grind against the bridge and break themselves on its piers. On the other side, I turned westward, deliberately avoiding the crowded Southwark streets clinging to the towering bulk of St Mary Ovey's priory church and the Bishop of Winchester's even more impressive palace, and jogged along Bankside. Steadily I put behind me the monastic hostelries and the fashionable houses built for nobles and bishops which gazed across at London and Westminster. A gaggle of onlookers were down by the royal barge house taking the opportunity to have a close look at the king's magnificent river craft, which had been brought out and moored at the wharf for its annual redecoration. Three men were applying fresh crimson paint and gilding while others worked inside the windowed cabins. Apart from them, there were few people abroad on this raw winter's day. That suited my solitary mood. I followed the river round the wide bend to Lambeth and rode on past Archbishop Cranmer's palace. A bleary sun was wrapping itself in folds of translucent cloud as I rode out on to Kennington Common. I gave Dickon a canter to the top of the hill, unpeopled save for two bodies dangling from a frost-rimed gibbet in the breezeless air, and in their company I stopped to eat my simple meal.

But not for long. The sky was darkening ahead, threatening snow. It was time for Dickon and me to retrace our steps. We had reached the semi-cultivated area known as Paris Garden and were just passing the bear pit when a sudden roar from one of the creatures caged there startled my horse. He skittered sideways, caught a hoof in a frozen rut, stumbled, recovered and broke into a frightened canter. I was almost unseated. It took me several moments to regain my balance, rein Dickon in and pat his neck to calm him. Then after a few more paces I realised that something was wrong. The poor animal was walking awkwardly. I dismounted and lifted his left foreleg. It was as I had feared: Dickon had cast a shoe.

Unless I could find a farrier, I faced a long walk home. Either way I needed to make haste. Dusk would be early and I wanted to cross the bridge before the bascule was closed for the night. Southwark, a haunt of whores, cutpurses and criminal gangs, was no place for honest citizens after dark. Only months before, the king had tried to close the bawdy houses. He could as well have ordered the river to stop flowing for all the good his edict did. This side of the Thames fell under the sway of Bishop Gardiner of Winchester, one of Henry's own councillors, and that good man of God earned too much from the rents paid by harlots and their panders to have the area cleared of the 'Winchester Geese', as these women were known. I took hold of the reins and set off, leading my horse, towards Southwark.

I had not been walking many minutes when two riders coming in the opposite direction halted and greeted me. I eyed them carefully. The elder of the two seemed to be a man of some substance. Though his heavy cloak was well wrapped round him, I glimpsed beneath it short trunk hose of a style fashionable at court some dozen years or so earlier and the hilt of a short sword. His boots were shiny and of good hide. The other man, in a leather jerkin and worsted cloak, I assumed to be his servant. They looked respectable enough but many of the thieves and ruffians who infested our roads were masters of deception. I was automatically on my guard.

'Good day to you. Do you have a problem with your horse?' the senior enquired with a polite doffing of his cap.

I was aware that Dickon and I were being scrutinised as carefully by these strangers as I was evaluating them. Well, I had taken no care of my dress. If they were contemplating villainy, they would have seen a dishevelled young man with three days' stubble on his chin, who was unlikely to be carrying much money. There was, however, no disguising Dickon's pedigree. He was bred out of sturdy, dark-haired Friesian stock but had taken his Irish mother's colouring and easy temperament. It did not need a wily coper's eye to recognise a beast that was strong, fleet and willing. He would be a considerable prize for any murderous villain. 'Lost a shoe,' I said, preparing to continue along the road. 'Just my luck. It seems we're in for snow.'

'Do you have far to go?' the older man asked.

'Not too far,' I replied non-committally. 'But I must keep moving. God speed you.'

The strangers exchanged glances and the servant nudged his mount sideways, blocking the path. 'Take care, young sir,' he said. 'This ain't the best place for a gen'leman travelling alone.' By the man's rough speech I marked him for a countryman, probably from Kent. 'Why, if you knew the number of poor travellers what's bin waylaid on this bit o' road . . . Ain't I right, Ned?'

'You are, indeed, Jed. Now, sir, might I suggest you give my companion and me the pleasure and privilege of accompanying you as far as your lodging?'

I glanced along the road. There was no one else in sight. 'That's remarkably kind, but I couldn't allow you to delay your own journey for me.' I tried to sound more relaxed and casual than I felt.

''Tis no more than our Christian duty, sir.' 'Ned', or whoever he was, turned his horse. 'Jed, let the gentleman have your mount. We cannot allow him to trudge the road like a wretched vagabond. You can lead his poor, afflicted beast.'

I had to think quickly. I waited while Jed dismounted. Then, as he handed the reins to his companion, I leaped back into Dickon's saddle, pulled his head round and legged him hard. There was no point in riding back along the road. The discomfort of the missing shoe would slow my horse down and I would have been swiftly overtaken. So I plunged in among the trees of Paris Garden. Despite its name, part of the area was still tangled and wooded and had the reputation of being a hideout for criminals and a place of assignation for those whose affairs called for secrecy. Desperately, I hoped that its deep shade would provide me with a hiding place from my assailants.

The trees were very close together and the undergrowth beneath them a jumble of ferns and briars. We made what pace we could, dodging around trunks, slithering into gullies and leaping over fallen, rotting boughs. I had no idea how close we were being followed. All my attention was given to peering ahead through the gloom for obstacles and low branches. It was such a branch that I did not see which proved my undoing. It caught me full on the temple and knocked me clean from the saddle. I felt myself thrown to the ground and sudden pain as my shoulder struck something hard. Then nothing.

Chapter 2

My first sensation when I came to myself was the smell – a mingled odour of latrines, stale sweat and something sickly sweet. When I opened my eyes I could only make out a blur of timber beams and mottled paintwork. I turned my head in an effort to identify my surroundings and was rewarded with a flash of pain across my temple. Then I sank back into welcome unconsciousness.

When I awoke again the pattern of ceiling beams was clearer. They were wide, suggesting another floor above. They had been painted, as had the plaster between, but long since, for the surface was flaked. This was not my room, nor any room I recognised. I turned my head slowly and carefully to the right. A good-sized chamber with plain wooden walls and over a simple chimneypiece a single candle burned. Night, then. Painfully I shifted my position and the truckle bed creaked its protest. Immediately there was movement in the room. A young woman's face and shoulders entered my vision. She wore her long, dark hair unbound but I could see little of her face which was in shadow.

'So, Master Treviot, you have decided to rejoin us.' The voice was soft but somewhat deep for a woman.

I groaned. 'Who is "us"?'

She laughed – something between a trill and a chuckle. 'Us? We are the Sisters of the Unholy Order of St Swithun.'

'My head is bursting, woman. Don't tease it with riddles. Be so good as to tell me where I am and how I came here.'

'That is soon said. You are at the Sign of St Swithun in Southwark, close by the Clink prison. You had an accident not far from here and were unhorsed. Luckily for you, a couple of Samaritans discovered you and, not knowing what else to do with you, they brought you to us to tend till you regained your wits. Do you remember anything yet?'

'Near the Clink, you say? Then I am in the Stews and you are ...'

'An honest woman serving the needs of travellers and fine citizens, like yourself, Master Treviot. Don't pretend you've never been here looking for some comforting company away from home.'

'Never. And how is it you know my name?'

'Why, all London and half the country around knows your name. There have been bills posted everywhere and search parties out looking for you. It's not every day a rich City goldsmith disappears without trace.'

'Then I assume you have sent word to my home. My mother will be anxious ...'

'One matter at a time, Master Treviot. When you are fully yourself we can make arrangements for your return – and discuss suitable terms.'

'Ah, I see. I am kidnapped and to be held to ransom by you and your accomplices.'

The whore stepped back from the bed and for the first time I could see her features. The candlelight revealed pale, somewhat flat cheeks, and glinted from dark eyes. She had the slim figure of a woman not yet in her prime. Though faint lines had already appeared around her mouth, I judged that she could be no more than eighteen. She stood, hands on hips, glowering down at me. 'Kidnapped, is it? If it weren't for my "accomplices", you'd be lying out there rotting under a foot of snow, waiting for the foxes and crows to make a meal of you!'

'Well, then,' I replied, 'if I'm free to leave I'll be on my way and put you to no more inconvenience!' At that I tried to sit up. Pain juddered through my back and neck and I collapsed with a gasp.

She laughed. 'Going to stumble all the way back to Cheapside, are you, with a bruised head and a broken shoulder bone? The bridge is closed and no boatmen working the river as long as it's littered with floating ice, so I suppose you'll swim the Thames.'

Gingerly I felt my left shoulder. It was tightly bound with linen strips. 'Whose handiwork is this?' I asked.

'Our apothecary. We do have such things here, you know. We're not quite the dregs of society you think us. Now you just go back to sleep. I've still work to do and a living to earn.' She ran her fingers through her hair and patted her cheeks to bring colour to them. She left and I heard the rasp of a door bolt as I drifted once more into unconsciousness.

Light filled the room from a wide, unshuttered window when next I woke. Inner illumination also seemed to be clarifying my thoughts. For the first time I remembered clearly the encounter on the road up to the moment of my flight into the

Paris woods. I tried to imagine what must have happened thereafter. I envisaged the two supposedly solicitous strangers following me and coming upon my unconscious body. They would, undoubtedly, have stripped me of anything valuable and taken possession of Dickon. Why had they not, then, left me to perish of cold or despatched me themselves? There could be only one reason: I was worth more to them living than dead. So they had brought me here to this bawdy house to be patched up by their female partners in crime.

Slowly, carefully, I urged myself off the narrow bed. With my dangling left arm thrust inside my doublet for support, I limped across to the window.

What I looked out on was a courtyard enclosed on all sides by an old timbered structure three storeys high, the upper floors overhanging the one at ground level. Several windows had open shutters and, while some were glazed, many were filled with panels of grimy hempen cloth as protection against the cold. The weather had obviously improved a little since I had been brought here for the ground was covered in slush, churned into muddy mounds where wheels, hooves and boots had trampled it. Three urchins were playing a desultory game of snowballs, scooping up handfuls of the dirty, frozen mess to hurl at each other. Washed clothes hung on lines stretched between upper windows. Beyond this enclosed yard I could not see, for opposite my window the large doors that gave on to the street beyond were closed. This was clearly an inn lodging that had seen better days. Once the town house of a prosperous lord or, perhaps, a monastic hostelry for travellers to the City, it had, like many buildings in overcrowded London and its environs, been divided into tenements taken up by the poor and 'undesirables'.

The door behind me opened and, turning, I saw one of the

villains who had waylaid me on the road. The one who had called himself 'Ned'. I was able to get a better look at him and beheld a stout man of about fifty years, with thick white hair and a ruddy complexion. His doublet and hose were faded but clean and his beard was well trimmed. He wore an apron tied round his waist which bore streaks of what might have been blood and he carried a satchel. His confident and genial air suggested that in the community of this wretched dwelling he probably passed as a gentleman.

'Master Treviot, how good it is to see you on your feet.' He set down his bag on the bed.

'No thanks to you,' I growled. If there had been any strength in my body I would have lunged at him with my fists.

He shook his head. 'Now there, I fear you do me a disservice. Had my assistant and I not searched long and hard, found you and tended to your needs ... well, you would not be standing where you are now with every prospect of a full recovery from your accident.'

'Accident!'

Before I could find words to vent my anger, my visitor held up his hand. 'I must confess, sir, that the original fault was mine. I should have introduced myself properly when we met. Of course, I could not know that you would take such alarm at our appearance but ... yes, I see now that you had some reason to suspect that we might be ruffians bent on taking advantage of your predicament. Yes, yes, I see that. *Mea culpa, Domine.*' He lifted his eyes briefly heavenwards.

'Then perhaps you will make good your omission now. Just who are you?'

'Edward Longbourne at your service.' He made a slight bow. 'Late of the Priory of our Lady at Farnfield.'

'A monk?' I laughed and a stabbing pain in my shoulder made me regret it.

'An ex-monk.' He sighed. 'The time is not far off when we shall all be ex-monks.'

'What's that supposed to mean?'

'The writing is on the wall for those who choose to see it. Royal commissioners sent to all the abbeys to poke and pry. Sent to find proof of irregularities – and to make up what they cannot prove. But that is nothing to the purpose.'

He busied himself unpacking the satchel. 'Now, let us have that shirt off and see how your shoulder is faring.'

'The woman – I don't know her name – said I was tended by an apothecary. Was that you?'

'It was. Come, let me see if the bandages need tightening.'

I had no option but to allow his examination and stooped so that he could ease off my shirt.

He ran his eyes appraisingly over my torso. 'Hm, yes, very fine. If I mistake not, you are a keen archer, Master Treviot.'

'I practise regularly, as the king ordains ... At least I did until recently.'

'What deterred you? I prescribe regular exercise to all my patients. Now, turn round to the light.' He ran his fingers over my upper back and neck and his touch was gentle but firm – like a woman's.

'Tell me, rather, how you came to leave the life of holy contemplation for this squalid haunt of whores and other outcasts,' I said.

'Did not Christ himself live among whores and outcasts? This may hurt a little.' He pressed firmly on the broken bone. 'This is what we medical men call the *clavicula*. It is particularly vulnerable to fracture but mends itself readily. What we have to do is make sure that it is straight when it reknits. You don't want that fine physique marred by a crooked shoulder, do you? So we just tighten this binding a bit . . . like this.' I winced as he did so.

'Three weeks should see it completely mended,' he continued, 'though you should wait a little longer before you draw a bow again.'

'You avoided my question,' I said.

'How came I here? I was the infirmarian at Farnfield for more than twenty years. Looking after the health of a community of men – many of them aged – provides one with a wide knowledge of simples and poultices, broken bones and fevers, herbs and tinctures. I had a good teacher and I also read the standard texts – Galen, Mundinus, even some of the Arab anatomists in Latin translation. But we were a small house and getting smaller, year by year. It's hard to recruit novices these days. Young Jed – he was my companion on the road the other day – was the last to join us. Our prior was old and close to death. So, when Master Cromwell sent his commissioners out, Farnfield was ripe for the picking. We were all offered generous bribes to abandon our vows and threatened with being accused of unnatural vices if we refused. We took the easy option.'

'But why come here?'

Longbourne shook his head. 'That's enough of my story for one day. Let's get your shirt back on. I've a sling here for your arm and a tonic of mugwort that will rebuild your strength.' He gave a throaty chuckle. 'You could say it was mugwort, or *Artemisia*, that brought us together. Jed and I were out gathering roots along the roadside on Tuesday when we came upon you.'

'What day is it now?'

'Saturday. You had a bad concussion but, God willing, there is no reason to fear permanent damage.'

'Then, I may go home?'

'Whenever you wish – though I would counsel another two days of rest to build up your strength. Jed makes a very efficacious chicken broth with leeks, and the women keep a good pottage on the go. Your horse is not yet rideable. He's been reshod and I've poulticed his pastern. Come Monday he should be fit for duty again.'

'You've taken a deal of trouble. I'm sorry I took you for a common highway thief.'

Longbourne was busy repacking his knapsack. 'You had reason. 'Tis not for nothing Southwark has its reputation. There are many of our neighbours who would have cut your throat for the clothes you stood up in. But not all men are bad and most men are not all bad and no man is so bad as to be beyond redemption. You might want to think on that.' He shouldered his bag and left. Once more I heard the door being bolted.

Still a prisoner, then, despite the apothecary's assurance. I prowled the room, looking in vain for some means of escape. Manoeuvring through the window with one arm was out of the question. There were two doors but one led only to a tiny latrine closet. The stench suggested that the bucket had not been emptied for days and I quickly shut the door again. Sitting on a rickety chair beside a small table (these were the only items of furniture besides the bed), I assessed my situation. Should I watch for a chance to break free of my confinement or trust these strange people? How much easier it would have been, I reflected, if Ned and Jed *had* been murderous ruffians; if they had despatched me and thus reunited me with Jane.

23

I was still nursing these melancholy thoughts when the woman came in. She set down on the table a kettle, from it ladled soup into a wooden bowl and plonked a small loaf of grey maslin bread beside it. It looked and smelled good and I stared at it.

'Well, eat it,' the woman said, hands on hips. 'Or perhaps you think it's poisoned.'

'Would that it were,' I muttered.

'Oh!' She gave a light laugh. 'Weary of life today, are we? In that case I won't waste good food.' She stooped to retrieve the bowl.

'No,' I said hurriedly, taking up the spoon. 'Thank you for the soup.' I began to eat hungrily.

'I'm sorry if I appeared ungrateful yesterday,' I mumbled, not catching her eye.

'You did not *appear* ungrateful; you *were* ungrateful.' She shrugged. 'But that's no less than we're used to.'

'I don't know your name,' I said, trying to thaw the atmosphere.

'Lizzie.'

'Just Lizzie?'

'We have no use for family names here. We're all family.'

Now that I could see her more clearly I realised that this young woman was quite pretty – in a basic sort of way. No vulgar stain coloured her lips. Her cheeks still had the bloom of youth and needed no creams. There was about her a strong smell of rosewater, presumably another concoction of Master Longbourne. Southwark had yet to turn her into a jaded bawd.

'Your apothecary suggested I might walk free,' I ventured. 'Yet I see the door is still kept locked.'

'There's too much of the monk about old Ned.' She scowled. 'He says, because you're a gentleman, you'll see us right. Well, I don't set no store by gentlemen. You see this?' She pulled her hair back and turned her head to the light, revealing a long, livid scar across her neck. 'That was done by a gentleman. Gentle is as gentle does in my reckoning. We aren't a charity. I've given up several customers these last days, looking after you. Well, I deserve payment for my services, don't I?'

'Of course.' I finished the soup and held out the bowl for a refill. 'As soon as I get home I'll have money sent to you.'

She threw back her head and laughed. 'Oh yes, my fine merchant. Part with the goods now and accept payment later? Is that the way you do business? When you walk through that door that's the last I see of you, isn't it?'

'Then come with me and collect your fee in person.'

'And have your servants send me off with a flea in my ear? I don't think so.'

'Lizzie, I don't know what else to suggest. There has to be trust somewhere.'

'What I trust is silver with the king's head on it – here!' She held out her hand.

I could see her point. The question was whether I could make her see mine. I seized the hand and held it. 'Look, we seem to have made a bad start. I'm sorry. Blame the bang on my head. You ask how I do business. Well, the answer is only with people I trust. And I find that trust breeds trust. That whole city over the water has its foundations in trust. Without trust London would not be one of the greatest trade centres in the world. I owe you a debt. You and your friends probably saved my life. I will honour that debt. Trust me. Please.'

She withdrew her hand but her frown had gone. She looked thoughtful. I tried to read the thoughts behind her dark eyes and she quickly turned away. Then she stood suddenly. 'Very well. I'll probably regret this but I'm prepared to put your "honour" to the test. Come with me and I'll show you something. Make a run for it and I'll know what a sham your "honour" is.'

She led me out into a corridor that had been formed by reducing the size of what had once been interconnecting rooms so that each chamber now had its own door and enjoyed privacy. We descended the original wide staircase into a hall where half a dozen women sat huddled around a hearth in which logs blazed. An outer door led into the courtyard, which we crossed to the main gateway and so passed out, under the creaking signboard with its image of a mitred saint, into a busy, narrow street.

'This way,' Lizzie said, taking my arm. We turned to the right and followed the lane until we were confronted by the high stone wall of Winchester Palace. Sometimes my guide nodded to or exchanged a word with passers-by – members of her own close-knit community. At one point a woman leaning from an upper casement called out, 'Who's your new darling, Liz?' and Lizzie stuck out her tongue by way of reply. After we had passed the palace gatehouse, where she paused to flirt with the guard, my guide steered me off the lane and on to a track, barely distinguishable under the melting snow, which crossed the bishop's parkland. A few more paces and she stopped.

'There, do you see it?'

I scanned the empty expanse of white, dotted with trees.

'Where am I supposed to be looking?'

'Just here, in front of us.'

The ground closest to us was uneven, broken by a series of little mounds. There was nothing to attract attention.

I shook my head. 'I can't see . . .'

26

'Exactly. Just an unremarkable stretch of land, generously donated by His Grace, the Bishop of Winchester. It's called the Unmarried Women's Graveyard. You know, of course, what "unmarried women" means. This is where we end up – where I will end up – buried in unconsecrated ground, an unrepentant sinner not worthy of Christian burial. The bishop takes our rents. His priests use our services. But at the end the Church turns its back on us. We enter purgatory with no shriving, no passing bell, no sacrament. We can go to hell for all the Church cares.'

There was a long silence. I stared at the bleak, unmarked hummocks and thought of my Jane's memorial in the Berentine Chantry in St John Zachary with its carved, fresh-painted effigy; the tomb where I had often imagined myself being laid beside her – together again and supported by the obits of the priest performed every year's mind. But for this girl-woman beside me no such comfort. It had never occurred to me before that respectability was just as much a barrier in whatever lay beyond death as it was in the London and Southwark of the living. We had begun our walk back to St Swithun's House before I said, 'At least you have one church-man who seems to care.'

'Old Ned?'

'Yes. How did he come to be here?'

'I don't know. Perhaps he regards it as a sort of penance. He and Jed had to quit the monastery.' She paused, and seemed to be choosing her words carefully. 'At St Swithun's we ask no questions and make no judgements. Anyway, he's useful to have around.'

'For treating the pox and carrying out abortions?'

I had not meant the words to sound judgemental but Lizzie stopped suddenly, glaring. 'Mother of God, you spleeny,

27

puffed-up ingrate! Ned and Jed should have left you to freeze to death. The folks here are flesh and blood, same as you. We get sick, same as you. Just because you can afford fancy physicians and barber surgeons don't think you're any different underneath your fine clothes.'

We completed our journey in silence.

That evening I asked for pen and paper and wrote a brief letter to the only man I could take into my confidence; a man whom I knew would provide ransom money without demur and without alarming my mother – Robert Packington. He was a prominent member of the Mercers' Company, had been my father's closest friend and was now a great stay to my mother in her widowhood. To me he had always been a sort of unofficial uncle, somewhat austere in demeanour but always understanding and encouraging. Without disclosing my whereabouts, I asked him to entrust to the bearer a sum of money that, I calculated, should more than compensate everyone at the Sign of St Swithun for my board and lodging. I showed it to Ned Longbourne for his approval and he arranged for Jed to deliver it and return with the cash.

So it was that after spending six days in the Southwark Stews I returned to Goldsmith's Row and respectability – and to the inevitable inquisition that, I knew, would await me.

Chapter 3

I had a tub of hot water brought to my chamber, washed myself thoroughly and changed my clothes before going to my mother's rooms on the upper floor. I found her in the window seat with one of her women bent over her sewing. As soon as she saw me she jumped up, the needlework falling to the floor.

'Tom! Oh Tom! Thank God! Your father and I have been so worried, haven't we, my love?' She gazed past my shoulder into the empty space beyond. 'We have had the servants out every day scouring the City. Your father posted reward notices and alerted the constables to look for you. We distributed your portrait – the one done for your sixteenth birthday. Master Holbein made a copper engraving. No one saw you anywhere. You really must stop going off by yourself without telling anyone. If you must go a-riding take one of the servants. What would happen here if any ill befell you? Tom, I don't know whether to be cross or happy.'

I was saved from responding to this torrent by a familiar footfall on the stair. A moment later the tall figure of Robert Packington was framed in the doorway. He was dressed in his usual black with a simple gold chain round his neck. The square cut of his grey-streaked beard made his frown look even more formidable. With scarce a glance at me, he strode across the room, scuffing up the herbs which the servants always kept fresh-laid. He made a slight bow.

'Isabel, how are you today? I see the prodigal has returned.' He turned to me. 'God be praised for our answered prayers. Someone entered the shop and told me you'd been seen. I came round straightway. You've been attacked, I see. I'll send straightly for Doctor Drudgeon to examine that arm.'

'I thank you, Robert, but there is no need. 'Tis no more than a broken collar bone – my horse stumbled – and it's been reset by ... er ... a professional.' I had not yet decided how much I would tell Robert about my adventure. I was sure he would never understand the people at the Sign of St Swithun.

'Excuse me, Mistress.' My mother's woman was hovering in the doorway. 'The horse litter is here at the door from Mistress Galloway's.'

'Mistress Galloway?' My mother shook her head, trying to remember.

'Aye, Mistress, her time is nearly here and you promised to call.'

My mother rose with a sigh. 'Ah yes. Now, Tom, you're not to set foot outside the house till I return. Stay and tell your father everything. Everything, mind! You understand?'

When she had left, Robert drew a joined stool up to the window and perched himself upon it. 'I've told her nothing about the letter or the uncouth fellow who brought it,' he said. 'It would confuse her, or, I should say, increase her already growing confusion.'

'Thank you, Robert. That was thoughtful. And thank you even more for helping me. I could not leave my hosts without showing my appreciation. Before you leave I'll reimburse you.'

'You'll do no such thing. I'm just happy that I was there for you to turn to. Now, tell me what happened.'

'I really remember little about it. Poor Dickon stumbled in the icy ruts and I had a bad fall. I was unconscious a long time. Fortunately some kind folk found me and nursed me back to health.'

Robert held me in an unblinking gaze. 'And where did all this happen?'

With a great effort I managed not to look away. 'Somewhere south of the river. As I say, it's all a blur in my mind.'

'Hmm.' Robert regarded me with a quizzically raised eyebrow. 'Last week I was offered six bales of fine silk by a Spanish merchant who claimed to have imported them direct from the Orient. The price was good but I turned it down. Something about the man did not ring true. Later, news arrived that a Venetian merchantman had been waylaid by pirates off Coruna and despoiled of a cargo of silks. As I grow older I find my first impressions are usually reliable.'

I stood up. 'I'm forgetting my manners, Robert. Let me pour you some wine.' I stepped across to the livery cupboard and returned with a goblet of Canary. 'I'm sorry about all the fuss and worry I've caused but I really did contact you as soon as I could.'

He waved a hand. 'And I am sorry that you feel unable to take me into your full confidence. But, no matter, we've more important things to talk about. Solomon wrote, "A foolish son is grief to his father and bitterness to she who bore him." If your father were here now he would, indeed, grieve to see how much you have let yourself be overwhelmed by the loss of Jane. As for your mother, she has had her own cross to bear these last months and you have seen how hard it is for her to bear it. You should have been here to comfort her instead of disappearing, day after day, to brood in private. And you must look to your standing within the Goldsmiths' Company. Reputations are easier lost than gained.'

I stood by the window, staring out at the busy street. 'No man can know how deeply the loss of a loved one will affect him.'

'Do you suppose you're the only man to lose a wife? I have buried two.'

I struggled to control the resentment boiling up within me. I turned to face my old friend. 'Robert, you mean well and I am grateful but I have not come home after an unpleasant ordeal to be chided like a child.'

There was no irritated response. I do not recall ever having seen Robert give way to anger. It would have been easier for me if he had. As it was, I could only stand there regretting my outburst but unable to apologise for it. Robert stood, slowly drained his goblet and set it down carefully on the stool he had vacated. 'Then it is time for the pedagogue to withdraw.' He walked towards the door. Halfway across the room he stopped. He turned, stood for a moment as though in thought, then thrust his hand inside his doublet and drew something out. He walked back and placed it on the stool beside his cup. 'You might find this a valued companion on your lonely wanderings. But don't let anyone know you have it.'

From the oriel window I watched him emerge into West Cheap, turn right and stride purposefully through the throng towards his own home in nearby Sopers Lane. 'Meddling fool,' I muttered to myself and knew, even as I did so, that I did not mean it. After some minutes I picked up Robert's parting gift.

It was a small book, bound in hide and designed for the purse or pocket. I turned to the title page and knew immediately why Robert had advised me to keep it clandestinely:

The New Testament, yet once again corrected by
William Tyndale,
whereunto is added a calendar and a necessary table
wherein easily
and lightly may be found any story contained in the four
Evangelists
and in the Acts of the Apostles.
Printed in the year of our Lord God MDXXXIV

I dropped it on the table in sudden alarm, as though it had burst into flames. Flames indeed – this was the notorious book men were burned for reading. I was astonished, shocked even. William Tyndale was a renegade priest who had fled to some Lutheran enclave on the Continent from where he had been smuggling his heretical text into England. Now the bishops were busy seizing every copy they could find and making bonfires of them – and sometimes of the men and women who owned them. What was Robert doing with such a dangerous book? I knew a couple of young men who boasted about reading Tyndale's *Testament*. They were Inns of Court students – bold anti-establishment fellows who liked to consider themselves 'advanced' thinkers. But Robert Packington? No one was more staid, conservative, respectable and orthodox than Robert. He was the very epitome of the correct and successful London merchant. He had grown rich from his trade in woollen cloth and risen to be Upper Warden of the Mercers' Company, overseeing all its affairs. He was on the Common Council of the City and a member of parliament. Could such an establishment figure be a covert Lutheran? The idea of connecting him with the wild-eyed preachers who stood in the public pulpits ranting against the evils of Rome was absurd.

It was a puzzle – but one I did not tax my brain with. Religion was something I was content to leave to the bishops and the learned doctors. However, I had become the surprise recipient of a dangerous book and Robert had, wisely, warned me to keep it away from prying eyes. I slipped the little volume in my purse, carried it to my own chamber and locked it in a coffer, meaning to get rid of it at the earliest opportunity.

Chapter 4

Until my shoulder healed and I had fully recovered the use of my left arm, I could not venture out on solitary expeditions, nor was the dismal winter weather conducive to them. Despite myself I was obliged to give more attention to matters at home and in the workshop. My son had been put to a wet nurse who was provided with quarters on the top floor of the house. As far as I knew his progress was satisfactory. I saw little of him but any neglect of mine was more than compensated for by the attention and adulation lavished upon him by my mother and the women of the household. Business matters were less easy to avoid.

The morning after my return, my deputy, John Fink, presented himself in my chamber carrying a ledger. He was a small, spare, saffron-haired young man who wore a permanent frown of concentration and who stood now almost apologetically in the middle of the room.

'You'll be wanting to check the accounts, Master,' he suggested.

'I'm sure they're all in order, John,' I replied. 'You've been doing a splendid job these last weeks.'

He stood rooted to the spot. 'I really would rather you took a look, Master.'

I sighed. 'Very well.' I cleared a space on my table and settled into my wainscot chair.

John set down the large leather-bound volume and unlocked the metal clasp. He drew up the joined stool and perched on it. The first thing I noticed as he turned to the most recent entries was that there were fewer of them on the later pages.

'Business slackening off?' I asked.

He nodded mournfully. 'Some customers will only deal with you personally, Master. My Lord Basing's man called several times but ... well, Master ... what with your affairs so often taking you from home ... I believe His Lordship took his order to Master Leyland. Then there were the loans. I issued some for smaller amounts, as you can see.' He turned the pages and pointed out four or five entries. 'But anything over a hundred pounds I durst not sanction. Sir Arthur Talbot became ... well ... rather abusive when I tried to explain; though I think, Master, you would have turned him down yourself. As you know, he gambles heavily at court. He said he would make sure that it was well known how ill we used the king's friends.'

'Poor John.' I smiled at him. 'I have been preoccupied and I see what a burden that has laid on you. Don't worry about Talbot. He's angry because he knows how heavily he is already indebted to us. He's in the process of mortgaging his family into penury. I have no plans to be absent in the next few

weeks. Leave me a list of customers you have had to disap-
point and I'll contact them.'

Promises are easily offered.

I did make an effort. I spent more time in the workshop. I
talked with the goldbeaters. I examined the gem-setters' work.
I discussed with the draughtsmen the designs they brought in
for new jewellery. I despatched letters to our more important
customers assuring them of my personal attention to their
requirements. Yet my heart was not in it all. It was not just my
yearning for Jane that frequently burst in upon my waking
thoughts and kept sleep at bay; I could not get the St
Swithun's people out of my head.

Shrove Tuesday in 1536 fell on 3rd March. That afternoon
I was obliged, with all members of the Company, to attend the
Shrove Feast in Goldsmiths' Hall. After mass in St John
Zachary we processed across Maiden Lane into the hall – or,
it would be truer to say, we scurried, for it was a day of squally
rain and we had to tread quickly but carefully to avoid soiling
our shoes and hose with mud or our livery gowns with the
water trickling from the roofs. Once inside we were glad of the
good fire roaring in the hearth and the light from the cande-
labra overhead from which smoke spiralled into the dim
recesses of the rafters high above us. Ours was not a large
building by comparison with those of the other merchant
companies and could in no way be compared to the impressive
edifice of the Mercers' new hall, but none could rival us for
display. All along high table and the long table that ran the
length of the hall, at right angles to it, light glinted on plates,
salts, goblets and dishes of gold and silver gilt, while other no
less impressive items stood ready for service on the livery cupboards and buffets along the walls.

We were seated in strict order of precedence, which meant

that I was closer to the screens passage than the high table where our Prime Warden, Sir William Beaumont, and senior officers sat with the guests of honour.

'I thought Gardiner was on embassy in France,' Will Fitzralph, my friend and left-hand neighbour, observed, indicating the man on Sir William's right, resplendent in a scarlet cope festooned with gilt embroidery.

'He's just back for a brief visit, reporting to the king,' someone further down the table responded. He leaned forward to make himself heard against the clatter of dishes and the buzz of conversation. 'Those in the know say the good Bishop of Winchester is determined to keep a close eye on the monasteries bill.'

'What bill is that?' I asked.

There was a flutter of laughter around me and Will asked, 'Do you never listen to gossip, Tom, or are you still off on rural rides most days? Everyone's talking about the king's plans for the abbeys. They say that it is all the fault of the queen – Henry's concubine as some call her. She is supposed to be in league with Cromwell to drag us all into Lutheranism.'

The man opposite me, Simon Leyland, was not laughing. 'That's just rumour, spread by papists and other troublemakers who do not like the king's efforts to reform the Church. I trust you're not among their number, Will.' Leyland was a choleric man, well known for picking arguments. He glowered across the table, his high colour accentuated by the candles' glow.

Will stood his ground but replied in a calm, almost casual voice, 'No empty talk, Brother. I had it from a member of the Commons house.'

Simon glared back belligerently. 'You don't want to believe everything politicians tell you, especially those who have fallen for this fashionable heresy they call "New Learning".'

He wrinkled his nose in a sneer. 'Do you really think Henry so foolish? People grumble about idle monks and lascivious nuns but if the government tried to turn out all the religious from their convents, folk would soon band together in their defence.'

'Very likely, Simon.' Will refused to spoil the festive atmosphere. 'Anyway, when the bill is debated Gardiner and the other bishops will, doubtless, make sure that it is voted down.'

I turned to glance up at the high table. The Bishop of Winchester ('Wily Winchester', as people called him) seemed to be enjoying himself, sharing a joke with the Prime Warden. I had never seen him this close to. What I observed was a man in his fifties with dark eyes that sparkled in a fleshy face. He wore no beard but his upper lip was adorned with what the Italians call a *mustaccio*. So this was the master of the Southwark Stews; the bishop Lizzie and her associates loved to hate. I ran over in my mind what little I knew about him: career cleric; one of Henry's new men raised from obscurity to help secure the break with Rome; appointed royal secretary and very close to the king but a jealous guardian of the Church's privileges, which was why – or so men said – he had been sent on various foreign embassies, as a result of which another upstart, Thomas Cromwell, had taken over as secretary. I looked wistfully along the table at the faces of my brothers. Was it my imagination or were they more grave than they had been in previous years? I had always enjoyed our convivial gatherings but now it seemed we were all looking at each other through a grey haze of politics.

Conversation flagged as we fell to on the first mess set before us by the servants – a course of conies, venison and teal with sundry sauces. While Simon was busy skewering morsels from the dish, I asked Will quietly, 'What exactly did your Commons friend say?'

He poured the two of us cups of Rhenish. 'That a bill is being drafted to close down just the smaller monasteries – ones sitting on large endowments but with too few members to keep up the prayers their patrons paid for. There are plans for the money to be used for educational purposes.'

'That seems reasonable,' I said.

'Aye, but many folks are saying that this is but the beginning.'

'I am reluctant to admit it,' I muttered, turning my head close to Will's ear, 'but I'm inclined to think Brother Leyland is right on that score. *All* the abbeys to go down? England would be a different country – unrecognisable. The people will never stand for it.'

'Think you so, Thomas? There were those who said "the people will never stand for it" three years back when the king kicked out the pope and made himself head of the Church – and all for love of a woman.' Will grinned. 'And that is enough politics talk for one day.'

The feast extended well into the hours of darkness and all of us were feeling extremely mellow by the time we had disposed of the courses of meat, fish, cheese, elaborate sweetmeats and finally arrived at the voider of apples, nuts and hippocras. Eventually we left the table and, for a while, stood around chatting in groups. It was then that Simon Leyland drew me to one side.

'How is business, Brother?' he asked. 'It is difficult when there is a change at the top. Your father was much respected.' He crossed himself and wrinkled his brow into a frown of concern.

'You have benefited from it, I gather. Some of my customers have moved along the Row to your shop.'

He shrugged. 'We cannot stop men doing business where they will but you must believe me when I say I take no pleasure in seeing your trade decline. I will do anything in my power to help you back on your feet.' He tried to smile. It seemed to take a prodigious effort.

'Treviot's is not on its knees,' I replied, with an equally insincere grimace.

'Of course not. Of course not.' He paused, then lowered his voice – unnecessarily, for there was little chance of his being overheard in the general hubbub. 'You will, I suppose, be seeking a new wife 'ere long.'

'I'm in no hurry to forget my late wife,' I said quietly, struggling to keep my temper.

'No, indeed, but we all have to look to the next generation.'

'I have a son and heir.'

'Indeed, but a viol must have more than one string and life is so very uncertain. Think of the trials of our poor king – nearly thirty years married and only two girls to show for it.'

'Brother Simon,' I said, 'is there a point to this line of talk? There are one or two others I want to catch before they leave.'

'Just this, Brother. I have a niece – my ward, actually, daughter of my late brother, Edward. She will soon be of child-bearing age and is comely and remarkably accomplished ...'

I hitched up my gown and turned aside. 'You must excuse me, Brother. I need a word with Under Warden Hayes.'

'You will remember what I said,' he called after me.

'Indeed, Brother, when I feel inclined to cradle-snatching I will certainly let you know.'

I moved towards the upper part of the hall, through the

thinning crowd and stood to one side to allow two servants to pass supporting between them a member who had taken more advantage of the pre-Lenten bounty than was wise. In doing so, I glanced back at Simon Leyland. He was standing where I had left him fixing upon me a glare of smouldering hatred.

Chapter 5

Two weeks later I attended a celebration of a very different kind. It came about as the result of a chance encounter. I was still having trouble sleeping and would often wake from some hideous dream with sweat oozing from every pore. My mother pestered me to take some remedy. She herself was an ardent patroness of apothecaries and had in her chamber a cupboard containing numerous pots, jars and bottles for dealing with the various ailments from which she suffered or believed herself to suffer. Eventually I agreed and, thus, one bright spring morning, I walked the short distance along West Cheap as far as the Great Conduit and turned right along narrow Bucklersbury, the street where all the best grocers, perfumers and apothecaries did business. Smells from the bags of dried herbs and fruits and the onion strings hanging in open windows mingled with the acrid and sweet fragrances from open jars and simmering cauldrons. It all seemed particularly pungent that day in the mild, breezeless air. At the bottom end, at the Sign of the Boar, Stephanus Magnus plied his lucrative trade in a wide-fronted shop that, when the shutters were folded back, revealed a cavernous interior where several assistants were employed with pestles, mortars, measuring jugs and balances, while in the gloomy rear of the premises servants were bent over cauldrons on a stove. To one side, wrapped in a blue robe embroidered with mystic symbols and stained by his various concoctions, the proprietor was seated on a raised stool below a shelf of old vellum-bound books. He held a sheet of parchment and appeared to be reading it while, at the same time, keeping an eye on his underlings.

I approached and introduced myself.

He peered at me briefly before returning his attention to his manuscript. 'See my man there. Give him your urine and your birth date and threepence consultation fee.'

'I have not come for a horoscope. I need only a sleeping draft,' I explained.

'We will know what you need when we have completed your zodiac reading and assessed the balance of humours in your body.' Master Magnus seemed to be addressing his remarks to his reading matter rather than me.

'I really do not need . . .'

'Threepence,' he muttered and wafted a hand.

I did not know whether to shout angrily or laugh and contented myself with turning abruptly and striding out into Bucklersbury. I had gone no more than a few paces when I heard my name called. Walking towards me, carrying a basket, was Ned Longbourne.

'Master Treviot, well met. The shoulder gives you no more trouble, I trust?'

'No, indeed, it has mended excellent well. I am very grateful to you ... and to Lizzie for her care.'

He chuckled. 'I am sure she enjoyed playing nurse ... not that she would ever admit it.'

'No, she made it quite clear that she doesn't approve of me.'

He smiled. 'There is only one thing about you that she does not like.'

'What's that?'

'You are a man.'

'Yes, I suppose from her standpoint we are beneath contempt; creatures who deserve to be exploited because we are obsessed with fornication.'

'Oh, it goes deeper than that. It was her own father who put her to the trade she now plies.'

An image of Simon Leyland flashed into my mind. Was there any difference, I wondered, between a poor man who sold his daughter into prostitution and a rich man who offered his niece for marriage in order to become even richer?

Ned broke in on my thoughts. 'I am here to replenish my stock of herbs but what brings you to Bucklersbury? I do hope you haven't been patronising that charlatan who calls himself Stephanus Magnus.'

'I needed a sleeping draft and my mother suggested—'

'Pah! You need say no more.' In our brief acquaintance I had not seen Ned look so angry. 'Stephanus Magnus – Stephen the Great, as he likes to call himself – is a considerable success with the ladies. He impresses them with his potions and his magical fee-faw-fum. He poses as a scholar plumbing secrets far deeper than mere mortal men can understand. He calls himself an alchemist and apothecary. That's an insult to men who follow those callings honestly. The man is a fraud, a dissembler, a shammer. He started out as pedlar of

45

farthing cures, travelling from market to market. Then he discovered that showy play-acting was an easy way of impressing weak minds. Master Treviot, you should warn your mother to steer well clear of him.'

'That won't be easy but, yes, having had a brief taste of the man and his way of doing business, I'll take your advice.'

'Good, good. I'm sorry to hear about your sleeping problem. Sometimes pain or discomfort, caused by something like a broken bone, makes sleeping difficult and, even when the sensation has gone, we may find it hard to regain an untroubled night's rest.'

''Tis not the shoulder that troubles me, Ned – unless there's a demon sitting on it.'

He smiled. 'A demon?'

'Forgive me. Just a foolish fancy. Sometimes I feel an evil presence around me. I've learned to banish him from my daytime mind but at night he nips me sore.'

'Then, young sir, your "demon" lodges not on your shoulder, but in your spleen. 'Tis from there those vapours rise that bring on the melancholic humour. I have seen it often in the convent. Novices smitten with doubt about their vocation, overscrupulous brothers tormented by their supposed sins. Seek a physician, Master Treviot, and, above all, avoid quacks like Stephanus. As for the sleep problem, with your permission I'll have some dried valerian root prepared and delivered to you. I think you would find it calming and beneficial.'

Ned was as good as his word. A couple of days later a package of evil-smelling valerian root arrived, with careful instructions about dosage and the preparation of an infusion. It certainly worked. I began to enjoy better nights than I had experienced for months.

Lent passed, and Easter. I was proved wrong about the

monasteries bill. Parliament did pass it and Secretary Cromwell wasted no time in sending out his agents to receive the surrender of small religious houses and pack up their treasures. There was no rebellion. Most people seemed stunned. Stunned and confused. Radical preachers (the ones Leyland had referred to as 'New Learning' men) were put up by the king's council to applaud this new snub to the pope. It seemed that England was sliding into heresy; moving towards the kind of religion that had taken root in parts of Germany, some of the Swiss states and Denmark. But then, after another couple of weeks, all went topsy-turvy once more. King Henry had his new queen arrested and charged with adultery. Anne had, or so rumour had it, been lying with several men of the court, including her own brother. She and her lovers were tried, convicted and sentenced to death. Most Londoners were delighted. They had never liked the 'concubine'. All their sympathies had lain with old Queen Catherine and her bastardised daughter, Mary.

I had no strong feelings one way or the other. However, I was not to be allowed to distance myself from the king's affairs. One day in early May I received a summons from Under Warden John Hayes and dutifully walked along to Goldsmiths' Hall. There were half a dozen brothers present. We were informed that the king required representatives from all the crafts to be present at the Tower on the nineteenth of the month to witness the execution of the ex-queen and that we had been selected to represent the Company. The news was received with mutterings of annoyance.

'I know exactly what you are all thinking,' Warden Hayes said. 'The nineteenth of May is our patronal festival.'

St Dunstan's Day was, indeed, the most important date in the Company's calendar. Not only did we celebrate the life of our patron saint at solemn mass, we also went on procession with our banners and a choir, inaugurated our new wardens for the year and changed the date stamp applied to all assayed items of gold and silver. Of course, the celebration ended with another great feast.

I was, perhaps, more irritated than most of my brothers. I was trying hard to take Robert's advice and re-establish my reputation as a reliable and dutiful member of the Worshipful Company, so it was important for me to be seen as participating faithfully in all our rituals. Having to watch Queen Anne's execution would be as inconvenient as it would be distasteful. If only I could have known just how drastically the events of St Dunstan's Day, 1536, would change my life.

'How are we expected to be in two places at once?' someone protested.

Hayes nodded. 'It is, indeed, very unfortunate, but His Majesty has decreed it and we have no choice in the matter. You will have to miss the mass and join the rest of your brothers as soon as you can.'

Later that same day, as I sat at my desk in the workshop, another message was handed to me by one of my men. 'Brought to the front, sir, by an uncouth fellow none of us recognised,' he explained. 'He's waiting for a reply.'

The letter was in a neat hand and, shutting out the din from the workbenches, I read its few lines.

To Master Thomas Treviot. I commend me to your remembrance, good sir, and am in hope that you are in no worse case than at our last meeting. You spoke then of a *daemon* that troubled you and I was so bold as to recommend you to seek the ministrations of a *reliable* physician. I have thought much on what you said then and you will, I hope, forgive me if I venture some further observations. There are several ways to regain a balance of the humours. I have sometimes found borage and black hellebore efficacious in cases of melancholia, and hot, moist food expels dryness from the spleen vapours. Yet, I must not make great pretence to the physician's art lest you think me as big a quack as that dissembling cozener, Stephanus. However, there is a balm that, in my experience, soothes the melancholic spirit. I refer to company. Time spent with agreeable companions is better than overmuch solitariness. To that end my friends and I are in hopes that it might please you to come to us for supper at the Sign of St Swithun at five in the afternoon of the eighteenth day of May. The bearer will bring your reply.

Your assured friend,

Edward Longbourne

I reached for my quill and inkpot to write a reply offering regrets and explaining that I could not accept an invitation to a party on the eve of St Dunstan's Day, when I would be extremely busy and would certainly need to have a clear head. Even now, I know not what changed my mind at the last moment. Perhaps it suddenly seemed churlish to turn my back on people who had shown me kindness. Lizzie's taunts had certainly stung me and it may be that I hoped to convince her that I was not the haughty, judgemental swellhead she took me for. Whatever my reason I accepted the invitation, promising myself that I would not stay long at the party and that I would be safely back in my own bed by nightfall. So, the following Thursday I set off for Southwark, naturally without letting anyone know my destination, for what I imagined would be but a few hours' diversion.

I heard the party before I saw it. As I entered the courtyard of St Swithun's House the steady beat of a drum reached me, accompanied by a bagpipe's wail. These sounds led me to a ground floor room of moderate size already half-filled with revellers. In the centre a circle of men and women were caught up in a lively dance while the spectators encouraged them by clapping the rhythm. It was noisy and very hot. The air was filled with the mingled smell of sweating bodies and cooking meat. I made my way along to the far end where trenchers of food and jugs of ale were laid out on a long table. An older woman with a heavily painted face pressed a flagon into my hand and I had just taken a sip when Ned Longbourne clapped a hand on my shoulder.

'Welcome to our humble feast, Master Treviot. How like you Wily Winchester's ale?'

'Gardiner has provided this?' I asked in some surprise.

A wispy-bearded little man standing next to Ned laughed through blackened teeth, half-choking on his drink. 'Oh, aye,' he spluttered, 'only he don't know it. Ain't that so, doctor?'

'What Long Ben here means,' Ned explained, 'is that a wagon of barley on its way to the good bishop's brew house from one of his manors met with the same fate as the man who travelled from Jerusalem to Jericho – it fell among thieves. Somehow it ended up here.'

That sent Long Ben into a paroxysm of laughter. Ned steered me away. 'Come and meet some of your fellow guests.'

The company was more diverse than would have been found in any other gathering within the capital and its sprawling settlements. There were men wearing the aprons or breeches that indicated their trades, young students from the

Inns of Court in their gowns and others whose stylish clothes suggested a possible connection with the royal court. The favours of the St Swithun's ladies, it seemed, were a cloak spread over the whole of society – or, at least, those members of society who cared little for their reputations. In an adjoining room there were tables for cards and dicing. I moved among the crowd, hoping for a glimpse of Lizzie but it was some time before I saw her enter the room with a customer in an unfastened doublet, who had an arm round her waist and was slobbering over her neck. It was no very great surprise that this 'supper' was also a way of increasing the bawdy house's clientele or that Lizzie would be simply doing her job but, somehow, I found the sight distasteful. Coming here, I realised, had been a mistake. Robert was right. It was foolish of me to put my reputation at risk for such people. I decided that I would drink my fill and then leave. I found a corner near the table to lean against and from this vantage point watched the dancers who, as the evening wore on, became increasingly leaden-footed in their capers. From time to time one or other of the women volunteered to convey me to another room for 'extra entertainment' but I curtly waved them away.

When candles were lit in the sconces I judged the time was right to leave. The drink, the din, the heat and the smell had begun to cloud my head. I needed fresh air and my own bed. I made an uneven progress towards the door.

'Not enjoying yourself, Master Treviot?' Lizzie appeared at my side and linked her arm through mine.

'It has been very pleasant but I must away home.'

She pouted. 'Before your wife starts asking awkward questions?'

I turned to face her. 'I have no wife – and if I had I certainly would not be spending my evenings here.' The words came out more angrily than I had intended and brought back Lizzie's familiar scowl.

'Till you tired of her charms. Then you would be back here soon enough.'

'Not so!' I protested and felt my cheeks burning with indignation.

'Oh, yes so!' Lizzie stood, shouting. 'God's blood, master self-conceited merchant, do you suppose we don't know all about husbands here? You want your wives to be as chaste as the Blessed Virgin, while you take your pleasure where you will.' Her sneer was ugly. 'You're all from the same mould as Lecher Harry. He grows tired of his wife, goes panting after little Mistress Seymour and when the queen protests it is she who must be charged with adultery.'

A circle had now formed round us and Lizzie was enjoying her performance. 'Don't you know why we celebrate today? This is our wake for Queen Anne, who will die tomorrow. The king protests that she's a whore. Well, then, she's our sister and we mourn her.'

There were cheers from the audience but also a few angry murmurs. A thin, yellow-haired young man in a fashionable doublet of sky blue silk stained with ale stepped forward. 'Who speaks ill of the king?' he demanded. 'I'll not drink with traitors.' He threw the dregs of his tankard at Lizzie and it splashed in her face.

She fell back a pace. The crowd roared their anger. The assailant sneered. With another jerk of his hand he threw the tankard at me. 'And there's for your whore-master!' he shouted. I stepped forward to confront him. He stood his ground, swaying slightly, cheeks flushed with insolence and drink. I called out something – I know not what. He responded by putting his hand to the poignard at his belt. I fumbled for my own weapon. The crowd closed in on us. Someone shouted, 'Fight!' and others took up the chant: 'Fight! Fight! Fight!'

Blue-doublet and I circled each other. My opponent made a sudden lunge. I twisted sideways to ward off the blow. His point tore my sleeve and I felt its sharpness against my flesh. With an oath I swung round for a counter-blow. The other man stepped back a pace. Behind me, Lizzie cried, 'Enough!' But my eyes were fixed on the courtier's blade, watching for his next sally. Ned stepped briskly between us. 'Gentlemen, gentlemen, there's no need . . .' My foe planted his left hand in the old man's chest and sent him sprawling among the rushes. My anger was now fully aroused. I hurled a mouthful of insults and made a leap forward. Blue-doublet sidestepped. Then, taking advantage of my impetus, he came at me again. He missed and lost his footing in a pool of spilled ale. As he struggled to right himself his upper body was undefended. I drew back my right arm and thrust my dagger at his chest. With a scream he dropped his weapon and fell to the floor.

At that moment I felt my hand grabbed and I was pulled away. Lizzie dragged me from the crowd, through a doorway and up a staircase. I was vaguely aware of entering a chamber and being pushed towards a bed.

After that I remembered nothing until I was shaken into consciousness in my own room on the morning of that fateful St Dunstan's Day with an angry Robert Packington standing over me, impatient to take me to my ordeal at the Tower.

Chapter 6

After Anne's execution, I did not attend the Company's St Dunstan's Day celebrations. I was in no fit state for a long day of formal activities and enforced camaraderie. Robert hustled me home and wrote a note excusing me on grounds of ill health. I signed it and had John Fink take it to Goldsmiths' Hall. Then I returned to my bed in hopes of sleeping off the effects of the previous evening. It was some hours and a couple more vomiting attacks before I began to feel myself.

Meanwhile, my behaviour had not gone unnoticed among the craft fraternity. The incident in the Tower provoked a formal complaint to the wardens of the Goldsmiths' Company. It also set tongues wagging, as I learned when Will Fitzralph called the following morning. He pointed out gleefully that I had missed a particularly good dinner.

'There was roast swan for us below the salt, as well as

above,' he enthused, 'and partridges, woodcocks and plovers aplenty. Our new cook is a wonder with pastry. His side dishes were very novel – payn puffs filled with ragouts of port, dates, raisins, spices and I know not what else. The minstrels gave us some of the latest airs from France.'

'I regret missing it,' I said, 'but I fear I would not have been able to do justice to it.'

'I was sorry for your absence.' He paused, suddenly solemn. 'There were those who were not. It gave Simon Leyland and his boon copains opportunity for gossip. They grumbled that you've been ignoring your business these last months. Leyland actually had the gall to suggest that you were well enough to visit the Stews but not to fulfil your obligations to the Company.'

'Leyland is a malicious troublemaker who hopes to advance his own business by ruining mine.'

Will nodded. 'That's well known, Thomas, but you'd be wise to mark him. He's not without influence, especially with one of our new wardens, Thomas Sponer.' He paused before looking at me with an anxious frown. 'There's no truth in it, is there – about your getting drunk witless in a bawdy house?'

'What does Leyland care about truth?' I blustered. 'He'll say anything to harm me.'

After Will left I sat for a long time in my chamber, think-ing hard. Something must be very wrong if I found it necessary to lie to my friends. It was ironical, I reflected, that, just as the ache of grief was slowly fading and my life was regaining some normality, I should find myself in fresh trouble. I roundly cursed my own stupidity. Just how serious my trouble was I learned that very afternoon. A messenger from Goldsmiths' Hall came to the sign of the Swan to deliver a summons. I was to appear before the Court of Assistants, the Company's governing body, to answer charges of 'disrespectful and disorderly conduct unbecoming a freeman of the Worshipful Company of Goldsmiths'. My first reaction was to spare my mother this disagreeable news. I arranged for her to make an earlier than usual departure for Hemmings, our manor in Kent. We usually spent the summer months there to avoid the plague and the fevers that haunted the City in the hotter weather. She was protective of her health almost to the point of obsession so that when I passed on a 'popular rumour' that the sweating sickness was about to pay a return visit, she readily agreed to have her coffers packed. I promised to join her within days.

My next move was to turn to Robert Packington for help. My friend's tendency to lecture me was tedious but I knew that there was no one else I could trust with my confidences and whom I could rely on for wise advice.

We met one noontime at Blossoms Inn in St Lawrence's Lane. This popular hostelry had two advantages. It was always thronged with businessmen – foreign visitors as well as citizens – and our presence would attract no attention. Second, Robert was well known to the innkeeper, who kept for us a quiet table in a corner away from the door. We ordered ale and cheese and when these had arrived I explained to my friend in a very few words the latest development.

He tugged at his beard, a gesture that, I well knew, indicated extreme irritation. It was some moments before he spoke. 'You know how serious this is.'

'Yes, I . . . '

'No, I think you do not.' He slapped the table with the flat of his hand. For a phlegmatic man unaccustomed to physical gestures this was further indication of his impatience. 'I have spoken to Master Hubbard.'

'Hubbard?'

He sighed. 'The man you vomited over. I explained that you have a weak stomach and were overwhelmed by the beheading. He understands and I have promised him a new gown. He is, I think, satisfied with that.' Robert stared at me fixedly.

I muttered my thanks, trying not to meet his eyes.

He sighed. 'You really don't see what that means, do you?' He paused. 'If Hubbard is not making trouble for you, then someone else is. This is not just about what happened in the Tower. There are stories about you going round all over town.'

'What sort of stories?'

'Some say Treviot's is heading for bankruptcy. Others say that the head of Treviot's has fallen beside his wits and wanders the country raving like a madman. They claim that he deserts his own kind and resorts to low company.'

'That is all absurd!' I protested.

'Of course it is but false rumours like these undermine business confidence – and business confidence is an exceeding fragile flower.'

I gazed despondently into my tankard. 'How can I put a stop to all these stories?'

'Two things.' Robert pointed his knife at me. 'Start behaving like your father's son. These slanders could not gain credence if there was not some truth in them. You have grieved long and hard for your double loss but the time has come to put an end to it. You cannot think that either Jane or your father would want you to continue your eccentric behaviour.'

'Eccentric?'

'Spending days in a haunt south of the river so notorious that you are ashamed to tell me about it is certainly something I call eccentric. Getting so drunk that you cannot—'

I held a hand up. 'Yes, yes, don't rub my nose in it, Robert. What is the second thing you want me to do?'

'Find out who is behind these stories. Such rumours do not spread themselves unaided. I have not the slightest doubt that someone wants to put you out of business. Can you think who it might be? Is there someone who bears you a special grudge?'

'Well, there is a member of the Company who may consider himself slighted by me but I don't think he would denounce me to the Council.' I told Robert about my clash with Simon Leyland.

He frowned thoughtfully. 'I do not know the man but I will make enquiries.'

We addressed ourselves to our simple meal. It was a couple of minutes before Robert spoke again.

'Will you suffer a further word of advice?'

I nodded.

'The fact that you have inherited a flourishing business makes you particularly vulnerable to rumour and innuendo.'

'What do you mean?' I asked.

'Simply this: younger freemen of your company look at you and see someone of their own age who has had success handed to him on a platter, while they have to wait for their fathers to die or work hard to establish their own business from nothing. That may well breed jealousy. Older freemen of your company look at you and see a junior craft member who has none of their experience but yet rivals them in wealth and prestige. That may breed resentment. Anyone who wishes you ill will not lack for associates.'

'I see. What about you, Robert? When you look at me, what do you see?'

He scrutinised me keenly across the table. 'I see a man who cannot yet see himself; who is sensitive to his shortcomings, which daily accuse him, but who has yet to discover all his strengths. Such a man should look into the mirror of Holy Scripture.' He lowered his voice, although there was no one close enough to overhear our conversation. 'Have you yet read Master Tyndale's translation?'

'I have sampled it,' I replied mendaciously.

'Look deeper,' he urged with an earnest gleam in his eye. 'It is God's very own truth. I especially recommend the fifteenth of Saint Luke.' After a pause, he continued in a normal voice. 'Now we must consider how best to handle your examination.'

That Robert was a secret Bible lover disconcerted me, but I was too preoccupied with my own trouble to give it much thought.

'What do you think the Council will do?' I asked nervously.

'You know that as well as I. It could be a fine or a spell in the Counter Prison. If they are really annoyed, they may suspend your freeman status for a while.'

'Is there nothing I can do?'

'There may be something I can do, though it will not be easy. Your Prime Warden is a friend of mine. We sit together on the Common Council of the City. I will have a word with him.'

I felt like a shipwrecked sailor who sights a floating spar.

'You are very kind, Robert – more, perhaps, than I deserve. Anything you can do . . . '

He waved my thanks aside. 'It is you who will have the more difficult task of convincing your seniors. Your immediate responsibility is to make sure you give no one any opportunity to blacken your name. Your conduct must be beyond reproach. Above all, avoid bad company.' Again he fixed me with his penetrating gaze. 'I think you know what I mean.'

I knew only too well. Robert was telling me to restrict my

movements to the north side of the Thames. But this I could not do. I had to pay another visit to St Swithun's House.

As the fog in my brain gradually lifted, I remembered the details of the hideous party: the drunken courtier's insult of Lizzie, the ensuing fight, Lizzie dragging me away. Anxiety hovered in my mind like a menacing hawk. I was worried about Lizzie and needed to know that she was safe. But it was fear of the still unknown whose talons I felt most sharply. I saw myself standing over a man in a blue doublet, his face distorted with pain. In my hand was a dagger dripping with blood. I had to go back to Southwark to find an answer to the question that would not be silenced – was I a murderer?

Chapter 7

For my visit I chose Sunday morning, when many citizens would be at mass and the streets less crowded. The sound of the priory bells filled the air as I turned Dickon into the court-yard of the Sign of St Swithun. It was almost eerily quiet. When I had dismounted I had to knock on a couple of doors before I could rouse anyone.

Young Jed eventually peered out. He seemed genuinely star-tled to see me and hesitant when asked if I might come in. Hurriedly he closed the door behind me and stood to one side, barefoot and in his shirt, as though just out of bed.

'I'm sorry if I've disturbed you,' I mumbled.

'What is it, Master Treviot? What do you want here?'

'I've come to find out exactly what happened on my last visit. I know I got into a fight but after that my mind is a blank. Tell me, Jed, I have to know, did I kill someone?'

He seemed relieved at the explanation. 'No, you passed out. Me and a couple of friends took you home. We was told you had to get back specially.'

'Thank you so much.' I leaned back against the door, my body sagging with relief.

The young man was now shuffling nervously from foot to foot. 'We was happy to help, Master Treviot.' He reached out his hand towards the latch.

'So the other man is all right? Thank God.'

Jed was trying to pull the door open, obviously anxious to be rid of me.

'Best you were not here, Master Treviot,' he whispered.

'Who's there, Jed?' I heard Ned's voice as an inner door opened.

I turned and saw the ex-monk standing in the doorway, tucking his shirt inside his breeches. He, too, seemed disturbed to see me but quickly recovered his composure. 'Ah, Master Thomas, how good of you to call. If you'll excuse me for a moment . . . ' He went back into the inner room and reappeared moments later, fastening the points of his doublet. He extended a hand. 'I hope you are more yourself now than when you left us last.'

'I fear your hospitality overwhelmed me. I must have put Jed and others to a lot of trouble.'

'It was a troubled evening.' He paused, as though deciding whether to say more. 'But come in. Come in. We've some violet cordial here that will slake your thirst and restore your spirits.'

I followed him into the room. It was a crowded chamber, obviously with many purposes. A wide bed stood in one corner. A large carved coffer beside it had an ecclesiastical look to it – salvaged from the monastery, perhaps. Three joined stools stood beside a table spread with books, bottles, jars and the other necessities of Ned's apothecary activities. He poured intense pink liquid into pewter mugs and we seated ourselves by the table. Jed perched on the edge of the bed.

It was I who broke the awkward silence that followed. 'As I told Jed, I came simply to find out what happened to the man I fought with. How badly was he injured?'

Ned waved a hand airily. 'It was nothing. A flesh wound. You scarcely drew blood.'

'That is welcome news, indeed. I've been worried. You spoke of a troubled evening – was there more violence later?'

The two men exchanged glances. Then Ned said, 'It would probably be better for you not to be involved.'

'You speak in riddles. If whatever happened concerns me in some way, then, of course, I should know.'

He sighed. 'Very well. While you were in a stupor upstairs, your would-be assailant continued to make himself unpleasant. He was shouting all manner of threats and determined to come and find you. Jed and a couple of other burly lads got you out a back way and made sure you reached home. When she was sure you were safely off the premises, Lizzie came down and foolishly thought she could calm the troublemaker.' He shook his head. 'She has always been too headstrong, poor child.'

'What happened?' I almost shouted.

'The fellow drew a knife. It was very sudden.'

'You mean he stabbed her, killed her?'

'No, no, no – nothing so dreadful. Although—'

'Ned, in Jesu's name, tell me!'

'He went for her face.'

The shock silenced me.

Ned continued. 'I tended her immediately ... in here. Wine to clean the wound, warm oil to ease the pain. Fortunately the cut was not deep; there was little bleeding. She bore it all very bravely – more concerned about how she would look than the possibility of some poisonous infection of the air. It is that that concerns me. I cannot tell if putrefaction has set in until I remove the bandages. I considered the possibility of suture ... I have seen it done by a brother who spent some years as a military chirurgeon ... but she feared the needle would cause more scarring and, of course, she was right. So I have drawn the flesh together as tight as I can and we must wait to see ... we must wait to see.' He drained his mug and fell silent.

'And what of her attacker?' I demanded. 'Who is he? Have you had him charged?'

Jed gave a bitter laugh. 'Don't be stupid! A gentleman of the king's court accused of wounding a whore. It would never come before the judges. If it did what would their verdict be? We have better ways of seeing justice done.'

Ned nodded. 'I cannot approve but what Jed says is true. Master Nathaniel Seagrave has paid for his crime. We wait to hear news from the waterfront that his body has washed up downriver.'

I gasped. 'The man is dead – murdered?'

'No less than he deserved,' Jed muttered.

Ned said, 'When you came knocking Jed thought it might be someone reporting the discovery of the corpse ... or bringing less welcome news.'

'What might that be?'

Ned turned away with a deep sigh. 'Master Seagrave has friends – powerful friends. Some were with him that evening. They have vowed not to let his death go unavenged.'

'Seagrave?' The name seemed familiar. I felt sure I had seen it in one of my business ledgers. 'Was he not a server in the king's privy chamber?'

'Aye, that he was, and typical of the preening halfwits who are drawn to the court like maggots to dead meat. He came here mainly for the gambling.'

Then I remembered. The name Nathaniel Seagrave featured on my blacklist of customers whose credit had run out. 'You do well to be cautious,' I suggested. 'The young members of the royal household are a proud and tight band.'

'So are we,' Jed muttered. 'If it comes to a fight we can take care of ourselves.'

'No doubt.' Ned ran a hand wearily through his fringe of white hair. 'But what of the women?'

'Do you really think Seagrave's friends are so cowardly as to vent their anger on them?' I asked.

'Why not? To such hypocrites whores are not really women at all. When they've had their fill of them they look on them as vagabonds, clapperdudgeon beggars, cony-catching card-sharps, highway robbers and general gallows fodder. A man like Seagrave would boast of what he did to Lizzie and think of it as sport.'

'Then Lizzie is especially in danger,' I said.

'I fear she may well be.'

'Then she should not be here.'

'Where could she go?' Ned shrugged. 'To the best of my knowledge she has no family now. A mother and sister died in the last outbreak of the sweat.'

'May I see her?'

'Why?'

'What has befallen her is my fault. I must see if there is something I can do.'

'She is greatly shocked. Indeed, I think she has suffered more in mind than body. She shuns all company.'

'At least I must try.'

Ned shook his head. 'We can go up to her room but I doubt . . . '

He led the way out of the chamber, up the staircase and along the narrow passageway. We passed two chambers, including the one in which I had been kept in January, before reaching a door on which Ned knocked, then entered. By the light of half-opened shutters I could see that there had been some attempt to make this room attractive. It boasted a wide cushioned chair that must have been expensive. There was a worn tapestry covering one wall that could only have come originally from a fine house and another wall had erotic wood-cuts pinned to it. The bed was of a good size and canopied. Lizzie lay under a coloured coverlet, her face turned away from us. I could see that some of her hair had been shorn and her head swathed with bandages. The air was thick with a pungent aroma, presumably from the herbal ointment Ned had used to dress the wound.

'How bad is the cut?' I whispered to Ned.

With his finger he drew a line across his own left cheek from ear to mouth. 'God be praised it missed her eye,' he said softly.

'Who's there?' Lizzie muttered without turning over.

'It's Ned.' He moved across to the bed. 'Let me look at your bandages.'

She groaned and turned over. Only her eyes and mouth were visible through slits in the dressings. 'There's someone else there,' she said, as Ned bent over her.

'Master Treviot has been good enough to call,' Ned explained.

'Treviot!' Lizzie sat up suddenly as though stung. 'Tell that smug, canting, posturing, self-satisfied moneybags to get his fat arse out of here!'

I stepped forward. 'Lizzie, I—'

'Out! Out!' she screeched, her eyes glaring at me through the visor of her cloths. 'You damned slack-brained clodpole! Look what you've done to me! You've killed me!'

'Not so, Lizzie—'

'Yes. Look at me. I was only good for one thing! Who will want to bed me now?'

Ned tried to calm her. 'The scar may not be that bad. We shan't know until—'

'Damn your lukewarm lies, monk! I'm as good as starved to death and you know it. Why did you ever bring your merchant friend here? Everything has gone wrong since then.'

I tried again. 'Lizzie, please listen. I can help. Perhaps take you somewhere where you can recover properly; where you'll be safer.'

It was no use. 'Do you think I'd go anywhere with you? Jolthead!' She lay down again and turned away from us.

We retreated to Ned's chamber.

'She's right, of course,' he observed mournfully. 'We're a tight, supportive community here but if she can no longer pay her way . . . '

'That's why I think I should take her into my own household.'

Ned's thick brows rose in an incredulous stare. 'Master Thomas. I commend your compassion, but to take a whore under your roof. The scandal!' He shook his head. 'Even if Lizzie agreed, I cannot think it would do either of you any good.'

'No one need know about her past,' I said.

Ned's laugh was mirthless. 'I doubt you could keep that secret from prying neighbours and gossiping servants.'

'I have an idea that might work,' I explained. 'My mother is away at our country house with a small household. It's very quiet there and my mother would value the company. If we tidy Lizzie up ... some respectable clothes ... Do you not think she could be made very presentable?'

'I have little experience of ladies,' Ned said, 'but I think your mother would not be easily fooled.'

'My mother, alas, is failing in mind. Sometimes she does not even know me.'

Ned stood for several moments, his brow furrowed. 'Thomas,' he said at last, 'I have seen what evil tricks guilt can play. I have watched brothers punish their bodies and minds with self-imposed penances. Scourging and hair shirts are all very well for the saints but they are not right for all of us.'

'I'm not suggesting this to quiet my own conscience,' I replied. 'At least I don't think so. You heard what Lizzie said about me ...'

'She is bitter and frightened ...'

'I know what she fears.' I recalled our visit to the unmarried women's burial plot. 'I want to deliver her from that fear if I can. That much I owe her. Do you have a better plan?'

Ned's mournful silence was my answer.

'Then will you try to persuade her to give my plan a try?'

Chapter 8

The next day I arrived at Robert's house in Sopers Lane in good time for our appointment with the Wardens of the Goldsmiths' Company. I was shown into the garden where his wife Margaret sat reading beneath a mulberry tree, which was just coming into full leaf. She rose to greet me and, in so doing, let slip her book. When I retrieved it she took it hastily, closed it and, placing it beside her, covered it with a piece of tapestry she had been sewing, but not before I had read the name 'Luther' on the fly leaf.

Margaret, a plump lady in her forties, was as serious in her demeanour as her husband. 'I am sorry Robert is not back yet,' she said as I seated myself at her side. 'He had to go to Bakewell Hall. A consignment of cloths in from Suffolk, I believe. You know how it is when the clothiers arrive; all the dealers converge like wasps on a honey pot. Of course, if it had not been the clothiers, it would have been Mercers' Company business, or City Council business or parliament – you did know he's back in the Commons house? – and as if that wasn't enough there always seem to be little jobs to do for Master Cromwell. What with one thing or another we rarely see him these days. 'Tis particularly hard on his children.'

When she paused to draw breath, I said, 'I know how busy he is. I feel guilty that this little affair of mine is taking up still more of his time.'

'Oh, no, Thomas, you must not think that. Robert is very happy to help. He was so very fond of your father. He regards you as almost one of his own children.'

At that moment Robert appeared from the house, striding over the newly scythed grass with his usual purposeful gait. As soon as he had greeted us, Mistress Packington took her cue and returned indoors. Robert took her place on the bench.

'Now,' he began, in his usual brisk manner, 'I have made enquiries into Brother Simon Leyland and the business he runs with his younger brother. It seems that they are not the most scrupulous merchants in London. There was a case of false weights a few years ago which they managed to escape with a small fine. Their clients include some of the highest in the land and that has created problems for them.'

'How so?'

'They have lent to members of the king's council and court who have been less than prompt in making repayment. As a result they have been obliged to borrow secretly from foreign merchants. They desperately need new customers.'

'Which explains why they have been poaching mine.'

'Exactly. Now, we cannot make accusations at your hearing. The Leylands are not under examination. But we might be able to make subtle references that the Court are sure to recognise.'

70

'Why do you say "we"?' I asked.

'You've never been present at a meeting of the Court of Assistants, I suppose.'

'No, I thank God. No one is summoned before that august body unless he is in real trouble.'

Robert allowed himself a slight smile. 'You should not be too much in awe of them; they are only a dozen fallible present and past wardens and they have to overlook every aspect of the Company's life. They will have several other matters on their agenda today. I suggested to the Prime Warden that your affair might be dealt with more expeditiously if I were to speak on your behalf.'

'But you are not of our fellowship,' I protested.

'The rules permit you to have an advocate present and they do not specify that he must be a member of the Company. So, I will be beside you and I suggest you take your lead from me. Above all else be sure to appear humble and contrite.'

We spent several more minutes discussing the forthcoming ordeal and, after a light dinner that I was too nervous to do much justice to, we set off for Goldsmiths' Hall. My examination by the Wardens' Court took place in what was called the Ladies' Chamber, a first-floor parlour of large size but comfortably furnished. It was here that members' wives and daughters were entertained and where the Court held meetings.

After a short wait we were admitted. The new Prime Warden, Sir John Mundy, sat behind a long table, flanked by eleven of his colleagues, all wearing their blue scarlet-hooded robes of office. At one end a scribe was stationed. The only sound was the scratching of his pen. Robert and I stood in the middle of the room.

Eventually Mundy looked up with a grave half-smile. 'Master Packington, it is an honour to welcome you. Brother Treviot is extremely fortunate to have you as his advocate.' Mundy directed his gaze at me and the smile faded. 'Brother Treviot, it is not the custom of this Worshipful Company to pass judgement on the private lives of members. We are interested only in preserving the high standards of workmanship and business practice for which we are justly famous. However, when the conduct of a brother attracts unfavourable comment and impairs his relationship with other members as well as customers, we have to take note of it. Do you understand?'

'Yes, sir.' I stood, looking, I hoped, suitably abashed, my eyes fixed on the herb-strewn floor.

The Prime Warden continued. 'It has been noted for some months that you have neglected your shop and effectively delegated the conduct of business to someone who is not a freeman. Furthermore, you have been recognised paying frequent visits south of the river to a place of disrepute, as one result of which you absented yourself from the St Dunstan's Day assembly. All this may suggest to some observers that you have scant regard for the privileges and responsibilities of membership of this Worshipful Company. If this council failed to take action it might appear that we condoned such a casual attitude. Can you produce any explanation that might influence the decision we have to reach?'

Robert now intervened. 'Masters, not twelve months since, your Worshipful Company and, indeed, the whole merchant community of the City suffered an irreplaceable loss in the death of the older Thomas Treviot. That loss, however, was as nothing compared with that sustained by his family. Before his grieving son could recover from that blow he sustained another in the decease of his young wife. The wise Solomon tells us, "There is a time for sadness and a time for mirth; a time to grieve and a time to dance." Who can say how long these times, set by God, should last? Grief may be like a cave a man enters, hoping to pass through it and emerge into the sunlight once more. Yet, if the cave be long and beset with twists and turns, he may despair of ever escaping from the dark. Such despair may turn to madness. Masters, should not those of us who are older and have seen more of the world's trials be lights in the darkness?'

It was Under Warden Thomas Sponer, a lean-faced, thin-lipped man, who responded. 'Eloquently put, Master Packington. We are well aware of our responsibility to help and we have given support in various ways over the last few months. But we do have to satisfy ourselves that the recipients of our beneficence respond by doing all they can to help themselves. As Prime Warden Mundy has said, our ultimate responsibility is to guard the good name of the whole fellowship and we cannot permit any individual to jeopardise it.' He turned a stern gaze upon me. 'Brother Treviot, this council is entrusted with certain disciplinary powers that it must exercise for the good of the Worshipful Company. Our ultimate sanction, as you are aware, is the suspension of a brother freeman from membership, either temporarily or permanently.'

Beside me, Robert coughed lightly and, when I glanced in his direction, he nodded imperceptibly. I took the hint.

'Sirs, I am very grateful for your wise advice and for the practical assistance you and other brothers have given me over these difficult months. I see now that my preoccupation with my own troubles has blinded me to the problems I have posed to the Worshipful Company. For this I beg Your Worships' forgiveness.'

Robert added, 'I can vouch for the fact that Brother Treviot has, indeed, carefully considered his former conduct. He has already reassumed full responsibility for his business. If Your

Worships are prepared to allow me to act as his guide and mentor, I believe it will not be necessary to take any drastic action at this stage.'

The councillors consulted in lowered voices. I watched nervously, my whole body taut with anxiety. From their gestures and glances I gained the impression that, while several were responding favourably to Robert's words, Under Warden Sponer was arguing for an example to be made of me. My advocate chose his moment for another intervention.

'Masters, it might help if I were to mention a not dissimilar incident that occurred some months ago in my own company. One of our brethren had fallen into financial difficulties. He was too proud to seek help from his seniors. Instead, he tried to recover his position by dishonest means. Eventually we summoned him before the wardens. Instead of answering that summons, he cut his own throat. To this day I feel guilty about that. I know that my colleagues and I should have intervened sooner. But worse was to follow. When we met to sort out the poor fellow's affairs, we discovered that members of our own fellowship had been seeking to profit from their brother's difficulties. I forbear to go into details. I simply wanted to assure you that I am only too aware of the responsibility you carry and the many factors you have to take into account.'

Some twenty minutes later Robert and I were walking back down Foster Lane, he in his usual steady stride, me with a decided spring in my step.

'Thank you so much, Robert,' I said. 'That was masterly. Perhaps you should not have abandoned the law.'

He waved a hand dismissively. 'My hypothetical case may have made them reflect more deeply.'

'Hypothetical?' I exclaimed.

'Yes, I did mention that it was simply an example of what

could happen, did I not?' He stepped ahead to sidle past a wagon that was taking up all the width of the lane because of scaffolding coating St Vedast's Church. I caught up with him as we turned into West Cheap.

'Did you see Sponer's face? He was furious.'

'You must have a care for friend Sponer. He is very thick with Leyland. And you must follow your wardens' injunction to the letter. You are on probation for six months and must appear before them again in December. Your behaviour between now and then must be impeccable and I have solemnly sworn to ensure that it is so. It will do no harm for you to be seen accompanying me to church sometimes. Above all, you must look to your own soul. I trust you are still reading the New Testament.'

It was after this that I *did* start to leaf through Tyndale's book in the seclusion of my own chamber. I began with the fifteenth chapter of St Luke's Gospel, to which Robert had particularly directed my attention. There I read about a graceless son who forsook his own home, wasted all his money in 'riotous living' and returned to his father, who welcomed him as though nothing had happened. I could not doubt that I had been directed to this particular text as the strongest possible hint that I should repent of my involvement with disreputable companions and return to mercantile respectability. I was now more than ready to comply. The days passed with no word from Ned and, as it was evident that Lizzie had spurned my offer of help, I satisfied myself that I had done all I could and, probably, more than I should.

Come early June I had put St Swithun's House and all its turbulent events behind me. That was when I received a message from Ned. He had, with great difficulty, persuaded Lizzie to accept my offer of a temporary refuge.

Chapter 9

There was much to organise if Lizzie was to be comfortably installed at Hemmings. First she had to be supplied with a suitable wardrobe. I had retained one of Jane's close attendants and now I had her make a selection of my wife's clothes. Jane's press had not been opened since her death and I still could not face going through her things. I left the task to young Susannah, saying that I was making provision for a friend of Jane's who had fallen on hard times. When a large coffer had been filled with what Susannah assured me were all the necessary garments, I sent word to Ned, who brought a wagon to collect it.

The move began on a midsummer day that promised great heat. Ned and Jed came to Goldsmith's Row to collect my *koch* or coach. My father had been one of the first in London to order a vehicle built to the latest design from the Continent and it made journeys to and from Hemmings much more comfortable for my mother and her attendants. It was also the envy of our neighbours – a fact from which my mother derived secret pleasure. Soon after the koch's departure I set out on horseback and reached my house near Ightham in the Wealden valley early in the evening. Thus, I arrived a full half day before the Southwark party and was able to prepare my mother to receive our guest.

I was in the small summer parlour overlooking Hemmings's broad lawn when that guest arrived. Mother sat by the window to catch the light on her sewing. Lizzie entered, holding Ned's arm. I had been faintly curious to know what she would look like in her new attire but was quite unprepared for the transformation that had come over her. Gone were the wrinkled chemise and the brown, drab woollen gown. Gone was the lustrous but unruly cascade of unrestrained hair. Lizzie now appeared in a dark-green embroidered kirtle, with sleeves of a lighter shade and a russet overgown. Her hair was combed and covered with a simple linen coif. She appeared every inch the modest maiden. The only thing that marred her appearance was the dark oval patch applied to her left cheek. When I introduced her she made a light curtsey.

'Mistress Treviot, this is so kind. I do hope I shall not be a bother to you. Oh, what fine needlework. May I look?'

My mother handed over her sewing frame, completely won over. 'You are more than welcome, Mistress . . . ? You must tell me your name again, child. Tom mumbles so.'

'Garney, Elizabeth Garney, but my friends call me Lizzie.'

'Come and sit here, in the window, Lizzie. I think Tom has told me very little about you but I do tend to forget things.'

'Dear Tom is such a secretive young man.' Lizzie threw a cynical smile in my direction.

I left them to become acquainted and withdrew with Ned to the hall.

'How did you persuade her to come?' I asked. 'I really thought she hated me too much even to consider my proposal.'

Ned chuckled. 'Ah, that was before I was able to offer her the bribe.'

'Bribe?'

'There are many women who would do almost anything for a fine set of fashionable clothes.'

'Whatever caused her change of heart, I'm glad of it. I hope this may be a fresh start for her. I'd like to think she can put her past behind her.'

'Would that salve your conscience?' Ned asked.

I did not answer.

For the rest of the summer I divided my time between Hemmings and Goldsmith's Row. The little female coterie in Kent was more than content to gossip and ogle my infant son. Lizzie was a great success with Raphael and when the wet nurse left, at the end of September, she slipped naturally into the role of his carer. The sweating sickness did, in fact, break out in high summer and there was no question of my family returning to town. London fell very quiet save for the frequent sound of the passing bell ringing from several steeples. One event that many had looked forward to – the coronation of the new queen – had to be repeatedly postponed because of the contagion and eventually the ceremony was not held.

Business was brisk that summer, thanks in no small measure to Thomas Cromwell's assault on the smaller monasteries (Robert had been right to prophesy the minister's dramatic rise). With thousands of acres of land coming on to the market, property speculation soared. Noblemen, gentlemen and yeomen ambitious to establish or extend country estates came to the City to sell or pawn their plate or jewels in order to raise capital.

In this atmosphere of bewildering change I came to rely heavily on Robert's advice and enjoyed discussing with him the events of the day. We fell into the habit of attending Sunday mass together at the parish church of St Pancrate's or the Mercers' Chapel and dining at his house afterwards. For the most part Robert welcomed the revolution that was sweeping the land. He had little love for the monasteries and, as I thought of Ned and Jed, it seemed to me that many monks generously pensioned off might find themselves useful occupations outside the cloister. Yet I could not be blind to the mounting mood of resentment becoming almost tangible on the streets. For every gentleman or merchant looking to profit from the dissolution, there were a dozen or more ordinary folk who cursed Cromwell and (when they were sure no court eavesdroppers were listening) cursed his royal master. Those, like Robert, in close touch with affairs abroad had even more disturbing things to report. As he explained to me, England's rebellion against the pope had so far succeeded because our neighbours, France and the Empire, were intermittently at war but, in August, these belligerents signed a treaty. Those in the know, Robert said, genuinely feared the possibility of a combined invasion.

The changing political situation made it necessary for Robert to cross the Channel in August for consultation with his business contacts in the Netherlands. I received occasional letters from him during late summer and early autumn and they only increased my sense of foreboding. He hinted at threats and even actual violence being offered to English merchants in Catholic lands. He wrote of secret emissaries being sent by Catholic activists to friends in England with the express purpose of promoting rebellion and promising money and troops to aid in overthrowing the anti-papal regime.

In the first days of October it seemed that their strategy was working. The long-feared storm broke in the distant northern counties. The first we heard of it in London, around 7 October, was that all Lincolnshire was up in arms, that the people were demanding the monasteries should be restored and Cromwell handed over to the leaders of the revolt. Wild rumours rampaged through the streets. A rebel army was marching on the capital. According to which story you believed, ten thousand, thirty thousand or fifty thousand angry Englishmen, led by gentlemen of the shire, were on the road south and picking up more malcontents as they came. The government firmly denied these rumours in leaflets hurriedly printed and distributed to every household. The rising, we were told, amounted to no more than a peasant rabble that had already been suppressed by the king's generals. This reassurance was received with widespread cynicism. If peace had been so easily restored, people wanted to know, why had the king and court hastened to take refuge in Windsor Castle, the strongest royal fortress in the land?

In the midst of the general panic, I received another letter from Robert. It was brief and, to judge from its uncharacteristic scrawl, written in haste.

My hearty greetings to you and your mother. Here is much grave news. The King of France has sent troops against the English port of Calais. It is believed he intends to secure it as a base for an invasion fleet. Here in Antwerp several foreign merchants have been arrested and imprisoned with no charges put forth. I am so far safe, praised be to God, but obliged to go very warily about my business. Yet the worst news is that Master Tyndale, that great servant of God, is dead. He had escaped detection for some years but was recently discovered and betrayed to the authorities by a wretch sent over from England for the purpose. Three days ago he was brought to the stake near here and there strangled before his body was burned. Thus does Antichrist muster his forces. We must be vigilant. I have written nothing of this to my good lady wife and I pray you to say nothing that would alarm her. Should I be unlawfully detained here or should anything worse befall, you may receive no more letters from me. I shall write when and if I can and am in hope to return safely in about two weeks.

Your assured friend,

Robert Packington

It was a relief to know that my friend was safe but I was worried that he spoke of Tyndale in this way, almost as a personal friend. Two weeks passed with no more news. Then three. Then four. I called several times on Margaret Packington, hoping to discover that she had heard from her husband, while at the same time not wishing to let her see my own mounting anxiety.

Meanwhile, the atmosphere in the City was becoming almost unbearably tense. We heard that the trouble in Lincolnshire had been dealt with. The ringleaders had paid for their treason with their lives and the country was quiet once more. But we were allowed scarcely a breathing space. By the third week of October the contagion of rebellion, though no longer a threat to the nearest shires, had spread northwards.

What we could gather from messengers and travellers suggested that the whole of England between the Humber and the Scottish border was in the hands of men who called themselves 'pilgrims' and who were intent on forcing Henry to reverse his policies. They commanded tens of thousands of followers – too many to be defeated in battle. The Dukes of Norfolk and Suffolk had been sent north with all the troops they could muster but no one believed that the royal army was big enough to crush the revolt or that, if it came to a pitched battle, the king's men would advance against their own countrymen. Many citizens who could do so were fleeing to the comparative safety of the countryside. I made sure that the members of my own household were safe. At the beginning of November I sent down to Hemmings as many of them as could be spared.

Then, in the midst of all this gloomy turmoil, there came a piece of good news. I had retired for the night on Sunday 12 November when one of my servants came to my chamber with a scribbled note: 'Thomas, thanks be to God, I am returned safely and have much to tell you. Come with me to first mass in the Mercers' Chapel. Robert Packington.' The early office was performed at five o'clock so I extinguished the candle immediately and settled to sleep, happier than I had been in weeks.

The following morning I was up and dressed in good time. I took a lantern and stepped out into West Cheap. It was dark and made the more so by a thick mist drifting up from the river which so mingled with the smoke from household fires that I could see no more than a few paces before me. I had just passed the bulk of St Mary Bow, whose coloured windows were illumined from light within, when I heard a loud noise ahead of me. It was something between an explosion and a heavy blow upon an anvil. I could not recognise it at all. I stopped. Listened intently. The street was now quiet again, save for the sound of water dropping from the eaves. As I set off again, a frenzied commotion broke out – screams, shouts and cries of alarm. Cautiously I lifted my lantern higher and strode forward. A small crowd had gathered around the Great Conduit, the square building housing the water fountain that stands at the junction of West Cheap and Poultry. There was nothing unusual about that; labourers congregated there every morning hoping to be hired. But there was something different about this gathering. Everyone was grouped around a tableau at the base of the west-facing wall. Drawing closer, I saw two men kneeling beside a third who lay on his back upon the stone paving.

'What's happened here?' I demanded.

One of the kneeling men looked up. His face was pale in the lamp's lurid glow. 'This poor fellow's dead ... killed ... But, I don't understand ... There was no one near him ... Yet ... well, see for yourself, Master.'

I bent forward. There was, indeed, a gash in the dead man's dark cloak and the lamplight glistened on what was oozing from it. I shone the light on his face – and recoiled in horrified recognition.

Chapter 10

'Witchcraft, that's what it was. Must have been.' The speaker –
a dark, straggle-haired fellow with the stench of the tannery
about him – stood up. His long face in the lamplight was pale
and lugubrious.

I was too stunned to make any reply. I could scarce breathe
for the emotions surging in my breast – anger, horror, grief –
and disbelief. 'This could not be,' I wanted to cry out. 'Dear
God above, this could not be!' I knelt on the wet stone and
peered closer at the lifeless face. It was strangely calm and
expressionless. But there was no doubt. Here was all that
remained of Robert Packington.

The tradesman was now raising his voice to address a rapidly gathering audience. 'Here is a great evil, Masters, the
work of Satan himself and his bondsman.'

Several people in the crowd threw questions which the

self-appointed narrator answered with gestures and a quavering voice that would have done justice to an actor in one of the Inns of Court plays. 'Why, here's this fine gentleman walking across the street, holding his lamp high – thuswise. Steps forward this foreigner from the doorway yonder.' He glared around, gathering his audience with his baleful eye. 'He shouts some curse or spell and points – like this. There comes a doomcrack from the very portals of hell. Our gentle neighbour calls out.' He paused and lowered his voice. 'But straightway he falls down—'

'What are you saying?' I came to myself and stood up, interrupting the performance. 'This was the work of a foreigner? Why say you this? Do you know the assassin?'

The speaker drew himself up to his full scrawny height. 'That I do not, young Master (he emphasised the word 'young'), but, sure, he had to be foreign. Who of the king's subjects would deal in such devil's work?' His words drew a murmur of assent from the other onlookers.

'Then you know nothing! You stood there not ten feet from the murderer and all you can tell us is that, in your precious opinion, he must have been foreign.'

'Do not take on so.' The man was not to be put out of countenance. 'I saw what I saw and I know what I know. It was a short fellow in a long cloak with the hood up and he spoke in a strange tongue.'

'What did he say?' I demanded.

'And I were a scholar who spoke foreign I could tell you.'

'And what became of this little "foreigner"? Can you tell me that?'

For the first time the grimy leatherworker looked less sure of himself. 'Why, he headed down Bucklersbury . . . I think.' He spun round to point at the narrow entrance to the street of grocers' and apothecaries' shops. 'Yes, down Bucklersbury. Heading for the river, I doubt not.'

'God's death!' I shouted. 'You make a useless witness. What about the rest of you; someone must have seen what became of the assassin.'

There was much muttering and shuffling of feet but no one came forward.

'Well, we waste time here. Four of you lift the body – gently – and come with me.'

'Hold fast, young neighbour.' The tanner was not to be deprived of his assumed authority. 'This is a matter for the crowner. We must not move the corpse without his say.'

'Stand aside, fool!' My anger burst forth and I half-screamed, half-sobbed the order. 'This man was my friend and a truer friend man never had. Bring him respectfully to my house.'

No one moved.

I glared around at the faces, dim in the lamplight. 'This was a fellow Londoner killed in cold blood. We must find the truth of the matter. Take him to my house hard by. There we'll send for the coroner, as the tanner here insists, and a physician will examine the body.'

No movement, only whispered conversations. Then I guessed the cause of their reluctance.

'If it's loss of a day's wages that worries you, I'll see that no man is the poorer for a simple act of Christian charity.'

Still they stood like members of a tableau in one of the old miracle plays. Then an apprentice nodded silently to his friend and together they stooped to lift the slain man's shoulders. Others gathered round to help bear the weight. I stepped forward to lead the way and thus our little cortège bore the body of Robert Packington to Goldsmith's Row.

By taking charge of the necessary investigation of this atrocity I was, as I think I knew even then, covering over the thoughts and feelings that would otherwise have overwhelmed me. I had poor Robert laid out on one of the gold beaters' benches while I sent for my physician and also for the coroner.

The coroner was the first to arrive. Master Kernish was a gaunt, black-clad lawyer who was accompanied by a secretary carrying his ledgers and writing materials in a large scrip. He came striding in from the street, where daylight was now doing battle with the mist, and immediately set about establishing his authority. He scarcely listened to my brief explanation.

'Who sent for the physician?' he demanded curtly. 'I'll thank you to leave such decisions to the proper authority – which is me. However,' he conceded with a deep frown, 'since the man has been summoned I will await his report on the cadaver. I suppose it is too much to hope that there were any witnesses to this fatality.'

'Six unskilled labourers and petty tradesmen,' I said. 'I have sent them up to my chamber to await your pleasure.'

He replied with a grunt and turned towards the stair.

In the chamber he seated himself in a cushioned wainscot chair drawn up to the table. The secretary sat beside him setting out precisely his ledger, papers, quill, penknife and inkpot like troops on a battlefield.

Kernish surveyed with every appearance of distaste the huddle of men who stood by the livery cupboard. 'This is the way I work: I will take independent testimony from you, one at a time. You will wait outside until summoned and, while waiting, you will not discuss the incidents of this morning. I will not have any collusion. The life of one of His Majesty's subjects has been taken, seemingly in a violent manner. If that is the case then a vile crime has been committed against the king's peace and the good order of this city. I am empowered to uncover the truth. This will be a preliminary investigation. If I deem it necessary, I will swear a jury and you all, or any of you, may be summoned to give your evidence before it. Everything you say in this room and at a subsequent full inquest will be recorded and you will be under solemn oath to restrict your answers to my questions to the simple truth. I want no opinions, suppositions or accusations that cannot be substantiated. Is that clear?'

There was a murmur of acquiescence.

'Very well, outside, all of you. Master Treviot, I will hear you first.'

When the other witnesses had shuffled through the doorway and closed it behind them, Kernish looked up at me. 'For the record,' he demanded, 'you must state your name and occupation.'

When that had been done and noted by the secretary's scratching pen, the lawyer launched his routine interrogation. 'Our first responsibility is to establish the identity of the deceased. I understand he was known to you. Is that so?'

'He was Robert Packington, mercer, leading citizen of London, member of the Common Council and of the parliament. He was also one of the finest men who graced the life of this city. I have known him all my life and was privileged to call him my friend. Master Kernish, the sooner we can complete the formalities and set about tracing—'

The coroner held up a hand. 'I repeat what I said just now: relevant facts are all I require at this stage. Rest assured that accumulating evidence is the best way of discovering whether a crime has been committed and, if it has, of bringing the perpetrator to justice.' He sat back in the chair and his tone changed. 'So it is Master Packington whose body lies below.' He crossed himself. 'That is a severe loss indeed. One which many of us share. He was one of this city's finest sons. I met him on many occasions and know something of his charitable works. There are many who have cause to thank God for Master Packington. It is hard to think that anyone would wish him ill. Mayhap your physician will find some natural cause—'

'He was struck down,' I blurted out. 'There was blood all over—'

Again Kernish motioned me to silence. 'We must have everything in order. Now, Master Treviot, tell me clearly what you saw.'

I shook my head in exasperation. 'I saw nothing. Would to God I had been there moments earlier. I might have—'

'Facts, Master Treviot. Facts, facts, facts!'

I explained that Robert and I had an arrangement to meet at the Mercers' Chapel, that I had come across a group of men close by the conduit and found them gathered round Robert's body.

'How was the body lying?' Kernish asked.

'He was on his back, feet towards the conduit. His cloak had fallen open and there was blood on his doublet.'

'Was there a weapon of any kind on the ground?'

'Not that I saw.'

'And none of the bystanders was holding a sword, knife or poignard?'

'I ... don't know ... but I can't imagine ...'

'We'll have no imagining, if you don't mind.'

'Sorry. It's just that if one of those men had struck my friend down, the others must have seen.'

'Unless they were all complicit.'

'You mean they might all have been waiting for him in ambush?'

'At this stage I must rule nothing out. Were there others abroad at that hour? Did you see anyone running or walking from the scene?'

'The Cheap is very quiet at night's end and it was dark. Yet, I am sure I would have noticed anyone hurrying away. There was a fellow there – a tanner – who claims that Master Packington was accosted by a foreigner in a hooded cloak who made off down Bucklersbury, but I saw nothing.'

'A foreigner, eh? A convenient tale. Strike down your victim and lay the blame on some stranger. Well, we shall see what your tanner has to say for himself. Daniel' – he turned to his secretary – 'bring the fellow in. Master Treviot, you may stay, if you wish.'

When obliged to appear before authority the voluble leatherworker seemed to have lost his tongue. He stood in the middle of the room nervously twisting his cap in his hands. He gave his name as Dick Fennel.

Though nervous and rendered even more so by Kernish's brusque manner, the tanner stuck to his story. He explained that he had taken his place by the conduit, as he did most mornings, in the hope of acquiring casual work. He had seen Robert approach, at which point a hooded figure, who apparently managed to be both 'a foreigner' and 'Satan', had pointed at him, called out something, then discharged 'a bolt from hell', whereupon Master Packington had fallen back dead.

The coroner was distinctly unimpressed.

'At this rate,' he groaned, 'we shall be here all day and no further forward.' He glowered at the cringing tanner. 'Put your mark to this statement. Then get out and send in the next witness. Pray God he is not as witless as you.'

Fennel scrawled on the paper where the secretary indicated and gratefully shuffled from the room.

What we learned from the next two witnesses took us no nearer to identifying the assassin or, indeed, to understanding the exact nature of the assassination. There seemed to be agreement that a cloaked and hooded figure had pointed at Robert, at the same time calling something out. One of the apprentices, a wide-awake looking young man with untidy fair hair, who gave his name as Benjamin Walling, provided the clearest and most succinct evidence, though it scarcely made sense. It was his firm opinion that the murderer had demanded – though with a thick and possibly foreign accent – 'Who's there?' and that Robert had replied, 'Thomas.'

I was still trying to make sense of that when the door burst open and Dr Drudgeon strode in. Harry Drudgeon, whom I had known all my life, was our family physician and I had had no hesitation in sending for him to examine Robert's body. He entered now, rubbing his hands on a red-stained apron. Always a fastidious man, he had been careful to cover his grey satin doublet but there was a streak of blood across one cheek and on his neatly trimmed beard. I had no need to introduce him to the coroner; most of the City's leading professionals were known to each other and I imagined that Harry was well accustomed to giving evidence at inquests.

'Welcome, Doctor,' Kernish said, waving the newcomer to a chair. 'Doubly welcome if you can provide us with any more substantial evidence about this sad affair. So far we have only heard from witnesses who talk of a hooded man, shouting unintelligibly and somehow stabbing his victim at several paces without leaving any trace of his weapon behind.'

'No mystery there, Master Kernish.' He opened his hand and allowed a small metal pellet to roll on to the table. 'There's your weapon.'

Chapter 11

We all stared at the tiny object. I expressed our bewilderment. 'That looks like ... shot, arquebus shot.'

Harry nodded, 'It *is* arquebus shot.'

'But that is not possible.' I pictured the weapons I had sometimes seen the militia practising with on Finsbury Field or stored in their racks in Leaden Hall. Four or five feet in length, they were quite unwieldy.

Kernish agreed. 'The assassin could not have discharged a firearm without being noticed. Even if no one saw the flame applied to the smouldering match, the flash and the explosion as the powder ignited must have been clearly visible from yards away.' The lawyer seemed personally affronted by facts that refused to fit together.

Drudgeon shrugged. 'My job is to decide the cause of Master Packington's death, not to explain the circumstances surrounding it. I was a surgeon with the King's army in 'thirteen and I know a gunshot wound when I see one. I removed that ball from Master Packington's heart and I will stake my career on the fact that he was shot with a firearm.'

We were all struck dumb. I wager the others were thinking the same as me: This sort of thing did not happen in London ... or England. In Italy, possibly, or the wilder parts of Germany, but London?

'Perhaps Fennel was right,' I muttered. 'All that talk about a hooded foreigner.'

Ben Walling spoke up. 'We did all hear a noise.'

'So we did,' I recalled. 'That must have been what Fennel called a bolt from hell.'

'Describe this noise,' Kernish demanded.

'Well,' I said, 'it was a sort of explosion. It echoed along the street.'

'So it could have been a gunshot?'

'I suppose so,' I replied lamely.

'That would mean there's an assassin loose on the streets of London,' the apprentice muttered.

Kernish re-established command of the meeting. 'We must not jump to conclusions. We have ascertained that the victim was shot and the witnesses I have so far seen agree that a stranger pointed at him. Was it a gun that he pointed?'

Both the apprentice and I shook our heads firmly. 'No,' I said, 'it takes two hands to fire an arquebus. Someone would have noticed. The murderer could never have discharged his weapon and got clean away without being challenged.'

'He'd have been a fool to try,' young Walling added. 'My friend Bart and I would have been after him straightway. We'd have made him wish he'd never set foot in Cheapside.'

'So what became of this stranger?' Kernish asked.

Walling thought carefully. 'When Master Packington fell we all moved forward to see what was amiss ... whether he needed any help.' He frowned. 'The killer must have made his getaway while we were distracted.'

'Fennel swears he saw the man run off down Bucklersbury,' I said, 'but what store we can set by his testimony ...'

Drudgeon removed his apron and smoothed down the sleeves of his doublet. 'Well, Master Kernish, that is a problem I must leave with you. I have patients to see and I've not yet broken my fast. With your leave, I'll sign my statement and be on my way. My condolences, Thomas. I know how close you were to Robert.'

While the physician was bent over the table, I drew Walling to one side. 'I'd be obliged if you and your friend could stay for a while. Go to the kitchen and tell my cook to draw you off some ale and find you some bread and cheese. There are a couple of things I'd like to go over with you in private.'

Kernish devoted another half-hour to questioning the witnesses. Then he made a cursory examination of Robert's body. Drudgeon had closed up his incision in the chest and replaced the clothing so that the only visible evidence of the crime was the caked blood on the shirt and doublet. The corpse could tell us nothing that Drudgeon had not already deduced. Strange and appalling as his findings were, there was no escaping the fact that someone had slain my friend with a gun at close range and then made his escape in the darkness and mist.

The lawyer departed to view the scene of the murder and ordered us all to accompany him. I went down to the kitchen where I found the two apprentices doing justice to a hearty breakfast. I informed them of the coroner's instructions and we left together to make the short return journey to the Great Conduit. As we walked I probed further what the young men had seen or, more specifically, heard.

'Ben, you said the assassin called out, "Who's there?"'

'Yes, something like that.'

'Definitely not words in a foreign language?'

'No, he had an accent but his meaning was plain enough. Well, it must have been or Master Packington would not have replied.'

'Now that is what puzzles me. Are you absolutely sure that he called out "Thomas"?'

It was Bart who replied. 'Oh, yes. That was quite clear.' Ben Walling's friend, tall and pinch-featured, had about him an air of studious seriousness that made it difficult to doubt what he said.

'Was it a statement or a question?' I asked.

Ben looked at me with a bewildered frown. 'I don't take your meaning.'

'Well,' I explained, 'did his inflection suggest that he was saying, "Yes, I'm Thomas" or "Thomas, is that you"?'

'I don't recall ... What happened next ... Well, we all saw ...' He shrugged. 'Anyway, does it matter?'

'It matters a great deal to me.'

We had arrived at the conduit house where a crowd had gathered. News of the tragedy had spread rapidly, as it always does in the City, and a solemn mood had descended on the thoroughfare and its market stalls. Shopkeepers, customers and passers-by had gathered and now watched as Kernish cleared a space and arranged his witnesses within it in the places we had occupied at the time of the incident. With his pernickety thoroughness he took each of us again through our recollections of the murder. At last he released us with strict instructions to present ourselves in the Mercers' Hall seven days hence for the formal inquest before a jury.

As we dispersed, Ben Walling clasped my hand. 'I'm truly sorry about your friend. This was a monstrous business.'

'Aye, and the murderer will be well away by now,' Bart added. 'I doubt Master Kernish will ever find the truth of it.'

'*He* may not but I will track the hellhound down and avenge Robert's death.' For the first time I gave expression to the passionate determination that had been forming in my mind.

'How?' Ben asked.

'For a start by asking some different questions – questions the coroner did not ask.'

The apprentices exchanged puzzled glances.

'Think about it,' I urged. 'Was this a random killing or was it planned?'

'It must have been planned,' Bart said. 'The assassin was lying in wait for his victim.'

'I'm sure you are right. But who was his intended victim? Can you spare me a few more minutes?'

'Oh, aye,' Bart answered. 'We've time enough. We've been suspended by our craft masters.'

For the first time that day I laughed. 'Oh, I see, caught in a drunken brawl, were you?'

Bart scowled. 'It was conspiracy. Business is bad and the freemen look for any excuse to wriggle out of their duties to their apprentices. I was accused of involvement in an affray and Ben's master says he tried to seduce his daughter.' He giggled. 'If you could see the girl in question! Even Ben is not that desperate.'

'Come with me, then, and I'll tell you what puzzles me.' I led the way back along Cheap. After a few yards we turned into the narrow entrance to Sopers Lane. Though the sun was now up, daylight still struggled with the gloom between the tall houses. We crossed the intersection with Needlers' Lane and stopped after a few more paces. I pointed across the street to a building with a hanging sign bearing the symbol of a man's leg.

'That is – or was – Robert Packington's house,' I said. 'Now, if you were an assassin come to shoot him, where would you choose to do it?'

It was Ben who came back promptly with an answer. 'Probably on the corner along there. You have a good view of the house and can make your escape past St Pancrate's or run on down here to Budge Row.'

I nodded. 'I agree, so why did our man take his stand in Cheap, where there were other people around?'

Ben ran a hand through his fair hair. 'Perhaps he did not know where Master Packington lived.'

'Or perhaps he did not know Master Packington by sight,' Bart said quietly. 'He had to position himself close to the Mercers' Chapel where he knew his victim was headed and get him to identify himself by calling his name.'

'But that's just it!' I exclaimed. 'If what you say is right, Robert did not identify himself. He called out, "Thomas."'

The young men looked at each other, then at me. Bart said, 'You don't really think . . .'

'I was also making my way to the Mercers' Chapel,' I said. 'Are you absolutely sure you heard a'right?'

Ben nodded. 'But there are lots of Thomases in London. Is there anyone who would want to murder you?'

I thought of the Seagrave clan. Could this be a revenge attack? 'It seems a strange coincidence that I was due to meet Robert there and that the killer was lying in wait for someone named Thomas.'

There was a long silence broken, at last, by the thoughtful Bart. 'Did anyone else know about this meeting?'

'Not unless Robert told someone,' I said. 'It was only arranged last night.'

'Then you must not reproach yourself,' he replied. 'You cannot know that the murderer mistook his target.'

'Don't be an ass, Bart!' his friend snapped. 'If the assassin made a mistake, Master Treviot has a serious enemy and may still be in danger. 'Tis that that worries him.'

'Nay, I've no care for myself,' I said. 'I would gladly have taken that shot in my own body to save the life of a better man than I will ever be. Thank you, gentlemen, for your help and your time.' I took a noble from my purse. 'Here's some recompense. I wish you better fortune with your churlish masters.' I set off back along the street.

All that day I gave little thought to my work. Customers came and went. John Fink had accounts and orders for materials that needed my approval. But I did no more than go through the motions. There was a numbness in my soul and a buzzing confusion in my head. As soon as the shutters went up for the day, I called upon Margaret Packington. I found her in shock and grief with two close friends who were helping her cope. I muttered a few woefully inadequate words and after a brief stay took my leave.

Most of the next night I wrestled, sleeplessly, with accusing thoughts and answerless questions. If Robert's death was, in some way, my fault, I would never be able to forgive myself. But was it my fault? I had enemies – that much was certain. Would any of them go as far as murder? Simon Leyland had made his hostility well known and had business difficulties but I could not imagine him resorting to such desperate measures. Seagrave's family? I recalled Ned's nervousness about a backlash to the courtier's death. How far might they go in pursuit of revenge? And, anyway, my thinking always came up against the same obstacle: how could any harbourers of ill-will possibly have known I was going to be on that street before dawn. The arrangement had been made only a matter of hours before and I, certainly, had told no one. Which left Robert himself as the only possible source of the information. Yet, if he had been the intended victim, how could the assassin's behaviour be explained? To waylay his victim in front of witnesses when he could have done so in the seclusion of Sopers Lane? To use a gun that would draw attention to the crime rather than a silent knife? Such actions did not suggest the work of a rational mind. Could it be that this was, after all, a random killing, the action of a madman?

At some point in the early hours I quit my bed's tumbled sheets and lit a candle. I became aware of noises outside and opened the shutters to peer out. I saw a group of men carrying lanterns and armed with staves. Two of them wore common soldiers' helmets. All were bundled up with thick cloaks against the dank night air. One appeared to be issuing orders and I recognised him as our current ward constable. He divided his force into two groups and led one further along West Cheap; the other set off towards the Standard and Poultry. So, I thought, the watch has been put on alert. A pity they were not more attentive twenty-four hours since.

I took out the copy of Tyndale's book that Robert had given me but before I began to read another thought struck me. Robert had but just returned from the Netherlands where, to judge from his brief letters, he had been in some difficulty, perhaps in danger. I recalled what he had said about Tyndale's death – strangled and burned for a heretic. Since Robert held the author in such high regard, could it have been that he, too, had fallen foul of the Dutch authorities? Might some agent of their Catholic rulers have followed him to London with orders to kill him? I recalled Robert's last, brief note, 'I am returned safely and have much to tell you.' What dark news had he been bringing from over the sea? Was he silenced to stop him passing it on?

So many questions. No answers. The coroner was seeking them in his own ponderous way but I had little confidence in his ability to uncover the truth. My easiest option would have been to leave everything to the authorities but that was not possible – not only because of the outrage I felt at my friend's brutal and cowardly murder, but also because I did not know whether I was safe. And, if my life was under threat, might not the same be true of those closest to me? Anxiety impelled me to make an urgent journey to Hemmings.

Chapter 12

I was out on the Rochester and Canterbury road by first light, riding with a pair of well-armed servants. I had to get down to the manor as quickly as possible. An ungovernable fear gripped me: might not the mysterious assassin or his paymaster have marked my mother and son for death? If I was their target, they would soon have realised that their plot had failed. The news of Robert's murder had been all over London within a couple of hours. For aught I knew, fresh plans were already afoot for another attempt on my life and, if on mine, why not also on the lives of those I loved?

There was another reason for my impromptu visit – I wanted to see Lizzie. One clear idea that had disentangled itself from the nocturnal jumble in my mind was that she might be able to help me. She had spent much of her life in the company of violent men – desperate vagrants, soldiers turned highway robbers, child-stealing gypsies, hucksters of every hue and cut-throats who would, as they said, 'skene a weasand-pipe' for a purseful of groats. The more I thought about the events of the previous day, the more convinced I became that the assassin must be a professional. That or a madman. He could obviously handle an arquebus with deadly accuracy (though just how he had managed it was still a mystery). He was bold enough to discharge his weapon in full view of other people, and agile enough to make his getaway quickly and safely. As I rode along the rutted road between trees silvered with frost, I tried to form a mental picture of Robert's slayer. If I discounted the idea of a lunatic, it seemed that the man we were dealing with must be one who was not new to his craft. He had killed before. Whether or not he was foreign, he must be someone existing on the margins of society, a member of the law-defying underworld. He could not live in total isolation. He needed accomplices; people he could turn to for contacts, for shelter, for information. If I could gain access to that criminal Hades, I might be able to find some leads.

We reached Hemmings late in the afternoon. I saw Dickon stabled, took a few loosening strides round the yard and splashed icy water from a butt over my face. Then I went indoors through the domestic quarters. Entering the small hall from the screens passage a wave of warm air met me. A good fire blazed in the hearth and a semicircle of chairs and stools was arranged before it. I approached this barrier and found Lizzie kneeling on the rushes with little Raphael. She was holding out a bright red apple to him and encouraging him to walk in order to grasp it. Both of them were absorbed in the game and I was able to watch unnoticed for several seconds. The boy seemed very sturdy as he wobbled forward, holding out one hand for the fruit and clutching his skirts with the other. His hair was darkening now and when I looked at him I did not automatically think of Jane. When he fell, Lizzie did not lift him; she simply waved the apple until Raphael got to his feet unaided.

'The boy is doing well,' I said quietly.

Lizzie looked up, a quick smile dissolving rapidly into a frown. I was pleased to see that she no longer covered her scar, which had faded to a thin white line. 'We are honoured,' she said, rising and picking up the child as she did so. 'Raphy, look, here's your father come to visit.'

The boy surveyed me uncertainly, then turned his face away and buried it in Lizzie's neck. She came forward and held him out to me. 'Here, you two need to get to know each other.' As I clumsily took the boy in my arms, Lizzie walked away. 'I have to prepare his food,' she said and strode through the screens doorway.

I sat in an armed chair with Raphael on my lap but immediately he squealed, slipped to the floor and tried to follow his nurse. After a few staggered paces he fell and lay on the rushes. His face creased into an expression of desolation and he let out an anguished wail. When I tried to pick him up he struggled and refused to be comforted. I picked up the apple and held it out but the child's interest in this colourful lure had waned. I set him on his feet and tried to help him walk but he pulled away with surprising force. In doing so he rolled over backwards. His head was within inches of the fire. I quickly grabbed him and pulled him away. This, of course, frightened him and he now began howling in real earnest.

Fortunately Lizzie returned at this moment carrying a bowl and spoon. These she set down and, with a scowl in my direction, picked up Raphael and jogged him gently until his tears had subsided. My presence was clearly superfluous.

'I had better go and see my mother,' I said, rising. 'Where is she?'

'In her chamber, as ever. She seldom leaves it.'

'Right. When I come down I shall want to talk to you.'

Lizzie shrugged by way of response and I left her to her duties.

The atmosphere in my mother's room was close almost to the point of being stifling. The windows were fast closed and the shutters only half open. Smoke seeped from the smouldering fire and the light was so dim that it was some moments before I could discern her. She was sitting to one side of the hearth, upright in a padded chair, wrapped in furs, staring motionless straight ahead.

'Good day, Mother.' I stooped to kiss her cheek.

She inclined her head slightly. 'Who's that?' Her voice was faint and wheezy.

'It's Tom, Mother, come to see how you are.'

'Tom? My Tom?' Her wrinkles seemed to deepen with the effort of understanding what I said. 'Tom isn't here . . . not any more. He's gone.'

'It's your *son* Tom. I'm still here. I've been in London . . . in the shop. I've ridden down to see you.' I took her hand in mine.

'Tom's gone,' she murmured. 'Gone . . . gone.'

I opened the shutters fully and, though the outside air was cold, I threw wide the casement, letting in a breeze to disperse the stuffy atmosphere.

'Where's your maid? Where's Margaret?' I demanded.

The only response was a puzzled frown and the repetition of the word, 'Gone.'

Distraught and angry, I hurried down to the kitchen. The cook was there with two scullions. They looked at me warily from across the table, as though they feared I might strike them. When I demanded to know Margaret's whereabouts they looked sheepishly from one to the other and it was the cook who answered. 'Left, Master Thomas. Not two days since.'

'Left? Why?'

There was no reply.

I slammed my fist on the table. 'Answer me, damn you! No servant of mine leaves without my permission.'

'Perhaps she was afraid of the Yorkshiremen,' the cook suggested. 'Is it true the rebels are camped on Smithfield?'

'Certainly not! That is a silly rumour. She had no cause to run away and leave her mistress. Who is saying such things?'

'Most of the people round about – and the servants you sent down from London, Master. They say there's panic in the City and like to be war, as in our grandsires' day. They reckon we'll be no safer here than in West Cheap.'

'That is foolish scare-mongering.' I tried to sound calm and reassuring. 'It was only as a precaution that I sent everyone down from Goldsmith's Row. The rebellion is all in the North. You are safe here. Now, who is looking after Mistress Treviot?'

Again the exchange of embarrassed glances. At last the cook said, 'That will be your ... friend, Master Thomas.'

'You mean Mistress Garney?'

The woman nodded.

I strode back to the hall. Lizzie was standing before the fire, cradling Raphael in her arms. Before I could speak she raised a finger to her lips. 'Wait while I put him down,' she said quietly.

When she returned and we were seated by the fire, I asked, 'What has been happening here? The servants seem terrified, Margaret has disappeared and my mother is getting worse.'

Lizzie nodded. 'Aye, I've seen less juggle-headed souls in Bedlam.'

'But why? Has there been trouble – strangers calling, people making threats? Is there danger? Do you think anyone has traced you here from Southwark?'

Her face twisted into its familiar scowl. 'If you think I've brought danger to your household, you can send me back. I'm only here as your conscience, anyway.'

'What is that supposed to mean?' I tried to keep the anger out of my voice.

'You sent me here to do what you've no liking for – to care for your mother and your son.'

'That is not true. I am trying to do the best for everyone. There are terrible things happening and I just want to be sure that you are all safe here. Can you not credit me with some finer feelings?'

Lizzie shrugged and stretched out her hands towards the glowing logs. 'Bad things are happening here, too,' she said. 'Three men were arrested in Ightham for speaking against the closure of a local nunnery and there was a brawl in the church on Sunday when someone tried to pull the preacher out of the pulpit. You talk about being safe, is anyone safe anywhere?'

'I don't know. All I can do is try to protect everyone under this roof.'

After a pause, I asked, 'What became of Margaret and why did she leave?'

'She found your mother difficult to handle. I tried to help. She resented it.' Lizzie stared into the red heart of the fire and added, 'They all hate me. They think I've brought bad luck to Hemmings.'

'You must not pay any attention to such nonsense,' I said. 'Anyway if anyone is a courier of bad luck it's me.' In as few words as possible I told her about Robert's murder and the mystery assassin.

Lizzie showed no emotion. 'Death and trouble seem to follow you everywhere,' she commented eventually.

'I was just wondering ...' I faltered. 'Look, I don't want you to take this the wrong way ... I'm completely at a loss because this creature lives in a world I know nothing about. Can you think of anyone who might be able to tell me something about such an assassin.'

Her reply was prompt. She turned to face me. 'No, and if I did, I wouldn't tell you.'

'Lizzie, I ...'

She stood abruptly. 'You talk about keeping us all safe and in the next breath you tell me you want to stalk a murderer. God, Mary and all the angels, I see now why your mother is beside her wits. 'Tis in the family. You're all mad!' She turned to walk away.

I stood in her path and grabbed her arm. 'Lizzie, I owe it to Robert. I have to find this villain.'

'Go on, then!' Her face was inches from my own, her cheeks flushed with anger. 'Get yourself killed. I'll lose no sleep over that. But what's to become of everyone here ... poor Mistress Treviot ... and little Raphy. He has no mother and now you want to make him an orphan. And all out of some petty thirst for vengeance. Do you think that's what your precious Robert wants? Is he looking down from heaven,' she crossed herself, 'and urging you to throw away everything, destroy even more lives? Some friend that! Now let go or, by the saints, I'll kill you myself!'

I retained my grasp. 'Lizzie, please listen. All you say is absolutely true and don't think I haven't thought of it. In fact, I've thought of little else these past twenty-four hours and more. But things are not that simple.'

'Why not?' She shook herself free. 'You can leave everything to the coroner and the constables. 'Tis their job. I doubt they'll find the assassin but your conscience will be clear.'

'I have no choice. If it was just a matter of getting justice for Robert and his widow, I might walk away. I don't think I would but it's possible and your arguments just might persuade me. But what if the murderer and his paymaster are really after me? Suppose Seagrave's family is determined to avenge his death. They blame me . . . and probably you. And they certainly have money enough to pay a professional killer.'

'But, you don't know—'

'No, I don't! That's the trouble. I just don't know what all this is about. What I do know is that until the mystery of Robert's death is solved, none of us may be safe . . . not me, not my mother, not my son . . . and not you. Whatever you may think of me, I have the utmost respect and . . . admiration for you. Do you think I can stand by and do nothing while there is just a chance that all our lives might be in danger?'

Lizzie sank on to a stool. She groaned. 'I should have known you were trouble the first time I set eyes on you. If I had not been such a fool and taken pity on you . . .' Her hand went to her cheek and she left the sentence hanging.

'I shall always be grateful for that,' I said. 'Is there really nothing you can tell me that might help settle this matter quickly?'

She sat staring into the hearth for a long time before answering. At last she said, 'Very well. Go to the Red Lamb beyond Southwark. Go in broad daylight and when there are many people abroad and, in God's name, don't go alone. Ask for Doggett. John Doggett knows everything but tells nothing unless he is sure it's safe . . . and unless the price is right. You might take Ned to vouch for you. Doggett and his associates don't care much for strangers.'

Chapter 13

The following morning, before I made the return journey to London, I called the whole household together. I had to exhort them to vigilance without alarming them – no easy matter. I told them not to believe wild rumours about the northern rebels. The king's army, I assured them, had the situation under control. London, I reported, was its usual busy but calm self. Nevertheless the disturbed times inevitably encouraged an increase in lawlessness and they were to be on their guard, especially if they encountered strangers. On no account were the doors of Hemmings to be opened to anyone unknown. In private I instructed my steward to employ all the extra men he needed to patrol the estate. He was also to find a competent and trustworthy replacement for Margaret. In the meantime, I told him, Mistress Garney would attend my mother as well as my son and should be treated with courtesy by all the servants, if they valued their jobs. Part of me – a large part – wanted to stay longer but if I was to have any chance of locating the man I was looking for, I would have to act quickly.

On my way through Southwark later that day I called at St Swithun's House in the hope of enlisting Ned's help. He was not there so I left a message asking him to call at Goldsmith's Row as soon as he could.

Ned came that evening and I settled him in my chamber with a glass of sack while I recounted the circumstances of Robert's death.

He stretched out his legs to the fire. 'We heard, of course, about Master Packington, but I had no idea that you were involved in that terrible business.'

'He was my truest friend and I am ashamed to say that only now am I beginning to realise just how much I owe him.'

'That is often the way,' Ned reflected. He stroked his chin and I noticed that he was letting his beard grow longer. 'We appreciate things most when we have lost them. Life in the cloister could be tedious and there was certainly too much petty bickering and rumour-mongering. Jed and I suffered much from sniggering innuendos. It was malicious tale-telling that made it easy for Cromwell's men to accuse the community of heinous sins, *contra bonos mores*, and threaten to close us down. Our abbot took the hint – and a sizeable bribe. So, those of us who elected not to be transferred to another house ended up back in the world. Only now do I realise how much I relied on – and needed – the holy routine and the fellowship of brothers who, like me, were certainly not perfect. Master Packington was, by repute, an honest man of charitable disposition, though some of the City clergy had him marked for a heretic. I sympathise with your loss.'

'Have you heard any more of the Seagrave affair?' I asked.

'Oh aye, I doubt his people will let that rest for a while yet. The coroner questioned several of our St Swithun's friends after the discovery of the body back in the summer but they told him nothing, of course. It was left to Seagrave's family to seek out the facts. They used different tactics.'

'Threats? Bribery?' I suggested.

'Nothing that subtle. More truth lies at a knife's point or the business end of a quarterstaff than you'll find in a court of law.'

'They came with armed retainers?'

'Oh not they! Gentlemen of the court don't dirty their own hands with score-settling. They hired an expert – a man called Doggett. Fortunately, those of our number who were involved in Seagrave's . . . removal heard that Doggett was on their—'

'Doggett!' I exclaimed. 'Lizzie mentioned his name. Who is he?'

'John Doggett is a useful friend and . . . well, you wouldn't want to discover what he's like as an enemy. How best to describe him?' Ned paused and sipped his wine thoughtfully. 'He comes of good family; his forbears were vintners. Their business still exists in East Cheap. John is a man of some style and education but he turned his back on a tradesman's life. Too humdrum for him, perhaps. Or it may be that he simply stumbled upon easier ways to make money than in importing wine. Whatever the reason, he has set himself up as a princeling among the outcast and base community. You may not realise it but there is a hierarchy in the criminal world as fixed and immovable as the one that holds together the society of honest men. To take but one example, all highway robbers and travelling beggars ply their trade by courtesy of the "upright men" who ordain who may operate in each locality. Now, if the upright man is a noble of the open road, Doggett is king or emperor over an even wider domain. The Howards and the Brandons are effectively the rulers of East Anglia and the Percies and the Nevilles control the northern counties. In the same way Doggett treats Southwark and its hinterland as his realm. He has a band of rakehell servitors, known, inevitably, as "Doggett's Dogs". They police the Stews and the gambling houses. They decide which beggars and thieves may operate. They sort out disputes. And for all these services they collect their dues.'

'They rob from the robbers.'

'Aye, and kill the killers. Criminals are more afraid of the Dogs than they are of any magistrate.'

'I don't like what I'm hearing about this Doggett fellow.'

'Among the human leys of Southwark he provides something that passes for law and order but he is certainly someone to be avoided by honest men.'

'But if the Seagraves have set him on my trail . . .'

'I think they are more interested in the men who actually killed their family member. They know you are innocent of that crime. As long as you keep out of Doggett's way . . .'

'I cannot do that,' I said. 'I must seek this fellow out and talk with him.'

Ned's eyes opened wide and he almost dropped his glass. 'I trust you are jesting,' he gasped.

'I fear not.'

I told him about the inconsistencies surrounding Robert's death, the inconclusive evidence given to the coroner, my visit to Hemmings and my conversation with Lizzie. 'It was she who – very reluctantly – advised me to make contact with Doggett,' I concluded. 'She suggested you might provide an introduction. But now you tell me that he is working for the Seagraves, as their agent of vengeance.'

Ned set down his empty glass on the hearth, covered his face with his hands and shook his head. 'Oh, Thomas, Thomas, Thomas. What a labyrinth you have wandered into.'

'Exactly, and as in a labyrinth there is a point at which return to the beginning is impossible, so I must now go on.'

'Pray God you do not lose your way.' He sighed. 'When we came to Southwark, Jed and I, we were shocked by what we discovered. We seemed to have fallen into a melting pot where all the seven great sins were stirred together. It is not the place I would wish to introduce an honest gentleman like yourself.'

'Yet you have survived,' I urged.

'Oh, aye. We have been accepted because those who hold sway there think we have talents to offer. I have taught Jed something of my medical skills and, in a place like Southwark, we lack not for patients. But those who venture there for their own private reasons are like to find themselves covered in leeches – and not for the sake of their health.'

'Are you saying you won't introduce me to Doggett?'

He shook his head and sighed again. 'I know not what to do for the best. My instinct tells me to advise you to meddle no further.'

'But—'

He held up a hand. 'I know – you feel you cannot disentangle yourself. You may be right. But how to proceed . . . ' He stirred one of the embers with his foot.

'Perhaps we can make enquiries without involving Doggett,' I suggested.

'That is what you most certainly cannot do. He will know of your presence within the hour. He does not like strangers asking questions.'

'Then I must go firm-footed into the Dogs' kennel and risk getting bitten.'

'Not so hasty; this wants careful thinking.' He stared at me long and hard, the reflected firelight giving his eyes a glow of added intensity. 'What exactly is it that you are hoping to discover?'

'Simply what Doggett knows of a professional assassin, possibly foreign, who is an expert with handguns. There cannot be many such.'

'Doggett is certainly the one man who will know the answer to that question. Lizzie was right about that. But what if the murderer you seek is someone to whom he has extended his protection?'

'Then, I suppose, he will tell me nothing.'

'More likely he will prevent you asking questions – for ever.'

'Lizzie said I should not risk my life trying to find out who killed Robert.'

'You would do well to heed her. She is wise and has learned her wisdom the hard way.' Ned paused. 'However if we must pursue this matter – and I do say "if" – we must take a more oblique approach. Perhaps I should go to Doggett in the first instance.'

'I would not want you to take risks on my behalf.'

'Oh, Doggett will not harm me. I nursed his favourite doxy through a fever.'

'But if he has been commissioned by the Seagraves to kill me?'

'We would have to keep your name out of our enquiries – at least until we knew the lie of the land.'

'Do you think that possible?'

Ned shrugged, his rubicund features quite bereft of their

usual bonhomie. 'If Doggett felt I was deceiving him … making a fool of him …' He drew a finger across his throat. 'As soon as I broach the business he will have his hounds out, sniffing for information. One way or another he will have the truth ere long.'

'Then we will have to trust him. Surely, even a man like Doggett would not want to shield a cowardly assassin, would he?'

'If he has been paid to protect your quarry, yes. If he feels more loyalty to one of his own kind than to a stranger, yes. If he scents some financial advantage in helping you, then, just possibly, no.'

We both fell silent. It was a long time before Ned spoke again. 'I can see only one faint glimmer of hope in the situation.'

'What is that?'

'Doggett has no love of foreigners. If the man you seek came from across the water to ply his trade in Doggett's territory, Doggett would be most offended and might be persuaded to cooperate. But then, of course,' he observed mournfully, 'we don't know that your assassin is an alien.'

After another lengthy silence, Ned rose to take his leave. 'Let me see what I can find out,' he said, with his hand on the door latch.

'Very well,' I agreed, 'but don't be long. Our killer may already have left London.'

'In which case you have nothing to worry about,' he replied, with an encouraging smile.

But worry I did and another night passed in mixed wakefulness and bad dreams.

In fact my impatience was not long stretched. The following afternoon Jed appeared in my shop. His message was simple: 'Ned wants you to come straightway. He said to bring a full purse and a discreet weapon.'

The November weather had turned foul. We took the narrower lanes between Bread Street and East Cheap but rain and sleet lashed us as we emerged into Grass Street, passed the impressive frontages of rich men's houses and jogged on down Fish Street Hill. Huddled in our cloaks and hoods, we made haste for the protection of the bridge, thankful only that the rain had washed the stench of Fish Wharf out of the air. Reaching St Swithun's House, we dismounted and hurried indoors. Ned met us in the ground-floor chamber he shared with Jed.

'His Grace, Lord Doggett, has graciously consented to receive us,' he said, with an uncharacteristic note of scorn in his voice.

'Good,' I responded. 'When do we go?'

'Directly. Doggett is planning to be away from town and has commanded our presence before he leaves. It would not be wise to keep him waiting. But first there are one or two points I must make. The first is that I have not mentioned your name; you are simply a wealthy merchant in need of some discreet service, for which you are prepared to pay handsomely.'

'That's true enough.'

'There's more: I have given my word that you are not an intelligencer for the beaks.'

'Beaks?'

'Magistrates. They sometimes send spies among us. 'Tis a hazardous occupation; the wretches tend not to survive more than a few days. Doggett boasts that he can smell them.'

'I can satisfy him on that score.'

'Third, your audience will cost you five sovereigns of the latest coinage, unclipped, paid in advance.'

I nodded.

'Finally, I am to warn you that if Doggett comes to believe that you are not being straight with him, that you are concealing anything, or that you are in any way trying to trick him, then . . .'

'Yes?'

'His exact words were "Tell your friend not to make any plans for tomorrow." If these conditions are not agreeable to you, Doggett says you may leave and he will have no interest in you. If you accept his conditions, then you will be entering a binding contract and must accept whatever consequences follow.'

'I am ready for that,' I said.

Ned walked to the door and threw it open. 'Then let us go and may Mary and all the saints preserve us.'

Beneath my breath I muttered a heartfelt 'Amen.'

Chapter 14

Apprehension mounted as we rode down Kent Street and emerged on to open ground. The buildings, which afforded some protection from the driving rain, became sparse but it was not just exposure to the elements that knotted my stomach and set me shivering. Nor was it Dickon's reluctant gait as he bent his head against the wind that sapped my enthusiasm for this foray. At any moment I could easily have turned back, excusing my decision by acknowledging that Lizzie and Ned were right to call my self-imposed mission 'madness'. I had no idea what to expect from the forthcoming meeting with a man held in esteem only by those who were alienated from decent society, and fear always goes hand-in-glove with the unknown.

The Red Lamb was slightly off the highway about three miles from the sprawl of Southwark. It stood out very clearly in the surrounding landscape. A high wall enclosed the stone house and its attendant outbuildings, which were substantial. It may once have been a manorial residence but of any village that might have owed allegiance to its owner there was no trace. Only waterlogged meadows surrounded it. If Doggett reigned over all he surveyed from here, his demesne was sparse in the extreme. Yet I could well imagine its present tenant espousing the strategic value of the unrestricted views of the country on all sides. The sign above the entrance arch looked fresh-painted but, though my judgement may have been clouded by what I knew of the place, I found it difficult to imagine any weary traveller thankfully turning in here for a night's lodging or a much-needed meal.

The unwelcomeness of the Red Lamb was further emphasised when Ned and I dismounted in the muddy yard. Two men lounged by a stable door and a third scurried past towards the house without a glance in our direction. We had to lead the horses in ourselves and find stalls for them. But we would have been wrong to think that our arrival had created no interest. As soon as the heavy portal was opened to us we were confronted by two men in leather jerkins. They were very visibly well-armed and blocked our entry with hands on sword hilts.

The taller of the two nodded at Ned. 'This your friend, Doctor?'

'Yes,' Ned replied. 'Master Doggett is expecting us.'

The other, a burly fellow with a thatch of rufous hair, said, 'That's right. We'll take your weapons first.'

Reluctantly I handed over my dagger. That was not enough for them. 'Cloaks off,' Red-head ordered.

When we had removed our sodden capes, his companion patted and prodded us. Having satisfied himself that we carried no concealed knives, he stood back with a curt, 'Follow me.'

The 'hall', now the inn's main room, had a scattering of tables. A dozen or so men sat drinking and playing at cards or dice. They showed no curiosity about us as we were led to a circular staircase at the far end. To my surprise, we did not climb to an upper storey, but went down to a cellar or under-croft. It was a long room, little more than a corridor, lit meagrely by two hanging lamps. The smell was foul – damp, decay and faeces. Along one side there were cells fronted by iron grilles. I tried not to look into them but at least two were occupied. Our guide made no comment. He simply turned at the end of the cellar and preceded us back to the staircase. This time we did climb to the next floor, then stepped through a doorway, crossed an empty chamber and halted before another door. The tall man knocked, opened it and ushered us in. When the door had been closed again, he stood inside with his back against it.

The room was large, with an impressive fireplace on one wall and a south-facing oriel opposite it. The overall impression was of good taste, affluence and comfort. The large tapestries that faced us as we entered were of recent import and would have graced any nobleman's chamber. The furniture was of good quality, and a standing cupboard beside the door had been carved in the latest Flemish style. The centre of the room was dominated by a long trestle table, above which was suspended an eight-branch brass candle beam. The flickering glow from this augmented the paltry light penetrating the window from the grey day outside. With its aid the man seated behind the table was reading a letter. At our entry he placed it carefully on a pile beside him. John Doggett was not what I had expected. Thin-faced and pale of complexion, he wore spectacles through which he now subjected us to a long, appraising gaze. But, though he had the air of a clerk in

Chancery rather than that of a feared and ruthless criminal, there was no mistaking the authority he exuded. His voice was sharp; his words clipped. I sensed that every one was calculated and none wasted.

'Good day again, Ned. This, I take it, is Master Treviot.'

My surprise must have been obvious, for our host continued, displaying no emotion. 'Of course I know your name. It was really rather foolish of you, Ned, to try to conceal it.' He indicated two chairs opposite him and we seated ourselves. 'Like you, Master Treviot, I am a successful merchant. Tell me, do you choose your clients carefully?'

'Yes, of course,' I replied.

'As do I. Before I embark on a business relationship I make a point of discovering all I can about my proposed associates. This is vital when one is dealing in valuable commodities. I'm sure you would agree.'

'Certainly.'

'You handle precious metals and gems – costly, indeed. But my trade is in something quite priceless: information.' He sat back in his chair. He seemed rather pleased with his allegory and developed it further. 'Information is more difficult to mine than gold – but infinitely worth the effort. You have seen my guest accommodation below. The inhabitants will tell me what I want to know – one way or another – and I already have customers for the information they will impart.'

''Tis information I have come in search of,' I said.

'Of course, and you have not, I hope, come empty-handed.'

'No.' I counted out on to the table five gold coins.

The crisp image of the enthroned king glinted in the candlelight. Doggett's eyes gleamed and he allowed himself a slight smile. 'And for this offering you want me to tell you who killed Master Robert Packington.'

It was a statement, not a question, but this time I was careful not to show any surprise. I simply nodded. 'If you know,' I said.

He sat back, hands forming a steeple beneath his clean-shaven chin. 'Well now, just for the sake of friendly debate, let us say that I do know. The question then arises what use I should make of this information.'

'If you want more money . . . '

Doggett shook his head. 'I'm sure Doctor Ned here will agree that money is not everything. Information is valuable but it can also be dangerous, and danger is to be avoided whenever possible. Don't you agree?'

I declined to comment.

'If I had the answer to your question,' Doggett continued, 'and if I gave it to you, what would you do with the information?'

'I would obtain justice for Master Packington's wife and children.'

Doggett laughed. 'Oh, please let us not confuse the issue with high-sounding words like "justice". The greater good might be served by this dangerous knowledge being withheld.'

'I think not – not if there's a God in heaven.'

'Ah, well,' Doggett responded, 'that is something we might well debate but it is little to the present purpose. We must always consider the possible consequences of our actions. What, I wonder, would happen if I were to set you on the trail of this assassin?' He turned to my companion. 'Ned, would you say that our young friend here is inclined to be head-strong?'

Ned responded cautiously. 'Master Treviot is very determined. He has, perhaps, a tendency common among young people to see everything in black and white.'

Doggett nodded. 'Would he, do you suppose, leave no stone unturned in pursuit of his friend's killer?'

'His interest is rather wider; he is concerned that he, and not Master Packington, might have been the murderer's intended victim and that consequently his own life is in danger.'

'Truly?' For the first time Doggett showed surprise. 'How so?'

I briefly described the circumstances surrounding Robert's death.

Doggett listened attentively. At last he said, 'Suppose I was able to set your mind at rest on that score, would you then abandon your pursuit?'

The man's cat-and-mouse tactics were beginning to aggra-vate me. 'I'll answer that question with another,' I said. 'If you knew the identity of this cold-blooded killer, might he pay you well to protect him?'

I felt rather than saw Ned's worried reaction. 'Master Doggett's business arrangements are no concern of ours,' he said hurriedly.

Doggett, however, showed no sign of irritation. 'As the good doctor has intimated,' he said, 'life is not printed in simple black and white, like a penny engraving from the print shop. You are a merchant, Master Treviot. Therefore you know the importance of peace. Where there is peace there is confidence. Where there is confidence there is trade. And where there is trade there is profit. I use my influence to maintain peace. Indeed, my reputation depends on it. Within my bailiwick there are many potential rivalries and feuds; men who have scores to settle, families intent on keeping old arguments alive. If I did not exercise firm control ... well,' he spread his hands in a wide gesture, 'chaos! I simply cannot permit you to go charging around like a loose colt in the marketplace quite possibly disturbing many people and seriously affecting my business.'

'Then I fear we are wasting each other's time.' I half-rose from my chair.

A firm hand pressed down on my shoulder. Another held a blade to my throat. 'You leave when Master Doggett says you leave,' the tall man said.

'It's all right, Jack. I'm sure Master Treviot meant no disrespect.' Doggett folded his arms and stared solemnly across the table. 'I will tell you what little I know and, if you are wise, you will be content with that and dabble in this business no further. Ned, you will stand security for your friend's satisfactory behaviour.'

'You have my word on that,' Ned muttered eagerly.

'Good. Well, then. The man you wish to identify goes under the name of *Il Ombra*, which is Italian for "The Shadow".'

'Italian!' I exclaimed. 'So the rumours of a foreign assassin were right.'

'He is an ex-mercenary captain who travels widely, offering his services to wealthy patrons. He is an expert in his chosen profession, equally skilled with sword, knife or gun. His favoured weapon is the wheellock, a killing device so effective that it has been banned by the Emperor and other princes.'

'Wheellock?'

'An ingenious weapon almost unknown in this country. I have seen one myself. Basically it is a small arquebus that can be wielded with one hand. It needs no lighted match because the powder is ignited by a mechanism that strikes sparks from a flint.'

'Mother of God, how diabolical!' Ned crossed himself. 'What evil will men think of next? Guns that can be carried in a purse or tucked inside a sleeve?'

I, too, was appalled but also excited. A vital piece of the puzzle was now fitting into place. 'Yes, that is how it was done!' I cried. 'The assassin must have kept the gun concealed beneath his cloak until the last moment. When he had identified his victim, he had only to raise his arm and fire. Before anyone knew what had happened, he could slip away. What a diabolical device indeed!'

'One that will quickly become the chosen weapon for assassins,' Doggett observed. 'You may take my word on that.'

'So,' I mused, 'that was obviously the manner of it but how can you be sure that this hell-bred villain was not looking for me?'

Doggett smiled. 'I mean you no disrespect, Master Treviot, but I doubt whether you are that important. Those who have met Il Ombra tell me that he is a professional killer only a very few can afford. He is at the height of his career and his fees are exorbitant.'

Now my mind was racing. At last I had information. Some glimmering light had been thrown on the mystery of Robert's death. 'Where is this man now?' I demanded.

'Gone whence he came, I believe. On the way back to his own country, his mission fulfilled. And now, Master Treviot, you have the information you came for.' Doggett scooped up the coins and dropped them into his purse. 'Our business is concluded and I bid you good day.' The tall man's hand fastened on my arm. He pulled me roughly to my feet and steered me to the door.

Minutes later Ned and I were riding away from the Red Lamb. The rain had stopped but the chill wind still rattled the leafless branches and shook droplets on us from the elms as we travelled back to the City.

Ned wiped his brow with his sleeve. 'Thomas, your tongue

will be the death of you – and possibly of me. Pray God we never see the inside of that place again.'

'Amen,' I muttered, occupied with my own thoughts. 'Where do you think this Italian could find refuge?'

'You heard what Doggett said,' Ned replied. 'The rogue has left the country and we are well rid of him.'

'Doggett was lying.'

'What do you mean?' Ned twitched his rein nervously.

'I know for a certainty that this Il Ombra, or whatever he calls himself, is still in England. All ships are laid up in harbour because of the weather. I have some friends who have been stuck at Dover this four days since, waiting for a crossing to Calais. Perhaps that's where I should go – Dover, I mean.'

'You cannot!' Ned was now really alarmed. 'You gave your word to Doggett that you'd let the matter drop.'

'On the other hand,' I was speaking my thoughts aloud, 'suppose he's not ready to leave yet. He'll have to collect his blood money before he goes anywhere. There may be a good chance that he will have to stay in hiding not far away and now that we know what sort of a man we're looking for—'

'You promised Doggett!' Ned almost shouted.

'I? I promised nothing, Ned.' I urged Dickon into a fast trot.

Chapter 15

Back in Goldsmith's Row I was met in the shop by John Fink, his young face, as ever, wrinkled by anxiety.

'Saints be praised for your return, sir.' He ran a hand through his thick yellow hair, which stood in untidy peaks on his head. 'Everything here is at six and seven. I had to close early; the place was full of idlers and gossips come to gape and gaze. People want to see where we laid poor Master Packington. They're full of questions: "Why was he brought here?" "Did we know the Dean of St Paul's has praised his killer for ridding the world of a heretic?" "Is Master Treviot a heretic, too?" It was terrible, sir. We couldn't get any work done. I had to turn everyone out and close the door.'

'Don't fret, John,' I said. 'You did the right thing. Everything will settle down in a day or two.'

He did not look convinced. "Tis the dreadfullest thing to

happen in anyone's memory. To be shot in the common street – horrible! And Master Packington such a fine man. Why would anyone call him "heretic", sir?'

I thought of the Tyndale Testament safely locked in one of my coffers. 'Just malicious gossip, John. Pay no attention.'

'Master Leyland was here again, sir, making trouble,' John grumbled.

'Oh, what was he doing?'

'Just telling anyone who would listen that someone who got mixed up with murder and mayhem was not fit to belong to the respectable merchant community.'

'Forget it, John. Leyland is just jealous of our success.'

'Well, sir, as to that—'

I cut him short. 'Not now, John. I've spent a lot of time in the saddle these last three days. I'm somewhat tired.'

As I moved towards the stair, John said, 'There were some messages left, sir.' He handed me a bundle of papers.

I had lamps lit in my chamber and sat at the table to read.

The first item I picked up was a grubby piece of paper torn from the leaf of a printed book, folded and fixed with unsealed wax. The scrawled message was brief and in an uncouth hand: 'Deth to heratiks'. I crushed the missive in my hand and tossed it into the fire.

There were three business letters. I made a mental note to go over them with John Fink.

That left a slim package wrapped tidily and addressed in an educated hand. Inside was a new pamphlet bearing the mark of the King's printer, Thomas Berthelet, and the title, 'A Sermon Made by M. Hugh Latimer, Bishop of Worcester, the Twenty-first Sunday after Trinity Sunday at Paul's Cross.' This interested me because Latimer's recent appointment to the episcopate had raised many eyebrows. His thunderous sermons against the pope and his minions had always attracted large crowds. Urged by many friends (including Robert), I had for some time intended to see one of Latimer's performances but this was just one of the many things that I had not got around to during the last troubled months. Latimer's attacks on church dignitaries, both in Rome and England, had often got him into trouble but his new dignity strongly suggested a shift in policy towards the more radical religion laughingly referred to by its detractors as the 'New Learning'. Intrigued, I moved my chair closer to the fire, placed my reading lamp on the wall sconce and settled to read the short text.

The sermon, delivered little more than a week before, was a ringing denunciation of the northern rebels and it was at once easy to see why this preacher was so popular. His words were couched in a homely vein and his illustrations were vivid and compelling, even in printed form. After announcing his text from the Epistle to the Ephesians – 'Put on the armour of God so that you may stand against the crafty assaults of the Devil' – he proceeded to develop the metaphor, showing that it was not the treasonous rabble in the North that his hearers should fear, but their general, the one who led their revolt – the Prince of Darkness. The preacher denounced the bishops and priests who resisted the truth set forth in the Bible as prime weapons from the Devil's armoury. These were revolutionary yet hypnotising words. I read on. Latimer faced his critics. 'You will say this is new learning but I tell you it is the old, the original Bible learning. You say it is old heresy, new scoured. Oh, no, it is old truth, long rusted with popish canker but now made bright and polished.' Leaving aside the princes of the Church, he went on to identify other diabolical weapons employed against true believers. Then I came upon a passage that made me gasp:

The Devil has handguns and bows which do much hurt. They are the accusers and slanderers of God's people. They are evil ordnance, indeed, these shrewd handguns and bows. They cause individuals great distress and often death follows when they shoot.

It was almost as though Latimer, preaching several days before the murderous attack on Robert, had spoken prophetically. Despite the heat from the fire, I found that I was shivering. The elegant – almost poetic – phrases of the sermon and the crude threat I had discarded had in common a passion that was frightening.

I had little time to brood on these missives for this was the evening designated for Robert's wake. As darkness fell I made my way to Sopers Lane to join the family and friends sitting up with Robert's body. I knew the short route as well as I knew the fingers of my hands and would normally not have given a second thought to walking it alone but now I took no chances. I had a servant go before me with a lamp and made sure that we were both well armed. At the house, Robert's younger brothers, Augustine and Humphrey, were receiving guests at the door. Like Robert, they were both of the Mercers' Company and I had met them quite often. Humphrey was similar to Robert in both appearance and bearing: on casual acquaintance anyone would have identified him as a grave and respectable citizen. Augustine, by contrast, was some ten years younger and still had about him vestiges of youthful brashness. His handshake was firm and warm as he led me into the hall.

The room was dimly lit by six candles on tall stands placed around the bier. Robert had been laid out in the robes of his livery and looked, despite his pallor, like one quietly sleeping.

I joined the line of people filing past, some making the sign of the cross, others holding their hands together in prayer. With a sudden shock I realised that I did not know what to do, what petitions to offer. What did I believe? Should I seek an easing of Robert's journey through purgatory? I suspected, from comments he had made from time to time, that he had abandoned belief in any such place. Peering through the crowd, I saw the florid features of Dr Edward Crome, appointed a year since to the rich living of St Mary Aldermary, by order of Queen Anne. He stood in a corner surrounded by a coterie of admirers. Robert, I knew, had held Crome in high regard and Crome had frequently found himself in trouble with the Bishop of London for his outspoken attacks on official doctrines – including purgatory. Yet, remove that stout buttress of the Church's teaching and what would hold up the edifice? What would become of all the masses and trentals recited for the dead – including those I had commissioned for my father and my wife? Now, as I moved on towards the further end of the long hall, I observed that the throng held few clergy, certainly none that would be readily recognised as strong upholders of religious tradition. This wake was, I began to realise, a gathering of radicals. I knew most of the people present, at least by sight, and I could count fewer than five who would have stood up for the religion of England as it had existed before Henry had begun his divorce proceedings against pious, Catholic Queen Catherine. Robert Packington had been my friend as long as I could remember. Now that he was dead I realised, with a shock, that I had never really known him.

I accepted a beaker of wine from a servant and moved towards the womenfolk gathered around Margaret Packington and Robert's older children. I fully expected to find her still greatly shocked, not only by the loss of her husband, but also by the manner of his death. It was a relief to discover that, for the moment at least, she was more angry than grief-stricken.

'Who could do this wicked, wicked thing?' she demanded after I had repeated my condolences.

'Whoever it was,' I said, 'we will find him. That I promise you.'

'I pray that you do,' Margaret replied, gripping my hand tightly. 'And when you do, I beg you, bring him here to me. I want him to see the children he has so cruelly orphaned.'

'I have already begun to make my own enquiries,' I said, 'just in case the coroner has difficulty—'

'Pah, coroner!' she exclaimed. 'I'd as soon trust the man in the moon to find my Robert's killer. Do you search diligently and if you lack for any help I can give, do not hesitate to ask.'

I thought carefully and, after a pause, I said, 'Robert was much loved and deeply respected by everyone who knew him. I cannot conceive that anyone . . .' I stumbled to find words that would not add to Margaret's distress. 'But it seems that somebody paid good money to have him attacked. Do you know of anyone who believed he had a real grievance against Robert?'

'Bishop Stokesley,' a voice behind me suggested, 'or the clergy of St Paul's, or My Lord of Winchester or the Duke of Norfolk . . . the list is a long one.'

I turned to see Augustine standing there, grim-faced.

'Do you really think it that simple?' I asked. 'Is the Church's faith so fragile that its leaders will break every law of God and man to protect it?'

''Tis not about faith,' Augustine replied bitterly. His eyes were agleam with fervour. 'We are at war with the forces of Antichrist.'

There was that military image again; the same Latimer had used in his printed sermon.

I drew Augustine to one side. 'I doubt such talk is helpful to Robert's widow,' I said quietly.

'Why not?' he responded truculently. ''Tis the truth.'

'Your brother was no heretic,' I said. 'It can only distress Mistress Margaret to hear him compared to simple-minded Lollards, rural clods with a smattering of theology who presume to challenge the doctors of the Church. Robert was well-educated, a man of standing, not an itinerant tailor or pedlar selling his home-made theology to silly women. The Church is certainly at war with such as them but not with Robert Packington.'

Augustine gripped me by the arm, so tightly that his fingers felt like talons. 'Robert said that you were struggling to come to terms with God's truth. Can you not see what is happening before your eyes? You talk of ignorant Lollards. Is Dr Crome a lean-witted yokel, or other university-trained men like Bishop Latimer and Archbishop Cranmer? And what of Master Cromwell? The King has placed him in charge of all church affairs and for certain he loves God's word. These are standard bearers of Bible truth, which must and will triumph, however many of us have to shed our blood for it.'

I was finding Augustine's zealotry uncomfortable and wondered whether he had drunk too much wine. For the moment I could not escape as he steered me into a space beside a large livery cupboard. 'I'll let you into a secret,' he whispered confidentially. 'Do you remember the big bonfire of Tyndale's Testaments the former Bishop of London, old Tunstall, made in Paul's Yard a few years ago? Well, can you guess who paid for all those copies? No? 'Twas Tunstall himself! What say you to that?' His self-congratulatory grin was nauseating.

I smiled, muttered something and tried to extricate myself, but he had not finished with me. 'This is how it was,' he said. 'I was in Antwerp with Tyndale and he was angry with the printers for certain errors in copies recently made. He wanted to set in hand a new printing but had no money for the work. So I said, "Leave it to me; I'll raise the money." I came back here and went to see Tunstall, posing as an ardent papist. "Will you pay me to buy up all the pestilential Testaments I can find?" I asked. He eagerly agreed and I bought for him all the faulty copies. So you see, Tunstall had the books, I had his thanks and Master Tyndale had the money for his new, better print run.' He giggled and now I knew that he was drunk.

'I must have a word with Humphrey,' I said, at last detaching myself.

'Aye, do,' he said, 'and help us find Robert's killer.'

I was only too glad, a little later, to say my farewells and return home.

Chapter 16

That night I lay awake for a long time. A wild wind rattled the shutters and occasional draughts penetrated my curtained bed, making the candle flame veer and tremble. By its light I read Tyndale's little book. Not systematically. It seemed that this supposedly seditious volume was connected with Robert's death, so I searched it for any violent denunciations of bishops, priests or abbots which might have provoked hostility from the religious establishment. I could find none.

My mind drifted from the unhelpful text to remembered snatches of conversation. Advice, observations, warnings Robert had offered a young man who, at the time, had paid little heed to them. He had told me that I was more aware of my weaknesses than my strengths. I knew, now, what he meant. Instead of standing up to the savage blows of fate, I had collapsed into self-pity and despair. Lizzie, in her more direct way, had made the same point when she accused me of unloading my responsibilities on to her. If I was to be truly a man, I would have to have faith in myself.

Perhaps this was what Tyndale was saying. He made several references to 'faith'. I took up the small volume again. 'Faith is the mother of all goodness and of all good works, so is unbelief the ground and root of all evil and evil works.' So the translator wrote. Dimly I began to see how the clergy might regard such teaching as a threat. If faith – something essentially personal – was all a man needed to live a good life, what need of masses and decked altars and elaborate ceremony? Tyndale and his friends were bidding fair to make priests redundant.

The following afternoon Robert's funeral was held. I arrived early at the small parish church of St Pancrate in Needlers' Lane, knowing that the event would draw a large crowd. Even so, I had to shoulder my way in through the west doorway. Many tradesmen on Cheap and the adjacent streets had closed their premises as a mark of respect and because they wished to be present at the obsequies. The coffin already lay on trestles in the chancel. An area at the front of the nave, before the rood screen, had been cordoned off for dignitaries and principal mourners. Some senior members of the Mercers' Company had already taken their places there. In their ceremonial robes they looked rather incongruous perched on the stools provided by the verger and his assistants. After a brief word with the verger, I was allotted one of these seats and took my place on the north side of the nave opposite the pulpit.

'A terrible business, this.' My neighbour, a corpulent grocer, opened a whispered conversation. 'In all my forty years in the City I've never heard the like.'

'Aye,' I agreed. 'Know you if the magistrate has made any progress tracking down the culprit?'

'I think not. Mind you, we all know who was behind it, do we not? 'Tis another clergy plot, like the old Hunne affair.'

'Hunne affair?' I queried. 'What was that?'

'Of course, you are too young to remember. It was ... what ... let me see, twenty years ago, mayhap more. Richard Hunne was, like Master Packington, a highly respected member of our merchant community. He had little love for the clergy and fell out right royally with his parish priest. He was going to take the fellow to court. The next we heard, he'd been arrested on a charge of heresy and clapped in Tunstall's prison. He was found there in his cell – hanged by the neck, like a common sheep-stealer.'

'Ah, yes,' I said. 'I think I remember something about it now. The bishop's people were suspected of murder but it never came to trial.'

'That's right. The bastards hushed it up. Had it judged in Tunstall's own court and acquitted the killers. Suicide, they said. Bastards!' He scowled. 'One law for them and another for the likes of us. Look at them.' He pointed to the clergy in their cassocks and copes, who were filing into the stalls on the other side of the screen. ''Tis always the same. They think their "holy orders" make them better than other men. Any breath of criticism or scandal and they close ranks. But times have changed. They won't get away with it now.' He fell silent as the choir began the *Dirige Domine*.

The doleful ritual followed its course and eventually reached the place allotted to the sermon. As the preacher – a tall figure in the habit of an Austin friar – climbed into the pulpit, a murmur of recognition and surprise rippled through the congregation. The man chosen to deliver the oration was one of the most controversial figures in London. You either liked or loathed Robert Barnes. His many enemies dubbed him a pestilential, argumentative Lutheran. The bishop had banned him from City churches but he was powerless to prevent private citizens nominating him to preach at their funerals. Robert, I knew, looked up to Barnes as a champion of the new, radical religion and that was why he was here this morning to speak at my friend's obsequies. The king had, apparently, wavered in his opinion. He had, on more than one occasion, had the friar thrown into prison but latterly had appointed him an ambassador to the German princes who espoused Lutheranism and were in league against the Emperor. Like many of my neighbours, I had long abandoned the effort of trying to understand the toings and froings of royal policy. Like them, I, too, wanted to hear what Barnes had to say. Would it bring me any nearer to understanding what Robert believed and what might offer some clue to his murder?

The preacher clutched the reading desk and for several moments gazed keenly round the congregation. Not a sound disturbed the expectant silence. When, at last, he spoke it was in a strong, deep, booming voice that brooked no contradiction. 'The fifteenth of St John in the fine English of William Tyndale, which I would that you all did read:

> "The servant is not greater than his lord. If they have persecuted me, so will they persecute you; if they have kept my saying, so will they keep yours. All these things will they do unto you for my name's sake, because they have not known him who sent me. If I had not come and spoken unto them, they should not have had sin; but now have they nothing to cloak their sin withal. He that hates me hates my father."

'Christ here speaks to us of masters and servants and enemies and I would that we dwell briefly on each of these. What, then, do we know of masters? "Why", you say, "they are even those that give us orders." Aye, and so they do. Yet do they not also feed you, pay your wages, commend your diligence and chastise your indolence? Even so, does our heavenly Lord, for sure it is you never had nor can have a more just, a more generous or a more caring master ...'

Barnes spent several minutes on this theme before moving on to his next heading.

'But what said this good Lord, this best of all lords, about servants? "The servant is not greater than his lord." You all know that to be true. What a topsy-turvy world that would be where servants tried to rule over their masters. Yet what do we see in our own land today? A rebel rabble in the North who would dictate to our sovereign lord the king the membership of his Council, the laws to be passed by his parliament, the ordering of worship in his church! Yet is there more to Christ's words than this: "If they persecuted me, they will persecute you ... If they kept my saying, they will keep yours." The servant is identified with his master. He wears his livery. He is known for his lord's man. He carries his lord's messages. He defends his lord's honour when others seek to besmirch his name. He goes to war in his lord's army. Mayhap he will die for his lord ... as has honest Master Packington. For why does his cadaver lie there?' Barnes made a dramatic gesture towards the coffin. 'For loyally serving his Lord Christ – even unto death. Be not deceived, good neighbours.' Barnes paused again to glare at the congregation and it must have seemed to every person present that the preacher caught his eye, and his alone. 'Be not deceived. Master Packington was slain for being good servant to his heavenly Master, for openly wearing Christ's livery. For speaking Christ's truth to all who would hear. And, even now, his spirit stands before his Lord to hear his gracious commendation, "Well done, good and faithful servant, enter into the joy of your Lord.""

It was true, then. For all his outward respectability, Robert had been a member – and, seemingly, a prominent member – of this heretical underworld. My mind recoiled at the thought but could no longer reject it.

Barnes was now working up to his peroration. The words tumbled excitedly from his lips and were reinforced by dramatic gestures. 'Thus we come to the third type of whom Christ spoke: his enemies. These are they, he says, who hate him and hate his Father. Why did men hate the good Christ? Who could possibly hate our good Lord? Hear again what he says: "If I had not spoken to them, they would not have had sin, but now have they nothing to cloak their sin withal." Christ denounced the priests and Pharisees of ancient Jewry for what they were – hypocrites, blind guides, men who paraded their false piety before the world to win the praise of the common people.' Barnes turned to gaze on the rows of clergy in their chancel pews. 'These were his enemies; sinners who were struck to the quick by his words of truth. Scripture tells us "He knew what was in men's hearts" and it was because Christ revealed to his enemies the truth about themselves that they tried to silence him.

'What is the question on every Londoner's lips in these days? Is it not, "Who has done this monstrous thing? Who has struck down our beloved Master Packington?" Well, I will give you now the answer: it is the enemies of Christ. The servant is not greater than his master. Robert Packington was proud to wear his Lord's livery and it was his Lord's sworn foes who set another to silence him. The Jewish leaders in Jerusalem would not soil their own hands with Christ's blood; they had the Roman governor, Pontius Pilate, do their evil work for them. Our modern hypocrites, the Roman priests of London, who are enemies alike to Christ and to King Henry, paid a desperate villain to slay Christ's servant, Robert Packington. So, my neighbours, as you pray for the soul of our dear brother departed, pray also that his enemies may be brought to justice. But pray, above all, that the true Gospel, for which Master Packington died a holy martyr, may be set forth among us with the blessing of our sovereign lord, the king, and to the confusion of Christ's enemies.'

For several breathless moments the only sound to be heard in St Pancrate's was the preacher's footfalls as he descended from the pulpit. Then pandemonium broke out. Men cheered. Others shouted, 'Shame!' 'Heretic!' or 'Lutheran!' It was fully five minutes before sufficient order could be restored for the service to be concluded. After the coffin had been interred and we all spilled out on to the street, the congregation split into groups. Some stood in the narrow lane. Others made their way homeward. But all were talking excitedly about what they had heard.

Chapter 17

It was difficult to maintain the routine of the workshop in those days. The beaters often laid aside their tools to discuss the latest incidents in our divided city and I had to beat the furnace boy for neglecting his task and allowing the fire to grow too cold. People who came in through the door wanted to gossip rather than spend money. In truth, there were few customers to be had. The times were too uncertain for people to be thinking of buying plate or jewels. Some there were who came to sell precious items or raise money against them, so that they could conceal coin against a better time. Neither I nor my neighbours were much disposed to lend in such an atmosphere of uncertainty. The threat from the northern rebels seemed to have passed but the feeling of insecurity lingered. A common rumour persisted that the Emperor and the King of France were joining forces, at the pope's behest, to invade the realm of England's 'heretic' king. One could never be sure who might be thrown into jail for speaking against the doings of our sovereign lord; for expressing opinions that were either too Catholic or too radical. Panic was, in fact, led by the government. Orders went out from Cromwell's office that every priest in the City was to be searched for 'offensive weapons'. Any item so adjudged was to be confiscated, with the exception of 'a knife for meat'. Citizens were abandoning their parish churches in favour of others where partisan preachers to their liking were to be found. Not that one had to listen to sermons to discover what the rival parties were advocating. The streets were awash with pamphlets and broadsides, printed or hand-copied, then passed surreptitiously from person to person or boldly nailed to doorposts at dead of night.

Saturday 18 November was the day appointed by the coroner for the inquest into Robert's death. Along with other witnesses I took my reserved place in a crowded Mercers' Hall. Punctual upon the appointed hour, Master Kernish entered with his clerk and called for silence. He swore in a twelve-man jury of solid citizens. It did not please me to see Simon Leyland of their number and I wondered whether we might expect some self-important intervention from him.

The coroner tried to conduct the proceedings in an almost icy calm but the atmosphere was hot with anger and speculation. The witnesses were called in order, starting with Doctor Drudgeon. We all repeated our recollections of Monday's events and no one added anything new. There was one absentee; Ben Walling was present but there was no sign of his friend Bart. Kernish called the apprentice's name twice and then asked if anyone knew his whereabouts. I noticed that Ben kept his head down and his mouth shut.

It was when Ben was giving his evidence that the almost

inevitable question came from Leyland. 'With respect, Master Kernish, might we have more information about the deceased calling out the name "Thomas"?'

The coroner looked quizzically at Ben. 'Can you add anything to your testimony on that point?' he asked.

The young man shook his head. 'As I said, sir, Master Packington's reply sounded like "Thomas" but I may have been mistaken. What followed was so sudden and unexpected that I could easily have got it wrong.'

'Did it seem to you that the deceased was calling out to his friend, Master Treviot?' Leyland demanded, in his whining voice.

Kernish frowned at the interruption. 'I will question the witnesses,' he snapped. 'The jury's task is simply to listen to the answers. If you wish elucidation on any matter you will ask me.'

Leyland put on an obsequious smile. 'Of course, Master Kernish. I beg your pardon if I spoke out of turn. I simply wanted to be as clear as possible about the relationship between the deceased and Master Treviot. There is much talk of them being of the same religious party.'

'That is nothing to the point', Kernish replied. 'You will oblige the court by keeping personal speculations to yourself.'

Leyland looked abashed by the reproof but he had done what he intended and I noticed the glances being cast in my direction by several members of the audience.

When all the witnesses had given their testimony, Kernish called upon the Chief Constable of Cheap Ward to say what progress had been made in tracing the killer. That official made a stilted, formal reply, grumbled about the shortage of manpower, hinted at 'leads' being followed. What it all amounted to was that he had not the slightest idea about the perpetrator of the crime and entertained little hope of discovering him. Kernish now summed up all that could be known about Robert's death and virtually instructed the jury to declare a verdict of murder by person unknown.

At this point there was a sudden commotion at the back of the room.

'We all know who did it!' someone shouted. 'The Dean of Paul's and his popish crew!'

There was an immediate uproar. I turned in my seat and saw two of the constable's men struggling with another, who continued to shout, 'Send for the Dean of St Paul's! Summon the bishop! Call for Canon John Incent! They know who killed Master Packington! Their gold paid for it!' The protestor was still screaming his accusations as he was hustled out. I recognised him as the grocer who had spoken to me at the funeral.

When order had been restored Kernish resumed his address to the jury. After a brief consultation, they did as directed and reported that Robert Packington had been fatally shot by an assailant as yet unidentified. The coroner's clerk entered the verdict in his records. Kernish explained that this verdict would be conveyed to the magistrates who would further pursue their enquiries.

As we all filtered out, I looked for Ben Walling and caught up with him beside the old walled orchard in Ironmonger Lane. 'Where's Bart?' I asked. 'Is he sick?'

'Only in his head,' the fair-haired young man replied, not slackening his pace.

'What do you mean?' I put out a hand to stop him and when he turned I saw the shadows beneath his eyes that betrayed a lack of sleep.

''Tis nothing,' he muttered, and made to move on.

I gripped his arm. 'Come and tell me this nothing over a jug of ale,' I said and steered him towards an alleyway that led through into St Laurence's Lane.

Minutes later we were seated in Blossoms Inn. I guessed that many days had passed since Ben had enjoyed a good meal so I ordered food as well as ale. When the maid had set before us a capon from the spit and slices of autumn-cured ham, together with wedges of maslin bread, I resumed my enquiry. 'So what of Bart? Have you two fallen out?'

The apprentice spluttered something through a mouthful of meat and I had to ask him to repeat it.

'Gone north,' he said.

'North?'

'Aye, to join the rebels, or "pilgrims" as he calls them.'

'But the rising is over,' I protested. 'The Duke of Norfolk has made a truce with the rebels at Doncaster and the Duke of Suffolk has pacified Lincolnshire. I have this on good authority from people at the royal court.'

Ben paused in his hungry devouring of the food to scowl. 'That's the official story put out to quieten the people. If the trouble is past, why do the king and his council still skulk at Windsor? The truth is the rising has spread north towards the border. Bart's family is in Cleveland and his cousin rode down two days ago to bring the latest news and recruit support. Have you seen this?' Ben fumbled inside his tunic and brought out a crumpled sheet of paper, which he passed to me underneath the table.

I ran my eyes quickly over the printed text, keeping the paper on my lap:

A Call to All the King's True Christian Subjects to
Come Together in a Holy Cause
Stand with your brothers in the North!

Demand

Return to the true Catholic faith

Restoration of all confiscated monastic property

Surrender of Cromwell, Cranmer and all base-born councillors

A new parliament to consider the people's grievances

Deliverance of all heretics to the church courts

Stand Firm Across the Realm to the Shedding of Blood for God's Truth

In Nomine Patris et Filii et Spiritus Sancti

I folded the paper and handed it back hurriedly.

Ben said, 'This is the rubbish Bart's cousin and other messengers have been spreading everywhere. He says lots of men have responded and are making their way north.'

'And that's where Bart has gone?'

'Yes, arsewipe fool!' He jabbed viciously at the meat with his knife.

'Your friend is a religious zealot, then,' I said.

Ben snorted. 'Bart? Not he! He's simply looking for what he calls "action". He'd join any mob, support any demonstration, sign up for any cause, just for the thrill of it. He came to London because he thought this place was more exciting than his Yorkshire moors. Now he's gone back there because that's where he thinks things are happening.' The young man dabbed his eyes with a shirt sleeve. 'Arsewipe fool!'

'And you?' I asked. 'What are you doing?'

He shrugged. 'Waiting. My master is still mad at me but he'll come round. I'm a good worker and he knows it.'

I pushed my trencher away and watched Ben eat the lion's share of the meal. 'Would you like to do something for me ... while you're "waiting"?' I asked.

'What sort of something?'

'Well, two things, really. First, see if you can find that noisy fellow who interrupted the inquest. I'd like to know whether he has any evidence for his accusations of the clergy or whether it's just his prejudice talking.'

'That's easily done,' Ben replied. 'What's the other job?'

'Have you heard of Il Ombra, "The Shadow"?'

Ben shook his head. 'No, what is it?'

'"It" is a he, a man, an Italian ruffian.' I lowered my voice, though the inn was by now almost empty. 'He is the one who killed Robert Packington.'

Ben raised his eyebrows. 'You're sure of this? Why didn't—'

'Why didn't I say anything at the inquest? Because if he knows I'm looking for him he'll take flight – probably leave the country.'

'Or he might mark you for his next target.'

'That had occurred to me as a possibility. It's another reason to keep quiet about what I know.'

'So, you are still determined to track this fellow down.'

'That I am. The problem is that if I am known to be asking questions, word will certainly get back to my quarry.' I did not mention Doggett by name nor his instruction to let the matter drop. By no means would I have wanted my honest and straightforward young friend to become involved with the devious host of the Red Lamb. 'Will you keep your ears open for any mention of Il Ombra or an Italian villain skulking in or around London? Listen out particularly for any reference to someone who knows about something called a wheellock.'

'What's that?'

I told Ben the little I had learned from Doggett about the assassin and his chosen weapon.

He nodded gravely. 'Yes, I can do that.'

'Thank you but do be very careful. You know the sort of hellhound we're dealing with. Don't draw attention to yourself.' I took some coins from my purse and placed them on the table. 'This will keep you fed and lodged for a few days. Try out the inns and marketplaces. Encourage people to gossip. Let me know if you hear anything.'

Ben looked happier when we parted, glad, I think, to have something to occupy his mind and relieved to know where his next meal was coming from. I just hoped that I had not put him in any danger.

After supper that night I went to my chamber and read some more chapters of Tyndale's Testament. I was intrigued to discover fuller accounts of stories I had seen vividly depicted on church walls or exuberantly performed in the mystery plays I had loved as a child. It was a strange experience to be able to ponder words spoken by Christ or the apostles and find my own meaning, rather than have interpretation thrust at me from the pulpit. Bringing my own imagination to the text made it somehow more personal and permanent. It would be false to say that I fully understood what I read but in a sense, that was unimportant. What mattered was that *I* was reading it and *I* would make my own judgement upon it. If it was this kind of intellectual freedom that the New Learning men were advocating, they were, indeed, revolutionaries.

I had just closed the book and locked it safely away in my coffer when there came a sudden rattling at the window. I peered out and saw a hooded figure in the street below. I opened the casement and called, 'Who's there?'

The reply came from the darkness in a voice somewhere between a croak and a hoarse whisper. 'Thomas, it's me, Augustine. For the love of God. Let me in.'

I took my candle, descended the stairs, went through the

shop and drew back the bolts. Augustine slipped quickly inside and I returned with him to the chamber. He held out his hands to the embers of the fire. I noticed that he had come without gauntlets.

'You must be frozen,' I said. 'Let me mull you some ale.'

He shook his head vigorously as he threw back his head. His dark hair was all atangle and there was stubble on his usually shaven chin. 'No thank you, this is but a brief visit. I've come with a simple urgent message: you must stop any enquiry into Robert's death.'

'What!' I stared at him aghast.

'Meddle in the matter no further.'

'I can scarcely believe what I'm hearing,' I protested. 'Is this the man who only yesterday urged me to discover the truth – even to the shedding of blood?'

He looked down at his feet. 'Much can happen in twenty-four hours,' he muttered.

'Sorry, Augustine,' I said. 'I have given my word to your sister-in-law. I'll not go back on it. In God's name, sit down and tell me why this fright has come over you.'

He shook his head. 'No. I must not stay. I came here as soon as I knew what was afoot. You are a marked man, Thomas. Look to yourself. Let one man's death suffice.'

Chapter 18

Augustine was hovering by the door, anxious to be gone. Seldom have I seen a man more frightened.

'What is it, man?' I demanded. 'Why this complete change of heart?'

He hesitated, a hand on the latch. 'All I can tell you is that Friar Barnes is arrested and thrown in the Tower.'

'Because of his sermon at the funeral?'

'Yes.'

'What has that to do with me?'

'Barnes is not the only one. Several others have been taken also.'

'New Learning men?'

'Yes.' Augustine now had the door open.

'I still don't see what I have to fear. I am not of their party.'

'That is not what many people say.' With that Robert's brother hurried out and clattered down the stair.

I followed and locked the street door after him, then walked through to the deserted kitchen, suddenly hungry. There was a kettle of rich pottage on the hearth, cooked for the servants' supper and still hot. I found a stoup, poured myself a bowlful and sat at the table, still damp from its nightly scrubbing, to eat – and think.

How seriously should I take Augustine's warning? He was not the most stable of men and, perhaps, it was not surprising that he was blowing hot and cold. But surely he could not really believe that I was in any danger from a new purge of radicals. Unless . . . Barnes had directly accused Stokesley and his minions of plotting Robert's murder. On reflection, I had dismissed this as the raving of a fanatic against authority. But what if it were true? Then those with guilty consciences would certainly stop at nothing to prevent further enquiry into Robert's death and they had their own well-tried methods to silence criticism: sudden arrest and trial in an ecclesiastical court where the verdict was a foregone conclusion.

Barnes was not the only one to point a finger at the senior clergy. In his outburst at the inquest, the grocer had called out one name in particular – John Incent, a member of the cathedral staff. I did not know Incent well but he was a familiar figure around the City. A tall red-headed man with a reputation for haughtiness, he was most often seen in public on festival days, when he appeared, resplendent in brocaded cope and attended by incense-wafting acolytes. He was certainly one of the most persistent preachers against heresy. Was it possible that he and his colleagues were Il Ombra's paymasters? If so, what could Robert possibly have done that could warrant a hideous act of foul slaughter – an act, moreover, that would immediately attract suspicion to themselves? Too many questions. Dangerous questions. Questions that Ned, Lizzie, Doggett and now Augustine urged me to stop asking. I began to think that my solicitous advisers might be right. Perhaps the time had come for me to abandon my quest. Perhaps it was dangerous folly to pit myself against powerful forces I did not understand – folly that, as Lizzie had pointed out, would harm others as well as myself. She had certainly learned self-preservation the hard way and her advice deserved careful consideration. Yet, there was still one person who was even more concerned than I to get to the truth. I resolved to call upon her the next day.

I found Margaret Packington in her chamber, with her maid, folding items of her late husband's clothes into a chest. 'They are to be sold for the benefit of the Mercers' Company charities,' she explained. 'The warden has been wonderfully kind. He is supervising the distribution of all Robert's bequests and helping with the formalities of Humphrey's takeover of the business. Everyone has been so good. I never knew Robert had so many friends.'

'I'm not in the least surprised,' I said. 'He touched many lives. In fact, that was something I wanted to ask you about . . . if you don't mind a few questions.'

'Not at all, Thomas.' She dismissed the girl and motioned towards the window. 'Let us sit here. It is the one place that gets much light at this time of year.'

We settled side by side in the window embrasure from which we had a clear view all the way along Sopers Lane. In the street below a pie woman was making her way up to Cheap market with two baskets laden with her wares. A carter, unable to pass her in the narrow lane, allowed his horse to clop along patiently behind. Two men, heads close together, stood arguing in a doorway.

Margaret watched wistfully. 'Strange, isn't it, how the world goes on, when your own life has come to a sudden halt. I feel like throwing open the window and shouting out, "Why are you all carrying on as though nothing had happened?"'

I laid my hand on hers. 'I know, Margaret. Believe me, I know and I wish I could say that feeling will pass quickly. 'Tis fourteen months since Jane ... but I am still like a church clock that has stopped and needs someone to set its cogs turning again.'

She patted my hand. 'Poor Thomas. You must find what comfort you can in the knowledge that God took Jane in his time and for his purpose. What happened to my Robert was so ... *wrong* ... so evil. The time was not ripe for him. I cannot believe God purposed it so. You will track down this villain, for me, won't you, Thomas?' she pleaded.

'I'll do my very best, Margaret. Can you give me any leads? I will do all I can,' I said cautiously, 'though this affair may run deeper than we know. There are many accusations flying around but no clear evidence. People say that the bishop and his clerical hounds ... but I find that difficult ...'

'Old Stokesley!' She pulled a face. 'How well named he is. Our good bishop, so men say, is never happier than when stoking the fire under those he calls "heretics".'

'Is it possible that he believed Robert to be a heretic?'

'If all who love the word of God be, in his mind, heretics, then, yes, Robert was of their number. But I don't think Stokesley would have dared to lay a finger on him. He was highly respected in the City. He was of the parliament house. And he was a friend of the king's most trusted councillor.'

'Cromwell?'

'Yes. Men say he is riding so high that no one, whether gentleman, earl or bishop, dares to cross him.'

'A pity this friendship did not protect Robert,' I said, looking at the widow, who sat twisting a kerchief in her fingers. I understood well her need to find an answer to the question, 'Why?' that was screaming in her head. Yet I felt sure that there were things she was not telling me – perhaps because she thought they might cast doubt on Robert's good name; perhaps because there were confidences she could not betray or because she was protecting other people. 'Margaret,' I said, as gently as possible, 'if I am to help, there are things I must know. I feel that Master Tyndale's English Testament lies at the root of this affair. Could Robert have known men who were involved in bringing copies of that book across the sea from the Netherlands?'

She sighed deeply. 'Robert knew many things about many people but he never confided them in me. He wanted to protect me. He said it was safer for me not to know.'

'It seems, then, that he had a private life; that he moved in a secret world.' I blurted out my frustration. 'How can we find out about that world? There must, surely, be someone who was party to his most intimate thoughts.'

Margaret frowned. 'Augustine was involved . . .'

'Augustine is frightened. He came to me last night to warn me off. Stokesley has ordered a fresh purge of New Learning men and Augustine is terrified of being netted.'

She shook her head. 'It does not surprise me. Augustine goes on and off the boil – like an unwatched pot. When he has drunk too much he is the bravest man in the world. Then comes the sober dawn and his ardour droops like a plucked rose. But perhaps he is right. If you were to come under suspicion; if something . . . happened . . . to you, as it did to Robert . . . well, I should never forgive myself.'

'Margaret,' I said firmly, 'you're not even to think like that.

If I decide to get to the bottom of his murder it will be entirely because of the debt I owe him. Over the years he did so much for me. There remains only one thing I can do for him. If it lies within my power, I shall not fail him. Now, is there anyone else who might also have been involved with Tyndale?'

She stood up and moved across to the fire, holding out her hands towards the crackling logs. 'I don't know if I should.' She looked round, obviously troubled. 'Robert made me promise. It was just another of his business ventures. Probably nothing to our purpose.'

'Margaret, I don't want to press you, but, if there is any chance . . .'

'Yes, yes, I do see that the Brothers might have something useful to tell you.'

'The Brothers?'

'That was what he called them – his Christian Brothers. There were usually three of them, though others came from time to time. They always met here late at night. I know not what they talked about. But Robert was insistent that I should never tell anyone they had been here.'

'Do you know their names?' I probed gently.

Margaret hesitated. ''Tis probably nothing, Thomas. They are all prominent citizens, no less so than Robert himself.'

'I have nowhere else to turn, Margaret. If any of these Brothers can shed some light on Robert's death, they will surely want to do so.'

'I don't know . . . He said there was danger for anyone who was identified.'

'Perhaps that prophecy has come true,' I urged. 'Robert may have been marked as one of the Brothers. In that case his friends could be at risk.'

Margaret sighed again – a long drawn-out sigh. 'Perhaps you are right, Thomas. But if I tell you, you must promise to tread carefully. Robert would ask no less of you.' She paused again, then spoke the names slowly, as though reading them from a list. 'Geoffrey Robinson, William Locke and Thomas Keyle. They're all mercers. Humphrey Monmouth of the Drapers' Company. Thomas Poyntz, grocer, but he was only here once ... or possibly twice. I don't know any of the other names.'

Shortly afterwards I took my leave but not before Margaret had several more times exhorted me to take the utmost care in my investigations. She was clearly as much in two minds as I was. However, it seemed to me that there could be no risk in contacting Robert's close friends. In all likelihood they would not agree to meet me but nor would they inform on me to the bishop's agents. It was not difficult to locate the men Margaret had named. I knew them all by name if not by sight. The mercantile and civic leadership of London is vested in a comparatively small community of successful traders who are jealous of their own dignity and regard their leadership of livery companies, City corporation and church guilds as essential to the wellbeing of the capital. Every ambitious freeman sees himself as being on a Jacob's ladder reaching to the heavenlies where these furred and velveted mayors, aldermen and company wardens exercise sway over the municipality. The names of the aristocrats who govern our little realm are common property. So, I knew, for example, that Geoffrey Robinson was Senior Warden of the Mercers' Company.

Knowledge was one thing. Making effective use of it another. How was I to approach these grandees and persuade them to discuss with me matters of the utmost confidentiality? That afternoon I carefully composed letters to the men

Margaret had named. I explained that, as a close friend of Robert Packington, I was concerned about the manner of his death and would welcome an opportunity to discuss that shocking affair with any who might be able to cast light upon it. The following morning (Monday 20 November) I despatched messengers to find the recipients and deliver my request. Scarcely had I done so when news arrived concerning one of the addressees.

I was with the Dean of Gloucester, who had called about a new suite of gold altar furnishings for one of the cathedral chapels. As with all important customers, I received the cleric in my parlour and we were in the middle of cautious haggling when I received news that Ben Walling was in the shop asking to see me on an 'urgent' matter. As soon as I could do so politely, I concluded my negotiation with the dean, who must have been surprised that I so quickly agreed to a figure well below what he had, undoubtedly, expected to pay.

Ben looked excited as he came into the parlour and he declined the ale I offered.

'I've found the grocer,' he said. 'Or, rather, I haven't.'

'In God's name, Ben,' I growled, 'try to speak sense. Sit down, if you can remember where your backside is.'

'Sorry.' He grinned as he pulled up a stool. 'What I mean is I've discovered *who* he is but I don't know *where* he is now.'

'That doesn't sound very helpful,' I muttered.

'Wait till you've heard the whole story. This morning I went gossiping along the grocers' shops in Bucklersbury, as you suggested. Of course, several people had heard about the disturbance in the coroner's court and they knew who was responsible. His name is Thomas Poyntz – something of a troublemaker by all accounts.'

I pricked up my ears at the name. 'Go on,' I said eagerly.

'Well, I went to his shop and asked to see the master. "He's not here," his assistant said. The man was quite clearly frightened. When I asked where I might find Master Poyntz, his lips closed tighter than a Whitstable oyster. Not wanting to seem too curious, I thanked the man and left – and not a moment too soon.'

'Why? What happened?'

'I'd not gone more than a few yards down Bucklersbury when I heard a commotion behind me. I turned and saw four armed men getting off their horses and marching into Poyntz's shop. I stayed around as a member of the crowd which straightway gathered to watch the fun. There was a great deal of shouting and crashing from inside the shop. Then the soldiers came out pushing three of Poyntz's men before them, their hands tied, and off they all went.'

'No sign of Poyntz?'

'No. He was long gone. I overheard some of the neighbours talking about him. It seems he left yesterday morning on horseback. Probably trying to make the coast. By all accounts he spends a lot of time in the Low Countries – Antwerp mostly.'

Antwerp. Where Robert had been until recently. I knew that he used the English merchant quarter there as his base when his business took him overseas. That was where there had been trouble ... where the heretic Tyndale had been tracked down. Tyndale! Wherever I turned in this maze I always seemed to come face to face with him.

'Well, let's hope Poyntz escapes the bishop's clutches,' I said.

'Oh, these weren't Stokesley's men,' Ben said.

'City militia, then?'

'No, not them either. These soldiers were in royal livery.

Odd, that. Why would the king bother himself with the rav-ings of a bishop-hating grocer?'

'To show he's no supporter of heretics, I suppose.'

Ben scratched his head. 'Odd thing is some folks were saying it was done on Cromwell's orders. I can't believe that. If Lord Cromwell is intent on pulling down the abbeys, curb-ing the power of the Church and putting up New Learning preachers in our pulpits, why would he try to silence people like Poyntz for foul-mouthing Stokesley?'

'There are people who blame Cromwell for everything they don't like.'

'Aye, no doubt that's the truth of it ... though I still can't see ...'

'If you want to keep a sane head on your shoulders, Ben,' I said, 'don't try to make sense of politics. Any news of this Il Ombra fellow?'

He shook his head. 'No, and I've been thinking about that. Why would someone "shadowy", someone who doesn't want to be identified, use a fancy name?'

'Bravado?' I suggested. 'This wretch is a craftsman. He's proud of what he does.'

'And a craftsman needs clients. How does he find them?' Ben brushed his bush of fair hair back from his forehead. 'Suppose you wanted to hire his services. How would you locate him? You couldn't look for a shop with a sign outside – "Get your murders here".'

I pondered the question. 'I see what you're suggesting,' I said. 'I would have to let it be known that I was looking for an assassin.'

'Exactly. You'd ask around in the places where thieves, whores and vagrants congregate – like Mother Bennett's, hard by Bethel, or the ale houses on the road beyond Finsbury

Fields. Breathe the name Il Ombra there and say you want to buy his services and, as sure as the Devil's in hell, your man will come and find you.'

The suggestion was brilliant, obvious, and I had been too mired in detail to see it. 'Of course! That's what I must do – make him come to me,' I said.

'Hold hard now, Master.' Ben looked genuinely alarmed. 'You can't just arrange a cosy meeting with a professional killer. I have a better plan.' The young man drew his stool closer. He looked excited. Too excited.

'Go on,' I said cautiously.

'Let me put out the word that a wealthy man – perhaps even one of the king's courtiers – wants to arrange a revenge killing. If our luck is in, Il Ombra will take the bait and suggest a time and place to see you. Now, it's bound to be somewhere secure. He'll be wary of a trap.'

'Then that's where your plan falls down.' I was beginning to see where Ben's ideas were leading. 'He'll be suspicious. He won't want to be recognised. As soon as he realises that I don't come in good faith he'll be gone.'

'Oh yes, and he'll probably kill you first,' Ben said cheerfully. 'That's why you mustn't go alone. I'll be waiting for him with some of my friends.'

I laughed, trying to make light of the suggestion. 'So that he can kill us all? Have you forgotten that this man is an expert with firearms?'

'I can gather half a dozen apprentices who are very nimble with cudgels and staves.'

I could see that he was very much in earnest. 'Ben, I really appreciate the offer but this is not your quarrel and it isn't a May Day frolic. If I went to meet this assassin I would take a band of the constable's men.'

'A brilliant idea,' he scoffed. 'Our friend would recognise them on the instant and disappear.'

There was certainly sense in what Ben said. Seeing my hesitation, he pressed on. 'I reckon this Ombra fellow will choose a busy place where he can vanish in the crowd if he suspects anything. Well, we can be anonymous members of that crowd. He won't escape all of us.'

'And suppose he decides to meet on open land where he can be sure no one else is around?'

Ben was ready with his answer. 'Then we'll be there well ahead of time, concealing ourselves behind any bush or rock or tree that lies to hand.'

'Wherever this encounter takes place,' I protested, 'someone's going to get killed. If not you, then one or more of your friends. Does that not worry you?'

He shrugged. 'What is life worth without risk?'

Suddenly, I realised that, at one time, I would probably have made the same nonchalant answer. How much I had changed in the four or five years that separated us. Just as others were telling me to be cautious, so I now wanted to urge my enthusiastic friend to be cautious. I said, 'Well, Ben, I'll give your idea some thought, but—'

He jumped to his feet. 'Good. I'll come and see you tomorrow.' With that he was gone.

Meanwhile, my own lines of enquiry were proving fruitless. Geoffrey Robinson sent back a polite reply regretting that he was unable to offer assistance. The messenger I had sent to William Locke's impressive house in Milk Street was informed that Master Locke was spending a couple of days at his lodge on Hampstead Hill. My other envoys met with curt refusals. Frustrated, I decided to follow up the only lead I had. I would ride out personally to Hampstead that very afternoon and see if I could persuade Locke to talk to me. Accordingly, I told John Fink where I was going and left him instructions to shut up the shop at close of business. I had a quick, light dinner and was about to leave when Ned Longbourne bustled into the shop, breathless and distraught.

'I've just had a visit from Lizzie,' he gasped. 'She was in great distress.'

Chapter 19

I hurried Ned into the parlour. 'Has something gone wrong at Hemmings?' I demanded. 'Has anything happened to my mother? Is my son safe? Lizzie had no business abandoning him.'

Ned dropped heavily into the chair opposite. 'She is an impulsive creature, as you know. She came to Southwark on a whim, bringing the boy with her. All at your house are unharmed but Lizzie fears they are at risk. She actually wanted to leave young Ralph with me to return to you. I had the Devil's own job to persuade her to go back.'

I felt a dagger thrust of panic in my stomach. 'What is the problem? Do they need more protection? Should I send more men to Hemmings to guard them?'

'You will have to ask her. I promised her that I would bring you to Hemmings to see the situation for yourself. She says the household is surrounded by enemies, like a besieged castle.'

'No hint of who these "enemies" are?'

'None.'

'She can come to no harm at Hemmings, Ned. Of that I am sure. Do you not think she is just letting her own worries get the better of her? She's in a strange place. She misses the support of her St Swithun's friends. She needs time to settle down.'

He shook his head firmly. 'Lizzie may be headstrong but she is not given to fantasies. If she is anxious she has good cause to be. You would do her a disservice to dismiss her fears as feminine whims.'

I thought long and hard. 'You place me in a difficult position. I am already committed to a plan to put an end to all our troubles. I am going to draw the assassin into the open. That's the only way to stop this nightmare and make sure that Lizzie and my family are safe.'

'In God's name, let it be, Thomas!' Ned glowered across the table with a look of anguish, such as I had never seen before. 'Don't go to the stake for your friend.'

I stared back momentarily stunned. 'What in the name of all the saints does that mean?'

'It matters not. Forget I said it.' Ned waved a hand, as though brushing words away. 'What matters is whether you will come with me to Hemmings to see what ails Lizzie and set her mind at rest.'

'Very well,' I agreed, 'but I cannot come today. I will meet you in Southwark in the morning – but only if we can make an early start. I must get to Hemmings and back again in a day.'

As soon as Ned had gone, I set out with three servants. We

rode up West Cheap and out through Newgate. We skirted Gray's Inn and the lawyers' quarter and headed along the busy road that slowly inclines via heath and woods to the ridge of Highgate. Grudgingly I paid the toll demanded of all who crossed Bishop Stokesley's hunting ground, wishing that His Grace was as assiduous in maintaining the road as he was in collecting his dues. We kept to the sides of the track, avoiding as far as possible the wagon-ruts and wide puddles that splashed our mounts with mud up to their chests. It was not raining but the pewter sky threatened a possible downpour and gusts of wind tore at our cloaks as we reached higher ground.

Locke's timber-framed house stood at the edge of a copse and, as we approached, a small party of horsemen emerged from the stable block. Leading the group on a magnificent black mare was a ruddy-complexioned man of middle years, huddled in a fur-lined cape. It was obvious from his expensive clothes, his fine mount and his beard of formal, yet fashionable cut, that here was a man of substance and one who, in all probability, moved in court circles. On his left wrist he carried a hooded lanner falcon. I introduced myself and Master Locke smiled his welcome.

'Ah yes, you are a friend of Robert Packington. I received your letter. That was a shocking business, deeply shocking. I'm just training a new hawk but by all means ride with us.'

I fell in beside him as he led the way out on to the heath. 'A fine-looking bird,' I said, by way of opening the conversation.

'Yes, I brought her back from France a few weeks ago. She's a little skittish but she's responding well to training.'

'You are fortunate to have this land close to London to hunt over,' I suggested.

''Tis the king's land but, thanks to our queen of blessed memory, I had grant of hunting rights and was permitted to build my little lodge three years ago.'

'Queen Catherine secured you these privileges?'

'Oh, no, no. Indeed no. I mean Queen Anne. I was her personal mercer. I furnished the silks, velvets and brocades for most of her wardrobe – and the little princess's.'

'I believe you were a close friend of Robert Packington,' I ventured.

'Yes, indeed. A fine man, a godly man. He had many friends.'

'And, alas, some enemies.'

Locke reined in his horse. 'As I say, he was a godly man. As God has enemies, so did he. This is where I train Jeanette.' He gently stroked the bird's feathers.

We were on an open, gently sloping tract of rough grassland. Yards away Locke's servants were struggling with the wind to get a small kite airborne.

'You know what they're doing?' he questioned.

'I've never taken up the sport,' I said.

'This bird has been hand-reared. So we have to teach her to hunt. My men are sending the kite up with a lure attached. You can see that bag there with yellow feathers on it. Jeanette already associates that with food. Now watch.'

He removed the hawk's hood, held her at arm's length and released his hold on the jesses strapped to her legs. The bird flew and quickly soared higher than the kite. I watched as she circled several times.

Locke dismounted. 'She was a falcon, you know.'

'Sorry, I didn't quite hear . . .'

'Queen Anne – her heraldic badge was the falcon. How high she flew. How high and how beautiful.'

I watched the gently gyrating bird, captivated by her grace-ful, effortless gliding. Then, suddenly, she became an arrow, cutting the air in speared flight, taking the lure and plunging with it to earth.

'And all at once, in a moment, she fell.' Locke stooped to feed the hawk her reward and gather up the jesses.

Later, the session over and the party returning to the lodge, I said, 'You must have been very close to the queen.'

'I brought her more than silks and news of the Paris fash-ions. She grew up at the French court and I kept her in contact with old friends and new ideas.'

'New ideas? Does that mean what people call the New Learning?'

'What scoffers and God-haters call the New Learning!'

We were silent for some minutes as we rode through a belt of trees, glad to be out of the wind.

'You said earlier that Robert's enemies were God's enemies,' I probed. 'Do you think he was killed on the orders of the bishop or his senior clergy?'

Locke gave me a sideways glance. 'Do not tempt me to name names, young man. I know you not well enough. Permit me rather to catechise you. Is it God's will, think you, for all to be saved through knowledge of his truth?'

'I must believe so.'

'And is that truth contained in God's holy word written?'

'So the Church teaches us.'

'Should all who are literate read that word for themselves? What says the Church to that?'

I stumbled around for an answer. 'Some say "Yea". Others say "Nay, it is too profound for ordinary men; it must be inter-preted by priests."'

'And what say you?'

'I . . . I am neither on one side nor the other.'

'You think it too dangerous to hold an opinion on such things.'

'Yes, I suppose so.'

'Then by the same yardstick I will not name Robert's killer.'

I groaned inwardly with frustration. It seemed that my excursion to Hampstead had been in vain. I decided to try one last, bold overture.

'Robert spoke warmly of a group he belonged to – the Christian Brothers.'

Locke yanked on his rein, bringing his ambling mare to a sudden halt. He turned her round to stand before me on the path and fixed me with a penetrating stare. 'You lie,' he said quietly.

I opened my mouth to protest but Locke went on: 'Robert would never break his oath. *If* any such organisation existed and *if* he belonged to it, he would not mention it to an outsider – no matter how close a friend such an outsider might be.'

'That secrecy did not save his life,' I muttered angrily, 'but it seems that it will protect his murderer.'

That obviously stung Locke. He raised his head, thrusting forward his grey-flecked, neatly trimmed beard. 'Robert was a brave Christian warrior who knew the risks he was taking for truth's sake. But he was not the only one, nor was he the greatest to lose his life for what he believed.'

'You are thinking of Queen Anne?'

He nodded.

'I was there,' I said, 'in the Tower. I saw. I heard what she said.' The memory was still vivid – the small woman in grey, standing beside the block, poised and untrembling, her hands clasped before her. 'She confessed nothing.'

'And had nothing to confess.' Locke's cheeks blazed with sudden anger. 'She was a God-fearing woman and a faithful wife. No king ever had a truer consort or one who used her position more for good. I know better than most what she believed and what she achieved. It was I who bought her books for her – Bible translations in French and English, works of devotion by the best scholars in France, treatises urging reform of abuses in the Church. His Majesty will never have a better wife, nor England a better queen.'

'Then why—' I began, but Locke's passionate devotion to the late queen was like a key to the coffer of his memory that, once unlocked, spilled out its contents.

'She did not merely study holiness; she practised it. Her reign was short but she achieved remarkable things. She had godly preachers, like Dr Crome, appointed to their livings. And bishops! Where would Latimer be were it not for her patronage? Or Archbishop Cranmer? Who set the king on his course to close the abbeys so that all their hoarded wealth could be used for the common good? How much more might she have done if she had been spared? She was zealous in rooting out nests of papists and would have purged even the chapter of St Paul's, given time. And the Bible! Oh, how close we came to having an English translation set up in all churches by royal command . . .' He paused for breath, then continued in a quieter voice scarcely audible above the whining wind. 'So, of course, she made enemies – God's enemies – as Poor Robert did.' He shivered and drew his cloak tighter round his shoulders. 'But dusk is almost upon us and you must make your way back to the City. Come, I'll show you a shorter route across the heath.'

As I set out on the return journey with my attendants I was deep in thought about what William Locke had said – and what I could deduce from what he had not said. Had I been less preoccupied I might have been readier for what happened when we had travelled a scant mile. We were passing a couple of cottages that appeared to be derelict when there was the sound of a gunshot. Dickon reared up. I was thrown from the saddle and fell heavily. I lay momentarily dazed and winded. Then, unthinking, I sat up. That was when I heard a second shot.

Chapter 20

I felt this one. The metal pellet tore through the thick folds of my cloak and hood. It seared the flesh of my neck. That brought me to my senses. I looked around. Two of my mounted companions were standing like statues. The third was trying to calm his skittering horse. 'Take cover!' I shouted. Easily said. The heathland was wide and empty. The shots had come from our right, almost certainly from a small clump of trees. To our left, some twenty yards away, stood the ruined buildings. 'The cottages!' I yelled. 'That's our only chance.' The others spurred their horses towards the shelter of the ruined walls. I pressed myself close to the damp grass. I looked around for Dickon. He was ten yards to my right, limping, holding one of his forelegs off the ground. I stared at the trees but could see no movement. Leaping to my feet, I charged towards Dickon at a crouching run. I had almost reached him when another shot rang out. Good, I thought. The attacker will have to reload. I reached the horse and grabbed the reins. Frantically, I hauled him towards our chosen refuge. We were a few paces away when I heard another shot. This one whistled past my head. We scrambled into the shelter of the broken walls.

'Is everyone all right?' I called out as we reached safety.

There was a reassuring chorus of replies.

I peered round the side of my refuge across the open heath. 'Can you see them? How many are they?'

'Two, I think,' said Walt, my groom.

'No, only one,' someone else added.

We crouched against the wall and stared across the darkening landscape. Almost immediately there was a flash amid the cluster of elms and a ball thudded into the decaying wattle and daub to my left. Then silence. I watched intently and moments later, another shot was discharged from exactly the same spot.

'One it is,' I agreed.

'God damn him!' Walt muttered. 'Whoreson highwaymen and footpads! This area has always been plagued with them.' He seemed more angry than frightened.

'Well, he's going to be out of pocket today.' I needed to encourage the others. 'It's one against four and he daren't come over here until the light has gone. That gives us time to get help.' I called out to the youngest and most agile member of the group. 'Simon, do you think you could reach Master Locke's and tell him what's happened?'

'Yes, Master Thomas.' The reply was eager.

'Good! Take Walt's mare. She's the fastest.'

Instantly Simon ran over and took the reins from my groom's hand.

'No wait!' I shouted. 'See if our attacker fires again. Then go while he is reloading.'

Simon's mare whinnied and backed away, sensing well the danger. We waited for what seemed long minutes. Then came the flash again.

'Go!' I shouted.

Simon leaped into the saddle, spurred his mount into a canter and was away up the track in an instant.

I sat down with my back to the wall, thinking hard. Highwayman? Footpad? Some infantryman from the king's wars using his knowledge of firearms for personal profit? Somehow, I doubted it. This assailant was no common robber lying in wait for fat-pursed travellers. If he had wanted money he would have confronted us in a place where the woodland gave him cover, threatened us with his weapon, grabbed his loot and made off through the trees. If he was intent on murder what would his next move be? He would realise we had sent for help. That meant he had little time to finish his job. But he would have to wait for darkness to mask his movements. I turned to peer at the space between us. Grey clouds crowding in from the west were hastening the dusk. The shapes of trees and bushes were already becoming blurred.

'Will help arrive in time, Master Thomas?' Walt called out quietly.

'I'm sure of it,' I said. 'Master Locke is an upright man. He'll waste no time before sending aid. Meanwhile, keep a careful eye on our friend out there. Watch for any movement, however small. I must look to Dickon while there's still enough light.'

I had tethered the grey to a broken door frame and he stood, now, patiently holding up his damaged leg and whimpering quietly. Blood was running down his flank. I peered at the wound closely, trying to see how deep it was. Dickon pulled away as I probed with my fingers. I made soothing noises and felt for the ball. If it was in deep there would be no hope for my horse and I vowed that his attacker would pay dearly for the loss of my faithful steed. But I could feel no metal and concluded with relief that the ball had not penetrated the muscle. It had, as far as I could see, cut through hair and skin, then emerged, leaving only a bloody furrow behind. I patted Dickon's neck. 'Be brave, old friend. Whoever did this will pay dearly,' I promised. I was more angry about the damage to my horse than about my own peril.

As I stepped back, I was suddenly aware that everything had gone quiet. The marksman had stopped firing. Had he gone? Was he creeping forward in the deepening gloom – coming to finish his task?

'What's happening?' I demanded of the others. 'Can you see him?'

'No.'

'Not a sign.'

Walt said, 'Shall I go out and have a closer look?'

'No!' I replied. 'That may be what he wants. We must turn the fading light to our own advantage. Time, I think, for a game of hide and go seek. If he wants to find us, he'll have to come looking. Collect your horses and come, with me – very quietly. We'll move back, using the buildings as cover.'

'Shouldn't we just wait for Simon to get here with help?' Walt asked.

'Our friend out there will know he hasn't much time. He'll come.' It now seemed that we might be able to turn the tables on our assailant. I certainly hoped so.

We moved back some twenty yards, until the cottages were

nothing more than a black mass against an ash-grey sky. We waited. And waited. And waited. Nothing. No sound but the wind ruffling the heathland grass. Then there came noises away to our right. Clattering hooves. Men calling. Our rescuers had arrived.

I was actually disappointed.

There was no point in searching for our attacker. We returned to the lodge. William Locke came out to greet us, solicitous in the extreme. He insisted that Dickon should be cared for in his own stable with Walt to look after him until the groom declared him fit enough to be moved. Then, when we had made the horse as comfortable as we could, my host insisted that I join him for supper and that we all spend the night under his roof.

We sat alone in a room that was something between a small hall and a large parlour. Though modest in size it lacked nothing in opulence. The walls were hung with impressive Flemish tapestries and the food was served on fine silver. Locke himself was no less impressive than his surroundings. He was dressed in the latest fashion and the pomander hanging from a chain around his neck was of gold. Here was a man who enjoyed aping his social superiors and had the taste and wealth to do it well. He made me recount my misadventure in minute detail but made no comment until he had dismissed the servants.

Then, 'You think it was the same assassin?' he asked.

'I am sure of it.'

'Why? We live in evil times. The realm is full of desperate men.'

'But none who lay murderous ambush and cut their victims down with handguns.'

Locke pondered for a moment, fingering his close-trimmed

beard. 'If you are right, this fellow must know that you are hunting him.'

'The criminal world has its own efficient information networks,' I said. 'That is something I have learned in recent days.'

'In which case, the sooner you find him, the better.'

'Aye, him and his paymaster.'

Locke closed his eyes and lines of concentration scored his brow. I noticed that his lips were moving slightly, almost as though he were praying. Then he looked up suddenly. 'Very well,' he said, 'there is something I will tell you for your own safety. We spoke earlier about Englishing the Bible – how some promote it and some oppose it. You declared yourself neutral.'

'Yes, I can see that there are arguments on both sides.'

He shook his head vigorously. 'Young man, you have already taken a stand. Whether you like it or not; whether you know it or not, you have joined the battle.'

'Not so. I simply—'

'Nothing is simple!' he snapped. 'Everything – ideas, beliefs, principles, convictions – they're all up in the air, whirling around like leaves in an autumn storm. What are men arguing about everywhere from the royal council chamber to the most verminous village inn? The king's divorce, his murder of his queen – aye, murder, I say, look not so shocked – the pope's setting up other princes to make war on us, the downfall of the monasteries, pilgrimages and fraudulent miracles, the abomination of jewel-bedecked statues and other fripperies in our churches, the greater abomination of the mass.' Locke's tone had risen almost to a fervent shout. Now he lowered his voice. 'Yet is there one issue that underlines all, defines all, decides all, judges all: shall we or shall we not base our life on God's word written?'

The man's zeal was undeniable – and worrying. 'You seriously believe all our problems can be solved by one book?' I asked.

He smiled. 'If you knew how that book is already changing many people's lives you would not be so sceptical. There are thousands of copies of Master Tyndale's Testament being read all over the land.'

'Much good that did Tyndale,' I muttered.

'There are other Tyndales. They are at work in Antwerp and Cologne. Soon we shall have a whole Bible in English to distribute.'

Now that Locke was speaking less guardedly he was confirming what I had come to suspect. 'Then, that is what the "Christian Brothers" were doing – distributing Bibles? What part did Robert play in this traffic?'

Locke sidestepped the question. ''Tis the bishop's laws not the king's that are being disobeyed. Last year the queen herself persuaded His Majesty to sanction an official English Bible. Had he done so, there would have been no more need for copies to be smuggled over the Channel in bales of cloth and barrels of wine. Now that Her Majesty has gone' – he shook his head sadly – 'the enemies of the Gospel have their tails up and think that by rebellion, and burnings and imprisonments – aye, and by murder in the streets – they will prevail. So the war continues and you have taken sides. By setting yourself to uncover the truth of Robert's death you have been marked as one of us. Tonight's work apparently confirms that.'

'Then you must know who was behind Robert's murder and this attack.'

'Know?' He shook his head. 'The enemy is hydra-headed. At court there is the Duke of Norfolk, the new queen and her whole Seymour brood and, of course, old Wily Winchester

Bishop Gardiner. None of them would scruple to hire an assassin. They are all in league with Chapuys, the Emperor's ambassador. He is as slippery and twisted as an adder. He has spies everywhere and the gold to pay for all manner of mischief. Then there's Stokesley and his priestly crew. They still have more loyalty to the pope than the king and some of them are fanatical enough to commit murder and believe they do it in the name of God.'

'A gloomy catalogue,' I observed. If Robert had such an array of powerful enemies what chance did I have of getting at the truth – assuming that I survived?

'Aye, but all is not lost. There are many Gospel-lovers around the king and he has complete trust in Thomas Cromwell. Norfolk and Gardiner hate Cromwell with a primal passion but they cannot dislodge him and he is a favourer of the Gospel.'

'Robert always spoke well of Cromwell.'

'Aye, he was in Master Secretary's confidence and often carried messages for him when he travelled abroad. So, young man,' Locke concluded, 'you see what a mire you have stumbled into.'

Indeed I did. Now I could understand why Augustine had tried to dissuade me from my quest. It may have been partly concern for my own safety but he and his friends also did not want people like me stirring up trouble and drawing attention to them and their plans.

Later, as I lay in Locke's comfortable guest chamber, I thought over the day's dramatic and revealing events. One thing was clear: I no longer had the luxury of deciding whether or not I would investigate Robert's murder. My involvement was already known to his associates and to his enemies. The only conviction they all shared was that Thomas Treviot should keep his nose out of what did not concern him. But the only choice before me now was either to unmask the assassin or wait for him to make another attempt on my life.

The next morning I arrived back in Goldsmith's Row to find the whole house in a state of great agitation. The servants rushed out to greet us as soon as we clattered into the yard. I had scarcely tethered the young bay Master Locke had generously lent me before John Fink stood before me, anxiety and relief chasing themselves around his youthful, fresh-complexioned face.

'Master, Master,' he gasped, 'are you all right? When you failed to return, we ...'

'All's well, John,' I said reassuringly.

'But, Master, what happened?'

'Someone tried to waylay us on our way home.' I walked briskly into the house.

The apprentice followed, close on my heels. 'Was it the same villain who shot Master Packington?'

'I don't know, John. He disappeared in the dark. Now, I have to leave again within the hour. I'm needed at Hemmings and this incident has already made me late.' I strode through the kitchen.

Fink was still close behind me. 'What if he tries again, Master?'

'Who?'

'The assassin.'

'Then we must make sure we're ready for him.'

As soon as I and my two servants had refreshed ourselves and I had given such instructions as were necessary, we set out again. At St Swithun's House Ned was with difficulty concealing his impatience. 'I wondered whether you might have reconsidered,' he said, with a hint of reproach.

'A promise is a promise,' I replied. 'I was ... unavoidably delayed. If you are ready let us be on our way.'

We travelled over frost-hardened ground on a crisp, brittle morning, the low sun etching long black shadows across the track. Wherever the ground was not too hard and treacherously deep-rutted we cantered the horses. Otherwise, we were constrained to proceed at an ambling gait. As we journeyed I gave my companions a censored version of the previous day's events. They would hear about Il Ombra's attempted ambush sooner or later and I would rather they received a version that was as bland as I could make it.

Ned received the news sombrely. 'I suppose this terrible experience has left you quite unchastened,' he said.

'Well, you did warn me,' I replied.

He shook his head. 'That gives me no satisfaction. I can only hope that what Lizzie has to tell you will deflect you from your stubborn path.'

At Otford we fell in with a group of devout travellers on the old pilgrimage route to Canterbury. As we jogged between ploughed fields whose ridges were being broken down by the frost a lean priest on an even leaner horse bemoaned the changing times.

'Belike this will be our last chance to pray at St Thomas's shrine.'

'Why so?' I asked.

'The king means to bring it down,' he replied with a sage nod of the head. 'I have that on the best authority.'

'That is right enough.' The speaker was a lady in a fur-trimmed hood, who travelled with her chaplain and three of her women. 'My cousin attends His Majesty in his chamber. According to him, that wretch Cromwell is forever urging him to lay his hands on the devout offerings presented to the saints. He claims this would make him the richest king in Christendom.'

'A curse on the Jostler! A curse on the unholy trinity!' The thin priest raised his piping voice in an outraged cry.

I turned to Ned, a questioning look on my face.

It was Jed who explained, with a raucous laugh. 'Surely you've heard of the unholy trinity, Thomas?'

'No.'

'Its members are the Jostler, the Ostler and the Whore.'

'The Jostler, I take it, is Cromwell.'

'Aye,' the priest agreed. 'He is a nobody; the son of a Putney brewer and violent lawbreaker, who has jostled his way into the king's council and elbowed aside greater men like Thomas More.'

'And now,' Ned added bitterly, 'he is jostling monks and nuns out of their homes and honest men on to the gallows.'

'So much for the Jostler,' I said, in an effort to lighten the conversation. 'Who is the Ostler?'

The priest sneered. 'Why, that is Cranmer, His Grace of Canterbury. "Disgrace" more like. He's better fitted to a groom's apron than an archbishop's pall.'

'But why do you call him the Ostler?'

'Why, the hypocrite is a twice-married man and his first wife was the daughter of a Cambridge innkeeper. His second he brought over from heresy-land – Germany. They say he hides her away in his manor at Ford and when she must travel she does so in a locked chest.'

I laughed. 'What lurid yarns enmity spins. I've heard the self-same story told of at least two abbots.' I pointed ahead along the road. 'Our ways part at the top of that hill.'

I was not to be allowed to divert them from their complaint. The lady spoke again.

'And the whore, of course, refers to the Boleyn creature. If it had not been for her and her Frenchified wiles we should not be in this mess.'

'Well,' I said, 'she can do no more harm now, wherever she is.'

'Oh, we know where she is,' the lady replied with a fragile laugh bordering on the hysterical. 'Burning in hell. Would that I were there to stoke the fire.'

'Perhaps one day you will have that privilege.' I spurred my horse and rode on ahead of the company.

Minutes later we said goodbye to our companions of the way and turned on to the narrow lane towards Ightham.

'You were a little hard on them,' Ned said as we rode side by side.

'I think they would not have been so piously indignant if they had been on Tower Green last May. I *was* there. What I saw was no scheming, painted strumpet. She was a frightened young woman who died with dignity and, to my mind, Christian fortitude.'

Ned threw back his hood. 'I am glad to hear that. Yet, I can only think that England is the better for her absence.'

'Because she urged the king to close monasteries and turned you out of your comfortable living?' It was an unworthy attack but I was feeling far from charitable.

Ned answered my question calmly, ignoring the innuendo. 'Who knows what a woman may drive a man to when he is in the grip of lust? Many evils are born in the conjugal bed.'

'You can hardly speak from experience,' I retorted with a sneer.

He did not respond to the barb. ''Tis common knowledge that the late queen introduced her husband to books by Tyndale and other heretics that told him what he wanted to hear – that he could flout the ancient laws of Christendom, turn his back on the pope and take upon himself powers God never intended kings to wield.'

'If these trees had ears,' I said, 'you might find yourself on a treason charge.'

He laughed but there was a bitter edge. 'Oh, I will do whatever His Majesty ordains. I am not made of the stuff of martyrs. I hope the same is true of you, Thomas.'

I pondered his words for some moments. 'Yesterday you told me not to go to the stake for Robert Packington. What did you mean by that?'

Ned shook his head. 'Forget it. I spoke rashly, angrily. I was upset by Lizzie's message.'

'Yet you meant something.'

He was silent for a long time, then said, 'You understand gold, Thomas. You can tell its purity by feel, by appearance, by weight. You know true coin from false.'

'In most instances, yes.'

'It has taken long years of training to achieve this mastery of your craft. If someone tried to deceive you with counterfeit coin you would be angry.'

'Yes, but—'

'Bear with a stupid old monk, Thomas. I do have a point. Is it right, do you think, that counterfeiting is punishable by death?'

'Certainly.'

'Which is worse, in your opinion, to strike and circulate false money or to make and circulate false religion?'

'That sounds like a scholar's trick question,' I grumbled.

'Only to someone who doesn't want to face the answer.'

There was another long pause before he continued, 'Our prior in the monastery was a strict but wise disciplinarian. He had a varied store of punishments. For minor misdemeanours, such as oversleeping or talking in choir he prescribed learning by rote long passages from the Church fathers. I'm afraid I accumulated several such theological bits and pieces and my head is still full of them. One of them is from the writings of Irenaeus, a very early Christian scholar. What he said about heretics was this: "they upset many, leading them away by the pretence of knowledge from him who constituted and ordered the universe". Well, upset many this unholy trinity certainly have. They would tear up our entire culture. Is not that the worst kind of counterfeiting, Thomas, and worthy of death?'

'What has all that to do with me?'

He turned his head to stare at me before saying quietly, 'Thomas, you know the answer to that question, even if you will not admit it to yourself. Your friend – your true, good friend – was a propagator of false religion.'

'You mean he was a heretic?' I was trying hard to control my temper.

'Heretic is a word for church lawyers to bandy about. I mean only that Luther and Tyndale and their disciples cannot be content with what Christians have believed for fifteen hundred years.'

'Are we not told to judge a man by his deeds rather than his words? Search those fifteen hundred years and you will not find a better Christian man than Robert Packington.' I glared at Ned and threw the words out as an angry challenge.

'Believe me, Thomas,' Ned replied, 'I do not say this to pain you but to save you from sharing your friend's fate. It is my opinion ... '

I did not stay to hear Ned's opinion. I dug my heels into the bay's flanks and rode forward, preferring my own company until we reached the gates of Hemmings.

I went straight to my mother's chamber to pay my respects and was met by a curious scene. The old lady and Lizzie were sitting by the fire, with Raphael on Lizzie's lap and they were singing. I recognised the childish ditty.

Man in the Moon, where have you gone?
I saw you peep around the ash
But then you ran behind the barn,
Fell in the pond without a splash.
Man in the Moon, where have you gone?

Engrossed in the old rhyme and helping the child with the actions, they did not hear me enter. As I gazed at them I was reminded of an altar painting in St Peter's West Cheap of the Virgin and Child with St Anne. It was Ralph who saw me first. He pointed at me, his tiny face creasing into a frown.

'Dad-dy,' Lizzie prompted. But the boy turned his head away. I reached out to stroke his hair, then quickly withdrew my hand. 'He doesn't know me yet,' I said with a shrug.

'How should he?' Lizzie said, giving me one of her dark looks. I noticed that her fingers still went often to the white scar across her cheek. Was it my presence, I wondered, that made her conscious of her disfigurement? Would she ever stop blaming me?

I stooped to kiss my mother but her response was as negative as my son's. She was still crooning the song in a low voice.

'She likes singing,' Lizzie explained. 'She only has four or five ditties but she sings them most of the time.'

'Does she never speak ... converse ... order the servants?'

'She retreats into herself much of the time but her head is

clear sometimes, like someone coming to a window and looking out from time to time.'

'Perhaps she doesn't like what she sees.'

'She's not alone in that. This is a dreadful place.'

'So dreadful that you ran back to St Swithun's House.' I
tried not to sound annoyed. 'Now tell me what has been happening here. Ned said there were new problems.'

Lizzie looked up. 'New? No. Just old ones getting worse.'
She stared out of the window. The only sound was my mother
softly humming another song which reminded me of my child-
hood. 'At St Swithun's we were all shunned,' Lizzie said at last,
'but only by respectable people. Priests and god-fearing citizens
kept well away – until they wanted to get between our legs.
But here? Here *everyone* avoids us. Some of the servants can't
take it. Two scullions left yesterday and we can get no one to
take their place. Everyone's saying Hemmings is like a plague
house.' She paused, a thoughtful frown on her face. 'Yes, a
plague house, but one smitten with an even more deadly dis-
ease. Shall I tell you what they call you? "Treviot the heretic
whoremaster".'

Her words struck me like a douche of icy water.

'What! That's ridiculous! They have no grounds for such
slander.'

'Village people don't need grounds for malicious tittle-
tattling.'

'But there must be someone spreading lies about me.'

'Oh aye. There's a snooping priest who's the hub of it all.
Chaplain to the Everards over at Cotes Court and very hand-
and-glove with the vicar here. Between them they won't let
anyone from the house go into the village church and they
stop any of the parishioners having dealings with us. The
steward has to send into Ightham and beyond for provisions

and, as often as not, the children throw stones and rubbish at them as they go to and fro. They say Sir Hugh Incent actually stands by and encourages the little hell-pups.'

'Who did you say? Incent?'

'Aye, he's the Everards' chaplain. For the last couple of months he and his crony have done nothing but stir up trouble. They look for Lutherans under every bush and snoop around people's houses to see if they have forbidden books. I think it's only a matter of time before they force their way into Hemmings. If you were here ...'

I had stopped listening. I was trying to jog into place ideas that were rattling around in my head. Incent!

'Lizzie, describe this chaplain to me,' I demanded.

Although she had only seen him a couple of times, her description was good enough for me to hazard a reasonable guess that this Hugh must be a younger brother of the heretic-scourge at St Paul's. That would explain how news of my interest in Robert's death had reached this quiet corner of Kent. Did it also suggest that John Incent had, indeed, been involved in Robert's murder, as some people seemed to believe? Here was another lead to be followed up.

I looked at Lizzie as she sat hugging Raphael to her with obvious affection – a young woman, old beyond her years but not yet in her prime and still a prey to girlish passions. 'I'm very grateful that you came back,' I said.

She fussed with the child's dress and did not meet my gaze. 'Yes ... well ... I changed my mind. Some of us have a sense of responsibility. Don't think I did it for you.' She kissed Raphael's forehead.

I crouched beside her. 'Lizzie, I can't make you stay. You can ride back to London with me today if you want to but I have two reasons for hoping that you won't. The first is, despite all the unpleasantness here, you are safer at Hemmings than in Southwark. There's a slow fuse of anger and resentment running through the City and heaven knows when it will reach the powder keg. The other reason is simply that you are now one of the few people I can trust. You have courage and a quick mind. You may not like me but I can see that you care about my mother and my son. I know that you won't desert them until I've brought this wretched business to an end.'

'You're determined to carry on with it, then.' Back came the old scowl.

'I have to but it won't be for much longer. That I promise you. Did Ned tell you about our meeting with Doggett?'

'A bit.'

'It went well. Thanks to him I now know who the assassin is and I have friends helping to track him down. As soon as we've done that everything should return to normal.'

Lizzie pouted. 'And then you'll have no more use for me.'

'No! That's not what I meant!' I shouted and Raphael turned to me in alarm. I continued quietly. 'When it's over we can discuss what's best – for all of us. Meanwhile, I've had another thought. Would it be a comfort to you if I could persuade Ned and Jed to stay for a few days?'

Her eyes lit up at the prospect. 'It would be good to have someone to talk to. I've been so lonely.'

'I'll have a word with them, then. If this Incent fellow pokes his nose in here Ned will be more than a match for him. He can hardly accuse a deprived monk of Lutheranism.' I stood up. I kissed my mother and walked to the door.

Lizzie followed, still with the child in her arms. As I reached for the latch, she looked at me with the suggestion of a smile. 'I think you're a fool ... but I didn't say I don't like you.'

It was easily arranged. I suggested to Ned that perhaps he might make the acquaintance of these troublesome priests and their London contacts. Then, I was able to set off on my return journey well before dark.

Back in Goldsmith's Row I found an excited Ben waiting for me in my parlour. I had scarcely removed my riding cloak when the exuberant young man blurted out his news.

'We've found him.'

Chapter 21

I took Ben straight up to my chamber and ordered supper to be served there. As soon as we were settled at the table I said, 'Tell me everything.'

'Well, as I promised,' the young man began, 'I rounded up several friends and we set to work straight away on Monday afternoon.'

'Did they all obtain leave from their masters?' I asked. 'I don't want to be accused of seducing prentices away from their work.'

Ben winked. 'I didn't hear that question. There are ways to escape the drudgery of the workshop when something more interesting turns up. Anyway, we made a list of the more likely drinking places where vagabonds and caitiffs gather and split up to see what we could find out.'

At that moment one of the kitchen girls came in with our

food. John Fink entered in her wake. With a disapproving sideways glance at Ben, he asked, rather pointedly, when I might have time to go through the day's accounts.

'Later,' I said, waving him away. 'Wait for me below.'

As soon as the door closed I asked eagerly, 'What did you discover?'

Ben hungrily tore a chunk of manchet. 'Well, the pickings seemed pretty small,' he said. 'We spent all day Tuesday and yesterday on the trail. Most people either didn't know or didn't want to tell what they did know about a dangerous foreign assassin lurking in or around London. It was only when we met up this morning to compare notes that we began to see a common thread. Three separate people had talked about an inn out at Walworth called the Red Lamb.'

My surprise must have shown but Ben was too busy carving himself a slice of salted pork to notice.

'Well,' he continued, 'I came round here to see whether you wanted us to check this Red Lamb Inn but you were away so we had to decide for ourselves. Of course everyone wanted to go and have a look at the place. No one was willing to be left out. We all set off straight away. So as not to appear suspicious we took a football with us and when we got to the place, we doffed our jerkins and began a kick about on the common ground. If anyone bothered to look, we were just a bunch of prentices practising for the next Christmas match. Just as well we did, too. This Red Lamb place is more like a prison than an inn; high walls all round and a burly fellow at the gate checking all who come and go.'

He drained his beaker and held it out for more ale. 'We made sure we played close to the wall and soon the doorkeeper was taking an interest. A couple of his fellows came out to watch and, after a bit, we invited them to join us. By our lady, you've never seen such hard-boned thickpates. We took a deal of knocks from them, and Jimmy Tungle, the poulterer's man, had a head blow that laid him out a good fifteen minutes.' Ben laughed. 'Your little army certainly suffered its fair share of battle wounds. But it paid off. We were soon bosom friends with the Red Lamb men and were invited in to slake our thirst.'

As Ben described the main room of the inn I recalled vividly its gloomy interior and the grim secrets lurking in its depths. 'I hope you didn't attract suspicion by asking a lot of questions,' I said.

'We were careful,' he replied. 'There's something about that place. Whoever owns it keeps a score of men you wouldn't want to argue with. All I wanted to do was find out if they'd heard of Il Ombra and then get away safely.'

Ben's words alarmed me. 'Did you ask about Il Ombra by name?'

'I didn't have to, fortunately. There was a rack of arquebuses in a corner and I showed some interest in them. One of the men – obviously an expert – took great pleasure in telling me about them – where they were made, how accurate they were … that sort of thing. Then I asked, all casual, if he'd heard about the new wheellocks that I'd been told were being used across the Channel. That set him off! He told me what wonderful machines they were – easy to carry, quick to fire. In fact, he said, there was one in that very house. "I'd love to see it," I said. "Any chance?" He shook his head. "Ooh, no," he said. "Belongs to an Italian gentleman what's a 'guest' here. He never lets it out of his sight."'

I felt a flash of excitement. 'Do you mean Il Ombra has been staying at the Red Lamb all this time … that he's still there?' I gasped. This confirmed my suspicions that Doggett had lied to me about the assassin's return to Italy.

'There's more,' the young man said. 'We were just about to leave when there was a bustle round the room and everyone jumped to their feet. A little man came down the stairs. Not much to look at but obviously their leader. He marched through the hall and called out, "Chicken broth for our Italian friend. He's looking better this morning and I want him fully active by the end of the week. I may have work for him." He bustled out and someone rushed out to the kitchen to do his bidding. "Your 'guest' unwell?" I asked the gun-enthusiast. "Laid up in bed these last three days," he said. "He reckons good English food doesn't agree with him – reeky foreigner!" So there you have it,' Ben concluded. 'That's where your quarry is at the moment and unlikely to be moving on immediately.'

My young friend's report had thrown my thoughts into confusion. To have located the assassin so soon was more than I dared hope for but there were other aspects of Ben's story that refused to explain themselves.

'You're sure that Il Ombra has been bed-bound for three days past?'

'That's what we were told – and it would explain why there's been no sign of him.'

'Yes it would. It's just that ...'

'What?'

'Oh, it doesn't matter. Did you gain any idea of how long he's been at the Red Lamb?'

'No. Do you think it was the leader of that crew who ordered your friend's execution?'

'Yes. How came this murdering villain here? As a private mercenary or at Doggett's invitation?'

'Doggett?'

Too late I realised that the name had slipped out. I had

wanted to keep from Ben the fact that I had some knowledge of the Red Lamb ménage. The less he and his friends knew about that dreadful place, the safer they would be. If Doggett ever suspected that they had been spying on him their lives would be worth little. Now it seemed that I would have to take him into my full confidence.

'What I'm going to tell you, you must keep to yourself. It's vitally important that your friends do not know. In fact, they must not be any further involved in this affair. Do I have your word on that?'

Ben regarded me with a wary frown but nodded. He listened intently while I related the story of my own visit to the Red Lamb. Then he sat back with a long exhalation of breath.

'What a venomous double- and triple-dealing whoreson villain!'

'Yes, and a very clever one.'

For a while we ate in silence. Eventually Ben posed the question we had both been wrestling with. 'How exactly do you think the assassin is involved with this Doggett fellow?'

'I'm not so sure. He may have been recruited overseas or he may have fallen in with Doggett here. It doesn't really matter which. The point is that he is now completely in Doggett's power because he needs protection, somewhere to hide, a refuge. You've seen the Red Lamb; there can be few places more secure.'

'And I suppose in return for protection he has to work for Doggett.'

'Aye, and what a valuable asset he must be. Doggett has connections in high places. He knows powerful people, rich people, people who will pay well to have their enemies removed.'

'God's blood! An assassination business!' Ben ran greasy fingers through his fair hair.

'I doubt it's a new business for Doggett. Think of all the unexplained deaths that happen every year. You recall the drowning of the Earl of Stamford's son? What a convenient tragedy that was for the young man's cousin when he inherited the estate.'

'Yes, and there was that case of Tennet, the Essex clothier who lost a fortune gambling. He was a ruined man until his wife had her throat cut on the way to market and he was free to marry the Walmsley heiress. You don't suppose Doggett ...'

I shrugged. 'Accidents do happen. People do get killed by unknown assailants. Doggett can't be lurking in the shadows of every suspicious fatality. But where death and money come together I'll wager the meeting often takes place in the Red Lamb.'

'So what's to do? Have the magistrates raid the place?'

I pushed my trencher away. 'Proof? Evidence? What do we say to Master Kernish? "There's a villain called Doggett who we think may have paid another villain who calls himself the Shadow to kill Master Packington?" No, a frontal assault would be a bloody business and would probably get us nowhere. We have to outmatch Doggett in cunning. Besides what we ... what I ... really want to know is the identity of Doggett's paymaster.'

'What then?'

'It's a problem that needs more thought.' I yawned. 'This has been a long day and my brain is sluggish.'

Ben stood up. 'I'll come back tomorrow.'

'No.' I shook my head firmly. 'You've done enough ... more than enough. I'd never have got this far without you.' I went to my coffer and took out a bag of coins. 'Here's more money for you and your friends. You have earned it but you must not be involved any further. You've seen the people I'm up against.'

Ben took the silver coins with obvious reluctance. 'Well, at least you can sleep easy. As long as Il Ombra is shut up in Doggett's lair he won't be hunting you.'

I said, 'That's very true.' I thought, If the Italian didn't try to kill me on Tuesday night, who did?

That puzzle played havoc with my attempts to sleep. But I soon had bigger problems to worry about.

Chapter 22

The following day, Wednesday 23 November, was one of torrential rain which went on for several hours. Few people were abroad in Cheap and we closed the shop in mid-afternoon. Scarcely had we done so when there came a heavy banging at the door. John Fink went to answer. When he came to find me in the workshop he was trembling so violently that I thought he might collapse.

'What's the matter, man?' I demanded.

'Armed men ... from the bishop,' he gasped.

I brushed past him into the shop. There I found four pikemen in helmets and long capes that dripped water. There was a captain in charge and he addressed me in a peremptory manner.

'Master Thomas Treviot, freeman goldsmith?'

'Yes.'

'You are to come with me, by order of His Grace, the Bishop of London.'

'Come with you? Where to?'

'Just come quietly, Master Treviot. If you will not, I have orders to manacle you.'

'But why? What is this about?'

'I'm sure all will be made clear to you later. Meanwhile I have orders to search the house.' He turned to his little troop. 'Go through the premises and bring everyone you find into here. Don't let them out of your sight till you've finished the search. Stay here and await my return.' He grasped my arm. 'Let's go.'

'This is ridiculous,' I protested. His grip tightened.

Shouts, cries and crashes came from the workshop as the soldiers set about their violent task. I looked round wildly. John Fink stood transfixed, mouth agape, clearly as terrified as I was. I made a grasp for dignity.

'Don't worry, John,' I said as calmly as I could manage, 'I'll soon sort out this mistake. Please go and fetch my riding cloak.'

'No time for that,' the captain said gruffly. 'Anyway, we're not going far.' He pushed me towards the door.

Outside were six more of the bishop's personal 'army'. They formed themselves into two columns and I was thrust between them. The captain gave an order and we set off along West Cheap trudging through mud and puddles.

I was in little doubt about our destination, although for as long as possible, hope wrestled with fear. Houses and shops stood fast-shuttered against the weather and there were few other citizens abroad to stare with questioning eyes at the little posse hastening along the wide street in the last light of fading day. We veered left by St Michaels at Querne, passed through

Paul's Gate and so entered the cathedral yard. With the vast bulk of St Paul's on our right we passed the preaching place, then the south entrance and the old bishop's palace and came to a halt before the east face flanked by two towers. They were identical but the one on the right had an atmosphere all its own, due entirely to its sinister use. This was the Lollards' Tower – a lodging place (often a final lodging place) for those designated as enemies of the Church.

A vigorous hammering on the iron-studded door brought a shuffling jailer to the portal. The captain entered, leaving the rest of us in the wet.

It was some minutes before he reappeared and it was obvious that he was involved in an argument with the custodian.

The latter, a squat creature with carbuncled, toad-like features, peered out and scrutinised me. 'If 'is lordship wants quarters for gentlemen 'e shouldn't send them 'ere. Separate room, indeed. Where am I going to find a separate room?'

'Hold your tongue!' the captain responded. 'You'll do well enough out of this prisoner. Master Treviot can afford to pay well for a few comforts.'

With a grunt the jailer opened the door wide and, still grumbling incoherently, led the way into the building.

'Just sign for him and we'll be on our way,' the captain ordered.

The two of them entered a room on the right that was obviously the jailer's personal domain. There the formalities were swiftly concluded. The captain came out and he and his men departed. Toad-face locked the outer door with a key attached to his belt, then double-bolted it for good measure.

'In 'ere.' He led the way into his sanctum, a narrow, evil-smelling cabinet strewn with rank straw that squelched underfoot. At a table scattered with the remains of at least one meal sat a younger version of toad-face, burly and with an unkempt mane of black hair. 'Young 'Arry 'ere will attend your honour,' the master of the tower declared, with heavy emphasis on the word 'attend'. 'You'll want blankets – all our guests do.' He indicated a heap of stained and torn woollen coverings lying in a corner on the damp ground. ''Elp yerself. Penny each. You'll be arranging your own meals, I dare say. Twopence each dish brought up to your cell. Twopence for emptying slops. All payments a week in advance. We 'ave to 'ave money up front so's you don't go to the stake still owing.' He smiled, obviously relishing the prospect of my imminent fiery destruction.

I was still so dazed that I could scarcely take in what was being said. Somehow I found myself stumbling up the winding staircase clutching a couple of the ragged cloths ennobled with the name of 'blankets'. Young Harry followed, urging me to the top level, where a door stood open. The chamber within was large enough to accommodate a rickety truckle bed, a low bench that obviously doubled as stool and table and, leaning ominously against a side wall, a set of stocks. The only other furniture was a wooden slop bucket. Wind and occasional flurries of rain blew in through holes in the glass of a high, narrow window.

'Best room in the 'ouse,' my guardian declared. 'We've 'ad some wonderful wild 'eretics in 'ere. See that there 'ook?' He pointed to a large iron half loop protruding from the wall some ten feet above the stocks. ''Unne, the 'eretic 'ung 'isself from that 'ook. Of course that was afore my time and afore Old 'Arry's time, too.'

The lugubrious jailer spent another couple of minutes itemising the rights and 'privileges' of prisoners. I might have anything brought in – meals, linen, writing materials, books (so long as they had been vetted by 'them as understands 'em'). I might also receive approved visitors. All these favours, of course, were available at the customary fixed rates. At last Young Harry produced a candle from his pouch, lit it from his lantern, handed it to me and left me to accustom myself to my new surroundings.

I sat on the bed, mentally and emotionally numb. 'Heretic. Heretic. Heretic.' The word hammered in my brain. What was it Ned had urged – 'Don't go to the stake for your friend'? Was I about to do just that? Or would my end be quick and private? In either case it would have been better if I had perished on Hampstead Heath at the hands of the mysterious assassin. But then what would have become of those I cared about? Well, at least they would not have been tarnished with my shame. Ralph would have been looked after by the Goldsmith's charitable funds. What chance would he have now, growing up with nothing but dishonour, because all his father's assets had been seized when he went to the fires of Smithfield as a condemned heretic. That word again!

I raised my eyes to the hook my jailer had mentioned. It was not difficult in this awful place to see why a prisoner, with only death by burning ahead of him, might take his own life. But, according to Thomas Poyntz, that earlier occupant of this cell had not committed suicide. He had been brutally murdered within inches of where I now sat. Since that tragedy more than twenty years ago how many wretched men and women had lain in utter dejection on this very bed, or been left overnight in the stocks, or manacled to the iron rings in the wall. I held the candle higher and saw marks scratched into the stone. Names. I made out 'James Sawyer, mercer' and 'Hugh Baldwin – Christian'. There were other writings, most of which I was unable to decipher in the feeble candlelight.

But one was clear – and – poignant: 'FATHER FORGIVE THEM THEY WOT NOT WHAT THEY DO.' God in heaven! What times we were living in! I laid down and drew my meagre coverings over me, shivering with what might have been either cold or fear. The candle I left burning, unwilling to surrender to the dark and the hideous images it harboured. I had little expectation of sleep.

It was, therefore, with some surprise that I opened my eyes to discover late-autumn dawnlight slanting in at the window. Stark and menacing though my surroundings were, there was something comforting about the confident sequence of night and day. The passage of the sun and moon in their orbits suggests a permanence, a cosmic normality that seems to reveal the affairs of men in their true proportion. I recovered from the panic that had followed my arrest and began to martial my thoughts. I was *not* a Lutheran. Nor did my enforced lodgement in the Lollards' Tower make me one of those truculent native fanatics men called Lollards. I was a respected member of a worshipful company. Surely that would count in my favour; if and when the bishop or his officers examined me, I would soon be able to clear my name of the stigma of heresy – or so I tried desperately to convince myself.

Meanwhile, I had more urgent matters to attend to. News of my incarceration would already be slithering along the streets, lanes and alleys of the capital, whispered from door to door, casement to casement, distributed by the carters along with their merchandise. Members of my household would be being besieged for information. They would all be worried and fearful. As soon as the duty jailer appeared (this time a younger, healthier-looking fellow by the name of Michael), I sent him out to fetch pen and paper. With them I wrote a carefully considered letter to be delivered at the Sign of the

Swan. It explained that I had been detained on the mistaken assumption that I had become tainted with heresy. This was untrue, as I would make clear as soon as I had the opportunity. Meanwhile, they were to carry on as normally as possible and heed John Fink's instructions as though they were my own. I addressed the message to Fink, with orders to read it to the assembled household and to assure all callers that Treviot's was conducting business as normal. I knew this would not make much impression either among my own worried people or among the wider community watching with interest, not to mention the wardens and brothers of the Goldsmiths' Company, some of whom would be delighted to see the fall of the house of Treviot. However, I could do nothing more *in absentia* and I needed all my energies to extricate myself from the mess into which I had fallen – or, to be more truthful, into which I had rushed headlong.

Chapter 23

Being shut away from the world did have one advantage: it freed my mind from distractions. Now I could *think*. The Lollards' Tower was cold, damp and uncomfortable but I had extra clothes and wrappings brought from Goldsmith's Row, as well as a supply of paper and ink. As soon as they arrived I huddled on the bed wrapped in my thickest cloak and tried to set down all the recent events, make some sense of them and banish the clouds of bewilderment. It took until the evening of my first day's incarceration to martial my thoughts in some sort of order. After much scratching out and rearranging this was the result:

1. Robert may have been a member of a secret band who called themselves 'Christian Brothers' and used their trading connections to smuggle into England

banned books by William Tyndale and, in all likelihood, other inflammatory material by men such as the German, Martin Luther, condemned by the pope as a heretic.

2. Robert had been in direct contact with William Tyndale in Antwerp during his business trips and was there when the translator was arrested and executed. According to Robert's last letter, he had information about that event that he could not put in writing.

3. He had almost certainly fallen under suspicion and was a marked man by the bishop and his cronies but they were hesitant about bringing such a prominent and highly respected citizen before the Church courts, particularly as he was known to be in favour with Thomas Cromwell, the most powerful man in England, under the king.

4. But in recent months the mood of the country had changed. With all northern England in revolt against the New Learning, traditionalists in the capital had grown bolder – bold enough to use any methods to force a change of government policy. It was against this background that Il Ombra, a professional assassin, had been brought into England to rid the Church of Packington the 'troublemaker' in such a way that his death could not be traced back to the religious hierarchy.

5. Il Ombra was now under the protection of John Doggett who, it seemed, intended to hire out the Italian to anyone prepared to pay a high price for murder. That meant there was no way that I could get to the assassin and force him to tell me who had paid him to kill Robert.

6. My enquiries into the circumstances of Robert's death had attracted the attention of those responsible, as Ned had warned that it would. Was that why an attempt had been made on my life and, failing that attempt, why I had been arrested?

7. Not necessarily. I had other enemies who wanted me out of the way. Simon Leyland was a ruthless competitor who would probably stop at nothing to force Treviot's out of business. Then there was Nathaniel Seagrave's father. His mind might be so deep-wounded by grief that only my death could salve it. Either of these might have been responsible for the Hampstead Heath attack. They might even have been acting in concert.

8. Whoever it was had made a clumsy attempt to copy Il Ombra's technique. That suggested an opportunistic crime that had not been well thought out. The instigator would be more careful next time.

9. So, what was his plan? He had laid evidence against me, believing that, in the current atmosphere of religious ferment, the bishop's officers would be bold enough to put me on trial. But that in itself would achieve little. In all likelihood I would be examined and released with a caution. *Unless false evidence was presented to the court.* Perjury was an all too common resort of people who wanted to make trouble for their neighbours. This was what I had to be prepared to face. My adversary would pay someone to accuse me of denouncing the Church's leaders or denying some basic doctrine. My denial would achieve nothing and I would be quite unable to disprove the charges. My only chance of escaping the fires of Smithfield would,

then, be to recant my supposed heresies and perform some public penance, such as being paraded through the streets bearing a faggot and with a placard pinned to my back declaring my detestable errors. That disgrace would be enough to put an end to my career. The Goldsmiths' Company would disown me. Such ruin would, in all likelihood, be as satisfactory to the perpetrator as my death.

I went through my notes over and over again, my spirits sinking lower with every reading. My adversary seemed to have forced me into a corner in which I was trapped. And yet there was something here, something I had written that, I sensed, offered a way of escape. There was a detail the enemy had overlooked and, try as I might, I was overlooking it, too. When the light faded and I was obliged to use a candle I set aside the papers and lay on the bed, hoping that rest might clear my head.

Minutes later the door was unlocked and Young Henry entered. 'Visitor,' he muttered, and stood aside.

Ben Walling strode in. It was a pleasant surprise but one I could not be completely happy with.

'Ben,' I said as he warmly clasped my hand, 'this is very good of you but you really should not be here. The jailer will report anyone who makes contact with me. You could find yourself in a place like this.'

He looked around the cell. 'Not too bad.' He grinned. 'You should see my lodging.'

'I assume the news is all over town,' I said.

Ben seated himself on the bench. 'Yes, you're quite famous today.'

'What are people saying?'

'What you might expect. Some are cock on the hoop. They say the bishop's men have flushed out another heretic. But I think more people are angry about the power of the clergy.

'Steeth! The whole City's gone mad. Neighbour denounces neighbour as "Lutheran heretic" or "papist traitor". Cromwell has bills posted forbidding preaching of "disputed doctrines" but that doesn't do any good. It doesn't stop the hotheads who think they're speaking in the name of God. Not only in the pulpits; you find them in every marketplace and they pluck you by the sleeve in the inns and ale houses.' He stood up, stretching his legs. 'Saints in heaven know how it'll all end. It's like a summer storm a-brewing out there. You can feel it in the air. Now, do you want to hear the latest rumours about Master Packington's death?'

'Yes.'

'It's being put about by the cathedral priests that the murder was ordered by one of the late queen's chaplains, Robert Singleton.'

'Singleton? Wasn't it him who caused a stir a couple of months back for preaching against purgatory at Paul's Cross?'

Ben nodded. 'That's right. He's a dyed-in-the-grain New Learning man. It's no wonder the dean and his arsewipe fellows want to make trouble for him.'

'And to divert suspicion from themselves.'

'Yes, most people think the cathedral chapter were behind your friend's death and they're desperate to cover it up.'

'And particularly John Incent?'

'That name is certainly being bandied about.'

'He's had his brother stir up trouble in Kent. Now, why would he do that if he wasn't worried?'

We stared gloomily at each other for several seconds. At last I said, 'I should have listened to a good friend of mine. He warned me that if I didn't leave well alone, things would be bad not only for me, but for my family and friends, too. How are they coping at my house?'

'They're all terribly shocked, of course. Shocked and frightened. That journeyman of yours ... What's his name? Finch?'

'Fink,' I corrected. 'John Fink.'

'Yes, well, he seems to have collapsed completely. When I called, I found him in a corner, sobbing. He obviously holds you in high regard. If my craftmaster were carted off to jail I'd go out and celebrate.'

'Then I'm glad I don't have you for a journeyman. Strange, though.' I pondered. 'John has always been level-headed. He usually copes well in a crisis. Perhaps I've grown too accustomed to pushing responsibility on to him.'

'Now, then.' Ben abruptly changed the mood. 'We have to get you out of here. What can I do to help?'

'Nothing, absolutely nothing,' I said. 'You're a good fellow, Ben, but this time I have to face things on my own. Do you know how heresy cases work?'

'Well enough.'

'Then you know the accused is completely on his own. No witnesses allowed for his defence. Not even a clear indictment. Just hostile interrogation.'

'Aye, and at the end of it all, just one choice: "repent or burn".'

I groaned, head in hands. 'I don't know what I'll be accused of, or by whom, or what evidence they have, or what false witnesses they've paid. I feel like a man setting out on a journey who knows that highwaymen have been primed to lay in wait for him but doesn't know where the ambush will be laid.'

And that was when it struck me. Suddenly I recognised the

missing link in the chain of events I had so carefully tried to record.

'That's it!' I shouted. 'Move along the bench, Ben. I need room to write.'

The sound of footsteps on the stone steps outside added urgency to my task. I grabbed pen and paper and scribbled a note.

The door opened and Young Harry came in. 'Time's up,' he announced. 'You've 'ad your pennyworth.'

I wafted the paper to dry the ink, folded it and handed it to my visitor. 'There is something you can do, Ben. Take this, as fast as you can, to John Fink. I must see him. Urgently.' Young Henry was quite puzzled at the speed with which I hustled Ben out of the cell.

That night I had much to think about: re-examining my notes, re-adjusting, re-evaluating, reconsidering my own behaviour. Most urgently of all, I had to decide what I would say to my long-serving journeyman apprentice. The man I now recognised as my betrayer.

Chapter 24

No less a person than Old Harry woke me. He rarely dragged his aged bones to the top of the tower, designating all routine duties to his more agile subordinates. The fact that he had come in person to rouse me suggested that it was a mission of some importance.

'Up yer gets!' he ordered, wheezing from the effort of the climb. 'Bishop wants yer. Be sure to tell 'im 'ow well yer being looked after.'

A glance up at the window told me that it was yet scarcely day. I cursed inwardly. It was vital that I saw Fink before my examination began. 'Look, I'm expecting an important visitor, someone vital to my case,' I explained in some desperation. 'Can this wait ... just for a couple of hours?'

A sound somewhere between a laugh and cough exploded from the jailer's mouth. 'What? Keep 'Is Lordship waiting?

More than my job's worth. Get a move on . . . and remember you've been looked after right 'andsomely in the Lollards' Tower.'

Outside, in Paul's Yard, I was met by the same captain who had brought me to the prison but this time he was in charge of a small troop of mounted men. They had a horse for me and, as soon as I had climbed into the saddle, we set off.

'Where are we going?' I asked, as we passed through Ludgate.

'Fulham Palace,' the captain replied. 'His Lordship will see you there.'

I had several other questions for my escort but they were either not disposed or had strict orders not to answer and we spent almost the whole journey in silence. With the untidy sprawl of royal Westminster behind us, we crossed open country to Chelsea beneath a scowling sky that threatened rain but did not deliver. Where the road narrowed through Parson's Green hamlet we were held up by two women driving a gaggle of geese – until the troops rode through them and laughed to see the owners pursuing the frightened birds over hedges and ploughed fields. By the time we reached the river the sun was a smudge on the lightening clouds to our left. Then we entered the bishop's park and so arrived in the courtyard of the palace, bustling with visitors and servants.

All the way from London we had attracted attention. Men stopped to stare at the prisoner and nod knowingly to each other. Women pointed me out to their children, doubtless warning them what happened to those who wandered from the warm embrace of Mother Church. But not until we arrived at our destination did we encounter real hostility. As I was led towards a side entrance a stout kitchen woman waddled forward and spat in my face. Another called out, 'Heretic pig!' A passing priest muttered, 'Burning's too good for your sort.' The guard room, when we reached it, was a welcome haven. Here, amidst off-duty soldiers, relaxing with tankards of ale or cleaning their weapons, I waited for my summons to the episcopal presence. And waited. And waited, anxiety mounting with every slow minute.

It was gone noon when I was marched to the chapel and thence, by a narrow stair in the wall, to a first-floor landing. My guard knocked on the only door, opened it and all but pushed me inside. It was a smallish room, comfortable and well furnished. Shelves stacked with books lined two walls. A third was almost filled with a full-length oriel window and the remaining wall was taken up by a large chimney place, which bore the bishop's coat of arms in vivid colours above the opening. Stokesley sat at a large table, placed close to the fire and I noticed that this old man obviously felt the cold, for his cap was drawn tight over his head and a furred cape was draped round his shoulders. He was a man of florid features with bushy brows over searching eyes.

Those eyes were fastened on me as I bowed respectfully. After some moments of scrutiny, he said in a gentle tone of voice, 'I am sorry to discover a young man of your standing and obvious promise in such a parlous situation.'

'What situation, Your Grace?' I asked.

Stokesley dropped the urbane pose, his eyes flashing with sudden anger. 'Do not pretend innocence with me. I have seen too many of your sort to be taken in by such hypocrisy.'

I did not know how to respond. Should I stoutly deny all and any heresy, which would only stoke his anger further, or maintain a silence that would appear to confirm my guilt?

'I have no time to waste on you.' The bishop tossed a book on the table. 'Do you deny this is yours?'

I knew, of course, what the little volume was but I picked it up and made pretence of examining it.

'Well?' Stokesley snapped impatiently.

'It looks like something that was lent me by a friend a few months ago, Your Grace.'

'You know that it is against the law to read the works of the heretic, Tyndale.'

'I haven't read it.'

He jumped to his feet. 'Do you take me for a fool? This was found in your chamber, locked away in a chest to keep it hidden. How can you deny reading it?'

My heart was racing but I tried to answer calmly. I glanced around the library shelves. 'Your Grace has an impressive collection of books. Can it be that you have read every one of them?'

'Mother of God! Is there no end to your impertinence?' He was shouting now.

Strangely, the bishop's agitation had a calming effect on me. The angrier he became, the clearer my thoughts presented themselves.

He grabbed up the New Testament and flung it into the fire. 'Come here and watch it burn,' he ordered. 'See it consumed by the flames, just as its wretched author was. Do you want to share the same fate? Have you ever seen a heretic burn?'

'Once, at Smithfield, four years ago. A lawyer.'

'James Bainham?'

'I think that was his name.'

The cover of Tyndale's book curled, and the pages browned, blackened and flared up. Stokesley stabbed at it with a poker. 'Bainham was not unlike yourself – an intelligent man; an honest man, as I think – but sorely deceived. I had him here for several days. Reasoned with him. Tried to save him, just as

215

I am trying to save you. But Satan had so clouded his mind that he could not see the truth.'

The fire was now making hard work of the tightly bound inner pages. I said, almost to myself, 'I will always remember what Bainham called out at the stake. "I feel no pain," he shouted. "'Tis a miracle."'

Stokesley turned to glare at me. 'Oh, you will feel pain, I assure you. It will be a pain that does not end when your body is consumed. You will know that pain for ever – in hell – unless you avail yourself of the mercy of the Church.'

'I would gladly do that,' I said, and I certainly meant it.

'Then repent of your heresies.'

'What heresies, My Lord?'

'Why must you prevaricate? Why do you people always wriggle and squirm? You know you have rejected the truth the Church teaches.'

'If Your Grace will but tell me which truths I am accused of denying, I will happily confess my error.'

He turned to the table and extracted two sheets from a pile of papers. 'Item,' he read, 'Master Treviot declared that all men should read Scripture in their own language. Item: he said those who keep men from Scripture are the agents of Antichrist. Item: he said Scripture teaches that we should not worship images and therefore all paintings, statues and the like should be removed from churches. Item: he keeps a private whore for his own use and said that he was no worse than priests who do the same. Item: he said he would as soon worship his whore as the Blessed Virgin. Item: he said that priests are no better than laymen and cannot make bread and wine into Christ's body and blood ...' He put the papers down. 'Shall I go on?'

I felt my heart grasped by icy fingers of fear. 'Lies!' I gasped.

'All lies, invented by jealous and malicious men. Who has written these things?' I reached out a hand to snatch the papers but the bishop's fist came down heavily on them.

'That is not for you to know. All you have to do is recant your heresies and submit to whatever penance I impose.'

'But, My Lord, how can I repent what I have not said and do not believe?'

'The Church will decide what you believe and what vile errors need purging. You will be taken before my court and you would be well advised to submit to our judgement, without any more time-wasting nonsense.'

'And if I do?'

'Then, if the court decides that your recantation is sincere, the Church in its mercy will clasp you to its forgiving bosom – after your performance of penance.'

'What sort of penance?'

'That will be for the court to decide. These are serious heresies and, because of the love we bear to everyone in our diocese, we must make an example of you, so that others come not to the same condemnation. You would have to make public declaration of your sins and renounce them severally. Then you would be kept in prison so that you could receive instruction from priests trained to deal with penitent heretics.'

'For how long?'

He shrugged. 'That I cannot say. Months certainly, possibly more.'

'By which time I would be utterly ruined.'

'But you would have kept your immortal soul. As to your worldly affairs?' He sneered. 'Well, you should have thought of those before you allowed yourself to be influenced by that verminous hellhound, that twisted limb of Satan, Robert Packington.'

Stokesley glowered at me and I stared back at his rage-red flaccid features. The silence that followed his outburst lengthened like an opening court roll. As the moment stretched and lingered the last wisps of mist lifted from my mind. Hazy images took on a new clarity. Here was no spiritual shepherd concerned for my 'immortal soul'. This raging prelate's passion was not for Christian truth but for the preservation of the ecclesiastical hierarchy. He was intent on silencing me – by threats, by incarceration, by shredding my reputation or by the fire. Why? Because the truth about Robert's death had to be suppressed. Had Stokesley authorised that death or had some over-zealous underling taken the task upon himself? The details were irrelevant. Foul murder had been done in the name of the Church and the bishop quite clearly saw his role as covering up the facts.

At last Stokesley held out his bony hands to the flames. 'The trial is fixed for the day after tomorrow. If you make your submission to me now I will register that and we can keep the proceedings short.'

'With Your Grace's leave, I would like time to consider Your Grace's kind advice,' I replied.

He looked at me sharply as though unsure whether there was a tone of sarcasm in my voice. 'See you do. See you do.' He waved a dismissive hand.

Back in my London cell that evening I felt a despair I had not known since the death of my beloved Jane. My mind was a black maze whose every twist and turn only took me deeper into itself. When my wife had died I had often contemplated following her by some desperate act of self-destruction. The same possibility occurred to me now. I stared up at the hook from which, according to the official story, Richard Hunne had hanged himself all those years before. Whether or not that version of events was true, I could easily imagine that the prisoner might have contemplated such a solution to his problems. The only glimmer of hope in my situation was that John Fink might respond to my note, repent of his betrayal and withdraw his accusation. That possibility was a faint one indeed.

Contemplating it throughout the sleepless night only prompted me to wonder why he had so far turned against me as to wish me dead. Undoubtedly the fault was partly mine. Wrapped up in my own problems, as I had been, I had pushed an unfair amount of responsibility on to him. He was of an age when he would be looking to set himself up as a freeman gold-smith in his own right and I should have taken more interest in furthering his career. Unspoken resentments had obviously built up within him and I had been too blind to recognise the signs. I was probably deluding myself if I thought that he would respond to my request for him to come to the Lollards' Tower.

My only visitor, the next morning, was Ben Walling and I could tell from his face that the news he brought was not good. He sat down on the bench, his shoulders drooping.

'Did you deliver my message?' I asked.

He nodded. 'I went straight to Goldsmith's Row. Your place was in a turmoil.'

'Why?' I asked in alarm.

'I'll come to that in a moment. First you'd better read this. It's a letter from Fink. I tried to deliver it yesterday but you had already left to see the bishop. I certainly was not going to leave it with that fat rogue of a chief jailer.' He handed me a sheet of paper, folded over and sealed with the Treviot seal. I opened it and read the message couched in the journeyman's formal style.

My hearty commendations unto your worship. This is to advertise to you that I sore grieve the case in which your worship finds yourself. I heartily repent me that I have been the foolish instrument to bring about your worship's sorry plight. Never did I wish to see you in so perilous a position. I beg your worship to believe that I was gulled by an evil man and blandished with offers of betterment. I never knew what he purposed. On my knees I beseech your worship to be certain that I never sought to gain my advancement at the cost of your worship's utter ruin or death. So take I my farewell of your worship, gratefully mindful of the many kindnesses you and your worship's father have bestowed upon me over many years. I pray with tears that your worship may escape the fate which now threatens you and that you may live long and come to think not too unkindly of your wretched journeyman,

John Fink

I looked up at Ben with an unspoken question and handed him the letter. He scanned it quickly.

He said, 'It was found beside him late on Thursday, the night after your arrest.'

'What do you mean, "found beside him"?'

'It was in his room, on the floor. He was on the bed. His throat was cut.'

The news was like a punch in the stomach. For several moments I gasped for breath. 'Poor John,' I muttered at last. 'What have I done to him?'

'What have you done to him?' Ben responded indignantly. 'More to the point is what he's done to you – arsewipe Judas. Bloody death was too good for him!'

I shook my head. 'It's not that simple, Ben. Oh, if only I'd realised sooner . . . '

'How did you work out that he was a traitor?'

'I didn't know until you came to see me here. You told me how very upset John Fink was and that seemed a bit out of character. Then, as you recall, we talked about how heresy proceedings worked and how the suspect was never told what he was accused of. And I said I felt like a traveller setting out not knowing that a highwayman lay in wait for him. Well, that reminded me of the attempt on my life out at Hampstead. So I asked myself what I should have asked long before: "How did the attacker know I was going to be there?" I realised that only one person had that information.'

'Fink.'

'Yes, before I set out that afternoon I told John where I was going.'

'And he must have told someone else. But who, and why would Fink want to do you harm?'

'I doubt whether he did. He was genuinely shocked when he heard about the attack.'

'That didn't stop him gossiping to whoever got you arrested. According to this' – Ben brandished the letter – 'he was "gulled by an evil man" into laying information against you.'

'And I have a shrewd idea who that was.'

'But what can he possibly have revealed to get you into this mess? You're no Lollard or Lutheran.'

'No, but if he listened at doors and noted some of the men who called to see me, he might well have drawn the wrong conclusions . . . and he obviously discovered my Tyndale New Testament.'

Ben's eyes opened wide. 'You had a copy? God's blood, that's a burning matter.'

'Yes it is. Now do you see why you must put as much distance as possible between you and me? Tomorrow I shall be tried for heresy – and found guilty. My accusers will want to know all my supposedly schismatic contacts. The bishop will set his hounds on to flushing out anyone who has had dealings with me. I don't want them coming after you. One man's blood on my head is quite enough. Ben, get out of London – and start now.'

I went to the door and banged on it till a grumbling jailer came up the stairs to open it. Ben protested loudly but I almost pushed him out of the cell. I listened to his descending steps. Then I sat down on the bed. Alone. Very very alone.

Chapter 25

The next day I waited. And waited. And waited. I had not been given a time for my appearance before the bishop's court. All I knew was that the hearing would take place in the cathedral's chapterhouse. The morning passed. Sunlight began to slant in at the west-facing window. I wondered whether the delay was deliberate, intended to stretch my already taut nerves to snapping point. It was almost a relief to hear, at long last, the scrape of boots on the stone steps.

Young Harry opened the door. "Ere's a surprise, then,' he said, before turning enigmatically and leading the way down the stairs. Outside were two mounted soldiers in royal livery leading another horse. 'Master Treviot,' one of them called out, 'be so good as to come with us.' I climbed into the saddle and, flanked by my escort, circuited the cathedral and rode out of the yard through Paul's Gate.

Bewilderment, hope and apprehension jostled around my head. We passed Saddlers' Hall and I wondered whether I was being escorted home. But we clattered on, leaving to our right the impressive row of goldsmiths' premises with their gleaming paintwork and the gilded statues of mythical beasts. I stared longingly at the house with the sign of the swan. All its windows were shuttered and there was no sign of life. As we continued along Cheap a terrifying thought struck me. Were we bound for the Tower? Had Stokesley and his consortium decided that I needed to be confined more closely or, more alarmingly still, that I had information to reveal that could be dragged from me only by the repertoire of torturers who kept their array of instruments in the royal fortress.

I looked closely at my guardians. Was there any point in asking where they were taking me? Would they be just as uncommunicative as the bishop's men who had conveyed me to Fulham Palace? While I was still wondering, the question burst unbidden from my lips. 'Where are we bound?'

The trooper to my left turned with a smile. 'Why, did the jailer not tell you? We are going to Lord Cromwell's house. He has sent for you.'

'Sent for *me*? But why?'

He laughed. 'His Lordship does not confide in the likes of us.'

With that I had to be content. Yet now my mind was in a wilder ferment than before. What purpose could Cromwell, now generally acknowledged as the king's most powerful councillor, the man who had come to displace all the nobles and bishops, possibly want with me? He would scarcely have snatched me from the bishop's clutches to discuss a loan or place an order for a set of gold plate. The idea was almost comical. Not so humorous was the thought that, in exchanging incarceration by Bishop Stokesley for detention at Master Secretary's pleasure, I might have leaped out of the cauldron into the fire.

Our passage along the City's main thoroughfare aroused interest. Passers-by stopped to stare. Some, recognising me, waved. At the Stocks Market I thought I caught a glimpse of Ben Walling but when I looked again, his lithe figure (if, indeed, it was him) had disappeared among the crowds thronging the fishmongers' stalls. We took the leftward of the three streets that debouche into the marketplace, jogged along Three Needle Street, and so to Broad Street, where the slender and graceful spire of the Austin Friars' church beckons passers-by into the seclusion of the priory yard. The most impressive town house fronting that open space was the mansion Thomas Cromwell had been extending and improving for the last couple of years and more. There was still scaffolding clinging to the north-east corner, facing the monastery. As we drew up, a mob of beggars made way for us – not altogether willingly.

'Idle wretches,' one of the soldiers grumbled. 'There are more of them every day turning up for the dole. His Lordship is too indulgent.'

We dismounted and I was led into the hall. The escort went to announce my arrival and I was left to look about me. It was immediately evident that this was the home of a man of wealth and taste. In keeping with the latest fashion, the ceiling of this long room had been lowered to allow for more chambers to be constructed in what had originally been the rafter space of the old hall. Large Flemish tapestries covered much of the panelled wall space and before them stood cupboards and presses, some richly carved and coloured in the Italian style. A page in Cromwell's livery appeared with a tray – red wine in a ewer, with a silver goblet and a dish of ginger and cinnamon biscuits.

'His Lordship is still at dinner,' he said, setting the tray close to the fire. 'Be so good as to wait for him.'

I waited. And wondered. What sort of man lay beyond that door? Robert had served Cromwell and held him in high regard. He had advised me to seek the minister's favour. On the other hand, Ned – and probably most Englishmen – regarded the 'upstart' as the fount of all the evils now pouring across the land. Curious and apprehensive, I waited.

It was some half an hour later that the page reappeared. I had expected to be led to a private dining room where the master of the house would be taking food with friends or distinguished guests but we entered a small room overlooking the garden. The man who sat facing the window at a table covered in a Turkey rug was surrounded by papers and books in neat piles. An open coffer set beside his high-backed chair where he could reach it contained more documents. A trencher and silver dishes piled at one end of the table indicated that Cromwell had just completed a solitary repast. These items were being cleared away by servants.

The door closed behind them but Cromwell did not turn to me. He continued writing – at considerable speed, as though determined to give form to his thoughts before they escaped him. He wore a plain black gown over a doublet, some of whose points hung loose. His head was uncovered. The most striking feature of his broad, unlined face was the dark eyes, which seemed to peer out as though through holes cut in the flesh. My first impressions did nothing to cast light on the enigma.

This great man's informality was disconcerting. This was a man who enjoyed the confidence of the king and spent his working days with councillors and ambassadors, yet he had admitted me into this private centre of his wide universe almost as one might admit a friend. I was loath to interrupt his thoughts but after standing for several moments in the centre of the room I felt I should make some comment.

'I am grateful to Your Lordship for releasing me from the bishop's prison.'

Cromwell nodded.

'May I ask whether this is a temporary respite?'

'We have better things to do than chase heretics.' His comment was almost an aside as he finished his letter and added it to the pile of others waiting to be sealed. I could not think of a suitable response. Suddenly he looked up. 'Have you ever seen an elephant?'

I shook my head.

'The Duke of Ferrara had two when I was in Italy – along with scores of other remarkable creatures. He used to try to make them fight each other to amuse his guests. Interesting spectacle. They trumpeted and stamped their ponderous feet and flapped their enormous ears. But they did not charge with their massive tusks. They walked backwards. They made a great display of ferocity until, at last, one of them turned. Then, and only then, did his adversary give chase. Stokesley reminds me of an elephant. He makes a lot of noise. He issues threats. He has his clergy shout defiance from City pulpits. But he'll never lock tusks. He's waiting to see my arse.' Cromwell chuckled. 'He's in for a long wait.' He paused. Then, struck by a new idea, he said, 'The King of Portugal does a good trade in elephants. I wonder if I can get one for His Majesty. We can call it Stokesley.' Master Secretary took a sheet of paper and scribbled a note, then looked up smiling, inviting me to share the joke. All I could think of was one very simple question.

'My Lord, am I free to go home and resume my business?'

He set down the pen and stared across the desk, no sign of drollery now in the eyes deep-set in his fleshy face. 'Does your usual business include seeking out Master Packington's killer?'

I considered my answer carefully. 'When he was alive, My Lord, he cared for me almost as a father. Now he is dead there is only one thing I can do for him, as a dutiful son. Sadly, my efforts only seem to be making things worse. I've decided to follow the advice of my friends and abandon the quest.'

Cromwell nodded. 'A good reply. Death does not cancel all debts. When the great cardinal was alive . . . '

'Wolsey?'

'Yes. When he was alive I was his closest confidant. When he died in disgrace, all those who had fawned on him and benefited from his bounty fell over themselves to curse his memory. Not me. I salvaged what I could from the wreck of his fortunes. Did my best to safeguard those projects that had been dearest to his heart. Friends feared that I would suffer for it. Enemies hoped that I would. But, as you see . . . ' Cromwell waved a hand, indicating the piled documents, 'His Majesty recognises loyalty. He knows whom he can trust . . . and that is important for kings. They are surrounded by sycophants and time-servers, men who throng the court seeking only their own advantage. If you knew the number of petitions I have to deal with daily . . . ' He grabbed up a pile of unopened letters. 'Suits for positions at court; requests for grants of land; appeals for intervention in legal cases – the list is endless. Few there be who serve the king out of unfeigned love. Loyalty is a rare flower and I cherish it. That is why I have rescued you from My Lord of London's clutches.'

I faltered for an appropriate response. 'I am more grateful than I can say . . . If I can serve Your Lordship in any way . . . '

For the first time he turned his attention full on me. I was even more conscious of those searching eyes. 'Did you see Robert on his return from his last visit to the Low Countries?'

'No, we were to meet on the morning of his death.'

'Had he written to you ... told you anything about his mission?'

'He mentioned Master Tyndale's execution but not in any detail. I had the impression that he might be in some danger ... that he felt it unsafe to put things in writing. Do you think he was followed home by enemies? Was it they who organised his killing and not the Bishop of London?'

Cromwell drummed on the table with his fingers. He frowned. 'Tell me what you know about Robert's death.'

I reported what I had discovered. It was little enough: the confusion on that dark, misty morning two weeks ago; John Doggett's acknowledgement that Il Ombra was the paid assassin; my efforts to track down the Italian gunman; the attempt on my life and the informers who had denounced me to the bishop (which might or might not be connected to my investigation).

Cromwell listened with every appearance of total concentration. Then he said, 'These things go deeper than you know and involve issues more important than you can guess. You would have been wise to follow your friends' counsel. Cicero tells us wisdom is the most valuable of human virtues.' He paused as though recalling the words of some text read long ago. 'However, he also says "nothing is more noble than loyalty". In this business of our mutual friend's killer you did have a choice between the prudence born of wisdom and the somewhat headstrong actions stirred up by loyalty. Now you no longer have that choice. You cannot wind back the clock and simply take up your life again.'

'My Lord?'

'You are too far into this business, Thomas Treviot. You are close enough to the fires of Smithfield to feel their heat and I am the only person who can deliver you. But my help comes at a price.'

I felt a sudden chill of apprehension.

Cromwell continued: 'Robert Packington was a good servant of mine. He was employed in affairs that carried some danger.'

I grasped the opportunity to obtain, at last, an unequivocal answer to the question that had forced its way to the front of my mind. 'Stokesley accused Robert of being a smuggler of banned books. Was he right?'

Cromwell scrutinised me silently for several seconds, stroking his chin with one hand. Suddenly he stood up. He stepped across to the window and beckoned me to join him. 'I'm making a new garden,' he said.

I looked out at a stretch of grass flanked by ancient mulberry trees whose bare, wide-spreading branches almost touched. Beyond were piles of earth and three workmen dismantling a stone wall.

'That means, not just putting in more plants; I have to take into account what was there before. Some things have to be reshaped . . . and others removed. The same is true of the new England some of us are making. It will be a nation with a strong monarchy, supreme in state and church, secure from foreign interference, rich enough to be able to solve the problems that now trouble us – poverty, vagrancy, corruption in the courts, clergy who are above the law. Most importantly of all, it will be a nation guided by the word of God. But first we have to clear the ground; get rid of obstacles; deal with grumblers who can't or won't share our vision for a new garden.'

'Like Stokesley?'

'I was thinking more of the northern rabble that His Majesty is now bringing to heel, but, yes, Stokesley is certainly one of those who are more at home with the old garden, running to seed and overrun with weeds as it was. Tell me, Master Treviot, you have a son. Which England would you like him to grow up in – the old or the new?'

I was too surprised by the minister's apparent knowledge of my family life to come up with an answer.

He did not wait for a response. 'But I'm rambling. What is important at this moment is this: I can help you in your quest but only if you help me. First I must know whether your little adventure with Stokesley has taught you anything. I need you to step into Robert's shoes. To do that you will need to temper your impetuosity.'

'My Lord, I will gladly . . .'

He smiled. 'As a lawyer, I must advise you never to sign a contract without reading it carefully. Listen to my terms. Robert was undertaking certain confidential work for me in Antwerp. He was killed before he could make a full report to me. I want you to go to Antwerp and find out what he had discovered.'

'But why me, My Lord? I'm just a simple merchant.'

'Exactly. There are many English merchants in that city. No one will pay much attention to the arrival of another.'

'But, My Lord, I have a business to run. I have just lost my journeyman. He was very capable. Whenever I had to be away . . .'

'Ah, yes.' He returned to the table and selected a slip of paper from one of his neat piles. 'John Fink,' he read. 'Foolish fellow.'

I gasped. 'Your Lordship is remarkably well informed.'

'I have to be. Everything depends on reliable information. So I gather intelligence in many ways and about many things ... including Robert's death.'

I stared at Cromwell, trying to grasp what was going on behind that expressionless face. 'As you say, My Lord, I have no choice.'

His reply was calm and emotionless, almost nonchalant. 'There is no one else who can keep Stokesley's hellhounds on the leash indefinitely.' He resumed his seat and picked up a small hand bell. 'Well?'

I nodded.

He rang the bell. Instantly a secretary entered. Cromwell handed him a pile of letters. 'These are ready for sealing and despatch. Take Master Treviot and give him the package that has his name on it.' Looking up at me he said, 'God speed you, Thomas. Make all the haste you can. Events have a habit of changing suddenly in these days.' With a sigh, he reached into the coffer for more papers. Did I hear or imagine him adding, under his breath, 'and with this king'?

Chapter 26

The rest of that day was a blur of impressions, decision-making and emotions: walking home and being stopped every few yards by people wanting to know what had happened to me; finding my household, shocked and uncomprehending, barricaded behind locked doors against the malice or mere curiosity of neighbours; trying to comfort John Fink's widowed mother, who was distraught, not only by her son's death but also by her parish priest's refusal to allow Christian burial to the suicide; arranging for another senior apprentice to step into John's shoes; and, on top of all this, trying to evaluate and understand the toings and froings of my own fortunes. It was well past midnight before I was able to retire to my chamber with the package I had brought from Broad Street. I lay on my bed fully dressed, broke the large seal and severed the strings around the linen-wrapped parcel. By the light of a candle I spilled out its contents on to the counterpane. But, before I could begin to examine them, I fell into an exhausted sleep.

By the time I awoke it was broad daylight. I had food brought to my chamber and examined Cromwell's package as I ate. The instructions for me were to the point: a ship called the *Sweepstake* was waiting at the Custom House Wharf to convey me to Antwerp where I was to report to Stephen Vaughan, the Chief Factor at the English House: I was to pass him the sealed packet that accompanied my instructions. I was to make full enquiries about Robert Packington's recent visits and make careful notes on everything I discovered – no matter how seemingly trivial. I was to return as soon as I was satisfied that there was nothing else to learn and report immediately to Cromwell, whom I would find either at his London house or at the royal court. Cromwell expected to see me back in England by the second week of December.

It was obvious that His Lordship expected me to set out on my mission within hours and I was in no doubt that he would soon know if I prevaricated. Yet there were still personal matters I had to attend to before I could leave England. My main concern was for my family at Hemmings. I was anxious lest news of my recent misadventures might have reached them. Since I could not spend time travelling down into Kent, it was imperative that I send them a reassuring message. I pushed my breakfast to one side and took up my pen to write a hurried note.

I was too late.

Before I had scrawled three or four lines I heard a commotion on the stair outside my chamber – angry, shouting voices. I jumped to my feet but had not taken a couple of paces before the door burst open. To my astonishment a dishevelled Jed strode into the room, pursued by two of my

234

men, who were trying unsuccessfully to restrain him. His head was thrown back, his hair was wildly ruffled, his boots were caked in mud.

Fear gripped my throat so tight that I could hardly croak, 'In God's name, Jed, what's the matter? Has something happened at Hemmings? Why are you here and not there? I waved the servants away as my visitor dropped unbidden into a chair and unclasped his cloak.

'Master Treviot,' he gasped breathlessly, 'is it really you? Thank God I find you safe!'

'Why should I not be? What have you heard? Here, man, take some ale and get your breath back.' I passed my tankard to him and sat down again.

Jed shook his head. 'Read this first,' he said, fumbling a creased letter from his purse. ''Tis from Lizzie.'

'I didn't know Lizzie could write,' I muttered, as I unfolded the paper.

'There's much you don't know about our Lizzie.'

Apprehensively I peered at the unsteadily formed letters. The writing was almost illegible but the message was very clear and typically Lizzie. She might almost have been in the room, shouting it at me:

Thomas Treviot, if they let you see this in your prison I hope it makes you . . . '

The next few words were heavily scrawled out.

You have gone and left me in a hellbred hole. That swell-headed pock-brained pious prating hypocritical priest Incent was here all agloat. He said you was taken for a heretic and would be burned within days. He said we must confess all our heresies to him or he would be sure we burned too. Well I aint going to burn and nor I aint going to let anyone burn Raffy. I'm taking him somewhere safe. Not going to say where in case your jailers get their hands on this. God send you better than you deserve.

Lizzie

I read the message over, again and again, speechless with anger, fear and guilt. Then I implored Jed, 'In God's name, where are they? Are they safe? What's happening at Hemmings?'

Jed drained the tankard and wiped a sleeve across his mouth. 'Everyone's safe for now,' he said. 'Our old abbey of Farnfield has a sister house in Sussex. Ned's taken Lizzie there with your son and your mother. The nuns will look after them as long as need be. But how is it that you are free? That whore-son Hugh Incent came to the house with the most terrible tales. Were they a pile of lies?'

Briefly I explained my extraordinary change of fortune. 'So I am now under Lord Cromwell's personal protection,' I concluded. 'There is nothing Hugh Incent or Bishop Stokesley or anyone else can do.'

'So what happens now?' Jed asked.

I stood up and paced the room. 'I don't know,' I moaned. 'What I long to do is saddle up this instant and ride with you into Sussex. I want to go to my family and Lizzie and take them back to Hemmings and assure them that they're safe. But I cannot. I must set out on a mission for Lord Cromwell.'

'Can that not wait?'

'No, my orders are very clear. I must set out this very day. If I fail My Lord, I will lose his favour. Then we shall all be at the mercy of Stokesley and the Incents and their like.' I stood by the window and watched the new day's light bring West Cheap to life. 'Joseph, Mary and all the saints, what do I do? It seems my choice lies between abandoning my family and abandoning my patron.'

'Well, Master Thomas, Lizzie and your lad and Mistress Treviot are secure for the moment. They will rejoice to know that you have escaped the bishop's clutches.'

'Will they forgive me if I don't come to them straightway now that I'm at liberty?'

Jed made no answer, nor could I expect him to resolve my dilemma.

I returned to the table. 'Go to the kitchen while I think,' I said. 'Get some food.'

When he had gone I crumpled my unfinished letter, tossed it into the fire and took up another sheet of paper. By the time Jed returned I had completed two letters, and handed them to him.

'Take this straightway to Lord Cromwell at his house close by Austin Friars,' I said, pointing to the sealed note that had 'Urgent' scrawled across it in large letters. 'Don't leave until you are sure he has received it. Then haste you back to Sussex with this message for Ned. Ask him to explain to the ladies. Tell them all that you find me well and out of danger. I shall be away two or three weeks. Persuade them all to be at Hemmings for my return.'

The young man looked doubtful as he placed the letters in his pouch.

'Trust me, Jed,' I said, with as much confidence as I could muster. 'All will be well. Now make haste!'

When he had left I had my own London household to reassure – and to interrogate. I wanted to discover, while memories were still fresh, why John Fink had turned against me, what grievances he had harboured and, above all, who had encouraged his betrayal. Of course, I had my own thoughts on that matter; Simon Leyland headed my list of suspects but I found it difficult to believe that even he would go so far as to denounce a brother goldsmith as a heretic.

The image of my late journeyman that emerged from these interrogations was of a troubled young man whom, to my shame, I had failed to understand and who struggled to run Treviot's single-handed. He had sometimes grumbled to other members of the household. When I asked whether John had shared his discontent with anyone outside the business, Leyland's name certainly cropped up. It was apparent that he had visited several times when he knew that I was away and had spoken with John in private. John had hinted after one such meeting that he would soon be leaving to set up his own workshop. When I pressed for more specific information about Leyland's comings and goings, the replies I received were much more vague. Had John spoken to the rival goldsmith the previous Monday – the day I was attacked on Hampstead Heath? My steward thought Leyland *might* have called that afternoon but he could not be sure. A young scullion, however, was certain that John *had* received a visitor that day.

'I thought at the time 'twas a bit odd, Master,' she said. 'I was just on my way back from the conduit with the water buckets an' I met this priest at the back gate. He said as how Master Fink 'ad asked him to come there. Then Master Fink came out and the two of 'em went to Master Fink's room.'

'Well remembered, Mary,' I said. 'Do you know who this priest was?'

'I suppose he was Master Fink's confessor, Master.' She worried the edge of her apron with nervous fingers. 'I think I've seen 'im once before – at some festival or other. I recognised him for his red hair. He's not our parish priest – that I do know.'

'Did you hear anything they said?'

Mary's cheeks flushed. 'Oh, I don't listen to other people's conversations, Master. That's wrong, isn't it?'

'It certainly is, Mary, and I know you are a good girl. But sometimes we can't help overhearing what someone says – even though we don't really want to.'

She frowned and bit her lip, still, I guessed, wrestling with her conscience. 'Well,' she said at last. 'It can't do him no harm now, can it? Master Fink, I mean. He was definitely agitated. "Praise God, you've come, sir," he said. "I am innocent, whatever men may say." Then the door shut. That was why I guessed the priest had come to hear his confession.'

I recalled John's great anxiety on the morning of my return from Hampstead. He had been full of questions about the attack. At the time I had imagined that he was simply shocked at the news. Now, I was not so sure. Could it be that he was desperate to find out what I knew about the failed attempt? If he had revealed my whereabouts to someone and only discovered afterwards that, by doing so, he had put my life in danger that could well explain his need to send for his confessor. Then, when he heard that I had survived, he might have fallen prey to a new fear – that I would discover his complicity.

These thoughts were still running around in my mind as I supervised the packing of my travelling chest, had it hoisted on to a wagon and despatched to the wharf. I delayed as long as I could over following it, hoping at any moment to receive a reply from Lord Cromwell. None came. I pictured him in his office with his pile of correspondence and wondered whether

he would trouble himself with my desperate appeal. The afternoon was half spent when I rode out of the yard, turned into
Bread Street and thence, via the broad thoroughfare of
Candlewick Street and Thames Street, reached the crowded
waterside between the bridge and the Tower. At Custom
House Wharf I enquired for the *Sweepstake* and was pointed
to a sleek two-masted craft at the furthermost end of the quay.
Waiting beside the gangway, I recognised Cromwell's page. He
stood stamping his feet and blowing on his hands. As soon as
he recognised me, he ran up, thrust a letter into my hands and
hurried away.

I immediately broke the seal. The message was brief:

This is to signify that I have received your letter and
have thought convenient to send men to the convent at
Ladborough to convey my lady your mother, your boy
and his nurse to your house in Kent and there to remain
as long as necessary to guard them during your absence.
I most heartily fare you well. Thomas Cromwell

Chapter 27

It is difficult not to be impressed with Antwerp. Standing on the *Sweepstake*'s foredeck as it rounded the last bends of the long Scheldt estuary, I beheld a city that seemed to explode from the wide flat expanse of meadowland and marsh in an upthrust of spires and windmills. The waterfront was thronged with the vessels of many nations, loading and unloading cargo, and our captain had to wait three hours for a vacant berth at the English Quay. I took advantage of the delay to send a message ashore to Stephen Vaughan, together with my letter of introduction. When I eventually disembarked I was met by a servant who conveyed me to the guest quarters in a nearby building.

The English House comprised a large group of warehouses, dwellings and business premises within a high, walled enclosure. I was conducted to a comfortable chamber overlooking the river and had just finished supervising the unpacking of my chest when I received a visitor. The man who almost bounced into the room was thick set, in his mid-thirties with an exuberant growth of beard. I say he seemed to 'bounce' because the overwhelming impression Stephen Vaughan conveyed to all who met him was one of enthusiasm. Having shaken my hand and expressed an effusive welcome, he seated himself on the bed.

'Lord Cromwell speaks highly of you, Master Treviot, and that is sufficient recommendation for me. I'll help you in any way I can.'

'Have you known Cromwell long?'

'Ever since he entered Wolsey's service. That must be ten years or more since. He advanced me in the cardinal's household and, because my mercantile activities brought me often abroad, I was able to prove useful to him.'

'As a messenger?'

'Messenger, diplomat, intelligencer – all those rolled into one.' He laughed – a deep-throated, hearty laugh. 'Is there a single word for it – "spy", perhaps? But tell me about yourself. How come you to be in My Lord's service?'

I briefly related the events of the last few weeks.

He listened carefully, almost ostentatious in sympathetic attentiveness. 'I was devastated to hear of Robert's martyrdom – we all were. He was much loved by the community here.'

'And by all who knew him,' I added. 'You speak of "martyrdom". Does that mean you know who was responsible for his death?'

'Oh, aye, you know what Paul says in the sixth of Ephesians: "We wrestle not against flesh and blood, but against rule, against power, and against worldly rulers of the darkness of this world." Robert was a man of the Gospel and Satan was deter-mined to stop his activities.'

'Yes, indeed,' I muttered, 'but do you know which particu-lar human agent of Satan paid an Italian marksman to gun down our friend?'

'Do you doubt that it was Stokesley or one of his papist crew? You have suffered personally at his hands. I know full well what that is like. In exactly the same way I fell foul of the bishop's predecessor, Cuthbert Tunstall. He had me to his epis-copal court. Were it not for Cromwell I would now be in glory, like Robert. And you and I are not alone; several of the people you will meet here in this haven of the English House have escaped overseas from the snapping jaws of papist pursuers. We praise the Lord for raising Cromwell to a position of power but that has made our enemies even more desperate. Since they cannot use their corrupt judicial system against us, they resort to other measures.'

Stephen Vaughan was obviously a man who enjoyed the sound of his own voice. As he rambled on I began to wonder whether I had made my long and uncomfortable journey in vain. If he and his colleagues could only trot out rumours wrapped in pious words, I would learn nothing useful about the activities that might have led to Robert's death. 'You believe the bishop and his ilk will not stop at assassination?' I asked.

'That and any violence and duplicity that will enable the pope and his acolytes to cling to worldly power. I recall being at dinner once with Cromwell when he was regaling the company with his wide reading on this very subject. "*Exitus acta probat*," he said, quoting some ancient Greek philosopher or other – "Results validate deeds." He went on to explain how this immoral, antichristian concept had recently been expounded by the Florentine politician Machiavelli, and taken up with enthusiasm in Rome. From that headquarters of Antichrist orders go out to the princes of Europe to exterminate all true Christians – *by whatever means come to hand.*' Suddenly the scowl left his face and he laughed again. 'Fortunately, here in Antwerp we are under the protection of Mammon.'

'Does your trade wealth really buy you freedom from persecution?'

'Our overlord, the Emperor, would dearly love to please the pope and allow the Inquisition free rein but with 70 per cent of the Netherlands' commercial revenue passing through here, much of it in the hands of men he would call "heretics", why he dare not. Without our taxes and duties he would be unable to keep up his war with France – and that is very dear to him.'

'This I well believe and yet when Robert was here, only a few weeks ago, he seemed to think that he was in some danger.'

Vaughan looked up sharply. 'Did he say what he feared?'

'I had only a brief letter from him in October. He did not detail his anxieties yet I sensed they were very real. He said he had something to tell me as soon as he got back to London. Unfortunately ... I can't help wondering if he was killed to ensure his silence. I think Lord Cromwell has the same suspicion.'

'And that is why you are here?'

'Yes. Do you know anything that was worrying Robert while he was here – perhaps something connected with the death of Master Tyndale?'

Vaughan's mood changed abruptly.

'I believe you have a packet of letters for me,' he said.

It was as though the mention of Tyndale had dammed the flow of his eloquence.

'Yes, of course,' I said, going across to my travelling chest. 'Forgive me, I should have handed them over straightway. I fear I shall make a very poor intermediary.' I passed him the package Cromwell had entrusted to me.

The loquacious factor now seemed in a hurry to leave. 'I must go through these carefully. There are sure to be many matters His Lordship wants me to attend to. We can talk at more leisure tomorrow. Meanwhile, please feel free to eat with us in the common hall. The servants will show you around.' With that Stephen Vaughan bounced from the room.

The following morning I received another visitor, a spare young man with thinning hair, who introduced himself as John Rogers, chaplain to the English community.

'Stephen thought you might find it useful to have a brief tour of Antwerp,' he said. 'It's a very compact city. Strangers can easily lose their way, particularly if they don't speak the local language.'

I was pleased to put my mission briefly from my mind and explore this city, so different from my own. London was a higgledy-piggledy of ancient streets and alleys but much of Antwerp was new built with room made for open squares and spacious courtyards. I noticed very quickly that our tour included few churches. Rogers was disdainful of the 'papist hovels' and their 'idolatrous shrines'. He did, however take me to the cathedral. It was not, I realised, as big as St Paul's but its nave was of a prodigious width. I commented that its regular congregation must be very large to fill such a space. He nodded noncommittally. 'We rarely come here. The authorities allow us to conduct our own worship. They don't like it but it's part of the sacrifice they have to make to the real god of Antwerp – money. Come, I'll show you where he is worshipped.'

We passed through several streets and eventually turned under a large archway into an open square enclosed by colonnades, which had the appearance of an abbey cloister. It was, however, more spacious than any ecclesiastical enclosure that I had ever seen and it was obviously of new construction. It was all athrong with men, most of whom were standing in pairs or small groups, locked in earnest conversation.

'Behold Antwerp's real cathedral, the Bourse, opened about four years ago,' Rogers declared, with an expansive wave of the hand. 'This sacred area is dedicated to trade. Even as we watch, millions of Spanish dollars are changing hands. These people are buying and selling spices, broadcloth, silk, diamonds – any and every commodity that can be turned into profit.'

'How useful having one commercial exchange building for all merchants,' I said.

'Yes, and in the offices behind the colonnade we have money changers, who keep a constant record of currency values – Spanish dollars into German thalers or Florentine florins or English sovereigns – and the market masters who set the specie values for the trade fairs. The more important merchants have their own premises here where they draw up bills of exchange, make contracts and arrange transport details.'

'Very impressive,' I said, and meant it.

'You think so?' Rogers questioned. 'Well, now I will show you where we deal in something infinitely more valuable than Guinea gold or even Calicut pepper.'

There was, on the face of it, nothing unfamiliar about the place to which Rogers now introduced me. I had seen print shops in London and recognised instantly the stacks of paper, the typesetters' frames and the heavy oak press. A dozen men were engrossed in their various tasks but the person in charge, who was now holding up a finished page to scrutiny, was a woman. Rogers approached her.

'Françoise, good day. How is the work coming on?'

She laid aside the sheet and wiped her fingers on an ink-stained rag. 'We have started the Second Book of Kings,' she said. 'You will have proofs next week, I think.'

'Excellent,' Rogers responded warmly. 'Let me introduce a visitor from England. Master Thomas Treviot is an envoy from Lord Cromwell.. He turned to me. 'Françoise de Keyser came here with her husband, Merten, some years ago. Sadly Merten died a few months since. Françoise now runs the business – and does so very well.'

'If Master Treviot comes from His Lordship, then he is twofold welcome. None of this' – she indicated a pile of printed sheets – 'would be possible without the good lord's support.' Françoise spoke with a pronounced French accent. She was a small woman but muscular and her strong features suggested energy and determination. Her dark hair was covered by a simple kerchief, her sleeves were pulled up to the elbow and a large apron protected her gown.

'Delighted to meet you, Mistress Merten,' I replied politely. 'What is it that you work on now?'

It was Rogers who replied with enthusiasm. 'Nothing less than the complete Bible in English. William Tyndale translated the New Testament, as you know, and he was working on the Old Testament when he was arrested by the Procurer-General—'

'Cochon!' Françoise spat.

'Yes, indeed, a despicable little man who far exceeded his authority in his persecution of God's flock. Well, as I was saying, he tried to seize all Tyndale's papers but we were too quick for him. We saved our friend's work on the Hebrew

247

Scriptures – he had completed about a third of the Old Testament. That is what Françoise is printing now.'

'That leaves a large portion of the Bible untranslated,' I said.

Rogers nodded with a satisfied smile. 'That, too, is in hand. We have other scholars sent here from England by Lord Cromwell. Even now there is a much-learned Hebraist by the name of Miles Coverdale working on the Psalms, and I, myself, have undertaken part of the work. Between us we will have the entire Holy Scriptures ready for despatch and distribution by the spring.'

'More books for the bishops to burn?' I asked.

'They cannot destroy the truth. The more people read Scripture, the more they want. Do you know how many New Testaments have escaped the episcopal flames?'

'Several hundred, I suppose.'

'Nearer ten thousand,' Rogers said in a tone of zealous triumph. 'And that doesn't include copies pirated by other printers. The demand is insatiable. This book will change society,' he enthused. 'When people can read God's word for themselves there will be an end to popish error. More than that, we will be able to establish a godly commonwealth based on justice, fairness and care for the poor.'

I recalled Cromwell's talk of a 'new England'. It sounded very attractive but did he and his supporters really believe that it could be brought into being by a book?

As we left de Keyser's atelier and made our way to the waterfront I took the opportunity to learn more about Robert's participation in the book-smuggling business. Rogers was obviously proud of the operation and was not at all hesitant about explaining how it worked.

'The organisation is complex and meticulously planned. The sheets go from here concealed in bales of cloth and other merchandise to be bound in English workshops. Robert was part of the small secret committee in London that oversees distribution. It is their task to keep one step ahead of the opposition. They know which harbours are safe for landing contraband and which must be avoided because the bishops are keeping watch. They carefully monitor the market. Most books go to the universities and the Inns of Court but we have some brilliant salesmen who travel the country selling testaments in towns and villages everywhere.'

'I had no idea Robert was involved in something so intricate.'

Rogers smiled. 'Intricate and secret. But, God willing, there will soon be no need for such subterfuge. We are in great hopes that Lord Cromwell will persuade the king to sanction the unrestricted issue of vernacular Bibles.'

'What makes you think he will change his mind?'

'Oh, you of little faith,' Rogers chided. 'This is a work of God. It will not be denied indefinitely. Besides, Henry knows that his church is backward in banning the Bible. It is available in the language of the people here in the Netherlands, in Germany, Denmark, France, Spain and even Italy. The bishops may throw up their hands in horror and cry "heresy!" but the Bible is freely read in royal and noble courts throughout Christendom. Our king will not want it thought that his realm is a cultural backwater.'

I was not convinced by this line of reasoning but had no desire to dampen the chaplain's enthusiasm. I still could not see what was remarkable about this book so many men were crusading for but they seemed to be intelligent people and Robert had certainly been of their number. The next day I was to come a little closer to understanding them.

Chapter 28

It was a Sunday (3 December). I had been invited to join with the English community for the main mass of the day and to dine afterwards in Stephen Vaughan's private quarters. The service was both familiar and strange. The chapel of the English House was traditional in layout, although there was no rood screen, which was certainly unusual. The coloured windows, painted walls and well-decked altars bore witness to the wealth and generosity of generations of merchants. The first object that thrust itself upon my attention was the pulpit. It was a large structure of carved oak with a canopy and was clearly of recent construction because it hid from sight part of a painting of St George and the Dragon on the north wall. It jutted out well into the nave and slightly restricted the view of the high altar. The church seemed to have two conflicting focal points and I found the visual dissonance slightly unnerving. Before the pulpit several rows of benches had been arranged. Opposite it, at the junction of nave and chancel, a small group of musicians were tuning their sackbuts, shawms and lutes. While servants and children stood in the rear part of the nave, some of the senior members of the community had already taken their places on the seats and Stephen Vaughan motioned me to join him at the front. I saw that he and his colleagues were holding what appeared to be printed pamphlets. I assumed that these were devotional manuals such as many devout literate people read to themselves while the priest performed his ritual acts on their behalf. This was a practice I had never adopted, preferring to tell my beads during the solemn moments of the mass, but I accepted the pamphlet handed to me by one of the servants.

The choir and clergy entered in procession and the liturgy began. The singing was beautiful and much enhanced by the contribution of the instrumentalists. It was some time before I realised that I was not hearing the mystic Latin, which had worked its way into my mind, without effort on my part, Sunday after Sunday, feast day after feast day ever since my earliest years – *Kyrie eleison, Christe eleison . . . Gloria in excelsis Deo, et in terra pax hominibus bonae voluntatis.* No, the mass was being sung in English! But if that was a shock, more was to come. When we arrived at the *Credo* the congregation stood and, reading from their pamphlets, declared, 'I believe in God, the Father Almighty, maker of heaven and earth . . . ' Then, at the distribution, everyone received, not just the consecrated host, but also wine from a common cup. By this time my brain was reeling and I knew not what to expect next. When the mass was over, John Rogers, having laid aside his vestments, ascended the pulpit and preached a sermon. It lasted the better part of an hour but, even then, the ritual was

not over. The musicians struck up once more. The congregation now joined with the choir in singing a hymn lustily. Once
more the words appeared on the printed pamphlets. I have my
copy still and whenever I read it I experience the frisson of
that first hearing:

> With you is naught but untold grace,
> Evermore forgiving.
> We cannot stand before your face,
> Not by the best of living.
> No man boasting may draw near.
> All the living stand in fear.
> Your grace alone can save them.

The group that assembled around Stephen Vaughan's table for
dinner was small. Our host excused the absence of his spouse,
who was still recovering from the birth of their latest child.
Rogers was there with his wife, a local woman who spoke little
English. Also present was Thomas Poyntz, the stocky grocer
I had last seen exiting hurriedly from Robert's inquest. Apart
from Mistress Poyntz, the only other person present was
another visitor, a man of about my age, who was introduced as
Thomas Theobald.

'I am relieved to see you safe and well,' I said to Poyntz, by
way of opening conversation. 'I heard that several people had
been arrested in Stokesley's latest purge and I feared you might
be among them.'

Poyntz laughed and the others joined in.

'Am I missing something?' I asked.

Poyntz laughed. 'I was quite safe. So were Barnes and the
others. It was not the good bishop who had us detained.'

'Who then?'

'Why, Lord Cromwell,' he said. Then, in response to my obvious surprise, he explained further. 'The Gospel tells us to be as wise as serpents and gentle as doves in dealing with enemies of the faith. We are to be subtle, devious even, and Cromwell is a master at that. When Barnes preached at our brother Robert's funeral he stirred up a wasps' nest. The papists were all abuzz with indignation and like to sting any true Christians they could find.'

'It seems that Barnes was not displaying the wisdom of a serpent,' I commented wryly.

Poyntz shrugged. 'Our dear brother is inclined to be headstrong. Anyway, before any harm could be done, Cromwell acted. He had Barnes and a few other of us put under lock and key until things had calmed down.'

His wife pouted. 'You may make light of it. Next time it *will* be the bishop who takes you. Then what will become of me and the children?' She turned to the chaplain. 'John, tell him it is madness to return to London.'

'My dear Madge,' Rogers replied in a soothing voice, 'things are getting better. Lord Cromwell tells me in letters brought over by Master Treviot that the rising in the North has made the king more determined than ever to bring papists to heel. His Majesty is still considering an alliance with some of the German Lutheran princes and is almost ready to sanction an official English Bible. When he has punished the rebels no one will dare oppose him. It will give him all the excuse he needs to make new laws to reduce the powers of the bishops.'

'That's right,' Poyntz urged, 'and I must go back to take care of my business.'

His wife pursed her lips in defiance. 'Well, I'm not moving from Antwerp.'

I took the opportunity to steer the conversation in the direction that interested me. 'Is Antwerp really so safe? Tyndale was captured and executed here, wasn't he?'

It was obvious from the glances exchanged round the table that I had stirred up a sensitive subject. Poyntz muttered, 'He was tricked.'

'What exactly happened?' I asked.

Vaughan explained. 'Our security here in the English House rests on a very simple foundation – we are commercially indispensable to the municipal authorities. Of all the goods passing through this entrepôt, our woollen cloth is by far the most important. It feeds hundreds of native workshops that dye and dress the cloth. It brings buyers here from all over Europe. If we moved our staple to another port – which, theoretically, we could do – the Portuguese, the Italians and the rest would follow us. So the city fathers cannot afford to upset us. Nor can their master, Emperor Charles. He relies heavily on the money Antwerp's trade pours into his coffers. That is why here within our walls we are virtually independent. So, we can worship in the Lutheran style, as you saw this morning. We can print Bibles and other books setting forth Gospel truth. We can offer asylum to brothers and sisters fleeing from papal persecution. Of course, in Rome they hate this. We are a real thorn in their flesh. They are constantly pressing the Emperor to eradicate heresy. But His Unholiness may huff and puff all he will; Charles dare not offend us.'

'So what went wrong in Tyndale's case?' I demanded.

'Treachery!' Madge Poyntz cried. 'The papists tried to lure him back to England but he was too clever to fall for their knavery. He knew how dangerous England is.' She glanced meaningfully at her husband. 'Then they sent a smooth-tongued villain to trap him with lies and flattery. I never liked the rogue – not from the first moment I set eyes on him – but you men couldn't see his true colour.'

Vaughan took up the story. 'Sadly there's some truth in what Madge says. Tyndale was lodging with the Poyntzes last year when this fellow, Henry Phillips, turned up. He was a gambler and a wastrel – though, of course, we did not know that at the time. Desperate to pay his debts, he had become a papist spy and informer.'

Misery was writ large on Poyntz's face. 'Phillips was so plausible. He posed as one of us and had all the right language to be convincing. Poor William was a trusting soul. If only I had been here on that day!'

'Don't blame yourself, Thomas,' Rogers responded. 'Phillips deliberately waited until you were absent on business. He went to Dufief, the imperial Procurer-General, and lured William out into the street where Dufief's men were waiting to pounce. They threw William into a disgusting prison and then actually had the temerity to force their way in here in search of his books and papers. Praise be God, we managed to foil them. Then we set about trying to get our friend released. No one worked harder on his case than Thomas here. He appealed to Cromwell and to other members of the English court.'

'And Cromwell did nothing?' I asked.

'On the contrary,' Vaughan responded. 'He did everything in his power to help. He appealed to the imperial authorities and sent several agents to investigate Phillips and his contacts. One was Robert Packington and another was Master Theobald here. We were very nearly successful. We were promised William's release. But the wretch Phillips had one more ace in his scrip. He denounced Thomas Poyntz as an accomplice of Tyndale and we were unable to prevent him being held under house arrest for three months. God be praised, we managed to engineer his escape. He got back to England and gave Secretary Cromwell a detailed report of the situation here. Unfortunately ...'

I tried to bring the conversation round to my friend's involvement. 'What exactly was Master Packington's part in all this?' I asked.

It was Theobald who responded. 'Robert and I were both sent over to identify the agents of Bishop Gardiner and Bishop Stokesley and to discover all we could about how they were trying to undermine Cromwell's policy. Phillips had hurried south to Louvain after his treachery here. He was too terrified of reprisals to stay anywhere near Antwerp.'

'If he'd come anywhere near me, I'd have given him cause,' Madge interjected.

'What did you discover?' I prompted.

'Oh, Phillips was very bold in that seething papist wen,' Theobald replied with a scowl of utter contempt. 'He boasted to anyone who would listen that he was part of a major oper-ation to have Tyndale, Barnes and other champions of the Gospel burned as heretics. He tried to impress the Church hierarchy with his own importance in the campaign against heresy.'

'Who was behind that campaign,' I asked.

Theobald shook his head with a rueful smile. 'Ah, that was the one thing he would never say. He railed against the king, mouthed all manner of vile slanders about Cromwell and Cranmer but never revealed who he was working for. I think Robert had his suspicions but ...'

Vaughan held a finger to his lips as a servant entered with a fresh flagon of wine. When the door had closed again, he explained: 'Some of our own people are not above being bribed to gather information.'

Poyntz said, 'I don't believe that rogue Phillips had such an important paymaster. He was a mere scavenger, picking up scraps of information and selling them wherever he could.'

'You may be right,' Theobald conceded. 'Anyway, we had a stroke of luck with one of his couriers, an English monk by the name of Gabriel Donne. He was studying at Louvain University and was due to make a visit home, carrying messages from Phillips to his contacts in London. Now Donne came from a London merchant family Robert knew well and he made a point of befriending him. Robert obtained a passage on the same ship and during the visit he persuaded the monk to change sides and betray Phillips to Cromwell. That was in the summer of last year and I heard no more about the matter until Robert returned here a few weeks ago with fresh instructions from Lord Cromwell.'

At last I felt I was getting closer to the centre of Robert's secret life. 'Did he say who Phillips' contacts were?'

'He was too busy trying to save William. We all were,' Vaughan explained. 'He mentioned that he had learned something important from Donne. Cromwell was apparently so pleased with it that he gave Donne the rich abbey of Buckfast in Devon. But Robert never told me what the information was. In fact we hardly ever met. Robert spent most of his time in Brussels, talking with the imperial officials.'

'We were all depressed but Robert seemed to be more deeply affected than any of us,' Rogers added.

'He was certainly greatly distressed when he wrote to me,' I said. 'Do you know why that was?'

Rogers pushed his trencher to one side, his meat only half consumed. He sighed. 'All he would say was, "I should have done more." That wasn't true, of course. Winning Donne over was very important. It must have exposed Phillips' network.'

257

Vaughan nodded. 'He had certainly put an end to Phillips' usefulness. That double-faced, hell-hated villain is good for nothing now but to crawl from town to town seeking in vain for anyone who will trust him.'

'But none of you has any idea which of his backers might have wanted to be revenged on Robert?' I pressed.

All round the table heads were gloomily shaken.

Rogers said, 'I don't believe his melancholy was caused by concern for his own safety.' He glanced round at his colleagues. 'At times he seemed almost bent on martyrdom. We all noticed it.'

The others muttered their assent.

I blustered my disbelief. 'That is not the Robert I knew. You must be mistaken.'

'You didn't witness Tyndale's end,' Vaughan replied. 'We all went to Vilvoorde, near Brussels, to give him what comfort we could. We watched William fastened to the stake. He was allowed to pray and he called out something to his friends at the front of the crowd. I didn't hear it clearly but Robert did. He was straining against the cordon of soldiers and let out a howl of rage and grief when the executioner strangled William. When the fire was lit I believe Robert would have cast himself upon it if he could have broken through the guards.'

Still my mind would not accept what I was being told. The man they were describing was not the urbane, wise, impassive Robert Packington I had known for years.

'His spirit was broken,' Rogers added. 'Only days before he had delivered a sealed letter from Cromwell to the authorities, an appeal for clemency. I suppose he believed that would gain William a reprieve. When his hopes were dashed . . . '

Vaughan said, 'Nothing would solace him, right up to the time he left here. He seemed doom-laden. I saw him on to shipboard and when we parted he grasped my hand firmly and begged me, with tears in his eyes, not to think ill of him. His last words were, "Till we meet in heaven, dear friend.'"

'Why should you think ill . . . ' I began, but broke off, realising that these people were as mystified as I was.

I stayed in Antwerp a few more days and eventually took ship on 7 December. I called on Vaughan before my departure and thanked him for his help and hospitality.

'Have you found what you came here seeking?' he asked.

'I'm not sure,' I replied. 'I fear I have not discovered what Lord Cromwell sent me to find.'

'Take my advice; give Master Secretary a very precise report of everything that has passed here. The details may not seem important to you but he has a genius for fitting together tiny scraps of information. He sees the big picture. We do not.'

I asked Vaughan to extend my greetings to his colleagues and asked, 'What will happen to Thomas Poyntz?'

He sighed. 'Poor Thomas. He is a marked man on both sides of the Channel. I think he plans to stay here until after Christmas, then return to England. He is still in hope to take his family with him but you have heard what Madge has to say on that score. She believes the children are safer here. We must pray that the times will change so that Christian families like theirs are not faced with such choices.'

The vessel I boarded was bound for London via Calais. I was now desperately anxious to be back in England, to make my report and then ride to Hemmings as quickly as I could. It was the weather that conspired to delay me and stoke my impatience. A sudden storm prevented us making landfall on the French coast and we were driven out into the German Sea. For four days we pitched about on moving mountains of water that cast the ship to and fro like a tennis ball. I could do

259

nothing but lie in my berth groaning. I was certainly not able to martial my thoughts or consider what, if anything, I had learned. As I rolled from side to side, cold yet sweating, hearing only the thud of waves and the creaking complaint of the hull's timbers, jumbled fragments of conversations banged around in my head – meaningless, yet persistent, as though they would tell me something, if only I could make sense of them: 'more valuable than gold or pepper'; '*exitus acta probat*', 'results validate deeds'; 'not by the best of living'; 'wise as serpents and gentle as doves'; 'reprieve'; 'reprieve'; 'reprieve'.

Chapter 29

By the time the tempest blew itself out we were well north of our planned route. As darkness fell on the evening of 12 December and the cloud veil lifted, we could see the lights of the English coast but the master did not dare take his vessel closer inshore and so anchored for the night. The following morning we came to harbour in the port of Harwich. I went ashore immediately and few travellers can ever have been more thankful to find unshifting ground beneath their feet. My next problem was reporting back to Cromwell with the minimum of delay. Our ship had sustained serious damage in the storm and the master told me that it would be several days before repairs could be completed and the voyage to London resumed. There was no alternative but to make my way overland. The decision was easy enough to take. Putting it into effect proved to be less so. I needed a reliable horse and a couple of sturdy countrymen to ensure my safety on the road. Enquiry at the hovel that called itself an inn proved fruitless as did my questioning of the taciturn fisherfolk and petty merchants. They seemed quite unimpressed when I told them that I was on government business and I had resigned myself to waiting for the ship to be ready when a well-dressed man on an impressive black mare rode up to the quayside. He introduced himself as steward to Sir Sebastian Humphrey, the leading gentleman of the area. News of my plight had obviously travelled swiftly and the name of Lord Cromwell had had an almost magical effect upon this rural squire, who insisted, via his agent, in offering me hospitality and seeing me safely on my way.

The later events of that day would have been quite amusing had I not been anxious to reach home and discover what had been happening in my absence. Sir Sebastian was of a good girth and his wife and two daughters scarcely less so. The ladies were eager for news of the latest fashions at court but the head of the household was more concerned about developments at the centre that might affect his own situation. Since I was an intimate of Mr Secretary Cromwell, he entreated, did I think His Lordship might be prevailed upon to intercede with His Grace, the Earl of Oxford. There was land in Dovercourt that bordered Humphrey's estate and had belonged to the Benedictine priory of Earl's Colne. On that house's dissolution back in the summer it had been acquired by Lord Oxford. Sir Sebastian would gladly have it if Lord Oxford was disposed to sell. I tried to persuade him that my influence in court circles was limited (which, in itself, was certainly an exaggeration) but my host dismissed this as false modesty and when he renewed his pleading I promised to mention the matter to Lord Cromwell.

Humphrey was effusive in his gratitude and the dinner he set before me, consisting of a dozen or so dishes, was more than my still delicate stomach could do justice to. The best plate was laid out and Mistress Humphrey's tongue lashed the servants whenever any of them displayed behaviour that might have appeared gauche to the 'distinguished guest'. Over the meal her buxom daughters competed for my attention, giggling and simpering as they helped me to portions of food or replenished my goblet. As I took my last sip of sweet, warm hippocras Sir Sebastian casually asked whether I would care to look over his stable. He was, he said, rather proud of his horses. I rose thankfully from the table, more than ready for some crisp, fresh air to clear my head. It rapidly became apparent that Humphrey was extremely knowledgeable about horseflesh and he had some admirable beasts. As we toured the stalls he described the pedigree and merits of each incumbent in turn. He asked me which I liked best. My eye had been caught by a compact grey gelding of similar conformity to Dickon, though a couple of years younger.

When I pointed him out my host nodded his approval. 'You are an excellent judge, Master Treviot. Golding is what I call a "stayer". He will go all day and still have the spirit for a gallop when he smells home. Would you like to try him?'

Minutes later I was in Humphrey's schooling paddock, putting Golding through his paces. My host called out flattering encouragements. 'He goes well for you, young sir. You've won his approval.' He strolled over and ran a hand caressingly down the horse's neck. 'He has a favourite trick he only performs for those he really likes. Lean forward, pull back on the rein, tap his flank lightly and whisper to him "Stand".'

I did so and the next moment was almost unseated. The

grey flicked his ears and reared on his hind legs, his front hooves pawing the air.

Humphrey roared with laughter. 'Excellent! Stoutly done! You were made for each other.'

I dismounted and patted Golding. 'Fine horse,' I said. 'He handles well.'

'Just the mount you need to take you back to London.' Humphrey smiled disarmingly but there was a glint in his eye – the look of a businessman sizing up a prospective customer. Somewhat belatedly I realised that the bluff, naive countryman pose was just that – a pose. Sir Sebastian Humphrey was, in reality, a cunning and professional horse coper.

'You would hire him to me?' I asked, matching his feigned innocence.

'Oh, Golding is no hack for hire,' he protested. 'He is just the mount for a wealthy gold merchant.' He emphasised the word 'wealthy'.

There was no doubt in my mind that the grey's name had been invented for my benefit. For some minutes seller and buyer performed the verbal galliard of haggling. Humphrey named an outrageous price. I recoiled in mock outrage. He enumerated the horse's 'outstanding' qualities. I indicated that I might be interested at a much lower figure. The compromise we eventually reached was more in Humphrey's favour than mine. He had the advantage. He knew that I needed a reliable horse if I was not to be left stranded in Harwich. So, I ended up paying dearly for Golding. As things turned out, I never made a better investment.

That afternoon I completed plans for my onward journey. I would leave early on the morrow accompanied by two of Humphrey's outdoor servants as escort. My chest was consigned to the ship master, who – for an additional fee – agreed to have it delivered to Goldsmith's Row when he reached London. It was early on Tuesday 13 December that I set out with my companions under a slate-coloured sky, our cloaks wrapped tightly round us against a cutting wind. We made good time across the flat, largely empty landscape and, as the last light faded, we were crossing the marshland bordering the Thames estuary. The smoke blown horizontally from Tilbury's huddled houses was the only sign of occupation and we had to hammer on the inn door to rouse the proprietor. A wretched night followed in the most cramped and draughty guest chamber I have ever encountered. In the morning I located one of the ferrymen and, after the usual ritual of bargaining over his fee, he roused the oarsmen from neighbouring cottages and we boarded his broad, flat-bottomed craft for the crossing to Gravesend.

What I planned to do from this point was travel to Hemmings, which was only seventeen miles away, check that all was well there, send Humphrey's men home, and continue on to London with some of my own servants. Alas for the vanity of human designs!

I could tell that something was wrong as soon as we entered the stable yard. Walt came running out to greet us.

'Praise God you're here, Master Thomas,' he said, holding Golding's head while I dismounted.

'Why, what's the matter, man? Is it my mother? Or my son?'

He shook his head. 'No, master; they are safe and within doors.'

'Mistress Garney, then?'

'She is well.'

'God's blood, man, tell me plainly what troubles you!' I shouted.

''Tis your other friends, Master Thomas. They . . . the magistrate . . . ' He struggled for words. 'Best let Mistress Garney explain.'

I rushed into the house and found Lizzie in the hall, leading Raphael by one hand as he made tottering steps over the strewn rushes. The relief at seeing them both safe was almost overwhelming.

'Thomas!' she gasped and, for once, actually looked pleased to see me.

'In God's name, what's been happening here?' I demanded. 'Where are Ned and Jed?'

She picked Raphael up and seated herself by the fire, with the child on her lap. She looked up. 'Thomas, you have to help them. No one else can.' I had never seen her more anguished, not even in the depths of her own problems.

'That will be difficult if I do not know what has befallen them. I've had no news this last sixteen days. What has been happening?'

Lizzie took a deep breath. 'Well, that's easily told. Incent, that snivelling, ranting, villainous hypocrite, came marching in here to tell us you were taken by the bishop's men and would be burned for a heretic.'

'Yes, yes,' I said impatiently. 'Jed told me that Ned had taken you for safety to the nuns at Ladborough. As soon as I heard I arranged for you to be under Lord Cromwell's personal protection.'

'Aye, and that we were. Three of his own guards came down. After four days they said it was safe to return here. Everything was well as long as the soldiers stayed. Incent was furious at being baulked but he could do nothing while Cromwell's men were here. But last Friday they were recalled by their master. Well, that hellfire-headed priest wasted no time. Three days ago, he came back, this time with the local magistrate ... Whatsisname ...'

'Sir James Dewey.'

'Yes, him. I was sitting here in this very chair, changing Raffy. "Slut!" he shouted. "Stand up in the presence of your betters. Go and fetch the buggers!"'

'"And who would that be?" says I, staying put. That made his face go as red as his hair. "Strumpet!" he screamed. "Don't play the innocent with me. We know you're turning this house into a filthy bordello." He raised his hand to strike me but Whatsisname stopped him. Then the magistrate explained that they'd come to arrest two men believed to have taken refuge here. "On what charge?" says I. "Why, buggery," he says. "And since when has that been against the king's law?" says I. "These three years since," he replies. Lying puttock!'

'No, he's right.' I said. 'It was made a civil law offence so that the government could wield a stick over monasteries they wanted to close.'

'Well, we haven't got a monastery here, have we?'

'No, but I know what the Incents are up to. They're angry because I escaped their clutches. This is their way of hitting back. What's happened to Ned and Jed?'

'The magistrate brought armed men with him. They put our friends in irons and took them off to Ightham jail. Thomas, you've got to do something.' She released a wriggling Raphael. Staring watchfully after him, she muttered, 'You are bad luck to everyone who knows you, Thomas.'

'That's a just rebuke,' I admitted, 'but I'll get them freed. God's blood, the Incents are not going to get away with this!'

I hurried back out, had Golding re-saddled and set off for the magistrate's house, some five miles off, at Hadbourne. Sir James Dewey was an old friend. His family and mine had been leaders of local society for a couple of generations. Many were the private gatherings we had enjoyed and the public events he and my father had organised together. I could not reconcile what Lizzie had told me with the man I knew. I had to talk with him face to face.

But what was I to say? As the local representative of the king's justice he had solemn responsibilities. When alleged violations of the law were reported to him he was bound to investigate them. I knew and respected James as a man of impeccable honesty and one not swayed by offers of bribes or by favouritism. If I were to persuade him not to proceed further with the case against Ned and Jed, I would have to make an unassailable case. As I jogged southwards beneath the bare-limbed trees I went over in my mind what little I knew about John and Hugh Incent and their interest in me and my friends. And, suddenly, I understood. Like sunlight breaking through clouds, my hazy recollections became hard-edged and vivid. Facts fell into place.

Chapter 30

I did not need to travel all the way to Hadbourne to find James Dewey. I came up with him a mile from his house and we journeyed on together. His welcome was warm, as I had known it would be.

'Thomas, well met!' His weatherbeaten countryman's face glowed with a wide smile. 'I hear you've been over to the Netherlands.'

'Aye, on business for Lord Cromwell.'

James' thick eyebrows rose in surprise. 'Moving in high circles, eh? Better than the business you were doing with Bishop Stokesley, by all I hear.'

'Ill news rides a swift horse.'

He laughed. 'You know our locals. They know everything about us and what they don't know becomes the subject of vivid imagining.'

'Like the behaviour of my guests at Hemmings?'

He looked at me gravely. 'I'm sorry for it, Thomas. But, a plaint being laid, I had no choice. I would to God that you had been present. That canting priest might not have been so bold.'

'What do you know about Hugh Incent, the Everards' chaplain?' I asked.

'Well, as you are aware, the Everards are no lovers of the king's new policies and they supported Queen Catherine over the divorce. Their priest is of the same colour, but a deeper hue. You remember that mad Barton woman folk called the Nun of Kent who went about uttering supposed prophecies against His Majesty? Well, Incent was one of her mentors. He was lucky not to end up with her at Tyburn a couple of years back. The experience doesn't seem to have chastened him. He's a pious troublemaker, always on the lookout for people to haul before the ecclesiastical court on heresy charges. This business of your friends would have ended up being heard by the archbishop if buggery hadn't been taken out of the Church's hands and made a common law offence in thirty-three.'

'Have there been any prosecutions under this statute?'

'Not that I'm aware of. It served its purpose in His Majesty's closure of religious houses. Several abbots and abbesses surrendered to prevent their perverted behaviour being exposed.'

'Yes.' I thought of Ned and Jed.

'What will happen to my friends?'

'I will examine them and if I decide there is a case to answer I'll refer them to the next assize sessions.'

'And what if Incent can produce no evidence?'

'Oh, I've no doubt he'll suborn some witness prepared to support his accusations by lying under oath. His sort are practised at perverting the course of justice.'

'*Exitus acta probat*,' I muttered to myself.

'What was that?' James asked. But we had now arrived at Hadbourne and I made no answer as we dismounted.

I declined my old friend's invitation to stay to supper but he insisted on offering me refreshment before I returned and it was as we sat with hot, spiced ale and cakes before a blazing fire in his hall that I said, 'All this is aimed at me. Will you help me put a stop to it?'

Again James' bushy brows rose gesturing surprise but he asked no questions. 'I will certainly listen to whatever you have to tell me.'

I gave him an abbreviated account of recent events and particularly what I was now convinced was John Incent's involvement in the attack at Hampstead.

When I had finished, James sat back in his chair, frowning. 'In my days at Gray's Inn,' he said quietly, 'we would have called that a circumstantial case. Attempted murder is a serious charge. As I understand it, the only witness is this servant girl of yours.'

'Yes,' I acknowledged, 'and at the moment even she does not appreciate exactly what she knows. But I've thought this situation through dozens of times and I can see no other explanation.'

'Very well,' James responded. 'Go over the essential details again and we'll see if I reach the same conclusion.'

I laid out the facts in order. 'Point one: on the afternoon of Monday 20 November I rode out to Hampstead. The only person who knew of my destination was John Fink, my journeyman. Point two: John was a man with a grievance against me.'

'That's conjecture,' James protested.

'No, he admitted almost as much in the letter he sent when I was in prison.'

'Proceed.'

'Point three: as soon as I was gone to Hampstead he summoned a priest to come to the house – secretly. This priest was seen by a kitchen girl. She thought he had come to hear John's confession.'

'A reasonable assumption.'

'Yes, but it misled her.'

'What do you mean?'

'Well – and this is my point four – the girl said John welcomed his visitor with the words, "I'm innocent."'

'So?'

'If John had been about to confess his sins, he would hardly start by denying guilt. What she really heard was not the word "innocent" but "Incent".'

'Mere speculation.' James frowned. 'If anyone produced that as evidence in my court . . .'

'Ah, but wait,' I said eagerly, warming to my story. 'She described the visitor to me. Like his brother, John Incent has red hair. There are not many such among London's priests. Anyway, it would be easy enough to have her identify John's visitor.'

James looked dubious. 'A sceptical judge might suspect that you had paid your servant to say what you wanted.'

I continued. 'Point five: later that same day someone lay in wait for me on Hampstead Heath and tried to kill me. Point six: when that attempt failed, John Incent went to the bishop to lay heresy charges against me. Once again, his attempt was unsuccessful. But the Incents didn't give up, even when they knew my household was under Cromwell's protection. As soon as the coast was clear, Hugh came to you with tales about Ned and Jed. This unscrupulous pair of priests are determined to blacken my name and discredit me. Now why do you think their persecution is so relentless?'

'You believe it's because you are enquiring into Robert Packington's murder?'

'I'm sure of it.'

James shook his head. 'Your suspicions may be correct but they'd not add up to much in a court of law. In any case, if you decide to proceed against John Incent for the attempt on your life, he will "claim his clergy" and have the case heard by the bishop – and we both know what the outcome of that will be.'

'All that is absolutely true,' I said, 'but it is not my intention to lay charges.'

'What, then?' James asked with a puzzled frown.

'Bluff.'

'I don't unders—'

I interrupted, eager to convince my old friend of the plan I had concocted while riding from Hemmings. 'I want to give Sir Hugh a taste of his own bitter medicine. Why do his threats have such an impact on the local clergy and people?'

'They know he has the power of the Church behind him.'

'Exactly. So what I propose is that we threaten him with the power of the king.'

'But you don't have His Majesty's backing.'

'I have the backing of Lord Cromwell and that is the next best thing. If I go to Incent and confront him with what I know ...'

'What you have guessed,' James corrected.

'Very well, but I'm sure I'm right. Will you come with me and take him into custody, pending His Lordship's pleasure?'

'Not so fast, Thomas.' James frowned. 'I have to keep order around here. That means, among other things, staying on good terms with powerful families like the Everards. If I arrest their chaplain without very good reason ...'

'James, James,' I pleaded, 'you're my only hope . . . and I'm sure you'd like to be rid of a troublemaker like Incent.'

My friend stared silently into the fire. I waited anxiously for his reply. When, at last, he spoke it was in a half-musing way, as though he were trying to persuade himself. 'He is already a marked man because of the Elizabeth Barton business and I would certainly be glad to see an end to his heresy-hunting crusade.'

'So you will come with me, then,' I urged. He nodded slightly.

'Let us see what effect your threats have. Perhaps they will be enough to make him crumble.'

With that I had to be content.

I returned to the demoralised household at Hemmings and brought everyone news that I hoped would raise their spirits. I announced that the house was to be shut up for the winter and that family and staff would be moving to Goldsmith's Row. The sense of relief was almost tangible and the servants began with a will the business of packing everything that had to be transferred to our other home. For the next thirty-six hours all was bustle and clamour and, as the time of our departure drew nearer, the atmosphere became almost cheerful. I sent a messenger ahead with a letter for Cromwell, announcing my return and telling him that I would be in Goldsmith's Row, awaiting his summons.

Chapter 31

I had arranged with James to visit Hugh Incent on Friday 16 December and on that morning I rendezvoused with him and two of his armed retainers at the Everard estate. We rode on to the chaplain's cottage close to the small chapel-of-ease which served the lord of the manor and his household. James approached the door and one of his men dismounted to knock. The door was opened by Incent's housekeeper, who, I could scarcely help noticing, was young and pretty. She reported our arrival and, moments later, her master appeared.

Hugh Incent was a small man whose paunch indicated that he was well fed. However, his most striking feature was his head of thick russet hair. Seeing James, he smiled and raised both hands in a gesture of welcome. 'Your Honour, this is a pl—' Then he saw me. For several seconds he stood, flustered and at a loss for words.

James dismounted. 'Good day to you, Sir Hugh. I have one or two questions to ask. May we come in?'

The priest tried to hide his reluctance as he ushered us inside.

When we were seated in the small main room of the simple dwelling, James began. 'I am here at His Majesty's express command. As you will appreciate, he is sore troubled by the rebels in the North, many of whom are clergy. Sadly, some of their brothers in other parts of the country have expressed sympathy for them. His Majesty has charged all justices of the peace to search out any mischievous people who are well disposed towards his enemies. Now, Sir Hugh, do you know of anyone, priest or layman, whom I should be investigating about this?'

Incent surveyed us warily but replied in a firm voice. 'No, Your Honour. I believe all hereabouts are loyal servants of His Majesty.'

'You are sure?' James pressed. 'There is no person you suspect of grumbling about the Royal Supremacy? No one who would like to see the Bishop of Rome reinstated as head of the English church?'

The priest shook his head firmly. 'No, indeed.' His brow was beginning to moisten with sweat.

'Hmm.' James stroked his chin thoughtfully. 'I am pleased to hear that. However, I'm sure you will appreciate that I may be obliged to detain some people for close examination. I must be thorough. His Majesty expressly desires above all things that his subjects should live at peace with each other. No more talk of "papists" and "heretics". The king remembers only too well the support in this area for the so-called Nun of Kent. He fears that disaffection may linger. Any such ... treason' – James emphasised the word – 'must be rooted out. As I recall, you, yourself ... '

Incent jumped to his feet. 'I denounced that fraudulent strumpet! I have taken the Oath of Supremacy! What lies have people been spreading about me?'

'No need to distress yourself, Sir Hugh. Please sit down.' James' manner was calm but certainly not reassuring. 'Since you ask, it has been noised abroad that your sermons don't seem to stress His Majesty's headship.'

Incent sank on to his stool. 'I ... well ... there have been other important issues to preach about.'

'More important than our Christian duty to support God's anointed king?'

The priest's mouth opened and closed but no sound came out. He turned his face from the fire and dabbed at it with a kerchief.

James continued calmly, with no outward sign that he recognised Incent's obvious distress. 'So that I may be able to report to His Majesty with complete confidence, I would like you to preach on the Supremacy every time you enter the pulpit for the next month. I take it you have no objection to that?'

'No, no, no, not at all, Your Honour.' The fat priest subsided with obvious relief.

James nodded and smiled. 'Well, I think that concludes my business here – for the moment. I'm sure His Majesty can rely on your complete support. Now Master Treviot has another matter he would like to bring up.'

Incent turned to me, instantly wary.

'My mission,' I began, 'is not totally unrelated to what Sir James has been saying. I have been charged by Lord Cromwell to investigate the scandalous murder of a prominent merchant shot dead on the streets of London last month. We have made various enquiries as a result of which we need to identify and interview a red-headed priest who appears to have some connection with the case.'

Incent was visibly shaken but tried hard not to show it. He had been deferential towards James but obviously did not know how to react to someone he had only recently denounced as a heretic. He tried humour. 'Is His Lordship proposing to round up every red-headed priest in England?' Incent laughed nervously.

'If necessary,' I replied solemnly. 'The victim of this atrocity was a personal friend of Lord Cromwell and he will not rest until the truth is discovered. I will need to establish your whereabouts on 20 November.'

Suddenly Incent lost control. 'This is all because I drew Sir James' attention to those two buggers you are defending, isn't it?' he cried in a shrill voice.

'Just tell me where you were on 20 November,' I replied calmly.

'I was here, of course,' he shouted. 'Here! Here! Here!'

'And you can prove that?'

'I need prove nothing to you. I am a holy, anointed priest. I answer only to my bishop.'

James intervened, raising his voice very slightly. 'The Vicegerent in Spirituals outranks all bishops, and Master Treviot is his representative. You will answer the question.'

Incent glowered. 'I can't remember exactly what I was doing a month ago.'

'Then you cannot prove that you were here and not in London,' I said.

'Of course I was not in London. I hardly ever go to London.'

'I see. In that case do you know any other red-headed priests we ought to question?' I asked.

He shook his head firmly. 'No, none.'

'Strange,' I said. 'Is not your brother of the same colouring?'

Incent's belligerence collapsed, like a fire when water is thrown on it. He covered his face with his hands. 'Someone has lied to you. This is all wrong,' he gasped.

On the contrary, I thought. Thank you for confirming my suspicion. I pressed home my advantage. 'And you yourself lied to us a moment ago?' To James I said, 'I see now how difficult a magistrate's job is. Lies, false accusations. Sometimes it must be almost impossible to come by the truth.'

James sighed. 'Yes, indeed, I fear we shall have to take Sir Hugh in for further questioning after all. Will you be so good as to call my men in?'

I rose and stepped across to the door.

Incent jumped to his feet again, trembling – though whether with fear or anger it was difficult to say – and shouting, 'That man you were talking of, the one who was shot, was a heretic! He spoke in the parliament house against the Church. He brought disruptive books into the country. He defied the authority of the priests.'

'And for that he deserved to be felled in the street by an assassin, even as he was on his way to mass?' I asked, trying hard to remain calm.

'Better that than the fire!' Incent ranted – and immediately realised that he had gone too far. 'Look,' he whined, 'my brother is one of the cathedral clergy in London, fighting hard to control these wretched New Learning people, but he had nothing to do with that man's death.'

'As to that, he can answer for himself,' James observed, 'and, doubtless, he will be examined by Master Secretary Cromwell. As for you, I counsel you to look to your own safety. Be content to live peaceably with your neighbours. Stop making accusations and seeking confrontation. For now,

Sir Hugh, having regard for your patron, I will leave you. But, if I have cause to come here again, do not expect any further lenience from me.'

As we rode away, James said, 'Let us hope he is suitably chastened. I'll have your friends released immediately and I suggest you advise them to remove themselves from here without delay.'

I thanked him and assured him that Ned and Jed would be returning to London with me on the morrow.

I dined with my mother in her chamber and, at my request, Lizzie joined us. It was difficult for me to be alone with my mother – difficult and upsetting. Sometimes she recognised me and sometimes she did not. Only when Lizzie was present did she seem less confused.

'She is very comfortable with you,' I said. 'She likes you.'

Lizzie shrugged. 'She has got used to me. I've become the only constant thing in her life. All the toing and froing of these last weeks has distressed the poor soul very much. And now we're going to make her move again.'

We watched the old lady as she sat methodically spooning up her pottage and staring vacantly into space.

'She's like this most of the time,' Lizzie said. 'Sometimes we have quite long conversations but they're less frequent now.'

As if to confirm her words, my mother suddenly looked up from her bowl with a smile. 'Is this man your husband, my poppet? He's a lusty young fellow, isn't he?'

Lizzie rose and went to her side. 'Mistress Treviot, this is your son, Thomas. Yes, he is a lusty lad, isn't he? Perhaps too lusty for his own good,' she added under her breath, with a flash of her familiar scowl.

But the old lady's eyes had glazed over again and she made no response.

Lizzie resumed her seat with a sigh. 'I sometimes think she's the only happy one here. At least she lives in her own world – wherever that may be.'

My mother began to hum an old tune and to rock from side to side with the rhythm.

'Yes,' Lizzie said. 'It's she who has her wits about her and we who dwell in a hellish Bedlam.'

On an impulse I rested my hand on hers. 'Don't be melancholic. Things will get better. They must.'

'Why must they?' She turned her head, eyes blazing. 'Every scrap of news we hear is worse than the last.' It was the sort of indignant outburst that was typical of this high-spirited woman. But she did not remove her hand.

'Well, from what I've heard on the road, it seems that the trouble in the North is over. The rebels have disbanded and been promised a royal pardon.'

'Oh, we've heard all about that!' Lizzie's nose wrinkled in a sneer. 'Ned says that's just a trick of the king's. He says as soon as the poor people up there have gone to their own homes, our Harry will send a fresh army to drag them out and put them to death.'

'Ned is a bit too sympathetic to the rebels' cause. I hope he will learn to be less free with his opinions. Perhaps his brief spell in the local jail will make him more careful.'

'Prison doesn't seem to have knocked any sense into you,' Lizzie snapped, and now she did remove her hand. 'But then you've become a copain of Master High-and-Mighty Cromwell, haven't you?'

I was spared the need to respond by a knock at the door. One of the servants brought the news that Ned and Jed had returned. I hurried out to meet them and Lizzie was at my heels. Our two friends had barely dismounted when she ran up to embrace them. 'Mary and all the saints be praised!' she exclaimed between tears and laughter. 'I prayed for you every day – every hour!'

Ned beamed and, with some difficulty, disengaged himself from her entwining arms. 'Then your prayers have been answered – though we must give due praise to Master Treviot as well as Our Lady.' He grasped my hand. 'Thank you, indeed, Thomas. Long years in the monastery accustomed me to confinement but a few more days in that damp, stinking hole ...'

'It's good to see you safe.'

'And you,' Ned responded warmly. 'We have much news to catch up on.'

'Yes,' I agreed, 'and best we do it well away from eager ears. Come with me.'

I led the way to the large wagon barn, next to the stables. Ned, Lizzie and I climbed to the loft and settled ourselves among the sweet-smelling hay. I described, as succinctly as possible, my arrest, release and visit to Antwerp.

'So,' Ned said, when I reached the end, 'you are now in the employ of the great man. What is your impression of him?'

I had been pondering that question myself ever since my surprise interview at the house beside Austin Friars and it took me some moments to offer a considered reply. 'I think Lord Cromwell is a man who speaks much and says little.'

'That agrees with what I hear. Those around the court believe that his rise to power has come from telling people (especially the king) what they want to hear. While he lulls them into believing all is well, he quietly pursues his own subversive policies. That was how he brought down Anne Boleyn.'

'Brought down Anne Boleyn! That cannot be!' Lizzie

exclaimed. 'Were they not both of the New Learning? Surely they worked together to pull down the monasteries? That's what everyone says.'

'That's just what the devious Cromwell wants everyone to say. Our contacts at court tell a different story,' Ned replied.

I laughed. 'Your contacts at court? Come now; what does St Swithun's House know about great affairs of state?'

'Don't scoff, Thomas.' I could see that Ned was quite serious. 'Gossip at the king's supper table is often common talk in the Stews by breakfast. As it happens, we've been finding out more about these "New Learners" at court. We had a pair of their friends to St Swithun's one evening a few weeks back. Some draughts of our excellent ale – embellished with a certain powder from my chest of simples – and they bade farewell to discretion. What they had to say about their betters would have made the Devil blush.'

I laughed but Ned ignored my mockery.

'You would be shocked to hear what goes on between the pious ladies of Queen Jane's chamber, the king's hunting companions and even the royal chaplains. But that's not to the point. Basically, it seems, we must abandon any idea that the "New Learners" are a close fellowship of Bible students, united around an agreed core of fashionable, novel doctrines. Having severed the cables binding them to Mother Church, they are adrift on a sea of treacherous currents that carry them in several directions. His Majesty's household is all asquirm with a myriad heretics. It is a cockpit where enemies of the truth unleash their talons against honest Christians. Some are hot to desecrate churches and pull down religious images but others distance themselves from such vandalism. Some proudly follow Luther's heresy, insisting that faith is all and good works count for nothing. Others point out that this only leads to unbridled licence and the abandoning of Christian virtue. 'Tis no wonder the realm is in such a state when those at the centre are so divided.'

Ned was becoming increasingly agitated and loquacious. I tried to head off his verbal stampede. 'Where stands Cromwell in all this?' I asked.

'Who knows,' he replied. 'As you say, His Lordship reveals little of his real thoughts. However, what our inebriated friends revealed was that Cromwell and the Boleyn whore had a fierce argument only days before her fall. It was about the monasteries.'

'I don't understand,' Lizzie said with wrinkled brow. 'Was the queen against their closure?'

'No, she wanted to use the proceeds for schools, poor scholars, and such like.'

'What makes you think Cromwell would oppose that?' I demanded.

'Because the only way that he had been able to get the king to agree to wholesale dissolution was by pandering to his greed.' Ned lowered his voice to a confidential whisper. 'All that was needed, he said, was a few Acts of parliament for all the Church's gold and jewels and rents to be poured into the royal coffers and make Henry VIII the richest king in the world.'

'And because the queen was trying to appeal to the king's better nature, Cromwell plotted to destroy her! The hell-bred, viper-minded, double-tongued hypocrite.' Lizzie glared at me. 'That's the sort of man you're working for!'

It was clearly time to change the subject. 'Enough of politics,' I said. 'Have you learned anything useful from these "court contacts" of yours?'

'As a matter of fact, I have,' Ned replied. 'I had asked our

Southwark friends to gather any information about the Seagraves. When Jed came up to town to deliver Lizzie's letter, he called in at St Swithun's House and picked up some interesting gossip. It seems they've been in touch with Doggett.'

'Why for?' I asked.

'Don't be so dim,' Lizzie scoffed. 'Doggett knows everything. If they want to find out who killed their sottish Jack Napes relative, Doggett would be the man to turn to.'

Ned nodded. 'That's right. And Doggett set his Dogs on to gathering information in their usual – very effective – manner. Unfortunately, in the course of their investigations, your name cropped up, Thomas.'

'But they can't still think I had anything to do with Nathaniel Seagrave's murder,' I gasped.

'They need someone to blame if they are to assuage their grief,' Ned replied sombrely. 'However, that is the bad news. The good news is that the parties have fallen out. The Seagraves wanted Doggett to arrange your murder. He refused.'

'The man does have a conscience, then,' I said.

'More like they fell out over money.' Lizzie gave a cynical laugh.

'Lizzie is probably right,' Ned agreed. 'Doggett's assassins don't come cheap.'

'Perhaps, then, they will abandon their dreams of revenge?'

'I think it likely they will seek other ways to destroy you, Thomas. You must stay on your guard.' Ned went on: 'Sir Harry Seagrave, Nathaniel's father, is a member of the Privy Chamber and a friend of the king. He is a born schemer, who has worked his way from rural obscurity to the centre of power by a calculated programme of ingratiation and betrayal. My guess is that he will watch his moment very carefully and only act when it is safe to do so. His only surviving son, Hugh, is quite another matter – headstrong, proud, jealous of his family honour and not very intelligent. Sir Harry has him at court to keep an eye on him but the young man is virtually uncontrollable. It might even be him who took a shot at you at Hampstead.'

'Will this nightmare ever end?' I groaned.

Chapter 32

By first light on Saturday we were all ready to set off. Horses were saddled, carts packed and my mother and son made comfortable in the koch, with Lizzie to cater to their needs. I hoped that the journey would last no more than two days because the weather had taken a very bitter turn. We were all heavily wrapped against the easterly wind which rattled the bare branches, snatched at our cloaks and carved the track into sharp ridges.

Progress was slow but our pace improved slightly once we had reached the Dover road near Wrotham. I rode part of the way with Ned for company. I wanted to press him further about what we had been discussing the previous day without alarming Lizzie.

'Now that I have met Lord Cromwell,' I began, 'I find it hard to recognise the picture you paint of him. He spoke to me about creating a new and better England. Now, whether you think that's a good thing or not, it's difficult to see what he had to gain by bringing down the queen. She, too, was all for reform. I've met men who were close to her. They praise her for her boldness in appointing preachers and bishops of the new persuasion and campaigning for an English Bible. Getting rid of her could only set back Cromwell's cause.'

Ned gave a cynical smile. 'And has it? Six months ago most people assumed that Queen Anne's disgrace and death would put an end to all this New Learning nonsense. They thought the king would make his peace with the pope, that the monasteries would be spared, that heresy would be rooted out, that Cromwell and his grovelling creature, Archbishop Cranmer, would be staked out as scapegoats to bear the punishment for unpopular policies. Has any of this happened?'

'No.'

'No. Cromwell is more secure than ever and hatching who knows what devilish plots to sink England deeper in the mire of heresy. The heroes who raised the North in defence of Christian truth certainly worried the king. They wanted to see the heads of Cromwell and Cranmer stuck up on poles but I fear the heretics are too firmly entrenched in royal favour.'

'You still believe he intends to put a complete end to the religious life in England?'

'Why would he stop now? The attack on the smaller houses was like a gage thrown down to see if anyone would take it up. Well, the brave northerners' challenge very nearly stopped him short. It was our last – our only – chance. If the Pilgrims of Grace, as they called themselves, had pressed home their advantage, we'd have seen an end to this headlong plunge into heresy.'

We moved into single file to negotiate a narrow packhorse bridge. 'Of course,' Ned continued, 'brave Harry would not have had the wit to think out this scheme for himself. It took your friend Cromwell to harness the greed of the gentry and would-be gentry. Distributing some of the confiscated land to eager estate builders was a clever move – diabolically clever.'

I thought of men like Sebastian Humphrey and could only agree. Such men would be invaluable allies for Cromwell as he set about creating his 'new' England.

'Do you miss the life of the cloister?' I asked.

He paused a long time before replying. 'That is a question I often ask myself. I was comfortable and secure at Farnfield. As a child I had been put there by my father and had no choice in the matter. I was the youngest of four sons and there was no way he could provide me with any inheritance. I suppose he thought it would be useful to have at least one member of the family pledged to pray constantly for his soul. I don't recall any time when I did not assume that I would live out my whole life in the priory. And I never doubted that my brothers and I were performing a useful service – praying for the king and the realm from one dawn to the next.' He sighed. 'Hubris! We had no real contact with the realm and certainly not with the king. How could we pray properly – particularly as our numbers dwindled. The world outside our walls was changing, spinning – perhaps to its destruction. Had we any right to be cocooned from that reality? Religious communities needed to be shaken out of their complacency if they were to serve this land turned topsy-turvy. There was a time when I thought that what Cromwell was about was a painful but necessary reform and that I might play some part in reviving monastic life. Self-deluding fool!' Ned laughed, mirthless. 'I think that is no answer to your question but 'tis all I can offer.'

'Well,' I said. 'I still think better than you of Lord Cromwell but, even if I did not, I would have no choice about serving him. I need his protection.'

'Then pray God you continue to please him,' Ned observed grimly, 'for we are all in the same case.'

'All?'

'Aye. You and me and Jed and Lizzie and your mother and little Raphael and all your household. We stand or fall with you. You have recruited us to His Lordship's service – without giving us any say in the matter.'

A young hind pranced across the road in front of us and made Golding prick up his ears. I was no less taken aback by Ned's statement. God forgive me, it was true. I had been dicing with the lives of people I cared about.

All I could think to say was, 'Well, please God, this business will soon be over, and we can all resume our normal lives.'

'A fond wish.' Ned stared at me solemnly. 'Life is not a trundling wagon you can jump on and off at leisure. For example, have you thought what's to become of Lizzie?'

'She's welcome under my roof as long as she wishes to stay. Raphael will need a nurse for several years. I don't know what other options she has – but then there's much about her I don't know. For instance, how did she learn to write?' It was a clumsy attempt to turn the conversation but Ned seemed as ready as I for a new topic.

'As far as I can gather from snatches of conversation, her father was servant to a wealthy merchant,' he explained. 'Lizzie grew up alongside this man's daughter and, when he hired a tutor for the girl, Lizzie also attended lessons. She even has a little Latin. That all came to an end when Lizzie's father fell out with his master – something to do with drink and missing money, I think. When the family were turned out, her father had no hesitation in putting his pretty thirteen-year-old daughter to work in the dockland streets to please sailors who came ashore with their wages.'

'Poor Lizzie.'

'Indeed. Fortunately she's a girl of spirit. It didn't take her long to calculate that if she was doomed to be a whore she would work on her own terms. That's how she ended up at St Swithun's. That's why I ask you what's to become of her. She deserves a better life.'

We stopped in Ash at the Sign of the White Swan to refresh ourselves and see the horses rested, fed and watered. After that I left the members of my little caravan to make the best time they could while I rode on ahead with a couple of servants. I wanted to get as close as possible to London before nightfall in order to reach home the next morning. If Cromwell had sent to summon me to his presence I had no wish to keep him waiting. We reached Deptford before a darkening sky obliged us to seek lodging. We had almost left it too late. The man I sent on ahead returned with the news that the inns were full. However, he had discovered that a certain Mistress Flower had a house near St Nicholas' Church on the Strand, where she sometimes welcomed guests. I, therefore, presented myself at her door and the good lady, having inspected me closely to ensure that I was what she called 'suitable', welcomed us in.

It was immediately apparent that, by good fortune, we had stumbled upon a haven much more agreeable than any of Deptford's bustling and overcrowded inns. We were comfortably accommodated and well fed. The only drawback was the garrulity of our hostess. Having had a substantial meal set out for me in her main room, she insisted on joining me at the table and regaling me with anecdotes about some of the impressive ladies and gentlemen she had welcomed beneath her roof.

"'Tis all on account of Placentia being so close by,' she explained.

'Placentia?' I asked.

'The palace at Greenwich.' She tut-tutted. 'I still call it by the old name. Can't get out of the habit. Lovely it is – and big, that I grant, but I prefer Eltham. It has the dignity of age, if you understand me, Master Treviot. But His Majesty prefers Pla ... Greenwich. So there you are.'

'Is the king coming here for Christmas?' I asked.

'Oh, indeed. He wouldn't be anywhere else. He used to spend a lot of time at that ugly, sprawling place upriver that was the Cardinal's.'

'Hampton Court?'

'That's right, Hampton Court, but between you and me, I think he's got tired of it. He likes to come here and see his ships being built in the new dock. Oh yes, he'll be here for Christmas, right enough. And his new queen, of course. Have you seen Queen Jane? I haven't, not yet. But I'm hoping to get a glimpse of her this time. They say she's taller than the last one. More stately, but, then, she could hardly be more *un*stately than the last one – that lewd Frenchified jade.' The lady laughed raucously.

Mistress Flower paused for breath and I managed to get a word in. 'I suppose the inns are always full when the court comes to Greenwich.'

'Yes, only 'tis worse this time. All these northerners, you see. Now that the rebellion's been put down we've got gentlemen and noblemen and churchmen and I don't know what else all coming here to prove their loyalty. They say – and I was told this by one of Archbishop Cranmer's gentlemen waiters ...

Now there's an odd man. Have you met him? I've seen him two or three times. Looks a bit of a dreamer to me. Not your typical bishop. He never seems, well, *comfortable* at court, if you understand my meaning.'

'What did he say?'

'The archbishop?'

'No, the archbishop's gentleman.'

'Oh, him. Well, that was funny. "The king has invited the ass to come down from the North," he said. Now what he meant by it, I can't think. Some sort of a court jest, I suppose. Can you think who the "ass" might be? They do have some funny ways, these court folk. I remember Queen Catherine's silk woman. She stayed here. Spanish she was, though her English was good enough. Insisted that I sat here and tasted all her food in front of her before she would put a morsel in her mouth. She thought that I would poison her! There's many folk would have been right put out by that. I just laughed at her funny ways. Of course, there's some as you can't laugh at. When one of the Duke of Norfolk's men was staying here, the duke himself came to visit him, along with the Bishop of Winchester. Can't say I ever liked the looks of him. Sat round this very table, they did, talking till nigh midnight – and no one allowed to come near them. Soldiers on the doors. What they were hatching only our Dear Lady knows. Not treason, I hope – not under my roof.'

It was late before I was able to disengage myself from Mistress Flower and go thankfully to my bed.

Flurries of snow slowed my progress the following day and it was gone noon before I reached the City. My first sight of the river above the bridge revealed islands of ice packing up against the stone piers and beginning to spread eastwards. Several lads had gathered at the bank and were testing the ice, daring each other to venture further and further out. I was glad to reach my own workshop where the refining furnace emitted a welcome heat and where a healthy fire blazed in my own chamber. There was, as yet, no message from Cromwell but, inevitably, there were many other matters that had accumulated in my absence and I was soon absorbed in writing letters, supervising the ongoing work and dealing with requests for new commissions. And I was enjoying it. It may not have been until months later that I reflected on the effects that recent events had had on me but I then came to see that, by the Christmas of that terrible year, 1536, I wanted nothing other than to be allowed to be no more and no less than Master Thomas Treviot, goldsmith of Cheapside in the City of London.

That was not to be – not yet. Late that afternoon I received an unusual visitor. The young woman who asked for me by name arrived unattended but was certainly not a servant bearing a message from a noble mistress. Equally clearly, she was not a lady of means, come to order a piece of gem-set jewellery. She was a slight creature of seventeen or eighteen, wearing a russet woollen overgown, which can have been scarcely adequate on such a freezing day. The auburn hair tucked into her linen coif paid no obeisance to prevailing fashion. The frost had pinched her cheeks to a high colour and the eyes that looked at me pleadingly were soft and brown – kindly, I thought, rather like those of a young foal. She had refused to disclose her business to my assistant and when told that I was very busy, she declared that she would wait. I went through into the shop with the intention of dealing with the woman quickly and getting on with more important matters. My assumption was that she had come on the embarrassing errand of seeking to pawn some precious object for much-needed cash. This was dispelled as soon as she curtsied and introduced herself.

'I greet you well, Master Treviot. My name is Sarah Walling, wife to Benjamin Walling.'

I hope I covered my surprise. 'Then, you are welcome, Mistress Walling. Your husband has been a good friend to me,' I said, leading her to the parlour.

When we were seated before the fire, I asked, 'Is Ben well? Is he not able to come with you?' I was suddenly anxious for the young man. I had strongly counselled him to quit the capital in case my enemies decided to pursue him. Could it be that he had ignored that advice and was now languishing in some damp cell awaiting interrogation by the bishop's officers?

'Thank you, Master Treviot,' Sarah replied. 'Ben is in good health.' She lowered her head. 'I fear it is shame that keeps him from your company.'

I was puzzled. 'Shame? I can think of nothing that he could possibly reproach himself for.'

'Then, by your leave, I must explain. Ben and I have been in love for more than three years. My father was furious when he found out. He made life very difficult for Ben but Ben stood up to him and told him that we wanted to be married. No daughter of his, my father said, was going to marry a penniless apprentice. They had a terrible argument and my father threw Ben out. The poor lamb was reduced to begging for work – any work. Ben is strong and clever and diligent and honest. If he can only get a start in life, he will be very successful. He got occasional labouring jobs and saved whatever he could so that, one day, he could make me his wife. And I promised to wait. But my father was very determined. He arranged what he called a "suitable" match. If Ben and I were ever to be together we had to act quickly. That was when Ben met you. He was standing by the Standard in Cheap, hoping to be hired as a day labourer, when your friend was so horribly murdered. When you paid him to make some enquiries, well ...' She hesitated. 'That seemed to be our chance. I escaped from the house and Ben gave the last of your money to an old priest, who married us. That was four weeks ago.' She sighed a long, shuddering sigh. 'I brought a few trinkets with me but they are gone – sold or pawned. And now we have nothing. I said to Ben, "Perhaps, you might turn to your friend Master Treviot for help", but he would not hear of it. "Master Treviot has his own problems," he said, "and I have not been wholly honest with him. I cannot face him." So I have come in my husband's stead to plead with you. He doesn't know I have come. I feel as though I am betraying him – but we are desperate.'

'You must tell Ben to have more faith in his friends,' I said in what I hoped was a reassuring tone. 'If he comes to see me I will certainly see if there's anything I can do ...'

'You have you not heard all.' Sarah stared mournfully into the heart of the fire. 'We have a room in a tenement in Love Lane, off Coleman Street. 'Tis small enough, God knows, but now we must share it with a great friend of Ben's, newly returned from the North.'

'Would that be a young man by the name of Bart?'

Sarah nodded. 'Aye, Bart Miller. Do you know him?'

'We have met briefly. I understand he went back to his own country to join the rebels.'

'Yes, beef-witted fool! Now he is here again, minus an arm and lucky still to have his head, from what he tells us.'

'And he is staying with you?'

'Aye, when his "great cause" collapsed he ran back to London to cast himself on his old friend, who is already at wit's end to know how to support a wife. Ben's trouble is that he is too soft-hearted – or, perhaps, it would be truer to say "soft-headed".'

'I can see it must be a great strain for you.'

Sarah nodded. 'Now you know all our troubles. Can you do anything to help?'

'Well,' I said, 'the least I can do is fill your bellies. Bring Ben and Bart here this evening and we'll talk about things over supper.' I recalled what Ned had said about the people for whom I was responsible. It seemed that the list was longer than I had thought – and still growing.

The next arrival that day was altogether more welcome. William Locke's head groom appeared, bringing with him a sprightly looking Dickon, now fully recovered from his injury. We welcomed each other warmly and the grey whinnied with pleasure when he was led into his old stall. Was this an omen that the bad times were behind us both? I dared to hope that it was.

Chapter 33

When my evening guests arrived I had supper served in the parlour. I had asked Lizzie to join us so that Sarah would not be the only woman present. I also hoped that her essentially sympathetic nature might help to dispel any awkwardness in the atmosphere. The three friends were a subdued trio and it was clear that there were tensions between them. Gone was the careless ebullience of youth. Ben and Bart bore the signs of young men pitchforked into responsibilities and experiences that had sapped their energies and troubled their minds. The transformation was most marked in Bart. The studious enthusiast who had spurred northwards to join in an uprising that would right the wrongs being perpetrated by the current regime had returned defeated and bearing the scars of battle. His left arm was missing below the elbow but that was not what immediately struck me as different about him. His thin face was scored with the lines that indicated strain. His clothes were shabby and his hair and beard unkempt. No longer was he ready with a jibe or a laugh. Ben and Sarah were equally reserved – two people divided by their love. Looks and gestures made it obvious that they had been arguing – and that they loathed themselves for arguing.

'Sarah told me I had to come and apologise,' Ben said, standing by the fire as the rest of us took our seats around the table.

'Then she mistook my meaning,' I replied. 'I am overjoyed to see you and to know that you have not suffered as a result of your association with me. If anyone should apologise, it is I for putting your safety at risk. Sit down, Ben, and let us hear no more of recriminations.'

He took his place at the table rather grumpily and for several moments we sat in awkward silence. The sombre mood might have lasted all evening had it not been for the excellent – and obviously much needed – food. While my guests ate I regaled them with an edited account of my recent travels and some of the people I had met. By the time I introduced them to Sir Sebastian Humphrey they were smiling and my description of the impossible Mistress Flower produced laughter.

'The ass from the North!' Bart almost choked on his hippocras. 'I know who she meant – Robert Aske. For sure the king has made an ass of him.'

'Who is he?' I demanded.

Bart sneered. 'He *was* our chief captain,' he said. 'He *is* our chief betrayer.'

'Can you give us a clear picture of what's been happening?' I asked. 'We get only garbled reports here.'

'I well believe it. All's been confusion beyond Trent and Humber too – rumours, squabbles, purposed misinformation.

All is at six and seven.' He laughed. 'Do you know there was even a story going round that the Duke of Norfolk, the king's general, was really on our side. Some said that he and Cromwell had come to blows and that the duke had stabbed Cromwell and killed him. How's that for an example of wishes giving birth to thoughts?' He drained his beaker and held it out for a refill.

'Speaking of killings,' Ben said, turning to me, 'has your quest for Master Packington's assassin borne fruit?'

'Yes,' I replied. 'It has been a confusing labyrinth of wrong turnings and misleading paths but I have, I believe, reached the truth.'

'And?' Ben enquired eagerly, setting down his knife.

"Tis quite clear that the man behind it was John Incent, one of the clergy at St Paul's; a Catholic zealot convinced that preservation of what he regards as truth justifies murder. He commissioned Il Ombra to gun down Robert and, when he thought I was getting too close to the facts, he hired some other villain – fortunately less efficient – to kill me. When that failed he had me hauled before the bishop. I suppose he reasoned that, even if I escaped conviction for heresy, I would be too frightened to pursue the matter of my friend's death. He reckoned without the king's Secretary.'

'I hope Cromwell strings him up from the nearest gallows,' Lizzie declared. 'Him and that red-headed demon brother of his. Mother of God, I'd do it myself and ask no fee.'

The others laughed at this outburst and Sarah asked, 'Who is this brother and what has he done?'

'What has he not? Goes round all the villages poking his long nose into everyone's business. "You must come to me for confession," he tells folk, "I've got a special licence from the pope to release souls from purgatory." Lying, power-crazed mammet! He thinks himself pope and cardinals all wrapped up in one. None of the parish clergy dare stand up to him. If anyone's stupid enough to confess any trifle, he pesters them to sneak on their neighbours and puts the fear of hell into them if they don't. He's recruited a little gang of busybodies to go prying into other folks' affairs. And all this prattle-prattle he writes up in a book. Ooh, how I'd like to get my hands on the hypocritical, canting rampallion!'

'Well,' I said. 'Sir James Dewey has doused Hugh Incent's flame for a while at least and I hope to bring his brother to account 'ere long. I'll be seeing Lord Cromwell in the next few days. I'll set the facts before him. It would be useless for me to take direct action against Incent but I'm sure Master Secretary will have cunning ways to obtain justice for Robert. But let's not talk of my problems. I want to hear everything about the northern rebellion. What can you tell me, Bart?'

Setting down his drinking vessel, Bart said, 'It was big. Thousands of us – all come together to show the king that he couldn't make his people victims of a few "new" thinkers like Cromwell and Cranmer. Radical ideas may sound very simple in the royal court or the parliament house – get rid of idle monks, pull down their houses, strip the churches of idolatrous images – but out in the country, well, it's like tearing the heart out of society.

'I got to York just in time for the council that gathered there to hear the king's response to the pilgrims' demands. Hundreds crammed into the Minster. The rest of us waited outside in the rain to hear what our captains decided. Too many captains, that was the trouble. Some were men the pilgrims had elected to speak for us but there were also nobles and gentlemen. They all wanted different things. By all accounts it was a babel inside the church.' Again Bart emptied his beaker at a gulp.

'What exactly was being discussed?' I asked.

'The pilgrims had sent their demands to the king: restoring of the dissolved abbeys; sacking of the king's evil councillors; a parliament to meet in York and an end to the making of all decisions in the South; free pardon for all the pilgrims ...'

'Yes,' I said, 'we've seen the list. No one with any knowledge of His Majesty could imagine him being dictated to like that.'

Bart nodded several times – emphatically. It was obvious that the drink was affecting his movements. I left his beaker empty and kept the flagon well out of reach. 'I know that,' he said. 'That's why I went north. What's clear here is not obvious to some of the folk up there. They really thought Henry would negotiate. Knot-pated fools! All he wanted to do was keep the pilgrims talking until the winter weather forced them to disperse. I told everyone I could think of, "Don't trust this king; use the power you've got; you'll never get another chance." Some of the commons – most, perhaps – were of the same mind. We had an enormous host – thirty thousand at least; some say forty thousand – and more ready to join us from Northumberland and Cumberland. We could have smashed the puny army that was all the king could send against us. Well, His Majesty had sent his reply – a compromise, of course – and that's what the captains were discussing. Those of us outside only got news by little and little but what became obvious was that most of the gentlemen and nobles wanted to disband the host and do a deal with the king. The size and mood of the pilgrim body frightened them. Huh!' He sneered. 'If we got what we wanted from the king, what would there be to stop us turning our attention to their exploitation of the people – enclosing common land, packing juries, maintaining gangs of armed ruffians?'

All this was putting flesh on the bones of what I had already heard about the northern rising and it seemed that Ned's assessment of royal policy was close to the truth.

'Tell Master Treviot about that Aske fellow,' Ben prompted.

'Aske? He's a gentleman, a one-eyed lawyer from Selby; clever. But for all his birth and learning he was one of us – or so we thought. At the beginning he had captured Pontefract Castle, taken Lord Darcy and the Archbishop of York prisoners and rallied the host to march south. But then he started listening to the other captains, the well-bred fainthearts, and he changed his tune. So all that came out of the York council was agreement for the captains to meet with the Duke of Norfolk at Pontefract. Another council. More talking ... talking ... talking.' Bart's head began to droop.

Ben nudged him. 'Tell Master Treviot about the ship at Hull.'

'Ship ... Hull ... Yes.' Bart shook his head and rubbed a hand over his eyes. 'Pontefract was a dis ... dis ... traction. Many pilgrims rode to Pontefract but we got news that a king's ship had arrived in Hull. It was loaded with ordnance for Norfolk and the army. Sir Robert Constable called for volunteers ... Never volunteer ... Never ... Never.' Bart slumped on to the table.

Ben hauled him upright and slapped his face but his friend only groaned and his head fell forward again, until it was resting on his arm on the table. Ben shrugged. 'I'm sorry,' he said. 'Bart's not fit for company. He's been through a great ordeal.'

'Let him be,' I said. 'What happened at Hull?'

'Bart and his "pilgrims" boarded the ship. There was a fight. That was when he lost his arm. Luckily someone got him to a surgeon, who did a proper amputation. He's still in pain but he refuses to give in to it. Meanwhile, the Duke of Norfolk had promised the rebels a complete pardon and agreed to all their terms. Aske disbanded the host and accepted an invitation to come south for personal talks with the king.'

'So it really is all over,' I suggested.

Ben frowned. 'I wonder. Bart doesn't think so. He's convinced that the rebels were tricked into going home. Norfolk was simply driving a wedge between the commons and their betters. Aske isn't the only one of the captains coming to London. They're all flocking here, eager to demonstrate their loyalty. Bart reckons there will be no pardon. As soon as the pilgrims are dispersed, the army will be sent in to exact the king's revenge.'

'*Exitus acta probat*,' I murmured, half to myself.

To my surprise, Ben responded. 'Oh yes, there's no morality in politics now. Perhaps there never has been.'

'Why has Bart come back?' I asked.

'He seems to think he has some sort of mission. As soon as he was able, he got on a horse and rushed to London. He aims to seek out the turncoats and confront them. You can see why we have to keep an eye on him.'

'Why us?' Sarah demanded sharply.

'Because he has no one else. He's broken his indentures by rushing off. Neither his family nor his old master want anything to do with him. We've been over all this a dozen times, sweetheart.'

Sarah pouted. 'I know you feel loyalty as his friend but he has only himself to blame and we have problems enough of our own.' She turned to me. 'Master Treviot, can't you make my dear dolt of a husband see sense?'

'I'm sure none of us wants to see Bart whipped through the City at a cart's end for begging in the street,' I said. 'Perhaps, between us, we can find him a job.'

'What jobs can a one-armed man do?' Ben asked mournfully.

'He has a mind,' I said, 'and it seems he knows how to use it.'

'Oh yes,' Ben agreed readily. 'He went to a grammar school and has good Latin. He isn't foolish. If anything, his problem is that he thinks too much.'

'Then, perhaps we can persuade him to channel his thoughts into something more positive than rebellion. I'll make some enquiries among my merchant friends. But you will have to sober him up – in more ways than one. No respectable businessman has room for a powder keg that's liable to explode at any time.'

Smiles of relief appeared on the faces of the newlyweds.

'As for you two,' I said, 'your first task is to make peace with Sarah's father.' I ignored Ben's scowl and went on. 'I don't think you want to remain at enmity with your family for the rest of your lives and I suspect they don't want that either. The longer the estrangement lasts, the deeper it will become. It will be worth a little humbleness on your part to put a stop to it now. May I suggest that Christmas would be an appropriate time for a reconciliation? If your olive branch is spurned, come and see me again but, please God, that won't be necessary.'

'You collect people with problems, don't you?' Lizzie said after the others had left. 'I feel sorry for that one-armed scapegrace.'

'Oh, Bart is his own worst enemy,' I replied, 'like someone else I know.'

Lizzie made a face at me as she left the room.

In the days leading up to the festival, London was, as usual, abuzz with excitement and anticipation. The food sellers were doing good business and staying open late. My shop was busy with customers buying jewellery to give as New Year gifts or negotiating loans to pay for their celebrations. Christmas is the season of generosity, when households relieve the gloom of midwinter with feasting on the last fresh meat of the year, from fowls and beasts kept and fattened for the occasion. But there were other reasons for the euphoria that pervaded the City in the Nativity season of 1536. News had spread that the northern rebellion was over. The fear that disaffection would spread and that southern counties faced a possible inundation by peasants brandishing billhooks and pitchforks in the name of Holy Church had evaporated. The feeling of relief was almost tangible and seemed to be shared even by many who were in sympathy with the 'pilgrims'. Also it was noised abroad that the king was coming.

The splendour of the royal court was very rarely seen on our streets. When Henry and his richly adorned attendants travelled to and from the palaces near the capital they almost invariably went by the river. The royal barge and a flotilla of other craft conveyed our social elite to Whitehall or Hampton Court or Richmond. But this year the king decided to keep his Christmas at Greenwich and to go there by road. This meant that his cavalcade would pass from Westminster, right through the City and across the bridge.

The immediate reason for the change of routine was ice. The river had a solid coating for a hundred yards or more upstream of the bridge and beyond that there was floating pack ice. But the bitter weather did no more than provide the opportunity for a royal show. Henry loved spectacle. Tournaments, pageants, processions – he was never the one to miss an opportunity for public display. And at no time did he have a greater need to remind the people of his power and magnificence than in the Christmastide of that woebegone year, 1536. The event planned for 22 December was to be a triumphal procession. Henry would appear before the citizens as their saviour, the warrior king who had delivered them from bloody rebellion. It mattered not that his victory had been achieved by guile rather than military might, nor that throughout the crisis he had not taken the field in person, but had skulked behind Windsor's ancient walls. He would claim credit for defeating the 'pilgrims' and appear before a grateful populace to receive their plaudits.

The day before this display I received Lord Cromwell's command to wait upon him at Greenwich on St Stephen's Day, 26 December. Before then there was much to do. All householders whose properties fronted the processional route were required to deck their houses with tapestry and rich cloth and to ensure that the street was covered in gravel of a regulation depth so that the finely caparisoned horses did not become besmirched with mud. The hard frost made this task easier. The attitude of the overseers sent from Westminster did not. They expected citizens to spread gravel twice – once for the royal baggage wagons that would come through on the twenty-first and once for the court personnel. Several of us went to the Lord Mayor to protest strongly the impossibility of complying. He, in turn, rode to the palace to discuss the problem with the Master of the Horse. After much arguing, it was agreed that some at least of the court's furniture and chests of plate would be transferred across the river from Whitehall and proceed from there along the south bank. The Lord Mayor agreed to allow the paraphernalia that could not be thus transported to be brought through the City and to keep back a supply of gravel to effect any repairs that might be necessary before the royal party entered via Ludgate and Paul's Yard. As well as decorating my own house front, I had to help with the impressive furbishment of the stretch of road allocated to the Goldsmiths' Company.

We were charged with decorating with cloth of gold the house fronts opposite St Michael's at Querne at the end of Cheap, close by the gate to Paul's Yard. However, it was not our gaudy preparations for the royal show that dominated our conversation as we supervised the servants clambering up ladders to attach our loyal tributes.

'Have you heard? He's been called to Westminster to be knighted by the king. Scandalous!'

As usual, it was Simon Leyland who was complaining. The 'he' referred to was Ralph Warren, alderman, sometime Master of the Mercers' Company and reputed the richest man in London. His nomination as the new Lord Mayor had been announced some weeks before and had divided the merchant community into warring factions. The Common Council had determined upon Sir Ralph Holles as the next holder of the leading civic office but had been overborne by the king, who had sent his mandate instructing the council to elect Warren.

'He has lent the king large sums of money,' my friend Will Fitzralph commented.

'That's not to the point,' Leyland retorted. 'The king likes not Holles for certain foolish words spoken in support of the northern rebels.'

'Are you, then, a secret sympathiser with these papist pilgrims?' I asked with a wink at Will. We both knew where Leyland's religious sympathies lay.

'Certainly not,' he roared. 'Holles is a troublesome heresy-hunter and I like not the man but there is a more important principle at stake. Our ancestors fought hard to establish our civic liberties and we should not allow the king to trample them.'

'I fear present politics count for more than ancient rights with our Harry,' Will said, being careful to lower his voice so that the servants could not hear. 'At the moment he is all for the new men.'

I was surprised to hear our new Lord Mayor named in that context. 'I had not heard that Warren is a religious radical.'

'Well,' said Will, 'he's very close with Cromwell and he has just been appointed the king's representative to the German merchant community here at the London Steelyard – and we all know what a nest of Lutherans that is. No, no, Peter, more to the left!' This last comment was addressed to one of the servants balanced on a ladder above our heads.

'I got up a petition to the Common Council while you were away from London – *again*.' Leyland glared at me and emphasised the word. 'I asked them to appeal against the king's order.'

'Which they did,' Will added. 'But Cromwell produced an old statute that, it seems, gives the monarch the right to interfere in all our elections.'

When the great day arrived, I breakfasted early and allowed all my household to gather in my chamber where they would have a good view of the street, while I donned my livery robe and went to take my place with my brother goldsmiths on the platform erected for us over against St Michael's Church. Even at that early hour the crowds had begun to gather, pressing against the cordon of troops who lined the route.

It was soon after ten o'clock that we heard the cheers from the direction of Fleet Street. Within minutes the procession emerged from the cathedral yard. First came the aldermen in their best liveries, then various officials of the court wearing rich furs against the cold and sporting jewelled bonnets. Then the escort of Gentlemen Pensioners marched past and we craned our necks to see the king and queen. It was then that I heard gasps from my neighbours. Leaning forward and turning to the right, I straightway saw what was surprising them. Immediately preceding the royal couple, in the position of honour, riding a richly caparisoned stallion, and carrying an ornate gilded mace, was Ralph (now 'Sir Ralph') Warren. 'God's blood,' my neighbour muttered, 'the king means to rub our noses in it!'

Whatever indignation may have been caused among the mercantile elite, there was no doubting that the royal show was a success. King Harry's flawless instinct for simple ways of pleasing the people once again served him well. Fear of the Pilgrimage of Grace had stirred ancient prejudices about 'uncouth' northerners and, whatever religious divisions might exist among London's citizens, there was unity when it came to their dislike of rebellion and their concern for the security of their property. Relief gilded their curiosity about Henry's young queen, small and demure as she trotted past in the wake of her corpulent husband. Both royal horses were caparisoned in yellow, symbolising, I suppose, sun-like brilliance and warmth triumphing over winter darkness and rebellion. The entourage made its way past ranks of robed company men, mitred bishops and abbots, and priests swinging censers, and was cheered all the way to the bridge. It was on such occasions as this, when the City's mercantile nobility were on display in their full livery, that I realised what a gap Robert Packington had left in the ceremonial and business life of London.

When Twelvetide arrived, I led the celebrations of my household on the first day. After mass in the morning we feasted and played various games over which the youngest scullion presided as our Lord of Misrule. The following days I gave permission for those who wished to depart and celebrate with families and friends to do so. I, of course, had much more serious matters on my mind, when, at dawn on 26 December, I had Golding saddled (I wanted to ease Dickon back into service) and set off for Greenwich and my meeting with Lord Cromwell.

Chapter 34

It was easy to see why the king favoured Greenwich Palace above his other residences close to the capital and spent most of his winters there. As I emerged from the deer park and began the gentle sweep down to the sprawl of red-brick buildings set amidst walled gardens, I was impressed by its sheer size and its location. On such a crisp, clear winter's day the palace could be seen to its best advantage, its towers and turrets outlined against the green-blue of the Thames. Looking down from a southerly approach was almost like seeing a map of this old royal home. I could make out the Italian-style gardens, where plants and grass were disciplined, in obedience to the latest fashion, into geometrical shapes intersected with gravelled walks. The tiltyard, Henry's own addition to the ensemble, was clearly visible. I could just see the craft moored beyond on the palace waterfront and upriver the tall masts of larger ships in Deptford dockyard. Placentia, or Pleasaunce, as it was sometimes called, seemed to have everything a cultured and fun-loving prince could want. I could only hope that this visit would 'pleasure' me; that Cromwell would receive my report and deal with Incent and his confederates. The prospect of seeing that red-haired head grimacing from the top of a pole at the end of London Bridge was one that I relished.

I left my two servants with the horses in the stable block and showed Cromwell's letter to one of the guards, who arranged for me to be escorted into the depths of the palace. We passed across courtyards, up staircases and through several rooms until we arrived in a large and busy antechamber. I presented my credentials to a secretary sitting at a table and took my place among a score of petitioners and messengers standing in small groups and all waiting to be shown into the great man's presence. I wandered across to a window embrasure commanding an excellent view of the river. I was peering idly at the marshland spur opposite held in, as it were, by the steep bend of the Thames when someone came up behind and quietly spoke my name. I turned and recognised the sombre face of Augustine Packington.

'Thomas, what brings you here?' he asked anxiously.

I explained briefly the commission that had taken me to Antwerp and that I had now come to deliver my report.

He plucked me by the sleeve and drew me into a quiet corner of the room where we could not be overheard. 'What did you discover about Robert's last mission to the Low Countries?' he demanded.

'That is confidential,' I explained. 'I am bound to report only to Lord Cromwell.'

'But I am Robert's brother,' Augustine pleaded, in a tone of reproach. 'Surely you can tell me.'

I considered carefully, then replied, 'What I can say is that Robert's friends told me he was in a state of very great distress over Tyndale's death.'

'I know that,' Augustine responded, almost tetchily. 'He said as much in his letters.'

'Did he say why he took Tyndale's execution so personally?'

Augustine shook his head and gave a mournful sigh. 'He described the burning in some detail. Apparently Tyndale's friends had paid for him to be strangled before the fire was lit. It was the last kindness they could do him. Robert was at the front of the crowd. He heard and saw everything.' Augustine's voice became muffled with emotion. 'He said the martyr's last prayer was, "Lord, open the King of England's eyes." Imagine that! Praying for the man who had done nothing to help him all those months in a damp, dark cell. Did they tell you in the English House that Tyndale's appeals for warm clothes and books to read had been denied?'

'Yes, but his friends were convinced that they had done all they could for him. Unfortunately, the severe restrictions governing his imprisonment severely limited their charity. Only Robert, it seems, carried a burden of guilt. He believed that he should have done more but I cannot see why he should have reproached himself.'

Augustine looked round the room, as though fearing that someone might have been listening or was suspicious of our private conversation. 'Tyndale was doomed,' he said at last. 'There could have been no other end. Beyond the English House he was a marked man and he could never have returned here.'

'Why so?' I asked.

He dropped his voice, although there was certainly no one near enough to hear what he said. 'He knew that his presence here would have played into the papists' hands. They'd have had the king's backing in hunting him down. And, if Tyndale had been burned at Smithfield instead of outside Vilvoorde Castle, do you think we would have had the remotest chance of seeing an English Bible in our lifetime? William was well aware of that. Rather than see his work come to nothing, he embraced perpetual exile.'

'I am confused,' I said. 'If His Majesty was so opposed to Tyndale, why did he send agents to intercede for him with the imperial authorities?'

'There are two things you should know about our king. The first is that he is a great hater. He takes any kind of disagreement personally, as proof of disloyalty. You saw what happened to Queen Anne. God alone knows what she did to turn his passionate love into frenzied hatred. There was a time when the king was an admirer of Tyndale. He praised him to the heavens as a wise and godly scholar – as long as he thought this genius could be useful to him in his battle with the pope. I once carried a message from Cromwell begging Tyndale to come back and produce books supporting Henry's governorship of the Church. He was promised a generous pension and every facility for his work. Then Tyndale committed the unforgivable crime.'

'What was that?'

'He had the effrontery to disagree with the king over his reading of Scripture,' Augustine said bitterly. 'Henry's case for having his first marriage annulled was that the Bible declared it unlawful. Tyndale knew that this was wishful thinking; the king was twisting the meaning for his own benefit. Now a prudent man – or a coward – would have kept silent. Not Tyndale. He was too much a stickler for the truth of Holy Scripture. He pointed out that Henry had misinterpreted the text and that, therefore, his marriage to Queen Catherine was valid. After that Henry's supposed love and admiration turned to black hatred. Without this Bible "proof" the king had no case. That was why he joined the baying pack screaming out that Tyndale was a heretic. After that there was no possibility of his ever returning to England. He was, and would always be, an outlaw. He had no citizenship, except, as he once said to me, "in heaven". And this great saint's last prayer was for the man who had abandoned him to his enemies!'

I considered Augustine's angry words. 'And what is the second thing I need to know about His Majesty?'

'That he is a master dissembler. Unless I am very much mistaken you will see that when you discover what happens to this Aske fellow. His visit is all the talk at court this Christmas. He was the chief instigator of the northern rebellion but now he is welcomed here like the Prodigal Son. All is forgiven. Aske is showered with gifts. Henry walks with him in the privy garden with an arm round his shoulder. Well, we will see how long this supposed friendship lasts. I'll lay you a hundred gold sovereigns that we see this little lawyer's head on a pole before Easter.'

My mind rebelled against this cynicism. 'No, Augustine, the picture you paint is of a capricious, feckless monster. I cannot believe such things of our lawful king. How could the realm possibly be governed if what you say is true?'

'We must praise God that Lord Cromwell is at His Majesty's right hand. He understands—'

'Master Treviot!' My name was called by the secretary and I went over to the table. 'His Lordship will see you now.' The man waved me towards the doorway behind him.

Cromwell's office was not large but its window commanded

the same wide view as that of the anteroom. The king's secretary had placed his table in such a way as to make most use
of the winter light. Like its counterpart in His Lordship's
London house, it was topped with papers, letters and books in
tidy piles. Cromwell was attired in an expensive black robe
with a fur collar over which he wore a gold chain of office. As
I entered, he set aside the document he was working on and
drew towards him another sheaf of papers.

'Ah, Thomas.' He looked up, all affability. 'I wish you a
good Christmas.' If I had been an old and trusted friend, his
welcome could hardly have been warmer.

'And I you, My Lord. I see you are no less busy in the festal
season.'

'If His Majesty is to enjoy celebrating the Nativity, some of
us must lift the cares of state from his shoulders. And what of
you, young man? Free of the worries that beset you when last
we met, I hope.'

'I am thankful that the Lollards' Tower is no more than an
occasional nightmare, My Lord.'

'Good, good ... and your personal quest to discover the
murderer of our dear friend, Robert Packington?'

'I am glad to say that I have reached a conclusion on that
matter. The culprit's name—'

Cromwell held up a hand. 'In time, in time, Thomas. First
I need to hear your report of what passed in Antwerp. Please,
take a seat.'

I had rehearsed several times the narrative of my visit to the
English House. It seemed to me that I had discovered little
that could be of interest to Cromwell and I was anxious lest he
should think me completely incompetent. Someone in
Antwerp had described His Lordship as possessing a mind like
the workings of a mechanical clock. As such a timepiece

317

ticked its way with relentless precision from minute to minute, so Master Secretary's thinking moved, in an orderly fashion, from fact to fact, detail to detail, spurning the irrelevant in its logical pursuit of the inevitable conclusion. I tried, therefore, to set out my account in an orderly fashion. Cromwell listened with total concentration.

I had scarcely begun when he interrupted. 'Did Robert deliver the message entrusted to him to the Regent of the Netherlands, the Emperor's representative in Brussels?'

'I believe so, but it distressed him greatly that Your Lordship's appeal for clemency was ignored. He seems to have blamed himself for that and become convinced that he had failed.'

Cromwell shook his head. 'Robert did not fail. No one could have saved Master Tyndale. All we can do is save his work and complete it. How goes the Bible printing?'

I reported my visit to Mistress de Keyser's printworks and Rogers' optimism about the progress of the translation. Again, he listened intently and I had the feeling that my words were being dissected minutely, as a surgeon explores a cadaver.

'Good, good!' For the first time real enthusiasm broke through the surface of logical calculation, like bubbles in a cauldron of pottage. 'That is a fine work and, praise God, we have excellent scholars like Master Coverdale to bring it to a conclusion.'

'Then we are to have an official Bible?' I asked.

His face became expressionless once more. 'If the king wishes it.'

'Would it not be ironical,' I ventured, 'if His Majesty were to give his blessing to the work of a man he had come to hate?'

'*Omnia mutantur nos et mutamur in illis.*'

'I'm sorry, My Lord, my father never put me to Latin.'

Cromwell smiled. 'Well, it is not too late for you to learn. I picked it up when I was about your age, travelling in Italy and elsewhere. That little piece of ancient wisdom might be translated, "Everything changes and we must be adaptable." He rose from his chair, stretching his arms and stifling a yawn. He stepped across to the window. 'Now here is a timely case in point,' he said, beckoning me to join him.

We looked down at the palace quay. A royal barge had just pulled alongside and the king was disembarking with his band of attendants.

'You see that small fellow.' Cromwell pointed out the man with whom Henry was deep in conversation. 'Two weeks ago he was the biggest traitor in England. Now he is His Majesty's honoured guest and special entertainments have been laid on for him. He has just been to Deptford for a tour of the *Henri Grace à Dieu*, the pride and joy of the English fleet. Situations change and His Majesty is wise enough to change with them.'

'So the rebels' demands are to be accepted,' I said.

For some moments the king's minister stood watching the royal party making its way towards the river gate. 'If only politics were that simple.' He sighed, then turned to me. 'It grieves me that Robert felt a burden of guilt over Tyndale's end. He knew that Phillips was part of a papist conspiracy. I had hoped that he would be able to gather useful information about those in the plot.'

'I believe he did his best. He befriended Phillips' confidant, Gabriel Donne, and won him over to our side. But, of course, Your Lordship will have heard all this from Donne himself.'

Cromwell looked thoughtful as he returned to the table. 'Indeed. Then it appears we shall never know what troubled Robert so deeply.' The remark was made casually but I had the faint impression that something lay behind it.

'I think it must have been the horror of Tyndale's execution. I've witnessed one burning and never wish to see another.'

'Only one?' Cromwell gave me a faint smile. 'How fortunate you are. I have seen things ... in the Italian wars ... that turned my stomach. But do you know what the worst of it is?'

I shook my head.

'I got used to them.'

There was a knock at the door and Cromwell's secretary entered. 'My Lord, forgive the intrusion.'

'What is it, Robin?' Cromwell asked.

'His Majesty has sent for you, My Lord.'

'Very well, I will be down directly.' Cromwell turned to me. 'I regret we must postpone this conversation till later. Stay in the palace and I will summon you as soon as I can.'

I bowed and turned towards the door.

Cromwell called out, 'One more thing, Thomas.'

'My Lord?'

'Everything that passes between us within these four walls stays within these four walls.'

I walked back through the anteroom in something of a daze. I had arrived with my thoughts well assembled and intelligently linked together. Now I found them disconnected, bumping into each other as they rattled uncontrollably around in my head along with other strange and unwelcome newcomers. I wandered aimlessly through the palace amidst hundreds of servants, guards and courtiers in their extravagant silks and velvets. Occasionally I was greeted by someone I recognised as a customer. I had to pause and exchange pleasantries but all I really wanted to do was find somewhere quiet where I could think. Until now I had been laboriously peeling layers from the onion of my problem. I had thought that I had reached the central truth. Now I saw that there were other, deeper strata still waiting to be uncovered. I was now convinced that the truth about the murder of my friend and all its implications was neatly filed away in the mind of the king's chief minister. Would he reveal it to me? Probably not. Yet if I could ask the right questions ... if I could be mentally ready for my next interview with Cromwell ... Eventually I found myself in the royal chapel. A priest was at the altar saying a mass assisted by two acolytes. I discovered some stone benches along a wall and sat down close to the west door where I would be least distracted by the murmured liturgy. I set myself to look with fresh eyes on the shifting cloudscape of political calculation, dissimulation and deceit.

Exitus acta probat – that was the justification everyone was using for their deeds. England must be saved from heresy, so the bishops could claim to be pursuing a holy cause when they sent desperate rogues like Henry Phillips to lure Tyndale to his death by lies and subterfuge. The translator's 'detestable heresies' must be prevented from circulating throughout the realm, so John Incent could excuse hiring a foreign assassin to gun down Robert Packington. Since the reputation of the ecclesiastical hierarchy must not be sullied, this unlawful action must be covered up. Therefore, Incent felt fully justified in having me silenced. When that failed, who could doubt that it was a pious stratagem to have me discredited by laying false information to the bishop or having brother Hugh make trouble for my friends and servants in Kent?

But what of Cromwell and his political allies? Their commitment was equally self-evident. They were striving to create a new England, one in which private and public life would be governed by the teaching of the Bible. Would they be as unscrupulous as their enemies in pursuing their 'holy' ends? Was Cromwell seeking to manipulate the king? His meteoric rise and the power he now wielded had taken everyone by surprise. Was he using his unassailable position to achieve his vision of the kingdom – *by any means?* Why had the minister saved me from Stokesley's clutches? Only because he thought I could be useful to him. To do what? The more I pondered that question, the more obvious it seemed that something had happened in Antwerp that Robert had been prevented from reporting back; something that might spoil his master's plans.

Then there were the Christian Brothers. They were no less committed to their cause. They claimed to be honest and pure-hearted believers in the written word of God. They risked their money in buying and distributing English Bibles, so that their countrymen could have easy access to the salvation plan set forth in them. Some were prepared to sacrifice their lives in this holy crusade. And yet they flagrantly broke the king's law. They defied the appointed leaders of the Church. They funded and encouraged firebrand preachers who disturbed the peace of the realm. Would they, no less than their enemies, stop at nothing in order to achieve their ends?

Behind all these questions stood the bulky figure of King Henry. He, too, had a vision of a new England but was it the same as Cromwell's? It would be a kingdom without the pope, without many of the monasteries, a land in which the ancient powers of the clergy would be seriously curtailed. But would it be a realm from which corruption and exploitation would be banished? Would his subjects be free to read the Bible in defiance of the bishops? Was he ready to embrace the New Learning or was he merely using Cromwell to achieve his immediate ends? If he could be equally devious and ruthless with men as different as Tyndale and Aske, could anyone guess where his real convictions lay? Suddenly, a picture presented itself unbidden to my mind. A slender woman in grey staring at me intently, almost imploringly, before a blindfold was fastened round her eyes.

I was aware that I was shivering. The stone seat and the icy draughts penetrating the chapel had chilled me to the bone. I needed to move my stiffening joints. Leaving the chapel, I emerged into the main courtyard. Before I had walked more than a few paces, I met up with Augustine again.

'Thomas, where have you been?' he asked almost accusingly. 'I've been looking for you everywhere. What did His Lordship say to you?'

'Not very much,' I replied. 'We were interrupted.'

He pulled a face and it was not difficult to read his thoughts. He suspected that I was keeping things from him. The reason was easy enough to see: he was keeping things from me and he found it difficult to accept that I did not share his own secretive nature. It was time to challenge his frightened reticence; to prise from him secrets that, as I now believed, were the keys to the death of his brother and all the circumstances surrounding it.

'Tell me about Robert's dealings with Gabriel Donne,' I demanded sharply.

'Who? What?' Augustine blustered but could not cover his shock at the question.

'You know very well who I mean. The Donnes are old friends of your family.' This was a guess but I saw from my companion's reaction that it was correct. I pressed home my advantage. 'Robert met up with Gabriel Donne in Louvain when he was on the trail of the hellhound Phillips. I imagine he must have been surprised to see a familiar face there. What more natural than that they should spend time together and exchange news? Your brother later made sure that he took the same ship back to London as Donne. The next time his Antwerp friends saw him, he was deep in melancholy and talking about having failed to save Tyndale. Now, by God's body sacred, tell me, man, what did he and Donne spend their days together discussing and what undermined Robert's spirit?'

Augustine banged his gauntleted gloves together noisily. "Steeth, I'm perishing with this cold.'

'Don't avoid the subject!' I protested.

'Very well, but, in God's name, let's find a fire first.'

We passed through several chambers and eventually chanced upon a small unoccupied annexe close to the main guard room where a pile of logs smouldered unenthusiastically in the grate. Augustine crouched down and made a great show of stoking the fire and blowing on the embers.

'So,' I prompted, 'Robert's conversation with Donne.'

'You'd better ask Donne,' Augustine muttered, staring at the tiny flames twining reluctantly round the wood.

'Donne is conveniently hidden deep in the West Country,' I said.

He shrugged. 'Anyway, who's to say that whatever they talked about has any bearing on Robert's death?'

I grabbed the hood of Augustine's cloak and hauled him to his feet. Turning him around, I thrust my face close to his. 'The only thing that convinces me that it does have a bearing is your reluctance to admit it.'

He shook his head and pushed me away.

'Very well,' I said. 'Let me tell you what I think happened. Donne told Robert who was behind Tyndale's persecution. Robert persuaded the monk to pass the information on to Cromwell, who, for some reason, declined to make full use of it. Robert believed he should have been more persuasive. That was why he blamed himself for Tyndale's eventual fate.'

'Truth is never that simple, Thomas.' Augustine drew his cloak more tightly around him. 'I must be about My Lord's business. The only help I can offer you is to repeat the warning I gave you weeks ago: you are sailing in tempestuous seas; return to harbour while you still can. Leave politics to those who understand it.' He grasped my hand in a brief, tight handshake, then turned and left the room.

I remained there for several minutes, nursing feelings of frustration, anger and despair. Somewhere among all the events and words I had encountered over the last few weeks there was a vital secret, like a vein of gold encased in obscuring layers of centuries-old rock. Robert had known that secret. Cromwell had ardently pursued it. Augustine had been a party to it or had guessed it. And, try as I might, it eluded me. I left to make my way back to Lord Cromwell's quarters. As I approached the antechamber a young page in plain blue livery stepped into my path.

'Master Thomas Treviot?' the boy enquired.

I nodded.

'My master would like to meet you and desires me to bring you to him. He would be honoured if you would join him for dinner.'

'And who is your master?' I asked.

'Sir Harry Seagrave,' he replied.

Chapter 35

I hesitated. The Seagraves had no reason to wish me well but surely they would not attempt any mischief here, in the king's palace.

The messenger had obviously been told to anticipate reluctance on my part, for he now added, 'Sir Harry instructs me to tell you that he wishes only to extend to you the hand of friendship.'

With that assurance, I allowed myself to be led to the courtier's chamber.

It was a smallish room overlooking an internal courtyard, its furnishings simple but of a good quality. Two men were seated by the fire but rose as I entered. The elder was a grey-haired man of about fifty, clad in sombre black but with a doublet chastely embroidered in gold. He stepped forward, smiling and holding out a hand.

'Master Treviot, I am delighted and much relieved that you have accepted my invitation. I had hoped to make your acquaintance earlier but was informed that you were overseas.'

'Yes, I was in the Netherlands, on business for Lord Cromwell.'

'So I understand. You are, indeed, fortunate to enjoy His Lordship's patronage.'

I listened carefully to see if there was an edge of sarcasm in the speaker's voice but could detect none.

Sir Harry continued, 'May I introduce my son, my *only* son, Hugh.'

Young Seagrave was something of a contrast to his father. He was, I estimated, about eighteen or nineteen years of age, tall, athletic of build and bonneted with the same straw-stalk hair as his brother. His court clothes – powder blue, heavily embroidered doublet over blue trunk hose slashed with yellow – suggested exuberance bordering on questionable taste.

'Good day to you, Master Treviot.' Hugh Seagrave's smile was not exactly enthusiastic. He turned to his father. 'I'll have the servants fetch dinner.' He left the room.

Sir Harry motioned me to a seat. 'Pray forgive the boy's manners, Master Treviot,' he said. 'He and Nathaniel were very close.'

'And he blames me for his brother's death?'

'Things appear very simple to the young. 'Tis only with the passing of the years that we can see their complexity. Do you not agree?'

'I think I'm beginning to understand that things are seldom what they seem,' I said. 'For example, your page intimated that your invitation was a gesture of friendship. Would I be altogether wise to accept that assurance?'

Seagrave gave the slightest of smiles. 'I doubt whether I would in your position. That means that I must try all the harder to convince you. My reasons for wanting to talk with you are not entirely altruistic.' He sat back in his padded chair and closed his eyes. ''Tis seven months and eleven days since they dragged Nathaniel's body from the river. Fathers should never have to bury their sons – 'tis against nature. I pray you never have that doleful duty, Master Treviot.'

'I am sincerely sorry for your loss,' I said, 'but Nathaniel's death was none of my doing.'

He waved a hand, as though brushing away a fly. 'What's done is done. Yet my grief, my family's grief, would be easier if we knew *why* it was done. Nathaniel set out one fine spring evening for an assignation with some woman or other – as young men do. Then, he simply disappeared. We had no news of him' – Seagrave dabbed his eyes with a kerchief – ''til some boatmen ... found him five hundred yards below the bridge. Why, Master Treviot, why? Was he so great a sinner that he deserved to appear before God unshriven?' He stared at me appealingly with red-rimmed eyes. 'He sometimes fell in with bad company. That we know. Possibly I had indulged him too much. Perhaps if I had kept him on a tighter rein ... Master Treviot, can you help us to understand? We don't want to know who killed our son. We don't seek revenge. We just want to understand.'

At this point servants bearing silver dishes of food from the palace kitchen appeared and set them out on Seagrave's table. As an attendant on the king, Sir Harry enjoyed bouge of court, the provision of all his meals. Hugh Seagrave rejoined us as we sat to table.

'Master Treviot was about to tell us what he knows of Nathaniel's death,' Sir Harry explained to his son.

'In truth it is very little,' I said. 'I met your son only once . . . at a party.'

'In a Southwark bordel,' Hugh sneered.

'Yes. He had drunk more than was wise. Probably I had, too. If our wits had not been befuddled, we wouldn't have fallen into an argument. It was foolish but it was no more than a brief flare-up. Friends separated us.' I shrugged. 'That's all there was to it. I never saw Nathaniel again.'

'We have been told that you were defending a foulmouthed, treason-spouting harlot,' Hugh said, glaring across the table.

'If you are so well informed you have no need of my testimony.' I tried to remain calm.

Sir Harry was quick to intervene. 'We have, of course, made enquiries elsewhere. There are different accounts of what passed that evening. We are merely trying to tease out the truth.'

'And I have no desire to conceal or distort it,' I said. 'Certainly there was a woman involved and certainly, in the heat of the moment, she made statements that were . . . ill-advised. We all know that women's tongues are apt to get the better of them. A wise man makes allowance for such foolishness. Sadly, on that evening, wisdom had temporarily deserted your son. He reacted violently. His discourtesy annoyed me.'

'And you threatened to kill him!' Hugh shouted.

His father's response was equally abrupt. 'Guard your tongue, sir! Master Treviot is our guest.'

'I take no offence, Sir Harry,' I responded. 'Master Hugh has every right to be angry. In truth, I cannot recall what I said in the heat of the moment but I solemnly swear that I had no part in what happened afterwards. I only learned about it days later.'

'Is it true,' my host asked, 'that you subsequently took the woman in question under your own roof?'

I nodded. 'She had been seriously wounded. She needed care. I felt in some part responsible for her misfortune.'

'And the "care" you offered – did it include revenging her injury?'

'On my oath, Sir Harry, such a thought never occurred to me,' I said.

Hugh muttered something I did not hear but his father said, 'You are an honourable man, Master Treviot. I accept your assurances.'

With a feeling of considerable relief, I thanked him and added, 'I would not have you think that I know nothing of what you feel. A very dear friend of mine was brutally murdered recently. My first reaction was to obtain justice for him but now I am coming to realise that retribution is like a briar. If it is not stopped, it spreads rapidly and takes root over and again.'

Sir Harry sighed deeply. 'You are right. Sometimes I feel that nursing grief is driving me to an early grave. Hugh, the time has come to call a halt. We have learned everything we can. Prayer is now all we can offer for Nathaniel. Let that be sufficient.'

The conversation moved on to pleasanter topics. It seemed that a weight had, indeed, been lifted from the older man's shoulders and he had a fund of interesting stories to tell about life at court.

'Is life very different here with the new queen?' I asked.

Father and son exchanged glances before Sir Harry replied cautiously, 'Queen Jane's greatest advantage is that she is not Queen Anne. She is quiet and submissive. No one could ever have described her predecessor as possessing those qualities.

Anne had a mind of her own and did not hesitate to express it – even to the king. Life around the court was never dull in her day. She was lively and sometimes indiscreet.'

Hugh sniggered. 'You should have heard what she said about her husband's performance in—'

'Hugh! Enough!' Sir Harry struck the table with his palm.

'Did you like Queen Anne, Hugh?' I asked.

'Well enough but her family were insufferable, especially her brother, George Boleyn.'

'What was wrong with him?'

'Always surrounded by preachers and trying to ram his New Learning down other people's throats.'

'Wasn't the queen of the same persuasion?'

'Oh, aye, she was always getting her companions to read holy books. But all that was, of course, in her own private chambers. On the king's side we saw little of it.'

'Yet, despite her piety, she was committing adultery with other men, including her own brother,' I suggested.

Hugh laughed. 'If you believe that—'

Once again his father intervened. 'Master Treviot doesn't want to hear all our court gossip. I have an idea: why don't you take our guest for a ride in the park? His Majesty is hunting this afternoon. You will be able to watch.'

'That's very kind, Sir Harry,' I said, 'but I have to wait upon Lord Cromwell's pleasure.'

'That won't be a problem. I'll have a man in Cromwell's chambers. He will find you as soon as My Lord summons you.'

'Cromwell won't be back in his office for some time,' Hugh said. 'His Majesty sent for him to the hunting field. I saw him leave. I think the king wants him to be present for informal talks with his "special guest".' His lips curled in a sneer.

'You mean Aske?'

'Who else? We all have to dance attendance on the traitor this Christmas. By the mass, it grates with me!'

I needed little persuading. It was important that I should buttress my reconciliation with the Seagraves. Added to that was the fact that the fire and a large dinner were making me drowsy, so the prospect of fresh air out in the deer park was appealing. Then there was also the intriguing possibility of a closer look at the man who had raised half the kingdom in revolt. I thanked Sir Harry for his hospitality and accompanied Hugh to the stables, where I had Golding saddled. Then, with my companion, I rode away from the bustle and noise of the palace.

For half a mile or so we jogged along beside the river. It was a bright, crisp, clear afternoon, the air so sharp that it made my throat tingle. Golding was also enjoying the outing. His ears twitched and he looked around him in apparent curiosity. Since Hugh was obviously less inhibited than his father about sharing court gossip, this seemed a good opportunity to discover more about the workings and personnel of the royal household.

'Have the Seagraves been longtime attenders on His Majesty?' I asked.

The young man was happy to boast. 'My father has been at court as long as I remember – some fifteen years, or so. He is a great favourite with the king ... especially at the gaming table. 'Tis only a matter of time before he is raised to the Council.'

'Even so?'

'Oh yes. He is very close to the Duke of Norfolk, who relies on him for news when he is away on campaign.'

'That must have been very valuable to His Grace in the last few weeks,' I suggested. 'I gather he has had a difficult task facing the large rebel host with only a much smaller armed force. Tell me, how much truth is there in the rumour that the duke has sympathy with the Pilgrimage of Grace?'

Hugh bristled. 'That's a calumny put about by the Cromwell crowd. You had best not give ear to it, Master Treviot. It springs from jealousy.'

'Jealousy?'

'Oh yes. The jealousy of a Putney brewer's son for the first lord of the realm.' The thin ice of Hugh's discretion was melting rapidly.

'Cromwell's strange and swift rise must be resented by the king's traditional councillors,' I mused. 'How do you think it can be explained?'

Hugh scoffed. 'That's easy. He promises to give His Majesty whatever His Majesty wants.'

'I thought that was what all royal councillors did, but, then, I know little of politics.'

Hugh took obvious pleasure in enlightening me. 'It isn't always possible. For example, when His Majesty sent the duke north to meet the rebels, he demanded a military victory. His Grace had hell's own job explaining that he would have to negotiate in order to get the traitors to disperse. The king was furious for two or three days. We all kept out of the way as much as possible. Eventually His Majesty realised that My Lord Norfolk was right.'

'I see. A councillor's job is obviously not an easy one.'

'Not with this king. The old cardinal discovered that right enough.'

'Wolsey?'

'Yes. Remember how powerful he was? Cock of the roost for a dozen years or more. And all by giving the king what he wanted – new ships, more taxes, military victories and so on.

Then the king said he wanted rid of his wife. Wolsey couldn't arrange it, so farewell cardinal.'

'Still, Cromwell seems to be doing very well at the moment. There must be thousands pouring into the treasury from the confiscated abbeys.'

'And when that source dries up and still the king wants more, what then? Master Cromwell ... Oh sorry, I should say My Lord Cromwell.' He sneered. 'He may look all powerful at the moment but eventually he will overreach himself. Then the king will see the wisdom of putting his faith in the great nobles and not in upstarts. Take my advice, Master Treviot, don't get too close to Cromwell.'

By this time we had turned away from the river and were riding deeper into the thickening woodland. We could hear the cries of hounds and the shouts of beaters away to our left. Rounding a bend in the track, we came to the edge of a large clearing. At a signal from Hugh I reined in Golding and looked across the open ground. It was ringed by royal guards. Opposite us was an enclosure marked out by flags. King Henry was seated within it, with Robert Aske at his right side, Cromwell at his left and a handful of other favoured royal companions.

I was puzzled at the sight. 'Does the king not hunt today?' I asked.

'Not this last year,' Seagrave replied, in a confidential whisper, enjoying airing his superior knowledge. 'He had a bad tiltyard accident – fell from his horse and the beast rolled over him. For several hours his physicians feared the worst.'

'I heard nothing of this,' I said.

'It was kept very quiet. He recovered ... after a fashion.'

'What does that mean?'

'Simply that he is not the man he was. And the court is not

the court it was. Few dances and maskings now. The king is troubled in his legs and moves about with difficulty. And he has had to give up his love of hunting. It irks him sore and when the king is irked ... well, let us just say he becomes difficult to serve.'

I stared across at the thickset figure opposite, talking jovially with his north-country guest and found it difficult to identify this ebullient figure with the melancholy sufferer described by my companion. Another thought that troubled me was why Hugh Seagrave was sharing with me information that must certainly be confidential. If the king really was a sick man and troubled in mind, he would not want it known and that would mean that if Hugh's indiscretion was detected he would be in serious trouble.

Suddenly a signal horn rang out away to our left. I saw the king raise a crossbow to his shoulder. Behind him and a little to one side one of his attendants also lifted his weapon. With a crash and a hullabaloo from the pursuing horsemen, a fine full-antlered stag burst through the undergrowth. I heard, rather than saw the crossbow bolts zing towards it. The animal's headlong flight carried him several more yards before his front legs buckled and he skidded into the ground, antlers tearing up the ferns. Immediately the watchers broke into loud applause and the king received their congratulations (though which bolt had struck the fatal blow, I cannot say).

As I watched I saw Cromwell lean across and say something to the king. Henry nodded. The minister rose and called for his horse. I pointed this out to my companion. 'We should get back to the palace,' I said.

He nodded. 'I know a short way. Follow me.'

We very quickly found ourselves in the thickest part of the woodland and on a narrow track that only allowed us to go in single file. After about fifteen minutes I saw Hugh rein in his horse with an oath and leap from the saddle. He stooped to examine his mount's near foreleg.

He looked up with a rueful expression. 'Sorry about this. Wretched creature's gone lame. You'd better ride on. I'll only hold you up. It's not far. This track will take you all the way.'

He drew his horse to the side to let me pass. 'Be sure to call in on us before you leave the palace,' he said cheerily as I rode forward.

I jogged on along a path that seemed to become narrower, with several overhanging branches beneath which I had to duck. It was after I had negotiated one of these obstacles and turned a sharp right-angled bend that I found my way barred by a man in a brown cloak, standing ten yards away and pointing a handgun at me.

Chapter 36

Startled, I brought Golding to an abrupt, protesting halt.

I was now no more than five paces from my assailant, a short, stocky man with a swarthy face. He was grinning at me along the short barrel of what I instantly knew was a wheel-lock pistol.

'Master Thomas Treviot,' the man said and his accent left me in no doubt whatsoever about his identity. 'I regret this, sincerely I do. But, unfortunately, you have enemies who wish me to do this. So, I must bid you farewell.' He took a careful sighting along the barrel but at this range he could not possibly miss. I had no space in which to turn my horse. The location for my assassination had been chosen carefully. If I cried out there would be no one to hear me. Escape was impossible. I was seconds from death. I mumbled the only thing I could think of.

'Look, however much you're being paid ...'

The man merely grinned, displaying a row of blackened teeth. 'Do not try the bribe, Master Treviot. I have my professional reputation to consider.'

Ned's words came back to me, his plea that I should not share Robert's fate. That was precisely what I was about to do. Why, oh why, had I not listened?

'You don't need to do this!' I called out. 'You have no grudge against me.'

'There is nothing personal about it,' he replied. 'I am a mere agent. If you have made enemies ...' He shrugged. I realised that he was savouring the moment.

Suddenly – miraculously almost – that realisation cut through my panic; allowed me to think. There was no one in these dense, silent woods who could come to my aid. Il Ombra knew this as well as I. He had no need to hurry. He had plenty of time to do a clean professional job. Could I, perhaps, play on his self-confidence ... make him relax, just slightly. 'Please, oh please, spare me,' I whined.

The Italian shook his head. '*Impossibile.*'

'Then, in God's name, give me a moment or two for prayer,' I implored with a show of trembling helplessness.

'Very well.' He nodded and lowered his pistol slightly.

That was my chance. I leaned forward, pulled on the rein and tapped Golding's flanks with my heels. 'Stand,' I whispered.

Immediately, the grey reared up, his front hooves thrashing air. The Italian staggered back, raising his hands defensively to cover his head. The pistol flew from his grasp, discharged with a bang as it hit the ground and lay hidden among the ferns. Il Ombra turned, looking for a path through the dense undergrowth. I did not wait for him to find one. I urged Golding forward, straight at the assassin. He fled along the track, his only means of escape. Within yards I ran him down. He flung himself among the ferns to his left. I leaped from the saddle and was on him instantly. We rolled around on the ground. He grasped my throat. I pummelled his face with my fists. My assailant was strong and lithe. He slipped from my grasp and staggered to his knees. I grabbed his legs and brought him down again. Now the fight began in earnest. My foe clawed with hands, struck out with booted feet and, when he could get close enough, tried to bite with his stained teeth. My responses were equally savage. Physically we were well matched but I had the advantage of unbridled fury. Weeks of grief and rage at what this man had done to my friend at last found their outlet. Anger at what I and others had suffered gave added puissance to my muscles. Slowly I felt my enemy weaken. He groaned. He shouted. He implored me, in his own language and in bastard English, to stop. His entreaties had the opposite effect. I pounded his face, my gauntlets tearing into his flesh. When eventually he lay silent I went on hitting him. Then I jumped up and aimed kick after kick at his inert body. Had I not been interrupted, I would certainly have killed the man but now I became aware of rapid hoofbeats and shouts.

I was surrounded by three of the king's guards, all with drawn swords.

'What's all this?' the captain demanded.

Struggling for breath, I tried to reply. 'This fellow ... tried to kill me ... You'll find his pistol ... over there, somewhere.' I pointed to the ferns and brambles where it had fallen. Then I sank to the ground, trembling all over.

The soldiers dismounted. One went in search of Il Ombra's weapon while another examined the prostrate Italian. 'He's breathing,' was the verdict, 'but only just.'

'Both of you have some explaining to do,' the captain said. 'Making affray in the purlieus of His Majesty's house is a capital offence.'

His subordinate returned from among the bushes and handed over the gun.

'Mother of God!' the captain exclaimed. 'What's this?'

'A wheellock pistol,' I gasped.

'I've heard of these,' he said, 'but I've never seen one.' He cast a professional appraising eye over the weapon. 'No one is allowed to carry firearms in the court except His Majesty's guard. To do so is treason. You say it was brought here by this fellow?'

I nodded.

'And how do I know it's not yours?' he asked.

'You could see which one of us is carrying powder and shot,' I suggested.

He gave the order and the Italian and I were searched. From a pouch still slung round Il Ombra's neck one of the soldiers produced a powder horn and a handful of lead pellets.

'Right,' said the captain, 'I'm not going to sort all this out. I'm taking you to the guard room.'

'Of course,' I said, getting painfully to my feet. 'But you should know that I was on my way to an appointment with Lord Cromwell. This rogue was determined to stop me. It might be in your interest to inform His Lordship that you have taken me into custody.'

We made our way back to the palace. The captain led, followed by Il Ombra slung over one of the horses, then me on Golding and the other king's men, one on foot. We were taken straight to the guard room where I was placed for safe keeping in the captain's own quarters. The Italian was laid on a pallet in one of the cells and a physician was called to examine him. I was glad to lie down on the truckle bed and ease my sore, pummelled body. I was bruised and aching all over and my limbs trembled uncontrollably. It was some time before I was able to think clearly about the afternoon's events. Then I remembered Ned's warning about Hugh Seagrave. He had been right. Nathaniel's brother had plotted my death and, despite his father's supposed falling out with Doggett, had managed to secure the service of Il Ombra. Did that mean that he had also been responsible for the attack at Hampstead? Had I been wrong to blame John Incent? I was still exploring these disjointed thoughts when I fell into an exhausted sleep.

I was woken by one of the king's guard. 'Up you get,' he said. 'Lord Cromwell has sent for you.'

'Gone six of the clock,' the man replied. 'You'd better smarten up.' He indicated a towel and a bowl of water on the table.

I looked at my image in a small square of polished tin hanging beside the door. My face was streaked with blood and grime and fronds of grass still stuck to my hair. I cleaned myself as best as I could and brushed most of the dirt from my clothes. When I asked for my bonnet the soldier shrugged and shook his head. I realised I must have lost it in the fight. When I had done the best I could to make myself presentable, I signalled my guardian that I was ready to be escorted to Master Secretary's quarters. Many were the curious looks I attracted as I was marched through the palace but when we reached Cromwell's antechamber the room was empty apart from the halberdier standing guard. After a word from my escort the inner door was opened for me.

Cromwell was standing before the fire, reading a book by the light of a lamp hanging from a high bracket. He set the volume aside as I made my obeisance. 'Thomas, Thomas,

Thomas, you seem to have a positive genius for getting into trouble,' he said, seating himself and motioning me to a chair on the other side of the hearth.

''Twas none of my doing,' I protested. 'The villainous Seagraves—'

'Yes, yes,' he interrupted. 'We'll come to that in a moment. First, I want to continue our earlier discussion. We were talking about Gabriel Donne. Have you met him?'

'No.'

'Are you familiar with the family?'

'I know his father and uncle by sight. They are leading members of the Grocers' Company but I have never had any dealings with them.'

'Very well and there's nothing more you can tell me about Robert's last trip to the Netherlands?'

I considered the question carefully before replying. 'No, My Lord. I believe he carried out his commission faithfully and was bitterly disappointed that it did not succeed in achieving Tyndale's release. If there was any other reason for his murder perhaps you will discover it by interrogating Il Ombra.'

Cromwell's eyebrows rose slightly at mention of the name. 'Are you sure about the identity of this assailant? How is that?'

'After my conversation with Doggett, it was not very difficult to recognise the man employed by the Seagraves in their trap. A foreigner, expert in the very latest firearm technology – it had to be Il Ombra.'

'Then your quest is ended,' Cromwell observed quietly.

'Almost, My Lord. Only two things now remain.'

'And they are?'

'To see justice done upon the assassin and to have his paymasters unmasked.'

Cromwell tapped his nose thoughtfully with the small book

he was carrying. 'As to the first, I can satisfy you immediately: Il Ombra is dead.'

I was stunned by the news. 'Dead? But his injuries did not seem ... I was sure I had not killed him ... Does this mean I'm to be charged ...'

He looked at me with a quizzical, cynical smile. 'You? Charged? What with?' The smile vanished to be replaced by a concentrated stare. 'Whatever occurred here this afternoon did not involve you.'

My obvious bewilderment must have appeared comical, for Cromwell laughed. 'Let me describe to you the unfortunate incident that occurred at Greenwich on the Feast of St Stephen in this year of our Lord, 1536. Princes, as you know, always have to be on their guard against assassination attempts. Regrettably, there are always madmen, fanatics and agents of foreign powers whose twisted thinking convinces them that the violent removal of a head of state will make the world a better place. Our gracious sovereign lord is no less a potential target than other kings and, like other kings, takes careful precautions for the safety of his person, especially in these troubled days. The palace grounds here are kept under constant surveillance by royal guards. This afternoon such a patrol came upon an armed desperado, skulking in the woods not far from where His Majesty was hunting. When challenged, this villain discharged his firearm at the king's men. There was a struggle in which the evil interloper was killed. The king was saved. The executioner was spared a job. All in all, a satisfactory outcome, would you not agree?'

I sat back with a gasp. 'This is what the king believes?'

'This is what the king wishes to believe and it is, therefore, true. Were the story any more complicated it might give rise to speculation, and, in politics, speculation should whenever

343

possible be avoided. Such incidents as this have to be dealt with swiftly and decisively. Then no awkward questions can be asked.'

I felt ... well, truly, I know not what I felt – outrage, relief, disappointment, distaste. I could only stare gloomily into the fire. 'Doubtless, that story will please the Seagraves,' I muttered.

'Ah, the Seagraves.' Cromwell nodded. 'I suppose you would like to see them dragged into the law courts and made to pay for their murderous attempts on your life.'

'I would like to see justice done, My Lord. I am a simple man and I hold to the simple man's conviction that law and justice bind a kingdom together. Without them ...' I shrugged.

'Without them,' Cromwell said, in a matter-of-fact voice, 'we have politics. It may not be as stout a cord as law and justice but when it is all we have, we would be wrong not to use it. Take the Seagraves, for example. A trial would have brought numerous facts to light that many people, perhaps including yourself but certainly including the king, would prefer to keep hidden. As it is, Sir Harry and his brainless son are now tight fastened by political shackles. They know that I have information against them that I can use at any time. Should they ever behave in a way harmful to His Majesty and the realm my sword of Damocles will fall.'

'They are close to the Duke of Norfolk, are they not?'

Cromwell looked up sharply. 'Why do you say so?'

'The brainless son boasted of it this afternoon and told me many things because he was sure I would not live to repeat his indiscretions.'

'What sort of things?'

'He warned me not to become too closely involved with

Your Lordship. He hinted that one day you would fall and that then the duke and his supporters would take control.'

Cromwell laughed. 'Aye, and whisk the country back to the baronial wars of the last century, when he and his kind wrestled for the crown. Well, we must make sure that doesn't happen, mustn't we?'

'He also said the king was ill and becoming difficult to serve.'

The minister avoided the subject. 'You will have no more difficulty with the Seagraves. I can promise you that,' he said.

''Tis strange,' I mused, 'that the Seagraves and John Incent both employed the same killer.'

'Not really,' Cromwell replied. 'You know, don't you, that they are related?'

'No.'

'They are of old Suffolk families. Sir Harry's brother is married to the eldest Incent girl. Together they all make up as nice a brood of papists as you could ever wish not to find.'

'And unscrupulous. Defending their doctrine excuses any evil, any crime. Is there a good reason, My Lord, why we should not proceed against John Incent for Robert's murder?'

'Absence of proof,' Cromwell declared quickly. 'Without Il Ombra there is no one who knows who paid for the murder.'

'There is one man who does know. I'm sure of it. His name is John Doggett.'

Cromwell laughed aloud. 'You've come across that scoundrel! You must know he'd be little help to us. If you could get him into a court of law – which is extremely unlikely – no sane jury would believe a word he said.'

'But could you not put pressure on him?' I asked.

'Oh, yes,' he replied, 'if I did not have a thousand and one other things to do.' He stood up. 'Thomas, be content. You have found Robert's killer and he has paid for his crime. You are beyond the reach of your own enemies. For tonight, lodging has been arranged in the palace. The guard who brought you here will escort you. In the morning, go back to your trade. Make a success of it. Be a credit to your father and to the Honourable Goldsmiths' Company. And may God prosper you.'

With those words I was dismissed. They were sensible words. There was no one who cared for me or had my interest at heart who would not have heartily endorsed Cromwell's sage advice.

So why was I unwilling to take it?

Chapter 37

'By all the saints, Thomas, what have you been doing now?'
Ned Longbourne was genuinely shocked when he called on
me the next day. Everyone was – and with good reason. My
face was badly bruised and one eye half closed. I walked with
a limp and a pain in my chest made me wince whenever I took
a deep breath or coughed. I was still resting on my bed when
Ned arrived. I got up, hobbled to the table and poured out two
tankards of ale. Then I reported briefly on the events at
Greenwich while Ned listened in wide-eyed wonder.

'God in heaven and all the saints be praised that Il Ombra
is dead, and at the king's order,' he said. 'I trust we shall see his
carcase in chains at Tyburn with a placard of his sins hung
round his neck.'

'I fear not. His activities and his very existence are to be
kept secret.'

'But why?'

'Cromwell's strict instructions. The armed assassin was captured in the palace grounds. If that news leaks out, it could cause general panic and also encourage the king's enemies. I shouldn't be telling you but I know you will let it go no further.'

Ned nodded and stroked his beard. This was now of collar length and streaked with grey. 'Was he interrogated? Did Master Secretary's torture specialists extract details of his crimes?'

'I don't know. If they did, the information is not for general circulation.'

Ned took a long draught of ale and set down the pot with a sigh. 'So you are no nearer discovering the identity of his paymaster.'

'Oh, I know who he was working for.' I took Ned through the process of deduction that had led me to the inescapable conclusion that John Incent was one of the prime movers of a campaign to stamp out supporters of Tyndale. 'Robert had unearthed important information about this plot,' I explained. 'That was why he had to be silenced. Then, when I began to investigate Robert's death, it became necessary to dispose of me too. Incent knew that his firebrand nephew Hugh Seagrave was also after my blood so it was easy for him to get that halfwit to lay in wait for me with his arquebus out on the heath.'

Ned listened carefully. 'You may be right,' he said. 'Probably you are. But it's all speculation, isn't it? You have no proof; nothing that would persuade a magistrate to open proceedings against Incent and his co-conspirators.'

'Very true. His Lordship made the same point. There are only two men who, I think, might be able to provide useful information. One is Doggett. The other is Gabriel Donne, abbot of a monastery in Devon. Lord Cromwell doesn't want me to approach them. In fact, he has ordered me to abandon my enquiries.'

Ned shrugged. 'Then that is what you must do, and I, for one, am not sorry for it.'

'Poor Ned,' I said. 'I've caused you much anguish over the last few weeks. You gave me your support even when you thought I was quite mad. I'm truly grateful. You are right, of course. Now is the time to call off the chase and return horses and hounds to the stable. But ...'

'But?'

'I just hate to see these fanatics go unchecked. To murder someone like Robert, simply for wanting to read a book ...'

'A book that might challenge the instigator's authority and the authority of all priests.'

'But how can the Bible and the priests be at enmity?' I demanded. 'And, if they are, which should we trust?'

'Now you're speaking like a Lutheran,' Ned said solemnly.

'I know very little about Luther but sometimes I wonder—'

Ned interrupted firmly. 'Then, I bid you keep your dangerous wonderings to yourself, Thomas.'

On 1 January I had a visit from Ben and Sarah. They looked radiantly happy and, though I could guess the reason, I allowed them to tell me how they had been reconciled to Sarah's parents and had moved back to the family home in Candlewick Street. They brought Bart with them but he said little and after a few minutes asked if he might seek out Lizzie.

As the door closed behind him, Sarah giggled. 'He's talked about no one else since we were last here. He wanted to know where she comes from, whether she's been married, all sorts of things. Now he's come bearing a New Year gift.'

349

'Does he know about her former life?' I asked. 'I wouldn't want him to find out by accident.'

'Oh, yes,' Ben replied. 'I made sure.'

Sarah added, 'He must like her for what she is, not what she was.'

'Well,' I said, 'if anything comes of it, Lizzie might be very good for him. He needs someone with a firm hand and I can vouch for the fact that she certainly has that.'

At the Sign of the Swan we celebrated Twelfth Night in style. I owed it to the whole household to signal that we had put behind us the anxieties and troubles of recent weeks. We filled the house with families and friends. All the lamps were lit and the walls hung with branches of holly and bay. The scene was set for a night of riotous festivity. The tables were piled high with food, a hogshead was kept replenished with hot wassail and the kitchen produced the biggest king cake I have ever seen. The workshop benches were cleared to the sides of the room to make space for musicians, dancing and performances by mummers hired for the occasion.

It was customary that a gold half-crown should be concealed within the cake and that whoever found it would be leader of the revels. On this occasion I cheated and ensured that Lizzie discovered the coin. She was by now very popular in the household and her nomination as revel queen was enthusiastically received. Many were the suggestive shouts, whoops and whistles when she nominated Bart as her consort. Together they presided over the night's events with bawdy good humour and the party ran on well into the early morning.

Three days later I called on Margaret Packington. A servant bade me wait below while his mistress was concluding a meeting with other members of her household. When I was shown up to her chamber, I saw a number of chairs circled round a table.

'We were having our prayers,' Margaret explained, as she rose to greet me. 'Robert always conducted them when he was home. I do my poor best to keep up the tradition, though I'm not as learned as Robert. But then, everything we need is in here, isn't it?' She pointed to the open book on the table – Tyndale's Testament.

'Should you not be more cautious about reading that?' I asked.

Margaret squared her shoulders and looked at me with unblinking eyes. I realised that something about her had changed. Her demeanour was more confident, even defiant. 'When Robert was here,' she said, 'I did sometimes worry that Stokesley's men might come a-raiding. But then I told myself that he and his crew would not dare make trouble for Robert. I see, now, that I was hiding behind my husband's reputation. Well, no longer. We have just been reading what is written here in Second Timothy.' She picked up the book and recited, '"I am not ashamed. For I know whom I have believed, and am sure that he is able to keep that which I have committed to his keeping." If the bishop wants to send someone to shoot me or drag me off to one of his Smithfield bonfires, so be it. He will be doing me a great service to reunite me with dear Robert.'

I could not find an appropriate response and, after a brief silence, Margaret continued brightly, 'So, Thomas, sit down and tell me what you have discovered. The last I heard was that you had been to Antwerp. Thomas Poyntz came to see me before Christmas – poor man – and told me that you had been busy over there.'

'How is Master Poyntz?' I asked. 'I thought he was staying longer in Antwerp.'

351

'He is in wretched case.' Margaret seated herself opposite. 'The Emperor's people made so much trouble for him that he had to leave the English House in great haste. His wife and children remain over there and are safe but he is staying with his brother in Essex. He cannot continue his business and is like to be utterly ruined. Thus does 'Stoker' Stokesley make honest Englishmen fugitives in their own country. Oh, the wickedness of these papists!'

At that moment, a maid appeared bearing a tray on which stood a jug and two glasses. She placed it on the table and departed silently.

Margaret poured out a deep yellow liquid. 'Escobar,' she said. 'My physician prescribes it as a remedy for melancholy and the damp humours. Unlike most of the concoctions he brings me, it is quite palatable.'

I sipped the sweet cordial. 'Very pleasant – as is the news I bring. Robert's murderer is dead.' I reported Il Ombra's detention and despatch, omitting any data that might be considered politically sensitive.

My hostess nodded solemnly. 'And you have sufficient evidence against Stokesley as the instigator of the assassination?'

'He was not the perpetrator,' I explained. 'The man who had a vendetta against Robert and, later, against me was John Incent, a member of the cathedral chapter.'

'Hoh!' Margaret uttered a scoffing laugh. 'That haughty lewdster with hair the colour of hellfire! I know him well. He is a sworn enemy of Bible people. He came here once – it must have been six months since – complaining about a speech Robert made in the parliament house. He said Robert should have more respect for the clergy. It will be good to see him brought to book.'

I was struggling to find words to explain, as gently as possible, that this was not going to happen, when the arrival of a new guest was announced. Moments later William Locke bustled into the room. He and Margaret greeted each other warmly and for several minutes we exchanged small talk. Locke had laid aside his cloak, revealing an exquisite doublet of dove grey, embroidered with black and silver thread. Now he unfastened the large purse attached to his belt and drew out a thick pamphlet whose pages were crisp and uncurled. 'I am delighted to find you here, Master Treviot. I brought this along to show Mistress Packington but it will interest you, too.'

He laid the document on the table and pulled up a chair. I stared down at the blank cover. No title. No author's name.

'Printed in Antwerp,' Locke explained, 'and arrived in London two days since. I bought it from a bookstand in Paul's Yard and straightway read it, cover to cover. When I went back this morning the stallholder told me his stock was all gone and he'd sent for more. "'Tis the talk of the City," he said, and I well believe it.'

'So, what is it?' I asked.

''Tis about the Hunne case,' Locke replied. 'You were a child when it occurred and may not have heard of it, but it caused much commotion at the time.'

'Indeed, I do know of it,' I said. 'In fact, I had the privilege of experiencing Master Hunne's accommodation in the Lollards' Tower. But this is an old story. Why should people be interested in it now?'

Locke smiled knowingly, excitement showing on his usually grave face. 'Now is precisely the time to publish a full account of that appalling affair. All London is talking about poor Robert's death – and we all know who encompassed that. Then there is the burning of Master Tyndale. People are still outraged about the sordid doing to death of a fine English scholar. Now, with the collapse of the papist rebellion in the North, the truth can finally come to light on all these things. Also, good news comes from the court—'

'Then the pilgrimage is definitely over?' Margaret interrupted.

'As good as,' Locke replied. 'When the king had the arch-traitor Aske to court and made much of him, the other leaders in the North felt themselves betrayed. The latest information is that the one-eyed lawyer has been shunned by former supporters and that his movement is falling apart in mutual recriminations. But, as I was saying,' he hurried on, 'good news comes from court. Cromwell, at the king's command, is to preside over a grand council or synod of clergy *and* laymen to debate the great doctrines of our faith. The bishops will be called to justify all their traditions from Holy Scripture.'

'All this is interesting,' I said, 'but how does it help us?'

'Don't you see?' Locke looked at me impatiently. 'It all affects the mood of the City. Now, though he might wish it otherwise, the king cannot afford to ignore London. He can threaten and dissimulate with the barbarous northern rabble but he dare not antagonise his capital. This' – Locke prodded the pamphlet – 'will inflame the populace and force His Majesty to expose the plot against Robert. Twenty-two years ago, a leading London merchant was brutally murdered in the Lollards' Tower. Why? Because he challenged the power of the clergy and because he put his trust in English translations of the Bible. Today we have another leading member of our mercantile community assassinated *for the very same reasons*. Anyone would have to be totally beside his wits not to make the connection. After the Hunne case the complicity of the Bishop of London and his cohorts was hushed up, largely because the king did not want to antagonise the clergy. This pamphlet explains how the truth was suppressed and prints documents of the time that were concealed. It will infuriate people. The clergy will not find the king so compliant now, especially after the support some of them have expressed for the rebels.'

'What exactly did happen to Master Hunne?' Margaret asked. 'I've often wondered.'

Locke picked up the pamphlet. ''Tis all here, in great detail – an appalling indictment of the lengths churchmen will go to to protect their own kind. It shows exactly how the bishop's chancellor, William Horsey, plotted brutal murder. Thomas, this will help you to expose the truth about Robert's death.'

Margaret shared his enthusiasm. 'Perhaps the tide is really turning at last, William. Thomas here has worked so hard in our cause and, as a result, the villain who shot Robert has paid for it with his life. I ought to say, "God rest his soul" but, in truth, I cannot. Now, it only remains to expose the ones who lay behind this crime and, as you say, the papists will not escape punishment this time.'

After that, how could I tell Margaret that my interest in her husband's death was at an end? For Locke's benefit I went over again my censored account of events at Greenwich. The three of us talked until the great clock of St Paul's struck eleven and the mercer scurried away to a business appointment. Before he said his goodbyes, he urged me to borrow the pamphlet. 'It will give you a better idea of what these papist fanatics are capable of,' he said.

That night I retired to my chamber to read the lamentable account of Richard Hunne's last days. Whoever had compiled this record had had access to official documents, hitherto 'lost' or suppressed, and had set them out clearly with a commentary that revealed the full details of his conflict with church authorities and the horror of the revenge taken by those authorities. As I read, my thoughts went back to that small, bleak oppressive chamber in the Lollards' Tower where I had spent dismal hours looking up at the hook from which that earlier occupant had been suspended. I identified with the poor man's fate. It both repelled and fascinated me.

Hunne's difficulties had begun in 1511 in a disagreement with his parish priest over a payment for professional services. The vicar took his stand on ecclesiastical law and Hunne countered with an appeal to civil law. Neither side would give way and the priest took the case to higher authority. The clergy closed ranks in support of their colleague and Hunne found himself facing a charge of heresy. He responded by bringing a civil case for slander against his accusers. It was to pre-empt this action that the bishop's officers struck first and had Hunne thrown into the Lollards' Tower, in October 1514. The whole City was now up in arms and waiting for Hunne's civil action to come to court. There was only one escape route for his enemies – the 'heretic' must die. They concocted a plot and carried it out one night in December 1514. The coroner's report set out all the vile details: the original plan was to make it appear that the prisoner had died from natural causes. They locked Hunne in the stocks in his cell while they made a last-minute attempt to persuade him to drop the charges. When this failed they dumped him on his bed with his arms bound behind him. There he stayed till past midnight, when William Horsey entered the cell, accompanied by John Spalding, a jailer, and Charles Joseph, a member of the bishop's staff. They lost no time in setting about their grizzly task.

356

Joseph heated a long needle in a candle flame. While the others held their victim down, he thrust this up Hunne's nose, aiming to pierce the brain and, thus, cause death without leaving any marks on the body. All this achieved was a massive effusion of blood, which stained Hunne's shirt and Horsey's jerkin. The prisoner was now screaming and writhing in agony, half on and half off the bed. The murderers panicked. They grabbed Hunne in an effort to silence him. They silenced him well enough: in the fracas they broke his neck.

Now they had to make the best of a bad job. That meant arranging a fake hanging. They cleaned the body and put a fresh shirt on it. Then they removed Hunne's sash, formed a noose for his neck, hoisted him up and tied the other end of their makeshift rope to the hook in the wall. They tidied up the cell as best they could but were so anxious to get away that they bungled the job badly. The stool the suicide was supposed to have used was placed upon the bed. His bloodstained coat was left lying in a dark corner. There was more blood on the floor. And in their zeal to make everything appear as normal as possible, the criminals carefully extinguished the candle that Hunne would have had to have used in order to fix the rope to hang himself. The coroner's jury could not fail to draw from all the evidence that Richard Hunne had been murdered.

While a search was instigated for the culprits, news of the atrocity gripped the capital. There were demonstrations of citizens, calling for justice against the clergy. The bishop and his accomplices were now so deeply mired that they could only press on in defiance of the evidence and the court proceedings. At a hastily convened tribunal, Hunne was posthumously declared a heretic, his body was duly burned and his goods confiscated, thus reducing his wife and children to penury.

It was late by the time I finished reading. I fell, fully clothed, upon my bed and extinguished the candle. My mind was still in a whirl. That was when the nightmares began.

Chapter 38

The dreams that invaded my sleep over the next few nights became so persistent that I scarcely dared close my eyes. The details varied but the main elements were constant. I was lying on the bed in the Lollards' cell, unable to move or cry out. Hideous, distorted faces leered down at me. They were chanting, chanting, chanting and my silent screams could not drown their monotonous, tuneless formula: *exitus acta probat, exitus acta probat, exitus acta probat!*

For two or three days I wrestled with a pressing, unwanted inevitability. An accusing conscience insisted that, whatever well-meaning friends might advise, whatever Lord Cromwell might order, whatever dangers might threaten, that which I had begun I had to finish. God in heaven knows I tried to stop my ears to that nagging inner voice. I immersed myself in work. I refused to think about murderers and heretics and

Bibles and when such subjects thrust their way into my mind I told myself that I had already done more than enough to avenge my friend.

Pragmatism would probably have won out in the end had it not come under attack, not only from my conscience but also from a very pronounced change of mood in the City. Locke was right. The anonymous pamphlet had stirred up virulent anti-clericalism. There was always an undercurrent of ill-feeling towards the senior clergy among the mercantile community but now the hostility was almost tangible. In every tavern, alehouse and marketplace, people were talking about the fresh revelations concerning the old Hunne case. Even Cromwell benefited from the change of attitude. People who had grumbled about the New Learning and its impact on their traditional activities now applauded the minister's initiative in bringing the overmighty ecclesiastical establishment to heel. Robert's murder offered proof that the arrogant and power-hungry senior clergy had not changed in the twenty or so years since they had done to death another respected London merchant. Thus it was that the conviction grew that I could not remain inactive; that I had a public duty to expose the crimes of the Incents and their accomplices. Perhaps I was being called to play a significant role in bringing about real reform.

As I brooded on this I could see only one way to achieve my objective. There was no one from whom I could obtain fresh evidence. The Seagraves might know something but if I approached them Cromwell would undoubtedly hear of it and exercise a firm veto. Doggett undoubtedly possessed the information I desired but I could see no way to obtain his cooperation. If Incent was to be delivered up to the magistrate, it would have to be with the support of his own confession.

Slowly I put together a plan – admittedly desperate – to obtain his signature to such a document.

While I was still pondering this initiative, a messenger called with an unexpected letter. It read:

> Master Treviot, be assured of my right hearty
> commendations.
> Please be advertised that I have today had the pleasure to
> call upon Mistress Packington. Being in Westminster for
> the great council summoned by His Majesty's Vicegerent
> in Spirituals, I took the opportunity to visit the lady in
> hope to bring her some comfort after the tragic loss of her
> husband. She received me graciously and was, I think,
> somewhat solaced by memories I shared with her of that
> fine gentleman. It was the lady's wish that I might call
> upon you and impart to you my recollections of
> conversations between Master Packington and myself as
> we came together from Antwerp into England and of our
> subsequent correspondence. These presents are to desire
> you to agree your conformity and goodwill thereunto.
> I pray you, Master Treviot, indicate by the present
> bearer if it might please you to give me welcome, as I
> trust it shall.
> Fare you well and the Holy Trinity have you in safe
> keeping.
> Gabriel Donne †
> From Westminster, this thirteenth day of January, 1536*

I sent word back inviting Donne to dine the following day. I also despatched a letter to Ned, asking him to join us. He

* The civil calendar reckoned the new year from 25 March.

would, I thought, enjoy meeting a fellow monastic and he might be able to help me understand Abbot Donne's point of view.

The kitchens were pressed to provide a good table for my honoured guest. As it was a Friday and, therefore, a fast day, I had my cook scour the stalls in Fishmongers' Row. The result was that I was able to set before my visitors oysters, stuffed trout, pike in a pastry crust and a supply of my best Rhenish. Ned, always a stickler for punctuality, arrived just as Paul's clock was striking noon but he was soon followed by the abbot, attended by two of his cowled acolytes. Donne was a tall spare man whose bald head provided little evidence of the tonsure that had once surmounted it. When we were seated at table in the parlour and the servants had withdrawn, my guests made relaxed conversation about life in the cloister. Only when Ned introduced that subject which, as I knew, was dear to his heart did Donne betray hesitation.

'Does His Majesty intend to close all the remaining houses?' Ned asked.

'Well, he is restoring some of the abbeys closed in the North, at the request of good Christian men there,' Donne replied, 'so I hardly think he is intent on putting an end to the religious life.'

'Is that not merely a bone thrown to the rebels to quiet them?' I asked.

'I prefer to think better of my king than that,' the abbot said, in a tone of mild reproof. 'There is no doubt that the system is in need of overhaul. Much of the rigour has gone out of cloister life. Numbers have fallen. Standards have dropped. Discipline wavers. You must have seen this, Brother Ned – I shall insist on calling you "Brother" – else would Farnfield not have closed voluntarily.'

Ned stabbed with his knife at a morsel of pastry. ''Tis a hard road, I grant you. Some embark upon it who lack the stamina. Others of us, I think, are placed there to test our faith.' He stared down at his trencher. 'We are called to love God only and we take the cowl because that is what we dearly wish. If our love is ever diverted from God to ... others, then we cannot sustain our high calling.'

'And that was the case at Farnfield?' Donne probed.

'Perhaps. To my mind, Master Secretary's visitors collected a little mud and built with it a tower of bricks.'

Time, I felt, to change the subject. Turning to Donne, I said, 'It was kind of you to visit Margaret Packington. She was a devoted wife. I fear it will take long for the wounds to heal.'

'A shocking business,' the abbot stated gravely. 'Such a good man. Uncomplicated. I knew him only a few weeks – we travelled together from Antwerp – and yet I felt that we became quite close. Being on narrow shipboard together sometimes turns acquaintances into friends.'

'People tell me that he was in a state of some distress over the fate of William Tyndale.'

Donne shook his head wistfully. 'Poor Tyndale. Such a scholar. He is a great loss.'

'Yet,' I persisted, 'Robert surely had no need to blame himself for Tyndale's incarceration, and certainly not his death.'

'He confided in me that he was devastated that he could not persuade Tyndale to change his mind but, as I tried to impress upon him, no arguments would ever have moved Tyndale.'

I was puzzled. 'Change his mind about what?' I asked.

'Why, about the divorce.' The abbot spoke as though what he was stating was obvious.

Ned clearly shared my surprise. 'Do you mean that Master

Packington was sent over to induce Tyndale to accept the king's rejection of Queen Catherine in favour of the Frenchified whore?'

A faint smile hovered over Donne's lips. 'I would not put it quite like that, Brother. Tyndale based his rejection of His Majesty's proceedings on his interpretation of Scripture. His Majesty was gracious enough to pardon his presumption and welcome him back on condition that he would admit that his exegesis had been wrong. Now, in my opinion, Tyndale *was* wrong, both on his reading of the Bible and his defiance of the king. He should have accepted the olive branch His Majesty was graciously offering. Sadly, he was too stubborn, too proud to admit his error. Nothing I or Robert or any of his other friends could say would sway him.'

By this point I was really confused. 'My Lord Abbot, are you saying that you were in Louvain acting on Tyndale's behalf? I thought—'

'That I was in alliance with that repulsive Phillips scoundrel?' Donne's smile was superior, indulgent. 'That is what Phillips and his backers and any other observers were meant to think. In fact, I was acting on confidential instructions from Lord Cromwell to learn all I could about the opposition to Tyndale.'

'So, you and Robert were employed on the same mission,' I suggested.

'Similar,' Donne agreed, 'though we did not realise it until we sailed together.'

I struggled to rearrange my thoughts. 'Then, Cromwell was eager to bring Tyndale back to England?'

Donne sat back in his chair. 'Lord Cromwell was – and is – eager to have an English Bible. This can now be stated quite openly. He said as much only yesterday to the Grand Council.

He has persuaded His Majesty that a new translation will put an end to dissension. Tyndale would have been useful, not only as a translator, but as a skilled writer, producing books and pamphlets to confound the enemies of vernacular Scripture. Such a pity that he refused to be reconciled to the king. Accepting the royal divorce would have been a small price to pay for seeing his Bible placed in every English church.'

Ned had sat scowling and silent during Donne's explanation. Now he spoke, obviously choosing his words carefully. 'My Lord Abbot, are we to understand that you are in favour of all this New Learning?'

'Not at all, Brother, but I have yet to be convinced that the Church is best defended by burning books and people who read books. I am not afraid of the Bible. Devoutly read and properly taught, it can only do good.'

'Even if it tells people to pull down abbeys?' Ned persisted.

'In point of fact, Brother, it says nothing of the sort, as any who read it will discover.'

Once again it was time to divert the conversation into a smoother path, not beset with rocks and ruts. I asked the abbot about his journey up from Devon and from this we moved to other non-contentious matters until it was time for my guests to leave. I accompanied them out to the stables and saw Donne mounted upon his horse. When he and his companions had left, Ned also climbed into his saddle. As I stood close by his stirrup he leaned forward. 'Mary and all the saints preserve us from men who don't know whether they are monks or politicians,' he muttered.

By this time my plan was well formed. It was bizarre, even grotesque, but I was determined to pursue it. I knew it would be risky but by now my anger was so great that I waved aside such considerations. In truth, the only thing that might have blunted my resolve was failure to recruit the accomplices I needed. I was still calculating how best to approach the men I had in mind when fate played into my hand.

On Sunday morning I was returning from mass at the Goldsmiths' Chapel with the rest of the household when I felt a tug at my sleeve. Bart was walking beside me and looking miserable. He had become almost a fixture in my house of late and my first thought was that he looked disconsolate because he had fallen out with Lizzie. I could not have been more wrong.

'Master Thomas, may I speak with you' – he looked around at the group of servants following us – 'in private?'

'Of course,' I replied. 'Let us take a turn around Paul's Yard.'

It was a bright, frosty morning and many people were enjoying the open space around the cathedral away from the dark, narrow streets. 'Well,' I prompted, as we strolled past the open-air pulpit.

'It's about Lizzie,' he began hesitantly.

'I rather guessed it might be,' I said.

'Then you know how I feel about her and she has feelings for me. We want to be together and I want to look after her. She's had a hard life but she's a wonderful woman and she deserves better.'

'I agree.'

'Well ... the thing is ...' He stared wistfully at a couple standing in the angle between transept and nave and throwing a ball for their infant son to catch. 'How can that ever be for us?'

'Why not?'

'Why not!' Bart's anger flared out. 'Lizzie lives on your charity and what am I good for?' He waggled his left stump.

I stopped and faced him. 'Lizzie does *not* live on my charity. She does an excellent job looking after my mother and my son. I depend on her enormously. As for you, if you could get rid of your self-pity, you could find yourself a useful occupation.'

He nodded glumly. 'That's what Lizzie says.'

'Was it she who told you to talk to me?' I demanded.

His downcast gaze was my answer. 'She has an idea . . . Oh. I can't ask it.'

'Then you will never learn my answer,' I prompted.

'Well, since John Fink . . . died . . . Well, your present senior apprentice is very good at his craft but, according to Lizzie, he can't keep the books properly.'

'That's true. I've often had to correct his figures.'

'Well, Lizzie's idea was that I might look after that part of the business for you. I have a good head for numbers. I wouldn't need much training. I could learn about the business quite quickly.' He looked at me appealingly. 'If I could earn enough, we might be able to get married in a few years.'

We walked on in silence for several moments. I deliberately gave the impression of thinking very carefully, although I knew what I wanted to say. When I spoke it was in a tone of great solemnity that was not entirely feigned. 'If you were to become a party to my business secrets, I would need to be sure of your complete loyalty. I would have to know that you would not go chasing off on some new crusade every few months.'

'Oh, I can promise—'

I interrupted. 'Don't make any comment until you have heard what I have to say. I have a test for you, something that will prove both your loyalty and your ingenuity. If you manage it successfully, then I will trust you with other affairs.'

Bart's face glowed with relief. 'Just tell me—'

367

Again I silenced him. 'What I am about to propose you may not like. You are free to refuse but, whatever your decision, you must swear to reveal it to no one.'

'I swear,' he replied eagerly.

We continued our circuit of the cathedral grounds and I unfolded my plan to him. He was surprised, shocked, as I had guessed he would be, but when I had finished he responded firmly. 'You can rely on me, Master Treviot.'

Having persuaded Bart, it was not too difficult to enlist Ben's aid. Ned was by far the hardest person to bring into my scheme.

'You are not the man for such devious plots,' he protested.

'I am a much changed man since first we met,' I replied.

'And you are determined to cast away what little innocence remains? If you use the methods of corrupt men, you become corrupt yourself. I cannot be a party to that.'

'Then, by default, you become a party to murder.'

Ned winced. 'That is unfair,' he protested.

'Is it? We are dealing with a priest who poses as a man of God but does not hesitate to use the Devil's own means to achieve his ends. What's worse, he lacks the courage to perform his evil deeds himself. He paid the Italian to kill Robert and he instigated Hugh Seagrave to shoot me. He weighed down John Fink's conscience and drove him to self-destruction. Not content with damning his own soul, he endangers the souls of others. Heaven alone knows what more mischief he might do if he is not stopped now. We have the opportunity to stop him. Can we, dare we fail to take that opportunity?'

Ned shook his head. 'I do not like it.'

'My dear friend, I would not involve you if I could conceive any other means of achieving my objective. The cause is just.'

'And, therefore, unjust means may be used to achieve it?'

That verbal thrust went home. Ned was accusing me of using the excuse I condemned others for employing: *exitus acta probat*. 'My means are not unjust,' I protested. 'Revenge would be unjust. Behaving as judge and jury over Incent would be unjust. I seek only to bring him into the law courts, where he will be able to speak in his own defence. Please help me.'

With the utmost reluctance Ned agreed eventually. It only remained to set the plot in motion.

Chapter 39

'Fish Wharf three o'clock.'

I had waited with growing impatience for a visit from Bart. Three days had passed since our discussion in Paul's Yard. Everything depended on him. It was Bart who had to set the wheels of my plan in motion. When no word came I casually asked Lizzie if she knew his whereabouts. She replied that she had not seen him since Sunday. I began to wonder whether he had had second thoughts about our agreement. Worse still, had he bungled his assignment and fallen foul of John Incent? It was, therefore, a great relief when a ragged urchin appeared at the shop door with a scrap of paper and solemnly demanded a penny for it, 'like the man said'. It was already well past two o'clock. I had Dickon saddled and rode, by way of Walbrook and Thames Street, down to the dock area for my rendezvous with Bart.

I found him leaning against a warehouse wall, talking with a fishmonger who was lamenting the decline in trade. As I dismounted I heard the man's complaint.

'Plaguy ice,' he muttered, spitting and staring gloomily over the river, still partially mottled with frozen blotches. 'Catches are down and what does get here comes by cart. Much of it's stinking by the time it arrives.'

We spent a few moments sympathising with the merchant before moving on down the almost-deserted quay. When we were quite alone, I asked, 'How are you getting on? Why haven't you been in touch?'

'That Incent's a wary one,' Bart replied. 'At our first meeting he said he was too busy to talk. Then, after we met a second time, he actually had me followed. I was on my way to report to you when, fortunately, I spotted the churl who was keeping an eye on me. I spent a whole day wandering the City aimlessly till the clodpole gave up.' Bart chuckled. 'I reckon his feet must be ready to drop off.'

'But what of Incent?' I urged.

'Snared,' Bart said, in a tone of triumph. 'He fell for my story. I told him all about my time with the northern "pilgrims" and how bitter I was that we had been betrayed. Well, I didn't have to make that up. I convinced him that I'm a kind of religious mercenary, ready for any dangerous exploit against the "New Learners". When I told him that the word was going around that you were out to make trouble for him, he really sat up and took notice. By Our Lady, he really hates you! He asked, straight out, if I was ready to rid the Church of a pestilential enemy – you. I said, if the price was right. We haggled. Eventually we agreed a figure.' Bart laughed. 'Do you want to know what your corpse is worth? Three new sovereigns.'

'I hope you weren't tempted,' I said.

'No, you're safe – at least from me – Master Treviot.'

'What happened next?'

'Well, it was a bit like a Twelfth Night play, at the Inns of Court.'

'What do you mean?'

'It was as though I'd written the part for him and he'd learned it by rote. He said exactly what I wanted him to say. I didn't have to steer the conversation. "How will I know you've done the job?" he asked. I said I'd show him the body.'

'And he agreed to come and check your handiwork?'

'Without a moment's hesitation. You should have seen the look on his face. It was as though he could see you lying before him, all cold and bloody. "Dead in a whore shop," he said. If he hadn't been so busy gloating, he might have questioned me carefully. He believed me because he wanted to believe me. "Master Nemesis" – that was the code name I'd invented – "Master Nemesis," he said, "you will be doing God's work and you can come to me for absolution." Rather odd, that. If I was doing God's work, why would I need to be absolved?'

'And you arranged a time?'

Bart nodded. 'I said I would do it tonight and he could come and see the body tomorrow morning.'

'Excellent, Bart. Bring him about ten o'clock. We'll be ready. Now we'd better leave separately to be absolutely sure no one sees us together.' I swung myself into the saddle.

As I turned Dickon's head, Bart called out. 'Will you give this to Lizzie for safe keeping?' He held out a gold sovereign. 'First instalment of my blood money,' he explained, before striding away down an alley between two warehouses.

I went in person to find the others and confirm our final

arrangements. Then I returned to Goldsmith's Row. That night I enjoyed the best sleep I had had in more than a week.

The next morning four very nervous conspirators gathered in Ned and Jed's room at St Swithun's. We assembled early to await our unsuspecting guest. Carefully we went over our plans, such as they were. Ben and our hosts all looked to me to preside over our business. For my part, though tense, I was eager for the confrontation. Though there were still a few gaps in the case against the priest, I was sure I had enough evidence to frighten him into a confession. We left the door ajar and Ben was placed beside it with a good view of the main entrance. Ten o'clock came, chimed from the tower of a nearby church. There was no sign of our visitor. We all exchanged silent glances. Ned said, 'You can't go by that clock. It's never right.' The words were scarcely spoken when Ben put a hand to his lips and quietly closed the door. I joined him behind the door. Jed lay down by the far wall and drew a coarse sheet over himself.

Moments later Bart strode in, pushing the door wide. 'There you are,' he said, pointing to the recumbent form. His companion hurried across the room, his eyes fixed on what he supposed was my lifeless body. Instantly, Ben slammed the door. He and I grabbed Incent by the arms and forced him to a stool. Jed threw aside the sheet and jumped up with a coil of rope he had ready and, while the priest struggled and shouted, he tied our prisoner's hands securely behind him.

'You may save your breath, Sir John,' I said. 'No one can hear you here and if they could they would know better than to interfere.'

Incent's first reaction was bluster. 'What do you mean by this outrage? How dare you lay profane hands on me! You'll regret this – all of you. I'll see you on a gallows for it.'

I let him rant. When he had subsided into surly silence, I said, 'Sir John, no ill will befall you at our hands. We are not thieves or murderers. We have brought you here for one purpose and one only.' I produced a paper from inside my doublet. 'Before you leave, you will sign this short document.'

'I'll do no such thing,' Incent snorted. 'What is it, anyway?'

'A confession of your implication in the foul murder of Master Robert Packington.'

'Pfah!' Our guest made a sound like a suddenly deflated pig's bladder. 'What nonsense! Master Treviot, I'm surprised at you getting involved with this bunch of knaves in order to play such foolish tricks.' Incent seemed to have recovered his composure slightly. I wondered whether perhaps it had been poor tactics to play my trump card straightway. If I was to shake the truth from the priest, I would have to build up my case stone by stone until he realised there was no escape. 'Well,' I said, 'we'll leave that matter for the moment. Let us consider first something that happened a mere two days ago. That was when you engaged my friend here to murder me for a fee of three sovereigns. It would be futile for you to deny that.'

Incent sneered. 'You are not going to take the word of this churl over that of a respected priest.'

'Your presence here gives the lie to your denial, Sir John. Why are you come, save in the hope of beholding my corpse?'

'I was tricked,' Incent snorted. 'It was a plot to get money out of me.'

'A plot that could only succeed if you wanted to see me dead,' I responded, 'and why would you desire that?'

Our prisoner's only reaction was to glower at us and wriggle in a vain attempt to escape his bonds.

'Let's leave that on one side also,' I suggested. 'We will go

374

instead to the afternoon of 20 November. That was when you made an unannounced visit to my home and persuaded my assistant John Fink to reveal my whereabouts to you. Having discovered that information, you arranged for me to be waylaid on Hampstead Heath.'

Incent shook his head violently but cracks were beginning to appear in the cladding of his choleric indignation. 'That was a pastoral visit,' he whined. 'Nothing more.'

'Then why,' I demanded, 'did you hasten to tell your nephew, Hugh Seagrave, all about it and why did he, with equal haste, ride out to Hampstead to lie in wait for me?'

The priest was thoughtfully silent for several moments, calculating carefully.

'Master Treviot, if the Seagraves have some quarrel with you, it is none of my doing.'

'So you say.' I pulled up a stool, placed it in front of the prisoner and sat down, our eyes on a level. 'But, again, let us leave that hanging in the air and come to other matters. The attempt on my life failed. Three days later, I was arrested at your instigation and clapped into the Lollards' Tower.'

'That was nothing to do with me,' Incent asserted, gazing straight at me. 'If My Lord bishop had you arrested, he undoubtedly had good cause to do so.'

I glanced around at my friends. They were looking distinctly uncomfortable. I decided on a change of tactics.

'Have you ever been inside that dismal prison?' I asked. 'That place where men are shut up for presuming to believe things other than you ordain? 'Tis a fearful place. If you set your ear to the stone, you can still hear the screams of Richard Hunne, brutally murdered by your predecessors.'

A sudden defiance flashed in Incent's eyes. 'Hunne was a heretic who hanged himself in a fit of remorse.'

It was Ben who responded. 'All the world knows that for a lie!'

'Indeed,' I said, 'but what does a lie matter if it rids the world of one heretic? That is your philosophy. You hate heretics, do you not, Sir John? Any crime, any bestiality, any sin that leads to their extermination is justifiable. Isn't that an article of your creed?'

Incent mumbled something.

'Speak up, man,' I said sharply. 'We did not hear your reply.'

He raised his eyes and again there was a touch of defiance. 'I am a priest. It is my responsibility to protect the Church from error. There can be no so-called "New Learning" if it does not come from our doctors and is not sanctioned by the pope.'

'Fortunately,' I continued, 'I was rescued from your evil designs by Lord Cromwell.'

'Cromwell!' Incent's sharp, raucous laugh took me by surprise. 'You young simpleton! You should choose your protectors more carefully. Do you really think His Lordship is interested in you? He cares only for his own power. He would betray you tomorrow if that would serve his purposes, just as he did Queen Anne and that deluded ninny, Tyndale.'

Our duel had reached the point when only a strong thrust would break through the man's stubborn defence. 'That is no matter,' I said. 'We must take one more step back in time to discover why you should want to destroy me. I am no heretic. There was no reason why I should figure on your list of "New Learners" to be exterminated – until you discovered that, like you, I was on a crusade. You learned that I was determined to discover the murderer of Master Robert Packington. That alarmed you.' I thrust my face close to Incent's and almost spat the words at him. 'Because you were the man who paid for his assassination!'

If I had hoped for a gasp of guilt unmasked or a gibbering denial, I was disappointed. Staring straight into the prisoner's eyes, I read surprise. I sat back to continue my interrogation. 'You are a self-appointed heresy-hunter and what worse heresy can there be than distributing the English New Testaments by that "ninny", William Tyndale. You knew Master Packington was a leading figure in that business. You knew that he was far too circumspect and too well connected for you ever to be able to bring a successful charge against him so you did what your predecessors had done to Richard Hunne years ago: you hired someone to murder him.'

'This is nonsense!' Incent shouted.

I stood up and towered over the trembling figure in the chair. 'No,' I said, 'not nonsense. The simple, naked truth.' I was forced to bluff. 'The Italian mercenary you paid has been apprehended and he has confessed all. The case against you is complete for all these crimes.'

At last the red-headed priest's composure was broken. He began gibbering about 'lies' and 'conspiracy'. In the commotion I did not hear the door open behind me. As I brandished the prepared confession in Incent's face, I felt someone clutch my arm. Turning, I was astonished to see Lizzie.

'Thomas, we must talk!' she said urgently.

'Not now,' I said, shaking off her hand.

'Yes now!' she insisted. 'Come with me.'

'Lizzie, I cannot! This is not the time.'

She refused to let go. 'It is the only time, if you value all our lives.'

Reluctantly I followed her out of the room and up the stairs until we came to what I recognised as her old chamber.

'What are you doing here?' I demanded angrily.

'I have come to prevent you committing a great folly,' she replied. 'When you gave me that money from Bart, I knew something was amiss. He could never have obtained such a sum honestly. I went to him last night and made him tell me what you were all planning.'

'You shouldn't have done that. This has nothing to do with you!'

'It has everything to do with me. If I hadn't ... But that's not to the point. The fact is you are making a grave mistake.'

'Really?' I mocked. 'And how do you know what I don't?'

'You remember, right at the beginning, I told you there was one man who knew the truth about your friend's murder.'

'John Doggett? Yes, but he refused to tell me.'

'Well, I have been to see him this morning. I have ways to persuade that you lack.'

'Do you mean you—'

She laid a finger on my lips. 'Not a word of that – ever – especially to Bart.'

'Are you telling me that Doggett confided in you?'

'No.'

'Well, then ...'

'He would not tell me because, he said, the information was dangerous. Instead he wrote something on a piece of paper, sealed it and told me to give it to you. He said he wanted you to know the truth to stop you blundering about in matters too deep for you. He hoped it would act as a warning. I was to tell you that if you persist in making a nuisance of yourself ... Well, knowing Doggett, you can guess what he threatened. And you know that he can carry out his threats. Please, Thomas, read his note and stop this business *now*.'

I unfastened the scrap of paper Lizzie gave me. The message was brief; curt in the extreme. It made no sense. 'This is ridiculous!' I shouted. Yet even as I did so, I was aware of a twinge of doubt, somewhere at the back of my mind. For several minutes I paced about the room. Questions tumbled around my brain: what was Doggett up to? How could his claim possibly be true? How could I give up my search for justice just when I was about to achieve it?

Lizzie stood there, hands clasped before her. 'Please, Thomas. I know what this means to you but you have done all you can. Doggett sent a couple of his Dogs with me. If you carry on with this ... inquisition ... you will not live to see another dawn. Nor will I or the others.'

I thrust the paper inside my doublet and stamped to the door.

In the room below I turned to Jed. 'Untie him,' I ordered. As a bewildered Incent shook off his bonds, I said, 'Get out. In future stick to your prayers and if anything untoward ever befalls me or my friends, expect a knock at your door.'

My companions stared at me and each other in mute astonishment. I did not stay to explain. I strode out to the courtyard, mounted my horse and rode away from St Swithun's. Not to London. Not across the bridge. Dickon and I ambled along Bankside and took the westward road between the Thames and Paris Garden. The ice was breaking up and the winter sun streaked the river with gold. It was, I realised, a year almost to the day that I had last come this way. A year? It might have been a century, crammed as it had been with bitter and bewildering incident. What had it all meant? What had I achieved? What had I learned?

Exitus acta probat. If any three words could sum up what I now knew about human nature and had not known the previous January, they were these. 'Results validate deeds' – it had been Stephen Vaughan who explained that Latin tag to me, with evident disapproval, yet it seemed to me that almost everyone I had encountered was motivated by this principle. Those who believed some objective to be good considered it legitimate to employ any means – illegal, immoral, cruel or inhuman – to achieve it. I thought of the woman in grey, silently appealing to her audience to believe her innocence. For what good reason had her life been severed by a French headsman? According to Hugh Seagrave, she had made fun of her husband's sexual inadequacy. If true, that threatened the dynasty. Kings must have sons. That is one of the rules they live by. Henry believed that the peace and security of the realm depended on his potency and his finding a wife who could give him the necessary man-child. No subject could be allowed to doubt the king's ability and determination to conceive an heir. To scotch any such anxieties was, seemingly, an objective he deemed it worth killing for.

As I followed the long curve of the river, the sprawl of Whitehall came into view on the opposite bank. Ahead of me stood the high wall encompassing the archbishop's town residence at Lambeth. State and church glowering at each other across the water. Rivals for power. Each believing in its own God-given authority and prepared to go to any lengths to defend it. Cromwell's new England would be a kingdom in which the pope no longer had any place and the bishops would be stripped of most of their power. To realise his dream, monks and nuns were being turned out of their cloisters and protesters executed as traitors. To defend the old ways, the ancient truths they and their fathers had grown up in, priests were stirring peaceful countrymen to bloody rebellion. Appalling means justified by desirable ends.

The track over which Dickon picked his way now lay across a narrow swathe of meadow between the river and a thick belt of trees. I dismounted, led him down to the water's edge and let him drink. Then, I tethered him to a severed stump to graze while I sat on a ruined wall – all that remained of an earlier generation's vain attempt to hold back the frequent floods that overran this area.

What of the Incents? I wondered. Were they not typical of priests who believed themselves called to defend their people from error and, in pursuing this holy vocation, were prepared to pry into other people's lives, to make accusations of heresy, to urge men and women to denounce their neighbours, to sanction imprisonment, torture and death by burning for those who did not believe the 'right' things?

Then there were the Seagraves. What had impelled them to seek my destruction? Revenge? Family honour? I pondered on the evils perpetrated in the name of rough justice. To my certain knowledge there were at least four fine families decimated and impoverished by feuds that had raged for generations.

I drew my travelling cloak more tightly round me and pulled the hood further over my head. A cutting wind was thrusting at me from the river. Yet I did not want to move. Not yet. Not till I had finished unravelling the coils that had bound themselves round my life during that dreadful year. I remembered my days in Antwerp. Were the members of the English House honourable people, uncorrupted by good motives? From their safe haven they were promoting revolution in their own land. The books they smuggled into England were inspiring literate men and women to defy ancient custom, to challenge the authority of the bishops, to tear down altars and shrines, to set neighbour against neighbour and even children against parents. They believed passionately in their New Learning and cared little what means must be used to drive out old falsehood. Tyndale had devoted himself tirelessly to translating the Bible into his mother tongue. What could be more honourable than that? But in so doing he had flouted the laws of church and state, defied his king and involved others in his intellectual and spiritual rebellion.

And that brought my thoughts back to Robert. Was that intelligent, noble, sensitive friend clear of the taint of using questionable means to secure desirable ends? Sadly, no. He and the other Christian Brothers were ardent in their belief that the Bible should be freely available to all who could read it and that this one book would change English society for the better. But to bring all this about they had, for some years, been operating a clandestine operation in defiance of king, bishops and the law. Their activities had placed many people in danger, including some of their friends. I thought of poor Thomas Poyntz and his family, separated – perhaps for ever – by his commitment to Tyndale and his work.

All these reflections met, inevitably, in one question: who ordered the murder of Robert Packington? It had always seemed obvious that the culprit must be found among the ranks of the clergy opposed to everything he stood for; men who hated the thought of an open Bible; men who loathed Tyndale with a passion and rejoiced at the news of his burning; men who thought that the translator's death was the signal for a major operation against those covert Lutherans, the New Learners who were disturbing the realm. And yet . . . I took out Doggett's note and stared at its simple message as though I thought that, somehow, it might have changed since I had thrust it inside my doublet. The four words were, of course, still there:

'Lord Cromwell ordered it'.

They still screamed their utter impossibility. But the writer had no reason to make such an extraordinary identification of the wretch who had masterminded my friend's death. He would know that I would refuse to believe it. Then, with the brilliance of sunlight bursting forth from clouds, I realised that that might very well be the point. No one would connect Cromwell's name with the murder of a man so closely committed to his own cause. They would assume, as I had done, that Robert had been killed on the orders of traditionalist clergy who were dedicated enemies of the New Learning. However, what fresh understanding might emerge if one allowed oneself to think the unthinkable?

One answer was that it provided answers to some awkward questions my mind had shuffled aside: how had Incent made contact with a professional Italian killer? How was he aware of Robert's movements? What *exactly* was it that had troubled Robert so much on his visits to the Netherlands? Cromwell had himself been a mercenary soldier in the Italian wars. He would know of men skilled enough and desperate enough to kill for pay. He could easily have brought Il Ombra over and lodged him at the Red Lamb, available to do his bidding. That would explain why Doggett had been so determined to throw me off the scent when I visited him. Cromwell was the only other person who could have known where Robert would be on that misty November morning, because Robert's first action on his return the previous day would have been to report to his patron. Time enough, then, for Cromwell to get an urgent message to his assassin-in-waiting.

But why? What possible motive could Cromwell have had for wanting his friend and colleague out of the way? This surely was the rock on which such a theory must founder. I stared across the water at the abbey and palace complex where, even now, Cromwell was probably presiding over his Grand Council. Abbot Donne was among the delegates. What was it he had said about the mission to the Netherlands? Robert had been in a profound melancholy because he had failed. Failed to save Tyndale from the flames? No, failed to save Tyndale from his own conscience. The scholar had refused to abandon his opposition to the king's divorce. Persuading him, then, must have been the aim of Robert's mission. Without such a change of mind the prisoner was doomed. The king hated him. Cromwell could not save him and would not have dared to try. Moreover, as long as Tyndale lived, the minister would not have been able to champion his translation. With Tyndale out of the way, however, Henry could announce to the Catholic world that he had disposed of a stubborn heretic. And Cromwell could throw himself wholeheartedly into promoting an English Bible that was substantially Tyndale's work. According to Donne, that was precisely what he was now doing. Either the translator or the translation could survive – not both. In view of Tyndale's obduracy, Cromwell could only withdraw his protection. Did he indicate to the imperial authorities that they could proceed with their prosecution of Tyndale without any official protest from England? Or did he simply let events take their course? Either way, Robert would have realised that Cromwell was nailing Tyndale to the cross of New Learning politics. That knowledge would have devastated Robert beyond measure. No wonder his Antwerp friends had described him as being broken by his complicity in such betrayal. Would he have been able to keep the bitter knowledge to himself? That might be a risk Cromwell could not afford to take.

He was a man with a vision. That had become obvious to me from our meetings. He was set on creating a new England with a new learning and a new Bible. His problem was that he was like a coachman trying to handle two ill-paired horses. The king was a plodding reformer, always sensitive about being dubbed a heretic. But several of the minister's allies were eager stallions, impatient for change. He needed the support of his royal master and of the 'New Learners'. I recalled Poyntz telling me how he and others had been locked up on Cromwell's orders to calm the overheated atmosphere following Barnes' sermon at Robert's funeral. If the minister feared that Robert might reveal Tyndale's 'betrayal' to his friends, then the loss of their support would have been a serious blow.

This very morning Incent had crowed about divisions in the visionary's own camp and reminded me how Cromwell had turned against Queen Anne. I closed my eyes against the glare of the lowering sun reflected from the water. And I saw once more that lady in grey, as it seemed, willing the silent crowd to know that she was innocent. She had perished because she had aroused the anger of her royal husband. He had wanted her dead and Cromwell, if he was to survive, had been obliged to make the necessary arrangements. He had survived. He lived still to achieve the goal he had set himself. He would justify any action that became necessary in the process. *Exitus acta probat.*

I tore the paper across and dropped the pieces into the water. For a moment or two they floated, then, as they dwindled into the depths, a shard of dirty ice drifted over them and they disappeared. I shivered. The cold was penetrating my clothes. I rose stiffly and stretched my arms. As I turned, a strange sight confronted me. Dickon was still contentedly nibbling the meadow grass. The winter-evening sun shone full on him, so that he seemed to glow with an almost supernatural whiteness against the background of the dense, grey-black trees. I went over and patted his neck. Gathering the reins, I hoisted myself into the saddle. Then I turned his head towards London and the future.

Historical Endnote

Many readers of historical fiction like to know – and rightly so – what elements of a tale constitute the core of fact around which the story is wrapped. It is important to believe that, while the events are contrived, they *could* have happened. Several of the characters in *The First Horseman* really lived and the major events that form the background to my yarn occurred in the ways I have indicated. Indeed, part of my reason for inventing this story was to recreate the tense and tumultuous atmosphere of the years 1536–1537 in England and, particularly, in London. It seems appropriate, therefore, to provide at this point a checklist of actual Tudor people who appear in the preceding pages (apart from obvious and famous characters, such as Henry VIII, Anne Boleyn and Thomas Cromwell).

Robert Packington was a prominent mercer, London citizen

and member of the House of Commons. He also belonged to that band of the 'Christian Brothers' who smuggled William Tyndale's books into England. He was assassinated in the manner I have described. His murderer was never apprehended.

John Incent was a priest, a canon residentiary of St Paul's and, later, dean of the cathedral. Some thirty-four years after the murder, John Foxe, in his 1570 edition of *Actes and Monuments*, repeated common gossip that Incent, a known enemy of the New Learning, had paid an Italian sixty crowns to do the deed.

Augustine Packington was Robert's brother and also involved in Bible smuggling.

John Stokesley, Bishop of London, was an active heresy hunter.

William Tyndale was, of course, the great translator of the English New Testament and parts of the Old Testament. His version formed the basis of the first officially sanctioned vernacular Bible, published, largely thanks to Cromwell's efforts, in 1537.

Stephen Vaughan was a close confidant of Thomas Cromwell and was for some years Chief Factor in the English House at Antwerp.

John Rogers was chaplain to the English community in Antwerp and was closely involved in the production of the English Bible.

Thomas Poyntz was a prominent London grocer who was imprisoned as a heretic in the Netherlands, escaped and spent most of his later years hiding from the authorities in England and separated from his family.

Henry Phillips was a ne'er-do-well who betrayed Tyndale to his enemies, though it is not clear who his paymasters were.

Gabriel Donne was a Cistercian monk who was associated with Phillips in the downfall of Tyndale, though his actual participation is far from clear. Instituted by Cromwell to the abbacy of Buckfast, he surrendered the house to the king within a couple of years and went on to enjoy a successful career as canon residentiary of St Paul's and a leading London ecclesiastic.

Thomas Theobald is a shadowy character but he was certainly employed by Archbishop Cranmer as an agent in the Netherlands.

Robert Aske was the main leader of the Pilgrimage of Grace. He was executed for treason in 1537.

And, yes, twenty-two years before our story begins, the wealthy and influential merchant, Richard Hunne, was, according to the coroner's inquest, brutally done to death in the way described in an anonymous pamphlet published within weeks of Packington's murder.

All the other characters in the story were either invented by me, or appear in the records merely as names. Invented or not, such people certainly existed and were caught up, in one way or another, in the appallingly violent events of 1536–1537.